Ladies in Waiting

Dear Zöe,

Ladies in Waiting

Jane Austen's Unsung Characters

Elinor Lipman

ELINOR LIPMAN

ADRIANA TRIGIANI

KAREN DUKESS

ELOISA JAMES

AUDREY BELLEZZA AND EMILY HARDING

DIANA QUINCY

NIKKI PAYNE

SARAH MacLEAN

11/25

G

Gallery Books

NEW YORK   AMSTERDAM/ANTWERP   LONDON

TORONTO   SYDNEY/MELBOURNE   NEW DELHI

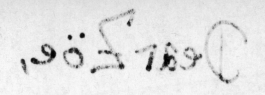

G

Gallery Books
An Imprint of Simon & Schuster, LLC
1230 Avenue of the Americas
New York, NY 10020

First Gallery Books trade paperback edition November 2025

GALLERY BOOKS and colophon are registered trademarks of Simon & Schuster, LLC

Simon & Schuster strongly believes in freedom of expression and stands against censorship in all its forms. For more information, visit BooksBelong.com.

For information about special discounts for bulk purchases, please contact Simon & Schuster Special Sales at 1-866-506-1949 or business@simonandschuster.com.

The Simon & Schuster Speakers Bureau can bring authors to your live event. For more information or to book an event, contact the Simon & Schuster Speakers Bureau at 1-866-248-3049 or visit our website at www.simonspeakers.com.

Interior design by Jaime Putorti

Manufactured in the United States of America

10 9 8 7 6 5 4 3 2 1

Library of Congress Control Number: 2025945373

ISBN 978-1-6682-0417-7
ISBN 978-1-6682-0418-4 (ebook)

CONTENTS

INTRODUCTION TO
Ladies in Waiting:
Jane Austen's Unsung Characters

The literary canon of Jane Austen is a glorious English garden, perennial and evergreen. Pick up any of her novels, and you will find yourself in bliss, following her down the same stone footpaths hemmed in boxwood where she walked in the Hampshire village of Chawton. You will look up to find the same unreliable English sun and hope, in that light, that love will bloom, fulfilling the most deserving characters and the readers who get lost in her storytelling.

Inside the pages of this book, nine American novelists, inspired by Austen's novels, have selected characters from her work and reimagined them, some even in time and place. Nothing inspires a writer more than reading the work of a master storyteller. Austen has remained relevant for 250 years because she wrote human beings as she saw them: full, dimensional, and real in the times in which they lived. She wrote about the lives of women in Regency England, where community, family ties, and friendship were essential, even if the pursuit of their own dreams was not.

Jane Austen may not have been encouraged to become an author, but she was compelled to write with ferocity. Austen wrote page-turners. The stakes were typically propelled by responsibility, a duty to family and society, set against the longing of the human heart.

In this collection, you will find some of your favorite characters from *Sense and Sensibility*, *Emma*, and *Pride and Prejudice*, in stories set in locations ranging from Austen's England to pre–Civil War New Orleans to the New York City of the moment.

Who are the ladies in waiting? Elinor Lipman chose Miss Bates, who interacts with the historical Jewish community in the Regency era; Karen Dukess stays in the same period and writes about Georgiana Darcy longing for *what if?* Eloisa James revisits the young Margaret Dashwood, who believes her sisters did not aim high enough when choosing their men. Her goal is to have a romantic adventure. Audrey Bellezza and Emily Harding create a new history for the first love of Colonel Brandon. Diana Quincy is intrigued by Lydia. Can she find love post-Wickham? Sarah MacLean imagines Miss Bates as the belle of the ball in a wonderful romance fantasy. Nikki Payne reinvents Caroline Bingley as a free woman of color in New Orleans, while I imagined Mary Bennet in contemporary Greenwich Village as the resourceful and last unmarried sister in her family, forging a life of duty over her own dreams.

Austen's six novels are among the most celebrated works in literary history. But we always want more. The authors who contributed their work to this anthology were inspired by Austen's themes of self-love, connection, passion, and purpose. So, the garden grows.

Adriana Trigiani
New York City, May 5, 2025

Ladies in Waiting

Miss Bates Bobs Her Hair

ELINOR LIPMAN

"Oh! very well," exclaimed Miss Bates; "then I need not be uneasy. 'Three things very dull indeed.' That will just do for me, you know. I shall be sure to say three dull things as soon ever I open my mouth, shan't I?—(looking round with the most good-humoured dependence on everybody's assent)— Do not you all think I shall?"

Emma could not resist.

"Ah! ma'am, but there may be a difficulty. Pardon me— but you will be limited as to number—only three at once."

Miss Bates, deceived by the mock ceremony of her manner, did not immediately catch her meaning; but, when it burst on her, it could not anger, though a slight blush showed that it could pain her.

"Ah!—well—to be sure. Yes, I see what she means . . . and I will try to hold my tongue. I must make myself very disagreeable, or she would not have said such a thing to an old friend."

Jane Austen, *Emma*

My choice of Miss Bates is embarrassingly pragmatic: *Emma* was my oldest and most tattered Austen, a paperback published by Washington Square Press in 1966. I knew I could make notes in its margins, highlight, and underline without feeling guilty. Inside the book was a clipping that advertised the PBS show *The American Short Story*. Among its adapted titles was "Bernice Bobs Her Hair," broadcast in 1976. That was that. A fan of F. Scott Fitzgerald's *Collected Stories*, of alliteration, of underdogs, and of happy endings, I chose to write about Miss Bates.

In real life, could there be a more annoying woman than the one ridiculed on the uncharitable pages of *Emma*?

I believe not. Most regrettably, that character's name is Miss Bates, and unfortunately she is me.

Her ceaseless prattling is an exaggeration, a composite, an unfair fiction created by Miss Jane Austen, who—as she writes about her eponymous heroine—"is used to having too much her own way and a disposition to think a little too well of herself."

But it is my honour to announce that, with the help of Emma Woodhouse herself, literature's most famous matchmaker, my goodwill and contented temper vouchsafed a happy ending: mine.

As a devoted reader of novels, I was no stranger to romance. Could a handsome, God-fearing, landowning man with a fine house—with gardens, servants, a handsome coach—ever ask for my hand? Didn't every heroine deserve a happy ending?

I was less and less hopeful.

The middle of my life had been devoted to the care of my mother. We lived in a very small way, in reduced circumstances. My clothes were hand-me-downs, offered to me, the late vicar's daughter, by widowers eager to make room for their new wives' frocks.

Despite Mother and me being the second or third tier of Highbury society, we were frequent guests at the Woodhouses' stately home, Hartfield. If I was at times "a great talker upon little matters," it was merely nerves, due to the privilege and possibilities of spending time with Highbury's grandest family.

When Mother died, and after a proper period of mourning, I was able to resume social intercourse. I often sat down to cards with Mr. Woodhouse, who fancied himself neglected by his daughters, fretting over all matters large and small. His was a nervous system that made no sense because older daughter Isabella was safe and happy in London, and Emma and her lovely husband, Mr. George Knightley, stayed at Hartfield after their wedding to keep her father sane.

It was these paternal anxieties that gave the Woodhouse daughters ideas. I sensed a campaign underway: to make Miss Bates their father's boon companion. I did not resist, having experienced, to my surprise, urges that were new to me, sitting opposite the widowed master of this great house.

At first I thought it was just Emma atoning for a slip of the tongue, a rather famous barb that humiliated me in public and on the page: the unpleasantness on Box Hill. But amends were made with softer words, with subsequent visits, and with sweet cake. Given my lesser social standing and my proclivity for forgiveness, I was hardly going to hold a grudge.

The daughters set to work. If they could turn their father's gaze onto me in a less platonic fashion, the first hurdle was my appearance. I had tried on my own, adding bows to my bodices and aromatic herbs to my wrists. It wasn't enough. Emma's mother had been a beauty. I knew this because a portrait of the late Mrs. Woodhouse in lavender silk and Alençon lace, with ropes of pearls and with Emma's luxurious yellow hair, painted by the talented Mr. Gainsborough of Bath, greeted visitors in the entrance hall, dampening the nuptial hopes of many female visitors.

Luckily, considering their father's age and idiosyncrasies, Emma and her sister realized that he had no need for a wife who turned other men's heads. Miss Bates would do.

Still, I required enhancement.

The word that best describes the rites and rituals I was obliged to undertake would be a *makeover*. It started with clothes. Enough time mourning in black; enough linen and wool and muslin as evening wear!

When they led me to their late mother's closet, I protested. Wouldn't Mr. Woodhouse recognize the provenance of these gowns and question my judgment?

No, he would not, they insisted. Pishposh. He was the last man in Highbury to notice what a woman was wearing.

"Then what is the point?" I asked.

They prevailed. The vintage dresses were still beautiful, the fabrics luxurious. Adjustments were needed, gussets added; voile panels stitched above the immodest necklines.

But it was my hair that provoked the most discussion. It had never been cut. My life could be measured in pigmentation, from the original chestnut (as my kind papa had described it) to duller and duller browns, and, now prevailing, brown streaked with gray. Emma, frowning, asked what I did with these braided ropes when I took to my bed at night? I admitted that so much heavy hair gave me headaches. But what does one do with it?

"It must be cut, and cut right," Emma ordered, and then, more softly, "it does you no favours."

How and by whom? It was Mr. Knightley's idea that we go to London. Surely someone who dressed the hair of gentlemen would cut a woman's, too. He wrote to Mr. Frank Churchill, whose journey the sixteen miles from Highbury to London for a haircut had been cited as an example of his vanity and profligacy. But needs must. An obliging letter arrived with our answer: a Mr. Fletcher on St. George Street, off Hanover Square.

Were Mr. and Mrs. George Knightley proposing that they travel with me to London for the cutting of hair? On one hand, borrowing from Ecclesiastes, "Vanity of vanities!" On the other hand, I'd never been to London. We'd be staying overnight at the home of Mr. and Mrs. John Knightley in Brunswick Square. Both the Woodhouse/Knightley sisters would accompany me to the tonsorial parlor on—they assured me— the poshest street in Mayfair.

Shock turned to mortification when we were turned away at the door by an angry wife, who informed us that her husband did not cut the hair of women.

The worldly Isabella whispered from the stoop, "She must think we're not gentlewomen."

Undaunted, Emma rapped on the door again. The woman yelled, "Go away!"

"Please, then—tell us who else will do it."

"No one!"

Isabella whispered to her sister, "Mention remuneration."

Emma said, "We will of course be paying your husband for his kind service."

"I bet you have plenty!" the woman yelled back.

That was quite enough! I asked the sisters, "Can't we just buy some shears and do it ourselves?"

"No!" said Emma, sounding cross. "We haven't journeyed to London to chop off a lifetime of hair without experience or finesse!"

What would my father have thought of this pursuit? Of this mission, the un-dowdying of Miss Bates? But what if—dare I even think it—a goal was met, if *their* father viewed me in a new and favourable light?

On the way back to Brunswick Square, in the carriage, Isabella said, "I know someone who knows someone who might be able to help."

The someone who knew someone was a bishop, a man of not only letters but broad-mindedness. And the person *he* knew was a religious leader of the Hebrew faith, a rabbi on Petticoat Lane.

I didn't know how that applied to my situation, but Isabella did. She explained it with some delicacy: Jewesses were obliged, before marriage, to cut their hair and cover it in public, under wigs. Surely they couldn't fit great lengths of hair under those wigs, could they? Someone had to cut it. We would start with wigmakers and work backward.

Did we even know that people of the Hebrew faith, outside the pages of William Shakespeare, were merchants? Though he'd never had reason to visit the East End, Mr. Knightley was comfortable stopping men we passed, bearded men wearing skull-caps, to guide us.

Signs above the shop were in letters I knew to be Hebrew, unhelpful, but wigs displayed in windows told the tale. Our entrance provoked eye-popping stares and exclamations in another language. But we were not turned away. The wigmaker's wife was present—necessary, I guessed, to maintain propriety, to fit the wigs on the affianced. A young man, stitching in a corner, translated.

Mr. Knightley yelled, "We are in need of someone who cuts the hair of women," pointing to me.

The young man told us that we'd come to the right place! His mamme often cut hair! Sentences were exchanged between Mr. and Mrs. Eichenbaum, not translated.

"Vimmins now!" she said, pointing to a curtain. Mr. Knightley excused himself and went outside.

I sat on a stool in the tiny back room. Emma and Isabella watched, Emma pointing instructively to her own tendrils, as if this wigmaker/barber were a magician. Untranslated, she added, "Leave enough so she can twist it into a topknot—"

But Mrs. Eichenbaum had a firm grip on my braid and, without warning, was sawing through it at the nape of my neck. When

I realized what had happened, and felt the nothingness left behind, I yelped.

"Nit gut?" asked Mrs. Eichenbaum.

"Noooo!" I wailed. "Noooo."

Emma and Isabella were both looking stricken. Isabella smoothed the remaining hair behind my ears and said, "It will frame your face."

"And it's all one color now," said Emma.

"Gamin-like," said Isabella.

Mrs. Eichenbaum appeared to be judging and weighing the liberated braid, unhappily. Finally, in English, "One bob I pay."

"*You* pay?" asked Emma.

Isabella said, "She thinks we came to sell your hair."

One shilling would buy a chicken. What was done was done.

"It'll grow," said Emma.

I whispered, crestfallen, "Now I need a wig."

"We're going to buy you a beautiful bonnet," said Isabella.

"Or two," said Emma.

When did it change, from cribbage to courtship? For all the years I'd been visiting Hartfield, I'd declined Mr. Woodhouse's offers of sherry or brandy. But with Mother gone, I accepted my first glass. He and I developed a routine: dinner, then music, if Emma was home to play and sing, then to the card table, fireside. If Mr. Woodhouse fell asleep over a slow game of honeymoon whist, I did not mind. Ever obliging, and with the horses ready, Jim drove me home.

One night, when Emma and Mr. Knightley were away on a trip to Bath, the very thing happened that made Mr. Woodhouse greatly agitated: It began to snow. He stated matter-of-factly that I could not return home.

I said, "It's a flurry. It won't amount to anything. And it's a short distance."

"You cannot go home!" He waved his arm toward the vast staircase beyond—"We have so many rooms"—which sidetracked him to one of his favourite wistful topics: why Isabella and her whole family couldn't move back from London and live with him.

The next words I uttered surprised myself. "I know you are nervous when the daughters are away. Perhaps . . . it's loneliness?"

He blinked hard, but he didn't answer. Instead, he returned to the task of setting up the chess pieces for the match I'd agreed to.

Didn't asking about a friend's loneliness deserve an answer? I found myself moving my ivory pieces aggressively, fueled by an unfamiliar ill temper. When I declared "Checkmate," it was without apology, without my usual offer to box the pieces. I announced I'd be retiring. Would there be a fire in the room?

"I'll summon Jim," he said.

We breakfasted at one end of the vast dining room table. Small talk was exchanged. The snow had stopped. How had I slept? he asked.

In an indifferent tone, I said, "Fine."

He informed me that I'd be staying until the snow melted.

Did he not know I needed changes of clothes and stockings and the emollients I used on my face? I explained that I hadn't anticipated an overnight visit. My birds were alone. Mr. Woodhouse declared, dismissing the very snow that vexed him, "Your birds are welcome here. Jim will drive you home. You'll collect what you need, and return."

"For what?" I asked.

"To keep me company until Emma and George return."

As his companion and helpmeet? As a governess to an adult man? Were his daughters' instincts faulty, their ministrations a waste of time? Mere companionship was not my fondest hope . . . but still the luxuries of this warm house, its cream soups, the fish and game, the puddings, the pennies saved.

I said, "If you think it's proper . . ."

He looked puzzled, and I sensed why. His expression was asking, *Miss Bates? How could her presence provoke anything but propriety?*

At home, I packed for all eventualities, practically my whole wardrobe, the new and the old, my knitting and my needlepoint, my diary, my parrots. How many books would look too ambitious? I packed just two.

Six days and nights passed before Emma and Mr. Knightley returned. I had had many opportunities—at breakfast, lunch, and dinner; over cordials and backgammon; on walks around the shrubberies—to take his arm and confess that I, too, was lonely, but I did not.

"Well?" Emma asked me in the manner of a bosom friend.

I said, "I keep busy during the day. We take walks. I write letters and read. I don't tire of the games at night because we vary them. And if I may be immodest, I think your father is less frantic over your absence when he has someone to fret with."

"You know it's a huge favour to Mr. Knightley and me?" Emma asked.

I did. But something was bothering me. I'd been to church and had returned to Hartfield in Mr. Woodhouse's carriage. Was I so plain, so unlikely a candidate for scandal, that no one in the village was gossiping about us?

My hair had grown an inch, and a vinegar rinse made it shiny.

A lock on either side of my face had been coaxed into a curlicue. I announced the obvious to Mr. Woodhouse one warm night after taking off my lace cap. "Until recently, I had very long hair—too long, a burden. It gave me headaches. It was like having an extra head on my pillow."

Finally, he looked up.

I said, "I think you know I visited your Isabella."

"London," he grumbled. "Always a sickly season."

"It was an adventure of your daughters' making."

No curiosity; no request for elaboration. "How are the children?" he asked.

I was accustomed to his conversational detours. "All in excellent health," I said. "I think Henry resembles his namesake."

Mr. Woodhouse was now attentive. "Me?"

"He's a very handsome lad," I said, then found myself prattling, once again the Miss Bates of old that I'd been trying to contain. On and on, the eternal talker . . . about Isabella's furniture, their garden, their cook, a roasted goose, a kidney pie, a lemon sponge. When I finally managed to hold my tongue, I held out my empty cordial glass.

He refilled his own glass, too. I let my shawl drop a hand's width from my shoulders. Was there color on his usually pale cheeks? I offered an explanation. "It's warm in front of the fire," I said, fanning my face, blotting my forehead. What did he understand? Had Mrs. Woodhouse died before the change of life? I smoothed my hair, smiling as if I took pride in it. "Your daughters thought I could do better with less. It was heavy and unwieldy. They encouraged me to . . . start over."

Mr. Woodhouse glanced up, but quickly returned to the cards splayed in his hands. I heard myself say—and where on earth did this come from?—"Mr. Woodhouse! Please! I've just shared the extremely personal news that I had my hair cut off in London, in the East End; in fact, at your daughters' behest . . . with some wishful thinking behind it."

He did not ask what their wishful thinking was. He did not acknowledge there was a new Miss Bates across the table. I heard not a compliment or an adjective. I stood up, causing my shawl to fall to the floor. "If it isn't too late for Jim to drive me home, I choose to do that," I declared.

"Miss Bates!" he exclaimed. "Did I say something to offend you? You sound cross, most uncharacteristically! Please sit down!"

Though stung, I kept my spleen. "It's fine. I understand that you're not susceptible."

"To what?" he asked.

To what? To shoulders and necklines and overtures—but hardly what a lady said aloud. Instead, I whispered, "I've grown quite fond of you."

"As I am of you, Miss Bates. You and your mother were always—"

"This is not the time to talk of me and Mrs. Bates in the same context!"

I then heard a word that startled me, nearly a term of endearment that signaled a breakthrough: He addressed me as "Hetty."

I sat down. I leaned across the table—a convexity above my decolletage could not be helped—and placed my hand on his.

Where did this courage come from? Was it my visit to Petticoat Street, its Old Testament flavour? Was I Samson in reverse, whose strengths were nullified by the cutting of his hair?

When my touch evoked a smile and a slow, meaningful nod, it meant we were betrothed.

Mr. Woodhouse was fearful that his daughters would be crestfallen to hear of a marriage.

"I think quite the opposite," I said.

He'd tell them in writing, yes?

The brave new me asked, "Can't you just say to all the Knightleys, perhaps with a raised glass, 'Miss Bates has agreed to be my wife'?"

He did exactly that, with me at his side. Emma hugged both her father and me at once, in such a way, and perhaps not accidentally, that I was pressed against his body.

"When?" everyone wanted to know.

"As soon as possible," I said.

I was oddly unafraid of what a man's marital privileges would mean. Though sheltered by my parents, I grew up in the country where the procreational impulses of dogs and horses were for all to see.

We were married at my father's church by Mr. Elton. Emma and Isabella and their husbands sat in the front pew, beaming. My beloved niece, now Mrs. Frank Churchill, came from Yorkshire to play the church's first organ, gifted by the gratefully liberated Knightley brothers.

I quite took to married life. Mr. Woodhouse, who for so long fancied himself neglected, was restored to a youthful vigor that shortened our hours at the card table.

Emma was able to move the short distance to Mr. Knightley's Donwell Abbey, having fulfilled her promise to stay at Hartfield as long as Mr. Woodhouse needed her. She and George would in quick succession have five children, one more beautiful and cleverer than the next. Though not a grandmother by blood, I became one out of tender devotion.

Happiness has freed me to recognize Miss Austen's kinder words, the ones describing Miss Bates as "a mine of felicity . . . a standing lesson of how to be happy."

Compliments, yes, but heard by me as an overdue apology.

Mr. Woodhouse reminds me I am a vicar's daughter. In the spirit of forgiveness, and with a healed full heart, I can wish Miss Jane Austen and her mostly beautiful words a fitting success.

The Bennets of Jane Street

ADRIANA TRIGIANI

"What say you, Mary? for you are a young lady of deep reflection, I know, and read great books and make extracts."

Mary wished to say something very sensible, but knew not how.

Jane Austen, *Pride and Prejudice*

As Mary Bennet knelt, she tried not to plunge her head too deeply into the cavern inside the cabinet under the sink because dark places in the old house gave her the creeps. She avoided the basement and crawl space under the stairs for the same reason.

Mary wore a headband with an LED light to illuminate the leak in the main pipe. It was the same safety headband her father used when walking the dog through the streets of Greenwich Village at night. Mrs. Bennet insisted her husband wear a light because he had taken a tumble on the cobblestones and wound up black-and-blue. "You never look where you're going! You're absentminded!" she chided her husband at the time.

When Linguini, their beloved puggle, died of old age soon after, Mrs. Bennet was less anxious about her husband falling because he no longer had to walk the dog. She could keep an eye on her husband indoors. (The new battery in the headband outlasted the old dog.) Mary assumed her mother would soon find something else to nag her husband about; for now, there was peace in the village.

As Mary directed the beam of light, she observed that the plumbing grid was a mess, a clutter of too many pipes, some open-ended copper tubes sticking up from the floor, others welded into weird, animal-cracker shapes. She groaned. Typical Bennet family repairs—nothing more than patch jobs. Decades of them. Mary unspooled a swatch of duct tape, made a tear at the top with her teeth, and ripped it from the roll. She carefully wrapped duct tape around the hole in the pipe as if dressing a wound on a battlefield.

Mary had decided not to tell her father about the leak because he'd just feel bad that they couldn't afford a plumber. Besides, at thirty-three years old, she needed to be able to fix whatever was broken. Mary had to be the adult in the family. Her four sisters and their husbands lived outside the city, close enough in case of an emergency, yet far away enough to relieve them of the day-to-day responsibilities of busted pipes, a leaky roof, and their demanding mother.

Her sisters had married and dispersed to the suburbs outside of New York City and beyond. Lizzie and Darcy had moved to Westport, Connecticut; Jane and Bing to Montclair, New Jersey; Kitty and Clem lived in Chestnut Hill, Massachusetts; while Lydia recently moved to Waterford, Virginia, with her second husband, Ethan, a career army guy. Her nieces were small (it turns out that all-girl families turn out all-girl families, at least in the Bennet crew). They gathered together once a year during Christmas. The holiday visits were fun but a tremendous amount of work for Mary, who prepared the house and the meals. Mary didn't complain; after all, she reasoned, her sisters needed a break at holiday time.

Mary was also left behind to care for her parents in the crumbling old house, but to her it was a palazzo. She saw nothing but potential in the sun-soaked rooms with peeling plaster and cracks in the ceiling where the house had settled. The black-and-white-checked marble floor in the foyer was a reminder of the grandeur of another era. The chandeliers, dripping with crystal daggers and strands of beads, were antiques, and despite missing pendants here and there, the overall effect remained dazzling, especially at night. Mary cleaned the crystals with a soft cloth and vinegar so as not to loosen the metal hooks. The parlors were spacious, dark wooden beams on the floorboards, the rooms stuffed with a collection of mismatched styles of furniture that together somehow worked. The Louis XIV chairs and settee were originally covered in pale green velvet, but the fabric had faded to a dull gold. Mary imagined the current patina was every bit as lovely as it had been when it was new years ago.

A crazy-quilt hodgepodge of books, some with jackets missing, others penciled with notes, most with dog-eared corners on their pages—a canon of all genres, colors, and sizes—were jammed into a pair of glass-front chimney closets in no particular order. The closets anchored the black marble fireplace in the back parlor. Their beloved children's books, including Karla Kuskin's *The Philharmonic Gets Dressed* and Syd Hoff's *Danny and the Dinosaur* were wedged between Montaigne's *Essays* and an almanac collection that went as far back as 1942. Mary loved nothing better than choosing a random book and taking a day off to read in the velvet chair, under a bright lamp with a pot of hot coffee and her specialty, chocolate-caramel brownies, close by to snack on. Reading and eating *à deux* never disappointed Mary Bennet. It shored up her soul.

The piano, a Steinway concertina, with a veneer as shiny as black patent leather, was tucked in the front parlor, between the windows that faced the street. Her father had acquired the piano from an ad in the *Village Voice* and given it to his wife on their wedding day in 1980. The piano had a story—a Wall Street banker, addicted to cocaine, sold off his belongings in a fire sale, making Mr. Bennet the beneficiary. The piano had a past, and Mary believed it made the music sound sweeter.

Mary left her sheet music in stacks on side tables and chairs. She would play whenever she had a few minutes. She taught piano lessons to students three days a week and found it exhausting. Organizing the annual recital was so taxing it nearly put her in the hospital, but when it was over, she felt a sense of accomplishment that she experienced nowhere else in her life. She enjoyed complaining about her students and their families, even though they were her bread and butter. Mary had to admit, as much as she identified with her father's calm nature, like her mother, she had bought more than one ticket to the emotional roller coaster. Restraint was the goal, though Mary did not ever meet her own standard. Despite her shortcomings, there were things that brought Mary joy.

A cup of sharpened pencils balanced on the nearby windowsill. When Mary wasn't teaching, she wrote plays. HB Studios was a two-minute walk away, which made it convenient for Mary to take playwriting classes. She had been trained over many years by Donna DeMatteo, a stellar playwright who encouraged Mary's work. Mary's ideas were nurtured by DeMatteo, something she lacked from her upbringing. The dark rehearsal space, lit by ghost lights, was her church. If HB Studios was Mary's place of worship, the family homestead was her factory. The scent of chalk and paint were the perfume of her creativity.

Mary had everything she needed on Jane Street to teach music and write plays, with plenty of space to wander when she chose to procrastinate. Throughout the day, she followed the sunlight up the five floors, to work and do her chores. There were two spacious rooms per floor, front and back, and three bathrooms—one on the second floor, where her parents had a bedroom and dressing room, and one on the third floor, where she endured with the faulty pipes and used to live with her sisters. A third powder room on the parlor floor had not been operational in fifty years. It was on Mr. Bennet's to-do list, but so far, renovation had not been done.

The sun rose on the front rooms and set on the back of the house. Mary never looked at the clock—there was no need—she followed the light. In this way, she was one with the family homestead. Old houses were idea factories, or at least they were to Mary Bennet. History had a way of speaking to her through wallpaper and paint, though she doubted anyone would understand her feelings.

The middle of five sisters, Mary assumed the role of the maiden aunt with an ease that can come only from resignation. Her fate was never to marry and to be of service in a different way, one that relieved her sisters of responsibilities. Mary was destined to take care of her aging parents and the house that went with them. Her mother had signs of early dementia, but Mary couldn't remember a time when her mother, even when she was young, didn't have a version of it. It seemed to Mary that everyone in her family was in denial about her mother's emotional short-circuiting, fluctuating anxiety levels, and sporadic forgetfulness. Mary assumed there was some depression afoot, because Mrs. Bennet had recently begun to take to her bed more often than she got out of it. Mr. Bennet knew when he married his wife that he had made his bed, and until further notice, they would lie in it together until the end. It was the kind of love that endured because of the sheer numbers. They had five daughters together and seven granddaughters. It was a family held together by girls and their velvet ribbons.

Mary's father had worked on and off as a freelance journalist through the years, and once in the 1980s he sold a book proposal that was sure to change the Bennet family fortunes, but it didn't. The book didn't sell, even though it was quite good. "And that's that," his wife said at the time, more disappointed at the failure than the author. When it came to finances, Mr. Bennet's single lucky break came in real estate. His parents left him Number 10 Jane Street, though it was not a straight inheritance, as it was encumbered by debt. The specifics of the debt had always been murky, and it did mean that the old house with the leaky pipes, shoddy electrics, and old windows on one of the most enchanting blocks in New York City would not be renovated by Mr. Bennet due to lack of funds.

The Bennets raised their daughters in Greenwich Village, which they could ill afford if the house had not been an inheritance. But as it goes with families, gifts often come with strings. There was debt on the building to the Collins family, Mr. Bennet's cousin, which her father assumed without complaint. Working and living under stressful financial circumstances was a Bennet family trait, like their predisposition for flat feet and adenoids. Her father believed, no matter what, it was his role to soldier on and hold on to the house.

Mary wished her father was not beholden to the Collins family. Surely they would allow the Bennets to remain in the house for as long as they lived, but it caused a deep sense of insecurity. Owning a home meant freedom from the tyranny of the landlord, a luxury the Bennets had never known. They would always be renters from the Collins family, who waited for Mr. Bennet to die so they might swoop in and sell the place. The reality of the bad deal, struck before Mary was born, made her shudder.

Mary's phone buzzed. She had propped it on the nearby toilet lid like a photograph in a frame, in order to follow the YouTube repair video. She banged her head as she pulled it out from under the sink. She cursed under her breath and tapped the screen.

"Mary Bennet?"

"This is she." Mary squinted at the phone, which said in big letters: BLOCKED CALLER. "May I ask who is calling?"

"Tsk. Lady de Bourgh, of course."

"Oh, Ms. de Bourgh! Forgive me."

Mary and her sisters found it hilarious that anyone would give their daughter the first name *Lady*. It was pretentious, like naming children after cities they hadn't visited (Paris), foods they hadn't eaten (Mignon), and designers they hadn't worn (Chanel). Lady de Bourgh had been the guest of the Bennet family many times, because she was the longtime president of the Greenwich Village Historical Society, and a cousin through Lizzie's marriage to Fitzwilliam Darcy.

"I have no forgiveness left, Mary. I'm calling because you have won one of the playwriting prizes—well, you're in . . . second place. Congratulations."

Mary could hear de Bourgh shuffling papers.

"Yes, second place," she went on. "A cash prize of five thousand dollars and a staged reading at the Transport Group."

Hot tears flooded Mary's eyes.

"Mary, are you there?"

"Yes, yes, I'm here. I'm so grateful. Thank you."

"That's nice. Frankly, I was surprised to see your name in the group of winners. The committee is composed of artistic directors of seven off-Broadway theaters. Your play must have rung a bell with them."

"I can't believe it," Mary said softly.

Lady de Bourgh went on, "So I imagine you're stunned that you won. The Bennet girls are intellectually elusive, in my opinion."

Mary had no idea what *intellectually elusive* meant, but it didn't matter. She had won a prize! Her play would get a staged reading, or even better, a production! That was all that mattered.

"Mary, are you there? Damn phone," de Bourgh muttered.

"I'm here! I'm here. I'm just happy, that's all."

"Well, then. Go to the website for further instructions."

Mary looked at herself in the mirror. The light on the headband gave a ring light effect in the mirror. She leaned in to take a good look at herself. She smiled. Her lips were thin but well shaped, coated with cherry ChapStick. Her pale skin and brown hair were mousy, but now that she was an award-winning playwright, she saw a certain sparkle that she had never seen before. Mary tilted her head in profile, like Virginia Woolf in her official portrait. *There*, she thought to herself. *I have character at an angle.*

Mary knelt down and collected her tools, placing them neatly in the kit, when, suddenly overwhelmed, she leaned against the doorjamb. She began to cry, which soon turned into a big weep. Mary Bennet was unaccustomed to good news, or any surprising turn in her favor. The news of a windfall based upon her work moved her deeply. She didn't dare think that a run of good luck had begun; instead, she would savor this happy news as a one-off. As a middle sister, she expected her portion and nothing more. What a portion this was! The beam of cold blue light on the headband bobbed as she cried, throwing shards of light on the pink linoleum floor and making circles on the speckled tile. Through her glassy tears, Mary saw a field of pink diamonds that filled her with a sense of her own possibilities, and her future, she hoped, in the American theater. She stood and wiped her tears on her sleeve. She turned on the faucet and peered under the sink to see if the duct-taped pipe held against the water pressure. It had.

MRS. BENNET

Mary carried a tray with tea and a fresh sugar cookie up the stairs to her parents' bedroom. She shoved the bedroom door open with her elbow and peered inside. Her mother, fully dressed in slacks and a blouse, lay on the bed and studied the television set. Her gray hair was pulled back into a low bun, which Mary had brushed into place that morning. Mrs. Bennet's brow was creased with worry lines as she listened to Spectrum News NY1, a local channel that covered stories about the city, from congestion pricing to the weather. Occasionally, the roving reporters would catch a crime as it was unfolding. It was essential viewing for Mrs. Bennet—even the questionable content.

"If we get another storm like Sandy, lower Manhattan will overflow like a bathtub." Mrs. Bennet's blue eyes were shiny and wet. "We'll bob in the filth and muck like plastic toys. You'll see." She waved her hand at the television screen. "This idiot is talking about sandbags. What good are they in a tsunami? How many blocks are we from the Hudson River?"

"Five blocks."

"Too close."

"There won't be a tsunami, Ma," Mary said, placing the tray on the chair by the bed. "And we're far enough from the river. The house is on an incline. We won't flood out."

Mrs. Bennet was not comforted. "You made me tea? My Mary."

"You asked for it, remember?" Mary smiled.

"I did, didn't I? I try not to be a bother," her mother said, not meaning it.

"You're not."

"I can't watch another moment of this." Mrs. Bennet turned off the television. "Television used to be entertaining. Now? It's a sump pump of nerve-inducing stories designed to upset people. It's constant. When will it end?"

"You're fine." Mary plumped the pillows behind her mother. "Lean forward."

Mrs. Bennet leaned.

"Now, lean back."

"Oh, you're an expert caregiver. You should have been a nurse. Or a PT. Or a doctor."

"I'm bad at science and math, remember?"

"Oh, please, Mary. Those are just excuses. When you have a weakness, compensate! A little elbow grease and common sense go a long way to counter low SAT scores."

That she remembers. Mary shook her head as she sat down on the bed. "You're right, Mom. I'm a compensator. Even my mechanical skills are improving. I fixed my sink. I'm a plumber without a license."

"See there? There is nothing my Mary cannot do when she puts her mind to it. She's a star." Mrs. Bennet had complimented her middle child as though she wasn't in the room.

Mary stood and began to straighten the space, hanging clothes draped on a chair and stacking magazines neatly. Mrs. Bennet had a way of pulling her daughter into her emotional twisters. Mary couldn't see her mother's rages coming, even when the signs were the same. Distemper led to fretting, fretting led to panic, panic giving way to a full-tilt meltdown. Mary had learned to ride them out. Her sister Lizzie was an expert at it. If only Mary could be more like Lizzie. Inside Mary's soul, she was a trash heap of steaming emotions, though on the outside, the only indications were the sweat and squirm, where she couldn't stand still and settled her nerves with busywork. Like now. She shifted from one foot to the other as she contemplated the end of the world and gathered empty teacups from the nightstands.

"Why are you sweating?" her mother asked.

"It's hot in here."

"It's freezing. Your father has the heat on sixty-five. Why?"

"To save money, Ma."

"Of course, I could've answered my own question. It's always about the purse."

Then why did you ask? Mary wondered. She believed, at her

age, in adulthood, she would've devised a way to cope with her mother.

"We will soon have to plan Christmas." Mrs. Bennet pulled a handkerchief out from under her bra strap and began to pull at the edges.

Mary recognized the sign and went to her, placing her hands over her mother's, which seemed to soothe her. "Mama, listen to me. You don't have to do a thing. I'll take care of it. All of it."

"You need my help with the roast."

"Happy to have you season it. You can help prep the potatoes, too."

"I love a delicate scalloped potato." Mrs. Bennet smiled.

"It will be perfect," Mary promised her.

Her sisters had it all figured out—they showed up on holidays with perfect manicures, wearing mommy/daughter Christmas dresses and carrying boxes of homemade cookies. Jane made a pineapple upside-down cake. Lizzie a cream-cheese Bundt cake. They'd deposit their desserts on the sideboard and roll up their sleeves to help serve the dinner Mary had made. Mary would decorate the tree, leaving one set of ornaments in boxes with hooks so the children could decorate the lower branches. Mary thought of everything.

MR. BENNET

Mary climbed the stairs with the threadbare runner to the top of the house, avoiding the holes and the spots where the wool buckled. Her father was sitting behind an old desk opening mail. The sun cut across the papers that were piled on the desk in neat stacks. The piles of paper had not changed since Mary was a girl. Her father had a system: Everything had a place, and the documents were organized alphabetically with clips, but nothing ever got done. The pile of bills were paid via snail mail. A large black binder holding the checks sat upright on the shelf next to the desk. Though Mary had tried, the thought of using online banking was anathema to her father. Mr. Bennet stretched his Social Security check like it was made of rubber from the Congo, but it never stretched far enough.

Mr. Bennet was tall, with fine features on a large face. His gray eyes tilted down in the corners. He forced his eyes to open wide over his reading glasses when Mary entered his office with a tray.

"Thank you, Mary."

Mary placed a tray with a turkey sandwich, potato salad, and a pickle on the desk. She handed him a tall glass of iced tea.

"I wish you wouldn't wait on me, Mary."

"If I didn't, you would never eat."

"Of course I would. It just wouldn't be delicious." Mr. Bennet took a bite of the sandwich.

"Dad, when I get the prize money for my play, I want to hire a plumber."

"Absolutely not! That's my responsibility."

"I could negotiate a good deal," Mary insisted.

"No question. But your prize money is yours. There are things you need and want, and you should have them."

"I have lots of years to save."

"You think you do, and one day, you wake up and you're seventy-eight years old and you've been patching and stretching for so long, you don't know any other way to live. I don't want that to be your fate, Mary."

"I'll be fine, Dad."

Mr. Bennet's expression softened. "Always positive. I wish I were like you."

"My playwriting teacher taught me never to make any assumptions about any character. Let them live in the scene and see where they take you."

"That's not easy to do. You write drama. I wrote nonfiction. History. The drama in history lives in the facts. You have to create the world and the characters from nothing. I think that's much more difficult."

Mary could not find a way to tell her father that she didn't write from nothing; she wrote from experience, the stories she heard in this old house, with her sisters and mother. With him. The hilarity and pain that ensued, all of it, Mary hoped, were in her play. There was even a good man who couldn't catch a break but found his happiness in raising his children. It was as if life in the outside world, including his career and ambition, were secondary to the family inside the house. But a father who does not achieve his dreams breaks a daughter's heart, because it might mean that her dreams won't come true, either. Mary wished her father had been rewarded for his contributions as a writer. Life had not been fair to Mr. Bennet.

Mary sat, leaned on the desk, and placed her face in her hands. She looked at her father, grateful for all of the one-on-one time she had with him. Mary had made a list of questions to ask her father, but that day, she was particularly curious about his artistry. When his eyes met hers, she asked, "Dad, why didn't you ever write another book?"

Mr. Bennet leaned back in his chair. "I didn't think I could write a better one."

"You said all you had to say?" Mary asked.

"I didn't say that." Mr. Bennet sipped his iced tea. "I didn't have the confidence to try again. It takes a level of belief in yourself to write. The page is filled with the person you are. Your observations. Your point of view. Your research. It's all very personal, in my estimation. How a writer sees things is who he is."

"It's your identity."

"In a way. And—it frightened your mother to be married to a writer. It seemed like a flimflammy way to live and bring up a family. And it was. That's why I took in copyediting jobs and tutored. We never knew when the money would land, if it did at all. It affected her nerves. The instability of it all. When you're an artist, a writer, a playwright, what have you, you cannot be tethered to anything but your work—the desk, the lamp, the paper, and the pencil are your life. And I fear if they aren't, the work is probably not very good."

"If the book had been a bestseller, we would be having a different conversation," Mary assured him.

"Do you think so? Or do you think that maybe I would have gotten a swelled head, grown out my sideburns, and left this old house for something new?"

"You're not the type, Dad."

"I often think I can't take another no." The ancient desk chair creaked as Mr. Bennet sat back in it. "But I do. I wish I had something to offer my children at this stage of my life—I wanted to leave you all something so you wouldn't end up like your mother and me."

"Everything isn't about money," Mary said quietly.

Financial anxiety seemed inborn in her. Mary couldn't remember a time when the topic of money didn't rattle her, and yet, she had to put on an act like it was the last thing on her mind. Mary wished she were wealthy and believed it would solve all their problems. There was never enough; her mother made sure her disappointment was obvious to her father, as if criticizing him would help him make more money. But Mary could see that his struggle was as much as he could handle—you couldn't add ambition and personal growth to his piles of obligations. All her father could do was push through, and Mary, a pragmatist, was just like him.

"My cousin the minister once said something in a sermon that actually made sense. He said, 'Money is always a problem, whether you have a lot, or a little, or just enough to get by, it's always a concern,'" Mr. Bennet shared.

"For Mr. Collins, it's a love affair," Mary said wryly.

MR. O'DONOGHUE

Whenever Mary sat on the stoop and watched folks walk down Jane Street, she observed them as though the action that unfolded before her was a movie and she were in the scene. She had a small peek into the lives of strangers through their conversations as they passed. Stoop sitting had made Mary Bennet a good listener, an essential skill in writing dialogue. Sometimes she rushed inside to fetch her playwriting notebook when a good line was uttered. Her favorite: A man, whose girlfriend's arm was laced through his, said, "Beth, the easiest person to cheat on is the one who trusts you." Mary recorded it exactly as she heard it. That line ended up in the play that had won her the prize.

Mary never tired of Jane Street, regardless of the weather or the season. The rectangle of blue sky overhead was precious. New Yorkers evaluated how much sky they could see from their windows as though it were valuable real estate. Jane Street had various charms through the seasons. In autumn, the leaves on the trees that lined the street were turning orange and red, moving in the breeze like feathers. The cobblestone street had fissures and pits that caused a yellow cab to buck on the surface as it passed.

Cobblestones were meant for horses, not cars, Mary reminded herself. She buttoned her jean jacket and turned up the collar against the wind. Mary checked her phone. The paving company was due to arrive any moment. She closed her eyes and enjoyed a few moments of solitude. Sometimes she was weary from going up and down the stairs, taking meals, clearing the dishes, and doing the laundry. It was as if she were the lady of the house caring for boarders, and sometimes, when her mother was particularly cranky, needy children.

The work van pulled into an empty space in front of the brownstone. A handsome Irishman and his apprentice emerged.

"A parking spot is always good luck." The man waved at Mary. "Kiernan O'Donoghue. This is my son, Kevin." Kiernan had sandy hair and a strong build. The son looked just like his father, a more slender version with a thicker thatch of hair. "You Mary Bennet?"

"Yes, sir."

Kiernan and Kevin went to the back of the van and opened the service doors as Mary studied the name of the paving company painted in emerald green on the side of the vehicle: *The Lucky Shamrock Paving Company, Sunnyside, Queens.*

Everything about the company seemed uplifting: its name, location, and the level of attractiveness of the stonemasons. Mary stuffed her phone into her back pocket. She crossed her arms across her chest and waited.

"Let's see what we've got here," Kiernan said as he approached the stoop.

"I got a summons from the city." Mary reached into the pocket of her jean jacket. She unfolded the letter she found there and handed it to Kiernan. "They tell me we have to fix the sidewalk. There have been complaints."

"You don't want anyone tripping on your sidewalk," Kevin said, smiling. He might be around her age, but she couldn't tell for sure.

"No, I don't." She smiled back at Kevin.

"You've got a crack here," Kiernan said. "This has caused the concrete plate to buckle."

"Can you patch it?" Mary asked.

"It's been patched before. If I were you, I'd fix it once and be done with it. We need to take up the sidewalk and repour the concrete; otherwise, we'll be back in a matter of months to fix it again. We're going to have a bad winter."

"I didn't know," Mary said. "How much will this cost?"

Kevin ran his hand through his hair. "You're just like my wife; you want to know the bad news up front."

Mary tried not to show that she was bummed that Kevin was married, but she should have known. Every month it seemed that more single men in her age category drained away from the pool of potential husbands. Mary Bennet was on the verge of giving up altogether.

"It's just an estimate," Kiernan began.

"An estimate is fine." Mary looked at him. "I won't hold you to it."

"We have to break up the old sidewalk, replane the ground, and pour the concrete. Looks like the curb is crumbling, so we need to redo it. We have to bring a cement mixer in. Five thousand."

"Five thousand dollars?" Mary said the number out loud.

It wasn't lost on Mary that she would be earning the exact amount in prize money that it would take to fix the sidewalk. But when she called the city and reviewed the fines that awaited the Bennets if they did not fix the sidewalk, they were far worse. Mary understood they would be saving money in the long run if they did the job once and properly.

Her father suggested a patch job, but Mary ignored him. "Dad, we can't wait on this. We've been kicking the can down the road for so long, we'll never find it," she told him. Mary was tired of fixing things only to last long enough for them to go bust again. The city of New York had a policy that the sidewalk and curb in front of a landlord-owned building was the responsibility of the homeowner. Mary could not bear the thought of someone tripping and falling because of fissures and cracks in the sidewalk. The Bennets could lose everything with one lawsuit. The reality weighed on Mary.

Mary put in her earbuds and listened to a podcast about the Brontë sisters as she washed the iron skillet and pans she'd used to make breakfast. She folded the dish towel and hung it on the hook when she felt the house shake. One jolt overhead.

She pulled the earbuds out of her ears and raced up the stairs. Her mother was screaming while her father lay on the floor next to the bed. Mary went to him. "Dad?"

He mumbled something, but Mary could not make it out over her mother's hysterics. She dialed 911. She informed the operator of her father's condition and their address. Mary turned to her mother.

"Not now, Ma. Enough with the drama," Mary said to her mother. She knelt next to her father. "The ambulance is on the way. Don't try to move, Dad."

"Ugh," Mr. Bennet moaned.

Mary looked over at the breakfast tray, untouched by her father and mother.

"I'm getting dressed." Mrs. Bennet got up from the bed. "Do not try and stop me."

DR. MARTINELLI

Mary handed her mother a cup of coffee. Mrs. Bennet wrapped her hands around the paper cup and sipped.

"Here's a cookie," Mary said, placing it on the table next to her in the waiting room. "In lieu of a proper breakfast."

"Who can eat? Who can think about eating? This is the end," Mrs. Bennet said as she stared off in the middle distance. She picked up the cookie and nibbled a corner of it. "Your poor father."

"He's not poor, and this isn't the end."

"The day I dreaded has come," Mrs. Bennet said wearily, ignoring her.

"That would be every single day, Ma," Mary countered.

"You wait. They'll come at us with a terrible diagnosis."

"His sugar was elevated. He may have crossed over from pre-diabetic to diabetic."

"Or it's *cancer*," Mrs. Bennet whispered the *C* word and looked at Mary. "Better to expect the worst and work back."

"Why?" Mary sat down next to her mother. "Why would anyone do that?"

"Because you can walk forward from bleak, but you can't walk back from high expectations."

"Ma, that's ridiculous."

"I don't expect you to take anything I say seriously. You girls look at me like I'm Nathan Lane in *The Birdcage* or Aunt Pittypat in *Gone with the Wind*. I see your faces. You think I'm a hanky-waving wing nut. Emotionally unhinged."

"Not true. I take most of what you say to heart—but this time, I just know you're wrong."

"I'm never right in your eyes."

"That's not true." Mary was tired of arguing with her mother. "Are you afraid?"

Mrs. Bennet put the coffee cup down. She fished inside her blouse and pulled a handkerchief out from her bra strap, then dabbed her eyes. "I'm terrified. I've been married to your father for half of my life. More, maybe. I think it's more. I was never good at math. Anyway, this is where it's all heading. Down the drain. All that time expended and nothing to show for it."

"You have five daughters," Mary reminded her.

"Who have left me for parts unknown."

"I left you for parts upstairs," Mary countered.

"You know what I mean," Mrs. Bennet snapped.

"Come on, Mama. You know where your daughters are. They're not far."

"I suppose I shouldn't complain. At least my Mary found it in her heart to stay."

Mary sighed. When her mother spoke about her in the third person in her presence, Mary knew she was cooked. She had no defense. Mary had stayed on Jane Street to care for her parents because she was needed, which in her mind was always the best reason to serve. Second, HB Studios was close. Third, if Mary were offered the option to live anywhere of her choosing in the world, she would pick Greenwich Village every time. How could she explain how much Jane Street meant to her? The winding lanes from another century, with the lights in the high-rises twinkling in the distance? The Hudson River, mighty and gray, with foam caps? The Statue of Liberty, with her blue-green gown, holding a gold torch, that cut a beam in the night sky and could be seen for miles? The wide expanse of the mouth of the Hudson, where it meets the Atlantic Ocean, where any explorer worth their salt had sailed through to find their idea of heaven? Mary could go on and on about how much she loved New York City, but no one understood, not even her father and mother, who had lived in the city all of their married life.

"My Lizzie!" Mrs. Bennet shouted as her second-eldest daughter entered the room.

Lizzie Darcy wore cuffed jeans and a barn jacket. Her hair was pulled back in a low ponytail. Her cheeks were flushed bright pink, which brought out the blue in her eyes. "I came as soon as I could," she apologized.

"I can't believe you got here this fast," Mary said.

"My angel!" Mrs. Bennet extended her arms like a three-year-old child who hoped to be lifted and twirled around the room.

Lizzie embraced her mother and sat down next to her. "Are you all right, Mama?"

"I'll never be the same again."

Lizzie looked at Mary.

"Dad will be okay. They ruled out his heart. And he didn't have a stroke."

"Thank goodness," Lizzie said. "We should be grateful."

"They have him doing tests right now. Could be diabetes," Mary fretted. She knew if her father needed medication, she would be the one to administer it; her mother was incapable.

"He can live with that," Lizzie said.

"Your father refuses to follow instructions and take the most basic of medications. I'd like to know how he could ever control his sugar." Mrs. Bennet sighed.

"He will have to—that's all. He will learn how to take care of himself," Lizzie assured her. Elizabeth Bennet was the most practical of the Bennet sisters. She saw a way through any dilemma by using common sense. Lizzie created order from chaos.

Jane arrived. She scanned the room from the doorway. Her sisters squealed when they saw her. Jane grinned and moved toward them, before her expression turned somber. It was wonderful to see her sisters, but she wished it were just for fun. Tall and willowy, Jane sashayed toward them. Her heels did not click on the linoleum because she glided over the floor like a dancer. She wore a wrap dress, and her chocolate-brown suede trench coat was open, the belt dangling from its loops. Her suede pumps matched the coat. Her blond hair fell in waves to the top of her shoulders.

"There they are!" Kitty entered the room behind Jane and pointed.

"Oh, Kitty, were you working in the garage?" Mrs. Bennet made a face. Where Jane was chic, Kitty looked like a farmer fresh from the plow.

"I was pumpkin picking with the girls." Kitty looked down at her muddy jeans and boots. Her hair was haphazardly pinned up with a series of small barrettes.

"Well, you make an excellent pumpkin picker," Mrs. Bennet said. "Evidently, you had to dig for them."

Mary, Lizzie, Kitty, and Jane looked at one another and laughed.

"I'm happy you find me amusing in my hour of despair," Mrs. Bennet said, blowing her nose into her handkerchief.

Mary checked her phone. "Lydia won't get here until the morning. She's taking the train from DC."

"Poor Lydia, living the peripatetic existence of an army wife. Do you think this country honors her sacrifice? I doubt it. She's nothing but heart, my Lydia, and a cog in the wheel of American defense."

"Her husband is a general. I don't think they do cogs."

"How many stars?" Mrs. Bennet asked.

Mary shot Lizzie a look. No one in the Bennet family could ever keep up with Lydia's love life. They were always polite but didn't get involved with her husbands. Lydia had more stepchildren over three marriages than Mrs. Bennet had grandchildren.

"Go ahead you two. Make faces. There is no title high enough for the husbands of my daughters," Mrs. Bennet insisted.

"You have a soft spot for Lydia," Lizzie said pleasantly. "And there's nothing wrong with that. It's hard not to choose a favorite daughter."

"I refuse! I love all my girls equally."

Dr. Martinelli entered the waiting room. He was tall, his jet-black hair combed back. He smiled and approached the Bennet women.

"Mr. Bennet told me to look for the girl group," the doctor said.

"That's us." Lizzie smiled and stood.

"Oh, Doctor, what is the news? How is my dear husband?"

"He is resting now. The tests showed us he has a blockage in his aorta. He's in and out of A-fib."

"I knew it!" Mrs. Bennet cried out. "A racing heart will kill him!"

"Luckily, your husband did not have a heart attack. This was a pre-episode. We're going to continue our testing. He may need an ablation."

"Surgery?" Mary asked.

"It's the least invasive of invasive heart procedures."

"Does that explain the fall?" Lizzie asked.

"It could. He may have been lightheaded, lying down, and then got up too suddenly."

"When can we see him?" Mary wanted to know.

"He's resting now, but you can go in any time you wish."

MR. BENNET'S GIRLS MINUS ONE

The machines beeped behind Mr. Bennet's hospital bed. The graphs of green, pulsating blue dots, dings, and beeps reminded Jane of her brief stint as a runner on the stock exchange floor when she was first out of college. Lizzie took the colorful lines on the screens as signs of hope. Mrs. Bennet looked up at the same screens utterly confused because she could not read their meaning. Kitty refused to look at the machines and instead kept her eyes on her father. She was internally beating herself up that she didn't do enough for him, didn't call, visit, or see him enough. Mary was confident. Her father was getting excellent care. He would bounce back. She was sure of it.

Mr. Bennet's eyes fluttered open. He looked around the bed at his daughters and wife.

"Have I died?"

Mrs. Bennet gave his arm a gentle jab. "Always with the jokes."

"I lived, didn't I? The grimmest joke of all."

Mary, Jane, Lizzie, and Kitty took turns kissing their father on the cheek.

"You need to be positive, Papa," Lizzie said.

"Why?"

"Because it makes it easier on me," Mary joked.

"Well, for you, Mary, I will fill to the brim and spill over with hope."

"Now you're talking." Kitty smiled.

"Kitty, you came so far. Did you walk?"

"I got muddy in the pumpkin patch."

"You tracked mud all the way from Massachusetts."

"And I'm glad I did. No one wanted to sit next to me on the Acela."

"I wish you would have called. There was no need for you to come all this way."

"I wanted to, Pa." Kitty squeezed his hand. "Am I still your favorite?"

"Don't tell the others," Mr. Bennet teased.

"I never would."

Lizzie put her arm around Kitty, but it didn't help, she cried anyway.

"Now, no tears," her father said.

Mrs. Bennet fished for her handkerchief and dabbed her eyes. "It's a pity to grow old and useless. All these years, all this affection, and for what? To wind up in a hospital being snaked by a copper coil?"

"You always know what to say to make me feel better, my dearest," Mr. Bennet said wryly.

"I do my best." Mrs. Bennet blew loudly into her handkerchief, startling everyone. She dabbed her tears.

Mr. Bennet closed his eyes. "Pay no attention to your dear mother, girls. You see, I'm on the comeback. Don't you worry!" Mr. Bennet opened his eyes and looked at them. "I have big plans. I have much to accomplish in my dotage."

"Like what?" Jane put her hand on her father's shoulder.

"Oh, a list of things. Getting from point A to point B, for starters."

"Good one." Mary laughed.

"Walking with a cane," Kitty offered.

"That doesn't even take practice," Jane said. "And you look regal using one."

"We'll see, Jane. I'm all legs, and they prefer to go akimbo. I have some neuropathy in my feet. When you can't feel your feet, good luck feeling the ground underneath them."

"There are more bones in the feet than in any other limb," Mary said.

"And all of mine ache," Mr. Bennet admitted. "Ladies, I want you to go home now. Mary will prepare dinner. Now go on. All of you. Home to Jane Street. I need my rest."

THE UNEXPECTED REUNION

Lizzie settled her mother in her bed.

"Call me if you need anything."

"I took a Klonopin," Mrs. Bennet admitted. "My nerves should settle now."

Before Lizzie could turn out the light, her mother was snoring. Lizzie went out into the hallway and down the steps. She stopped in the front parlor and took a look around before going through the pocket doors to the back parlor. This had been her favorite room in the old house. Books from floor to ceiling. Afternoon sun, she remembered. And the kitchen close by, to make a quick cup of tea to accompany her reading.

Lizzie turned on the small lamp on the side table before going through the door into the kitchen. Mary had set the table with a cloth and a candle. The soup bowls, Italian from Deruta, were stacked next to the Crock-Pot. The black-and-white marble floor was polished. The walnut table with the additional leaves was stretched to accommodate ten. Mary had not made it smaller since last Christmas because she liked to spread her scenes out on the table and look at them in small piles. She moved the action around on the table just as she hoped to do on the stage.

"Smells wonderful in here," Lizzie said.

Mary removed a loaf of bread from the oven. She placed a crock of butter next to it. "Let it cool," she said to her sisters.

"I can't believe you bake your own bread," Jane marveled. "Where do you find the time?"

"I found the old breadmaking machine in the basement," Mary said. "And wouldn't you know, our parents consume a lot of bread."

"You take such good care of them," Kitty said.

"Thank you, Kit. I made up all the beds. I'm sorry if your mattresses are on the lumpy side, but they're on my list to replace when we get some extra funds coming in," Mary said pleasantly.

"We can help put a fund together," Jane offered.

"You do enough. All of you. It takes five daughters to take care of two parents, evidently," Mary explained.

"Lydia says she'll be here by morning." Jane looked down at her phone.

"We'll have to take an official reunion photo once she arrives." Lizzie smiled.

"We'll go out on the stoop," Jane agreed.

"Better lighting out there," Mary joked.

The girls helped Mary serve the stew. Jane uncorked a bottle of wine and poured the burgundy Orvieto into glasses.

Jane raised her glass as Mary sat down and joined them at the table. "To Mary. Our brilliant artist. Our playwright. Our sister. God knows she can tell a story."

"And God knows she's got plenty to choose from," Lizzie added.

"Congratulations on your prize!" Kitty said as the girls clinked their glasses for good luck.

"It's not a big deal," Mary said.

"Oh really? We think it is! You've been taking classes at HB Studios since we can remember."

"I enjoy the classes. Winning the prize is extra."

"We'll all come to the premiere," Jane promised.

"Pa will be better by then," Lizzie said. "But we should think about the future."

"And the house." Jane nibbled at the stew.

"What are you thinking?" Mary's voice broke as she cut the bread.

"We have a guesthouse," Lizzie began, "and we could take Mom and Dad with us."

"What would happen to the house?"

"We'd sell it," Jane said softly.

"And what about me?" Mary asked.

Her sisters had not thought her fate through, or if they had, they weren't about to admit their plans to Mary.

"I would like to stay here and take care of the place as I've always done."

"The place is falling apart." Kitty looked around the room. "Needs a renovation."

"The downstairs bathroom has never worked properly," Lizzie said.

"Pa never had the funds to fix it," Jane said defensively. "Old houses are expensive."

"This house was always old. It was always in need of renovation. It was never brought up to code. But that's what's wonderful about it," Mary said. "It has history. It persists. It's not a grand brownstone; it's a home. And I love every corner of it. As long as I can climb the stairs and care for our parents, I don't think moving them to Connecticut is a very good idea. Mama is afraid of bugs and anything that tweets, including a phone. Papa works in his office every day, or pretends to, but it gives him a purpose to move papers around."

"He's been pushing those papers since we were little." Jane smiled.

"You know, our father is a writer. He never got much encouragement for it." Mary looked around the table at her sisters.

"He gave up too easily when his book was published," Jane said.

"Writers don't give up. Not ever. But we spend a good deal of time wondering how we can reach an audience who may see the world in the same way we do. If you want to know the truth, I would write plays whether I won a prize or not, but getting the prize validated all my years of working at it. Pa never had that—he never got that moment of recognition, that his work was amazing, which it is. He has gone unappreciated; sadly, our mother looks to the world to approve of his work, instead of offering it to him herself."

"Are you saying our parents are a bad match?" Kitty wondered.

"When it comes to Pa's writing life, there were challenges, for sure. But he loves her."

"He understands her," Lizzie said.

"Isn't that a form of love?" Jane asked.

"In this house it is," Mary said. "I see it every day."

"So what you're saying is, ride it out? Don't make a plan for our parents as they age and develop health problems?"

"No, Lizzie, that's not what I'm saying. I think we see how Pa does with this procedure, and once he's better, we can discuss this," Mary said.

"This in no way means we aren't grateful to you." Jane patted Mary's hand.

"Thank you. But please understand why I stay. I love them and I love this house—and I can't imagine living anywhere else in the world, even if you offered it to me."

"I felt the same until I moved," Kitty said. "You find you can make your home anywhere when you set your mind to it."

"You have a husband and children. That's different." Mary looked at them. "You all have husbands and children. I'm alone."

"You will fall in love someday," Lizzie assured her.

"Will I?" Mary wondered. "Well, it won't happen tonight, that's for sure. But I will put it on my list of things to do."

The doorbell rang. The girls looked at one another.

"Probably Amazon," Mary guessed as she went to answer the front door.

Mary unbolted the lock and peered through the chain. "It's Lydia!" she shouted. Mary loosened the chain and let her sister in.

Lydia wore pencil jeans and a tight sweater. She teetered on stiletto heels. Her hair was long, pulled up into a high ponytail that cascaded down her back.

Lizzie, Kitty, and Jane joined them in the vestibule.

"That was some train!" Lizzie said, hugging her sister. "You smell divine."

"Mademoiselle by Christian Dior. Thanks. I blew off the train. A corporal out of Fort Belvoir was driving up for a meeting and offered me a ride. Very handsome. Single. About thirty-two. Just right for our Mary. I had the most wonderful four hours looking at his perfect profile."

"How was he from the front?" Mary asked.

The girls laughed.

"Not bad. The eyes are a bit flinty, but a good strong nose and chin," Lydia reported.

"How do you grow your hair out so quickly? I might need biotin." Kitty patted the barrettes that held her hair in place.

"I don't grow anything. It's a weave," Lydia explained as she flicked it.

"Oh." Lizzie and the girls examined Lydia's hair like it was a sculpture in a museum.

"Are you hungry?" Jane asked.

"Of course. I hope you have carbohydrates."

"Tons," Mary promised.

Mary, Lydia, and Kitty went into the kitchen. Lizzie pulled Jane back into the front parlor as she followed them.

"What are we going to do about Mary?" Lizzie whispered.

"What do you mean?" Jane asked.

Lizzie ran her hand over the arm of the old velvet-covered chair. "She wants to stay in the house."

"New York City holds an allure for single women. It always has. This is no place to bring up a family."

"We were raised here, Jane," Lizzie countered. "And if I'm honest, I dream of the day I can return."

"I thought you loved your garden."

"I do. But there are all kinds of gardens. I could put a garden on the roof someday."

"I'm afraid the house will be long gone by then," Jane said.

"Mary loves the old barn. I would have liked to help her keep it. But where will we find the money to fix it? I have college to worry about." Lizzie bit her lip. Fitzy and little Mary were a few years away from college, but Lizzie was planning ahead. Her husband had done well, and Lizzie's marketing company was breaking even, but as with all women raised in homes with financial insecurity, the fear of poverty loomed in the corners of every endeavor, squashing ambition. Lizzie avoided risks, but it was necessary to take them to grow the business. Lizzie Bennet Darcy played it safe, even when she knew it would prevent her from reaching her potential.

"My husband and I will help," Jane said, looking around. "But look at this place. It's falling apart. We'd have to fix it up to sell it for the proper price."

"In this neighborhood? I wouldn't worry."

"Mary fixed a pipe upstairs by herself." Jane rolled her eyes.

"Poor thing."

"She won the playwriting prize, but every penny is going to fix the sidewalk," Jane said sadly.

"She shouldn't spend her money on repairs," Lizzie said. "She should spend it on what she needs, what she wants."

"Mary will never tell you what she wants. Ever," Jane said. "And now, Dad has gotten sick."

"He'll be fine," Lizzie assured her.

"You're always positive."

"And you worry too much," Lizzie said. "He has to take better care of himself."

"Mary is the one to make sure he will," Jane admitted.

"Are you gossiping about me?" Mary smiled from the pocket doors.

"We were just talking about how beautifully you take care of Mama and Pa."

"I am happy to do it." Mary didn't believe her sisters were chatting about her largesse. She knew something was up.

A VISIT FROM CHARLOTTE AND MR. COLLINS

Mrs. Bennet and her daughters were dressed, putting on their coats and grabbing their purses, about to depart from Number 10

Jane Street, when the doorbell rang. They looked at one another as the bell rang again, and Mary opened the door.

"Cousins!" Mary said a bit too cheerily. William Collins, fifty-ish, bald, and short, beamed while his wife, Charlotte, taller than he and ten years younger, searched the eyes of her cousins. Charlotte's empathy lived in every feature of her face, from her warm smile to the eyebrows that acted as arrows for her emotion.

Lydia groaned, and Mrs. Bennet shot her a look. Lizzie looked at Jane, who plastered a smile on her face. Kitty buttoned her jacket. She didn't care who stopped by; she wanted to be with her father.

"I'm so sorry, Charlotte"—Mary turned to Mr. Collins—"William. We'd love to visit, but we're on our way to the hospital," Mary said.

"That's why we came early." William smiled pleasantly and brushed Mary aside, entering the foyer. It was fascinating how high the chandeliers seemed when a man of slight stature stood under one. Mary wanted to remember the moment to write about it later.

"William, this is a bad time," Charlotte said. "The Bennet women are on their way out."

"I'll say," Mary laughed.

Lizzie embraced Charlotte. "It's never a bad time for a visit with you."

"See? What did I tell you?" William said. "I appreciated the text, Mary. I want you to contact us whether it's good news or bad."

"You're welcome." Now Mary was sorry she'd sent it.

"Shall we join you at the hospital?"

"No!" the all-girl Bennet Greek chorus rang out.

"Oh, all right then." William shrugged. "We can talk later. How is my cousin?"

"We hope he's even better this morning," Mary explained. "He took a little spill—"

"A great doctor once said if you want to make it to ninety . . . don't ever fall." William laughed at his own joke alone.

"Pa is not ninety."

"He's on his way. Ten years after eighty is like three. This is not meant as a slur; it's an achievement to grow old," William insisted. "An honor."

"Indeed," Lizzie said. "And knowing Pa, he will bounce back better than ever."

"Regardless of his chronological age." Kitty crossed her arms over her chest.

"I hope so—and I also hope that you ladies are making plans for your future. With your parents reaching elderly status—"

"I am already there," Mrs. Bennet said. "I'm knee-deep in old age with the bad knees to prove it, and I'm not ashamed of it."

"You shouldn't be. It's a natural part of life, for things to fall apart," William explained.

"William, please. Everything you say is sounding odd under the circumstances." Charlotte shook her head. "Can't you see our cousins are worried?"

"We're family!" William said.

"Yes, we are." Lizzie forced a smile.

Mary looked at William and wondered what his definition of family could possibly be. Was it to be of help to relatives? Or was it to sit like a spider until someone was ill and swoop in for the financial kill? The floor in the old house beneath Mary's feet suddenly felt soft, like wet sand. Was the foundation of everything she had worked so hard to maintain washing away? Were she and her parents going under with the outgoing tide? Where would they go? How would they live? Maybe she could call Charlotte later and reason with her to get to her husband. Maybe it was time to bring Lizzie in and have her deal with William Collins. She had had her altercations with him before, and Mary believed William was afraid of Lizzie. Surely her father had more rights than a renter!

"The ladies understand the situation. Their father has lifetime rights to the house, and upon his death, I take over the deed."

"Unless we pay off the debt." Mary folded her arms over her chest.

William Collins looked around the foyer and into the parlor. "That's always an option."

"Good to know," Lizzie said in a tone that meant she wasn't fooling around.

"We're due at our next appointment," Charlotte said.

"I cleared the afternoon." William looked at Charlotte, who glared at him. "We'll be off then. Next time, cocktails? Tea?"

"Sure. Sure," Mary agreed. William invited himself to the Bennets', which Mary thought was rude.

"We'll be happy to have you over once my husband is home," Mrs. Bennet assured him.

Mary opened the door and let her cousins out. She noticed that Charlotte turned to Lizzie and made a telephone receiver motion, hand to her ear, before closing the door behind her. There was a secret language between Lizzie and Charlotte, but whatever the case, it made Mary feel better to know that she wasn't alone in the fight to remain at 10 Jane Street.

"What was that all about?" Lydia wanted to know.

"He wants to sell the house out from under us," Mrs. Bennet said.

"I'd like to see him try." Lizzie squeezed Mary's hand.

"It's too late," Mary said. "He's like a vulture waiting for the worst to happen."

"Don't think about it," Kitty said.

But that was all Mary thought about.

MR. TARANTELLO

Mary sat alone on a folding chair under the ghost light in the HB Studios rehearsal space. She studied the marks made with tape on the floor and wondered if Tony Lo Bianco or Ellen Burstyn had ever stood at them to deliver a performance. Probably. There was more history in this small gray building tucked between the regal brownstones on either side than there was at the Whitney or the Metropolitan Museum of Art.

Sometimes Mary felt the past play through the space, like a cold wind blowing through old bricks, which made her shiver. She envisioned the past, back when Marilyn Monroe and Paul Newman took classes on this very stage. It probably had not been painted since they were young, and now they were both gone to actor heaven. She thought about Herbert Berghof, who founded the school, and how it had grown. Mary had no idea who paid the rent on the space, and how, after most of Greenwich Village had been upgraded and its buildings renovated, this compact, magical theatrical space survived. She knew only that she was happy it had.

A tall man around Mary's age stood in the door, backlit by the foyer lights. His appearance surprised her, which made her heart beat fast. As he moved into the studio, she remembered him. He was around her age and had a mop of black hair and the rugged build of a workingman. But he wouldn't be a workingman because they don't generally visit HB Studios. The men of HB Studios who took classes with her were pale, thin, and dyspeptic.

Mary remembered that he had sat in on a couple of classes, but she hadn't introduced herself because she had to rush home to make dinner for her parents. But today, she was free. Her sisters were staying over for one more night, and they promised to take care of dinner for their mother. Their father was still in the hospital, and that gave Mary peace of mind. She had a recurring nightmare in the days since her father fell. It was a strange dream where she was in the kitchen, heard the terrible thud, and raced up the stairs to find a hole in the floor, her mother shouting, and her father gone. It was the case of the disappearing father, which could not be solved in a dream.

"I know you." Mary smiled.

"How?"

"Didn't you sit in on my playwriting class?"

"It's your class?"

"Not just mine"—she blushed—"the one I take with everybody else."

"I'm teasing you." He smiled and looked around, spotting a folding chair along the stage wall. He crossed the stage, picked it up, and walked back toward Mary. She took a good look at him in the light. He had thick eyebrows and a straight but prominent nose. He was smiling, and had a beautiful set of white teeth and a dimple in his right cheek. Mary began to sweat.

He placed the chair next to hers and sat down. His scent was delicious, a little cedar and pine. Of course a rugged man would smell like a tree or a forest in snow or Christmas.

"I'm Joe Tarantello." He extended his hand.

Mary took his hand. It was like a paw. His touch thrilled her, but she pulled her hand away quickly so he wouldn't notice. "I'm Mary Bennet."

"I know. You won the playwriting prize. One of them, anyway."

"How do you know?"

"Mrs. DeMatteo said to read the plays. She let me sit in. I

know her husband and told her I was interested in plays, and she said, 'Why don't you audit?'" He smiled. "Here I am."

"So—you know people."

"Isn't that a requirement of show business?"

"I don't consider the theater show business," Mary said.

"Then what is it?"

"Literature with wings."

He laughed. "You're fancy."

"Do you think so?" Mary patted her bangs to make sure they were flat. Sometimes her bangs flew up like cheap window shades. She hoped she looked good. She had put on mascara that day, and only because she had time. Her sisters were doing all her chores, including the laundry. When she left, Jane was washing the front windows with vinegar and newspapers. For once, she was glad to have arrived at a destination early. "No one has ever called me fancy."

"You're pretty. For a writer."

"What does that mean?"

"I don't know. The beauty in the theater seems to go to the actresses."

"Because it doesn't matter what a writer looks like," Mary said defensively.

"God, you're cute," he said.

Mary blushed.

"That's a line from your play," Joe reminded her.

"Oh right." Mary instantly felt foolish.

"But you *are* cute, whether you wrote the line or not."

"Thank you."

"You seem disappointed," he said.

"I'm not disappointed; I thanked you for your compliment, didn't I?"

"I don't throw words around. Cute is step one on the way to pretty, which is one rung below beautiful."

Is this guy serious? Mary looked at him. Who is he? she wondered. She checked the time on her phone.

"Class starts in ten minutes," he said. "That's what it says online, but it never starts on time."

"You've only come to two classes."

"You noticed." Joe leaned back in the chair, which created a weird angle. He could observe Mary without her consent. So she scooted her chair back to be even with him. She turned to him.

"I notice everything. You wore a blue plaid shirt last time, and it reminded me of a blanket that was given to me when I graduated from high school. I see everything, and I feel everything. That's the job of a writer, even though I don't make my living writing. I teach piano."

"So you play?"

"Not so well, but I know enough to teach children the fundamentals. And when they have talent, I send them uptown to a great Russian teacher at the New York School of Music. Yulia Dusman. Now, *she's* a great pianist."

"And you don't think you are? Who told you that you weren't a great musician?"

"My dad."

"And you believed him?"

"Of course. He's my father."

"You should never believe anything your parents tell you. They make every decision based on fear. See, you were probably a great pianist, but your dad didn't want you to become a musician because it's a lousy lifestyle. You're working nights in dark rooms. Not safe for a woman, and then there's the smoke inhalation. Can't be good for your lungs."

"Or maybe I'm just not that good."

"I don't believe that."

"You haven't heard me play."

"Don't have to. You have beautiful hands. Beautiful hands mean two things: a person is adept at either playing an instrument or writing."

"Or sewing," Mary added.

"Or sewing. A lost art." Joe nodded in agreement.

"How do you know all this?"

"Because no one in my family wants me to write. And I was over at the DeMatteos, and the Mrs. caught on fast that I loved to write. And she gave me some encouragement."

"You're lucky," Mary said. "She saw who you are without you ever having to explain it."

"See, you get it." Joe grinned.

Mary looked away because the proximity of his mouth to hers was close. She slid away from him in the chair as far as she could. He slid toward her to make sure he remained close.

"So where do you live?" Joe asked.

"The village."

"Around here? Too expensive for me."

"It would be for me, too. I live with my parents," Mary explained.

"Why?"

"Because all my sisters moved away."

"Your parents are old?"

"On their way." Mary smiled. It made her laugh. If you asked her mother, she'd say she was ancient, but she just turned seventy.

"Mine, too." Joe squinted at Mary as if to read her or observe her in form and line like a painting. "The good news is you're from a big family so you have help."

"They try."

"Are you close to your family?"

"Very!" Mary blurted.

Joe put his hands in the air as though he was under arrest. "Hey, I'm just asking."

"I don't understand that question," Mary said. "A family is always close, even when they aren't in contact. It's the nature of what a family is in the first place."

"You think so?"

"I believe it."

"Maybe you're on to something. Can I ask you a question?"

Mary nodded. She was in a conversation with a man whom she was attracted to and a man who also intrigued her. She couldn't remember a time when both of those things had happened at the same time in the same conversation.

"Why do you write?" he asked.

"I don't know," Mary answered truthfully. "Why do you?"

"Because I have no other outlet for my feelings," Joe said, as though he had not admitted something so deep that perhaps should never be said out loud. He went on, "Writing is as good a way to connect to your feelings as anything else."

"True. But it's a lot of work. You can just have your feelings, sit with them, act on them in life—without becoming a writer."

"So, you *have* thought about why you write."

"Maybe because my father was a writer," Mary said. She discovered the truth as she said it. She had not made that connection before this conversation with Joe.

"Would I know his work?" Joe asked.

"Don't think so. He wrote a nonfiction book about shipbuilding—well reviewed, but it didn't sell."

"That's too bad."

"You know it's impossible to make a living as a playwright," Mary said.

"Maybe you will succeed where your father didn't," Joe said. "You're not the only person I know who went into the family business."

"Did you?"

"I have a day job," Joe admitted.

"What is it?" Mary asked.

"I'm a plumber. I do some electrics. Contracting."

Mrs. DeMatteo entered from the back of the theater. She was tall and thin, with white hair pulled back into a low chignon. Her full lips were bright red. She wore navy slacks and a white blouse, with an Hermès scarf tied loosely at her neck. She placed a large, open leather tote on a seat in the front row. "Good afternoon, Mary. Joe. Good to see you. How are you?"

"Better now. Is class starting on time?" Joe asked.

"Not if I can help it." Mrs. DeMatteo laughed. "Didn't anyone tell you that art is timeless?"

"Wouldn't work in the plumbing business." Joe smiled. "A burst pipe waits for no man."

TWO SISTERS

Mary lay in bed thinking. Lizzie slept in the twin bed under the window. The sheers ruffled where the window was cracked open. The pale yellow streetlight shone through the window.

Mary sighed.

"You awake?" Lizzie asked softly.

"Yep," Mary answered.

"This is like the old days." Lizzie sat up in bed.

"Not really. I was with Kitty and Lydia. You were with Jane."

"It's never been just the two of us," Lizzie said.

"Nope."

"Do you think Pa can handle the stairs when he comes home?"

"I was thinking about that. We could put a bed in the back parlor."

"But there's no bathroom," Lizzie said practically.

"And the stairs. Even from the street. The stoop is steep," Mary said. "Maybe William Collins is right. Maybe it's time to let go of this house."

"You can't give up, Mary."

"I don't know what to fight for. I couldn't imagine ever living anywhere else, but it's untenable. It's all too much. The debt. The repairs. Our parents and their bad knees and hips. It is too late to plan for the future. Here it is. Dad should've planned ahead. He should've thought about being eighty in an old, rickety house. Mama has never been strong. She's always been a mess. And now I have a wizened father and an emotional mother, and there's no way to hold them together along with the demands of this old house. If we let the house go, we get nothing. There's debt and taxes. Collins knows it."

"I can talk to Charlotte. They're wealthy. They could do a kind turn for our parents."

"Lizzie, the wealthy don't think like that. They sit on their money and wonder why everyone else isn't rich, too. To them, it's easy. But you have to start with something to be rich, and while Pa inherited this old house, it seems we won't end with it. What good is a house if you don't have the money to keep it up? We should be grateful to Collins and Charlotte; they're patient—and certainly have helped in the past—but it has never been a fair playing field. Collins always had money, because he was the only son in his family. Everything—on both sides—went to him. If Pa could have seen his way through, he could have kept this place in good enough shape to sell it and pay off the Collins family for their help through the years. But he only ever made enough money to get by."

"And Mom didn't work."

"Oh, please. Remember when she got a job in the shoe store on Eighth Avenue? They actually lost business because she talked people out of buying shoes. Said the leather wasn't good enough. Who does that?"

"Our mother." Lizzie laughed.

"So I don't know what to say, or how to say it, but we have to let it go." It was dark in the room, so Lizzie couldn't see Mary wipe her eyes.

"You can live with us, you know. My husband adores you."

"He wouldn't if he lived with me."

"Mary, you're important to us. To Darcy. To all of us. To Jane. To Kitty. To Lydia. We love you very much."

"I know that."

"And we want you to have everything you dream of." Lizzie's voice broke.

"I know you worry about me. I'm alone. I'm interested in things no one cares about anymore. Playwriting is like whittling or glassblowing or working a loom."

"That's not true."

"People don't read. They don't go to the theater. You know, I go to plays in preview—I get free tickets—and since I was a kid everyone in the audience was old. And now I'm grown up, and the audience is still old. I don't understand it."

"You enjoy playwriting, don't you?"

"I do."

"You work with interesting people. Donna DeMatteo—and actors and directors and designers. It sounds so exciting."

"It can be. You know when Lady de Bourgh called me to tell me I won the prize, I cried."

"Tears of joy!" Lizzie said.

"I don't know. They felt like sad tears—like, I won, but did it matter? And then in a matter of hours, or days, I can't remember, the sidewalk needed to be fixed or the city would come after us, and it was five thousand dollars."

"We'll help with that."

"Don't throw good money after bad, Lizzie. Your husband won't allow it. It's the first rule of banking."

"And my husband is an excellent banker."

"You need your savings for the kids. For your life."

"Jane said she'd take Mama and Pa with her."

"Jane isn't cut out for it. They'll drive her crazy."

"She said she doesn't mind."

"We should send them to live with Lydia—that would teach them a lesson," Mary joked. "They would learn that it's imprudent to get old in the first place. You never want to need our sister Lydia for anything. She is incapable of putting other people first."

Lizzie adjusted the sheers on the window and looked out onto Jane Street. "Maybe there's a way to fix this place up and make it work."

"An elevator costs half a million dollars, and I don't think there's enough space in the garden to install it." Mary lay back on her pillow; the thought of all this exhausted her.

"Maybe we'll get good news." Lizzie lay back on her own pillow. "I believe when you do the right thing, and live a life of generosity and kindness, good things come to you," Lizzie said.

"Elizabeth Bennet Darcy, you are out of your mind," Mary said.

"I do believe it!"

"Well, something good actually happened to me."

"Tell me."

"I met a nice guy," Mary said.

"You waited to tell me?"

"It's so weird, Lizzie. I believed it would never happen. And maybe it won't happen after all. But meeting him made me believe that maybe it *could* happen?"

"Of course it could," Lizzie said.

Mary felt strange confiding in Lizzie, as though she were intruding on the family order. Jane and Lizzie had always been the confidantes, and the truth was, Lydia and Kitty were close, too. Mary felt she was the outsider, the thin layer of jam in the middle of the bread and butter. Bread and butter satisfies, the jam is extra. You don't need it to survive. Maybe that was Mary's role, she thought to herself. Not essential. Not at all.

"Tell me about him," Lizzie said.

"He looks like a lumberjack. An Italian lumberjack."

"Is he an actor?"

"Oh no. A writer."

"Have you read his work?"

"I hope I never do. I don't want to know if he has talent, because if he doesn't, it will ruin the idea of him," Mary admitted. "And right now, I very much like the idea of him."

"Is he supportive of you?"

"Very. He sees me. He read my play."

"Did he like it?"

"He did."

"Well, that's a wonderful start. A love affair that begins on the page is already timeless."

"Lizzie, you're such a romantic. I'm not. I'm a pragmatist. A realist. A single woman on her way to being a curmudgeon."

"That doesn't have to be true."

"Well, it is. He took my hand, and I never felt so connected to a person in all my life. Is that how it was for you and Darcy?"

"We had a difficult road to love. And now that we're married and have children, we forgot all that. For me, being married is a moment-to-moment endeavor. Every day is new, because every moment brings new challenges and problems—and, you know, joy."

"Mama and Pa are proof of that," Mary said.

"They love each other," Lizzie said.

"I think when you're married as long as they have been, the love is the least of it."

"Mary, the love always matters. Always."

"Maybe."

"What do you think holds an old couple together?" Lizzie asked.

"Patience."

Mary and Lizzie were exhausted. They had said goodbye to their sisters and calmed down their mother. Their father was being sent to rehab for two weeks, which bought them time to make some decisions or, at the very least, gather some facts. They wanted everything to go well. The moon was high in that rectangle of black sky over Jane Street. Clouds moved over the light, long enough to cast a shadow in the old room.

THE PROPOSAL

Mary Bennet could barely keep up with her brother-in-law as they walked up Fifth Avenue in New York City. Fitz Darcy was tall, with long legs, which meant he had a stride that could cover a distance twice as fast as Mary. He moved like a shot, crisscrossing

Fifth Avenue as the lights changed. He had a technique whereby he never waited on a corner; he timed his steps so he never had to stop and wait. Impatience was a Darcy family trait.

"Come on, Mary," he called out to her to move quickly. "We don't want to be late."

When Mary Bennet dreaded something, and she dreaded this meeting with William Collins, she procrastinated. Maybe if she slowed down, they'd never get there, even though there was no logic in her thinking.

Darcy turned to her. "Mary, what is the problem?"

"I'm afraid."

"It's just your cousin."

"He has put the fear of God in all of us our whole lives."

"You have nothing to fear now," Darcy said. "I am going to get to the bottom of this, and we'll figure out how to proceed."

Mary wanted to believe her brother-in-law. She knew how Lizzie believed in him, trusted him. Lizzie swore she'd never marry, and the love was so all-consuming, she had to. Darcy didn't leave her any choice in the matter.

"We're here." Darcy opened the door of 154 Fifth Avenue. "Come on, Mary. We're right on time."

Mary followed Darcy off the elevator to the conference room where the meeting would be held. The walnut table was polished. Mary took a seat and poured herself a glass of water from the crystal pitcher. She poured Darcy a glass and placed it on the table in front of him.

"Are you all right?" Darcy asked her.

"I'll be better when this is over." Mary sipped the water slowly.

"I understand."

Darcy was a man who didn't blather; he shot straight, in Mary's opinion, and if he said he understood, it meant he had given what was about to transpire some thought. It was a gift that Lizzie had stayed behind to help after Pa's fall because it had given Mary a chance to tell Lizzie everything—when she could observe for herself Mary's experience caregiving for their parents. Lizzie must have imparted every detail to Darcy, because he took time to come into Manhattan to help her.

Mary could see Mr. Collins's shadow as he walked outside the glass bricks of the conference room wall. If she didn't know better, she'd think it was Take Your Son to Work Day; the shadow was half the size of what it should have been for a grown man.

"Cousins!" Mr. Collins pushed the conference room door open. His face fell when he saw Darcy. He was counting on dealing with the Bennet sisters, not their formidable brother-in-law. Mary, in her wisdom, knew how the world worked, at least when it came to banking, finances, and real estate. Her father had handled the family finances, and it was his family that owned 10 Jane Street. She also knew that the agreement between the brothers was fluid. Mary understood it was the moment to try to scare her wee cousin.

If Collins ever found out that it had been Charlotte's idea to bring Darcy into the mix around the discussion of the deed of 10 Jane Street, he would have been furious. The truth was, Mary couldn't handle this alone. She was worn down from taking care of her parents, and getting her father settled in rehab. He was coming home for good that week, and she had spent the time making a bedroom in the back parlor for him. Mary Bennet was no longer shy about asking for help.

Collins shuffled some files around. He opened one and removed papers, handing them over to Darcy. Darcy pulled his reading glasses from the breast pocket of his suit jacket. He put them on his nose and read.

"This is the original deed?" Darcy asked.

"Amended, but yes, the original is part of it."

"When were the amendments done?"

"Every few years. My cousin came in when he needed help," Collins explained.

Mary's face flushed with shame at the idea of her father coming to Collins for help. The burden of financial worry was one she shared with all of her sisters, excluding, perhaps, Lydia, who moved through the world without a thought about money and seemed to land on her feet no matter her circumstances.

"It is co-owned, Mr. Collins," Darcy said.

"Through our fathers, who were brothers." Collins shrugged. "I allowed some borrowing against my cousin's half," he explained.

"I see that."

"I recommend we sell the building to settle the debt and split the sale as described in the deed."

"May I see?"

Darcy handed Mary the document. She scanned it—she knew the numbers and the freight on the deed in terms of loans because copies of these documents were in the stack on her father's desk.

"William," Mary addressed Collins without affect. "The building, the lot, have increased in value. We have taken care of the building—my father for the last forty-three years. We have lived there. In New York City, there's a law that says in cases of joint ownership, sale will be determined by the tenant owner."

"If the co-owner wants his money, he can force a sale," Collins said without emotion.

"I understand. But we are living there—my father, my mother, and me."

"I suppose we can leave the sale open until the death of one or both of your parents," Collins said.

"I don't want to move them." Mary smiled. "Ever."

"Could you possibly wait to force a sale until such a time?" Darcy asked.

"I suppose," Mr. Collins said.

"Thank you." Mary looked around the fancy conference room, with its mahogany table, leather chairs, and expensive map collection on the walls. Mr. Collins had done well with his inheritance. If only her father had done the same.

AN UNLIKELY TURN OF EVENTS

Mary Bennet looked forward to her classes at HB Studios because she was becoming a better writer. Of course, since she had a meet-cute with Joe Tarantello, she also looked forward to seeing him and continuing their conversation. But he hadn't returned to class. Three classes came and went, long enough for Mary to conclude he had a girlfriend elsewhere—or that the theater just didn't work out for him. But Mary arrived early for her classes at HB Studios, just in case Joe showed up.

Mary Bennet had so much on her mind she wasn't even sad. She let it go. What could she do, anyway? Mary leaned against the front of the building on Bank Street. Up the block, students from the acting class checked their phones and smoked. They were clustered around the giant oak tree that grew toward the sky at a tilt.

Mary's play was soon to go into the casting process, and she was on the lookout for five women to play her fictional sisters and herself. She squinted at the group and wondered if any of them would audition.

"How are you, Mary?" Donna DeMatteo joined her. She wore a beige cashmere coat thrown over black slacks and a white blouse. A necklace of jade and pearl hung loose to her waist.

"You dress like someone going to Broadway, not a playwright."

Mrs. DeMatteo threw her head back and laughed. "Sometimes I have business before I teach."

"What kind of business, if you don't mind my asking?"

"I train women to communicate effectively in business. It's a little like an acting class, without scenes by Tennessee Williams."

"That's so interesting," Mary said, meaning it.

"A playwright can be a playwright as long as she has other jobs to support the habit."

"I understand," Mary said.

"Of all my writing students, I think you do. You get it, Mary Bennet."

"Thank you. I guess."

"I'd like to use your play in class today. You know, your Lady de Bourgh prizewinner. If you give me permission."

"I'd be honored. But why?"

"I love plays about family life. You really crafted a beauty," Mrs. DeMatteo said.

"I tried to write the truth."

"The mother character has dementia. Are you dealing with that at home?"

"A little. But my sisters believe that it's not technically dementia—it's been our mother's nature all along."

"That's why it feels so real."

"Thank you."

"And the loss of the home—when the girls are forced to sell. Is that true?"

"I hope not. But it may become real sooner than we hope."

"I'm sorry."

"There are remedies, Mrs. DeMatteo. And I'm hunting every single option down, and hoping for the best."

"I'm rooting for you. But whatever you do, wherever you go, I hope you keep writing. I'll see you inside." Mrs. DeMatteo entered the studio.

Mary looked at the simple sign that meant the world to her. HB Studios. White letters on gray stucco. It was a cathedral to Mary, a place of creativity and bliss. Tears stung Mary's eyes. She wiped them away quickly.

"Why you crying?" a voice said from behind her.

Mary turned. "Oh, hi, Joe."

Joe Tarantello looked handsome. He had gotten a haircut. He wore a white button-down shirt and jeans.

"Did you iron that shirt?" Mary asked.

"Yeah."

"I don't believe you."

"You shouldn't. I send them out."

"I figured."

"I wouldn't expect you to iron my shirts." Joe smiled. "You want to tell me what's wrong?"

"I didn't think I'd ever see you again," Mary said.

"And that's why you're crying?"

"It's so stupid. I hardly know you," Mary said, fishing for a handkerchief.

"But you do."

"I don't think so."

"You missed me, didn't you?"

Mary nodded. "I guess I did."

"And now I'm here. How do you feel?"

"Better."

"So, no need to cry," he said.

"I don't cry because I'm sad. I cry because it's a small victory to be happy. I don't need much. I cried when Lady de Bourgh called me. I cried when my father didn't have a stroke. And I cried when Mrs. DeMatteo said she was going to read from my play. And yes, Joe, I cried at the sight of seeing you again."

"Because I make you happy?"

"I don't know you well enough to say that," Mary said. "Please don't take offense."

"I came back to class to tell you that I wasn't going to take this class anymore. And I thought I could just text you, but that seemed like a cold option. And then I said, what is it about this girl? The first time I saw you, I was intrigued. And it took me a long time to approach you because you were always surrounded by people. Actors. Other playwrights. And I saw that they wanted to talk to you—to be near you—not that different from what I was feeling. And then I went on the portal and read your play. If you ever tried to hide who you are and what you feel, you'd be a failure. Your play describes something we all experience when we love. And I had to come back and tell you that."

"Well, I'm grateful. Thank you."

"And I wondered if you could go to dinner with me after class. Nothing fancy. Pizza."

"I'd like that."

"We could skip class." Joe smiled. His straight white teeth and full lips were like the moon, clear and bright. The sun was setting over Greenwich Village. It was just dark enough to see the moon—and him.

"I can't. Mrs. DeMatteo is using my play in class."

"So we stay." Joe took Mary's hand. "This will be fun."

Mary's hand in Joe's felt right. She didn't know what to be happier about—her play or Joe Tarantello or the possibilities of what might be. She wiped away a tear and called it a wash.

CHRISTMAS PUNCH

Mary centered the punch bowl on the side table. Slowly, she filled it with a mixture of cranberry juice, seltzer, and fresh orange slices from a crystal pitcher. She placed the glasses on hooks around the top of the bowl. The silver ladle rested on a doily next to the punch.

"Fancy," Mr. Bennet said. "I'll sample the Bennet way." He scooped a cupful directly from the punch bowl and took a swig.

"How is it?" Mary asked.

"It needs vodka," Mr. Bennet said.

"You're not allowed to drink."

"It seems to me the people in this world who most need to drink alcohol are the very people not allowed to imbibe."

"Oh, Pa. You don't need to drink. You have everything any man could ever hope for."

"Whatever you say, Mary."

Mary's father had bounced back from his health ordeal. He was slower and used a cane, but Mary didn't mind, as long as he was there to lead the family.

"Don't let that man drink!" Mrs. Bennet said, coming down the stairs one at a time, gripping the bannister.

"I'm not, Ma."

"Damn stairs. I will die without the benefit of an elevator."

"The stairs are good exercise," Mr. Bennet said.

"Your new room will be ready after Christmas," Mary promised her.

"You know I don't deal well with change," Mrs. Bennet groused. "And I don't know if I'll like the back parlor as a bedroom."

"But you will," Mr. Bennet assured her.

"Do I have a choice?"

"No," Mary and her father said in unison. The three of them laughed.

The door from the garden behind them blew open. Joe carried a cord of wood into the old house to the fireplace. He began to stack the wood.

"A fire! I love a fire!" Mrs. Bennet clapped her hands together.

"Merry Christmas, Mrs. Bennet," Joe said. Joe wore the flannel shirt that reminded Mary of her blanket. They had spent Christmas Eve in New Jersey with the Tarantellos. Mary had never experienced the Feast of the Seven Fishes, and now she hoped she always would.

"Ma, Pa, sit down." Mary helped her parents to the sofa.

Mary had put up the Christmas tree in the back parlor, as was the tradition. A tall blue spruce, fragrant and full, shimmered with lights and ornaments. Gifts wrapped in paper and ribbons were stacked underneath it. Mary closed the pocket doors between the front and back parlors.

"Whatever you're cooking smells divine," Mrs. Bennet said.

"I cooked all the traditional dishes—your recipes, Ma."

"I wish I could help."

"You made more than thirty Christmas dinners, Ma. I'm happy to do it."

"I did my share, that's for sure." Mrs. Bennet sipped her punch. "One never knows when they're in the midst of all that hard work if anyone notices it. I'm grateful you did, Mary."

Joe smiled and lit the kindling. Soon, the logs roared, with flames of orange throwing heat and light.

Mary leaned against the mantel she had decorated with candles and branches of pine. "It's a beauty," she said.

Joe pulled her close. "And so are you."

Joe kissed her, but it was quick and chaste. After all, Mary's parents were sitting a few feet away. But Mary didn't care. She kissed Joe again. She was in love, and she didn't care who knew it.

"Of all the wonderful sons-in-law I have, and believe me, I have them, and yes, I know it's a sin, but Joe is my favorite. I never thought one of my girls would marry an Italian, but here we are. And I am so happy for it."

"My wife likes your skill set with wire cutters and pipes and a hammer and nails."

"I'm happy to help," Joe said.

The doorbell rang. Mary excused herself. She threw open the front door. Her sisters, their husbands, and their children poured into the house, filling the place to the brim.

"The new sidewalk is so even!" Lizzie said.

"And the stoop—no cracks," Lydia marveled.

"We're getting there. One job at a time," Mary said cheerily. As the children ran to the tree, they peeled off their coats. Mary helped collect the coats of her sisters and brothers-in-law and sent them into the back parlor to see the tree.

"Joe built a fire," Mrs. Bennet announced as Darcy entered the parlor. "He remembered to open the flue," she added.

"Will I ever live that down?" Darcy turned to Lizzie.

"The black smoke Christmas?" Lizzie laughed. "I don't think so."

"We thought we'd die," Mrs. Bennet said.

"But we didn't," Darcy reminded her.

"Have some punch," Mary said. "Everyone."

Lydia ladled the punch into glasses. Kitty served. Jane handed out linen cocktail napkins that Mrs. Bennet had embroidered with small trees. Lizzie wrangled the children to the tree to look at the gifts wrapped underneath it, as the brothers-in-law joined their father-in-law on the sofa.

The girls clamored around the tree, squealing when they read their name on a gift tag.

"So this is a Bennet family Christmas," Joe said. "A lot of feminine energy."

"Is there any other kind?" Kitty joked.

"There is in New Jersey." Joe winked at Mary.

"How were the Seven Fishes, Mary?" Jane asked.

"Seven times seven." Mary laughed. "But not to worry. The feast inspired my new play."

"Good for you." Mr. Bennet grinned.

"My mother overdoes it," Joe said. "My father was hanging wallpaper five minutes before the guests arrived."

"That's a great opening scene," Mr. Bennet said.

"The Tarantello men are builders; they can do anything." Mrs. Bennet sipped her punch.

"I'll say. Joe, this brownstone never had so much love. The new bathroom is perfection," Lizzie said.

"For years, it was a water closet, now it looks like a powder room in Versailles," Mrs. Bennet said.

"Joe's masterpiece." Mary kissed him.

"I always wondered what it would look like, all fixed up. It's lovely," Jane said.

"Thank goodness somebody married a man who's handy." Kitty laughed.

"Hey," Bing said. His brothers-in-law on the Bennet side concurred. Perhaps they weren't talented in plumbing, electrics, and building, but they had other talents.

Lydia joined Joe and Mary by the fire. "Are you serious with that bathroom? It's gorgeous."

"Carrara marble. I figured you needed something Italian in this house."

"Besides you." Lizzie smiled.

"I love Italian everything," Lydia said. "You'll have to come to Waterford and build me a bathroom with spa features."

"I'd be happy to," Joe said.

"Oh, no, no, no!" Mrs. Bennet shouted. "Mr. Tarantello must never leave Jane Street!"

"I might," Joe said.

The sisters looked at one another.

"But I will never leave Mary Bennet," Joe said.

The sisters cheered. Their husbands had a laugh. Mrs. Bennet was smug. And Mr. Bennet was relieved.

Mary Bennet, for her part, was happy—the kind of happiness that's bigger than any dream, bigger than any house, bigger than Christmas—the kind of happiness that lasts.

What Georgiana Wants

KAREN DUKESS

"My sister, who is more than ten years my junior, was left to the guardianship of my mother's nephew, Colonel Fitzwilliam, and myself. About a year ago, she was taken from school, and an establishment formed for her in London; and last summer she went with the lady who presided over it, to Ramsgate; and thither also went Mr. Wickham, undoubtedly by design; for there proved to have been a prior acquaintance between him and Mrs. Younge, in whose character we were most unhappily deceived; and by her connivance and aid, he so far recommended himself to Georgiana, whose affectionate heart retained a strong impression of kindness to her as a child, that she was persuaded to believe herself in love, and to consent to an elopement. She was then but fifteen, which must be her excuse; and after stating her imprudence, I am happy to add that I owed the knowledge of it to herself. I joined them unexpectedly a day or two before the intended elopement, and then Georgiana, unable to support the idea of grieving and offending a brother whom she almost looked up to as a father, acknowledged the whole to me."

Jane Austen, *Pride and Prejudice*

Georgiana Darcy, the younger sister of Fitzwilliam Darcy, is critical to the plot developments in *Pride and Prejudice*. Only after reading a letter from Mr. Darcy about Georgiana's near elopement with George Wickham does Elizabeth Bennet begin to understand that her quick judgments about Wickham, as well as about Mr. Darcy himself, were wrong. And it is knowledge of what nearly happened to Georgiana (as well as his love for Elizabeth, of course) that propels Darcy to act on behalf of Lydia Bennet.

Yet despite her centrality to the novel, Georgiana Darcy has no voice within its pages. She appears only as others describe her and her words are never directly heard, only quoted by others. Georgiana Darcy is truly an unsung lady in waiting. It was an easy choice, and a great pleasure, to imagine her as a young mother looking back on her choices and pondering both what she has gained and what she has lost.

Not the Handel, please. Anything else."

At the pianoforte, my daughter, Anne, looks at me with an expression of petulance far beyond her seven years.

"But Mama, I've been practicing. I play it nicely now."

She sits up taller and shakes her head, golden ringlets glinting in the sun. She smiles at me and turns away, flips the sheet music as if she's not playing only the right hand and by memory. She is both pretty and defiant, a combination that amuses me now, but may bring us trouble when she is older.

Anne starts again, her playing halting but correct. I'm tempted to leave the room to be alone, but that will only make it worse. And the music didn't start this; the thoughts gripped me again this morning, shortly after I awakened, when the pleasant blur of my dream—bare skin, entwined legs, lips on my neck—clarified into a face, a figure, and a name.

Anne strikes a wrong note, bites her lip, and carries on. Her playing is slow and stiff, but still, it is too much to bear. Under my breath, I recite the tasks to which I should attend today—a letter to Lizzie, a dress fitting with the seamstress, a basket for that poor family with the sick child. Letter, dress, basket. Letter, dress, basket. Anne starts the song again. It's no use. Physically, I am here at Headsworth, where I am wife to the dependable Edmund and mother to Anne and Thomas, but in my head and my thrumming body, I am on holiday in Margate, just shy of sixteen years old, sitting on an unfamiliar piano bench beside George Wickham, under the watchful eye of my companion, Mrs. Younge.

"Position your hands," George had said, his silky, dark hair falling over his eyes. "Show me how to play."

I placed my fingers on the keys, curving them as I'd been taught. He rested his hands on mine. His scent, warm and earthy, was strangely familiar.

"Now," he said. "The minuet again. Handel."

"Like this?" I looked down at his large hands, which concealed my own. A sea breeze drifted through the open widow. It was warm, but I shivered.

"Yes, like this."

As I played, George's hands stayed with mine, barely touching but moving along the keyboard as if he knew where my fingers were going to travel. When we went up the scale, his shoulder leaned in. When we came down, he pulled back. I touched the right notes but barely heard the song, so overtaken was I by the catch in my throat, the tingling up my arms, the warmth in my seat. When we were finished, I didn't dare face him. Across the parlor, Mrs. Younge set down her needlework, stood up, and left the room. My heart hammered like a woodpecker—as it does now.

In front of me, Anne jumps down from the bench, slips, and falls.

"Ow, my knee!"

I help her up from the floor. She hops on one foot.

"You're fine," I tell her. "Run along and find your little brother. I think he's in the library with Miss Rookwood."

I take Anne's place at the pianoforte and practice scales, starting with the majors as always, C, then G, D, and A. Briefly, my mind is at ease. The pattern of the music calms me. I continue through E, B, and F, and then I start over, but the task is too slow and doesn't require enough concentration. A lock of hair tickles my shoulder where George once fingered a tendril that had fallen loose from my bun. I start the scales again from C, but play faster. Yet even as my fingers fly up and down the keyboard, my mind swirls with memories of those afternoons in the parlor—and the evening when George took my hand, turned it over, and pressed his lips to my palm.

"Annie! Come play with me!" I hear Thomas in the library. His excitement is palpable; he adores his older sister.

In the weeks after my brother brought me home from Margate, I spent hours at the piano. As if in a dream, I'd move from the drawing room to my bedroom and back again, tolerating company only at meals, during which I barely spoke. Being home at Pemberley was usually a comfort, but I took little pleasure in my surroundings. My brother assumed I was using music to drown out my shame at having nearly eloped, but shame was not all that afflicted me; I was heartbroken. I'd been so gullible and naive. And I regretted how virulently I'd argued with my beloved brother. We'd never before raised our voices at each other. After our parents were both gone, my brother had stepped in as surrogate father. I knew that many found him proud, but to me he was the essence of kindness and care. I still hate how I spoke to him in Margate.

"I don't care if George is after my money," I'd cried. "My thirty thousand pounds will be a factor in whatever match I make. Why shouldn't it go to someone I love?"

"Love?" My brother scowled. "You are an innocent child. What can you possibly know of love?"

"And you know so much about romance, Mr. Darcy?" I knew he despised when I addressed him formally in this way, like a stranger or a servant, but I was beyond reason. "George Wickham may not be perfect, but at least I have known love. You'll never marry because no one meets your impossible standards."

Worse, I accused my brother of being jealous of George, whose sparkling eyes, fine countenance, and happy manners brought him friends and admirers wherever he went. Everyone at Pemberley adored him, our father most of all.

Now, a rustle of skirts at the door. The governess.

"I beg your pardon, Lady Stoughton, may I take the children outside now instead of later this afternoon? There are clouds in the distance, and I'm afraid it might rain."

"Of course, Miss Rookwood. You don't have to ask permission. I trust you to do what you think is best."

She is still new, so young and tentative. I think she's scared of me. If only she knew how frightened I am of myself!

In the next room, Miss Rookwood speaks to the children, who clap and squeal, delighted to play outside. When I was their age, I used to roam all over Pemberley, looking for George. The son of the estate's steward, George grew up alongside my brother and, thanks to my father, was schooled beside him all the way through Cambridge. Though a decade older than me, George devoted hours to my amusement. He'd slip lemon drops into my hand under the table and sometimes tease me by tugging on my bonnet and feigning innocence when I whipped around. "Moi?" he'd say, confusing me with his French. "Mais non!" I loved fencing with him, a cattail as my sword, until he'd pretend defeat so well that I would cast myself upon him on the ground, sobbing only half in jest as I waited for him to lift his head, wink at me, and say something dramatic like "I live to see another day!"

If my brother was the sun of my girlhood, dependable and steady, George was the stars.

A horse whinnies. I go to the window. Outside, Edmund sits tall and straight-backed in the saddle as he prepares to ride out with the estate manager. He bends to adjust a stirrup and, as if he can sense my eyes on him, looks up toward the house. When my husband spots me, he grins and makes a flourish with his arm, like a court jester bowing to a queen.

I watch as he prods his horse and canters away. How lucky men are to have important things to keep them diverted from whatever rumbles in their minds. And how odd that I can move through my days as if I'm concentrating on a conversation, or the words in a book, or the stitches in my embroidery, while I am thinking only of long-ago moments that, even in memory, make my body vibrate like the plucked strings of a harp. I am thankful that no one can read my thoughts. My husband would be shocked. My brother would be deeply disappointed to know that, after all this time and all that we now know, I am still dreaming of "that wretched man."

"To think what he might have done to you had I not joined you here in Margate unexpectedly," he'd said, after I'd confessed our plan to elope. He told me that "Wickham"—he wouldn't speak his Christian name—was not to be trusted or believed.

"He aims only to satisfy himself," he said.

"It's not his fault that he lacks for money," I said.

"No? Our father left Wickham a living to enter the clergy, but he refused it and asked for money instead. I gave him money, but he squandered it. And then came back and said he wanted to enter the clergy after all, which was patently absurd, as he'd done nothing but pursue a life of idleness and dissipation. He was livid at my refusal, but I never thought he'd stoop so low as to lure you and your fortune into his trap."

"But he didn't," I'd countered. "We met him by chance when we were walking along the seawall."

I recounted how Mrs. Younge and I had been out strolling when the wind picked up and it started to rain. I was struggling to open my parasol when I heard a man behind us say, "It's only a mizzle; you won't melt." It had been years since I'd seen George, and I was so happy to discover him that I forgot my manners and threw my arms around him like I was still a child.

"Could it be? Miss Georgiana Darcy?" he'd said. "Look how you've grown."

I thought he was teasing me about my height—we were nearly eye to eye—but he spoke earnestly and declared me a proper young lady, which reminded me to act like one and introduce him to Mrs. Younge. He bowed elegantly. I was sure Mrs. Younge was impressed that I was on such familiar terms with a man as pleasing as George Wickham.

George had looped his arm through mine, and we'd walked forward in quick, long strides, soon making a distance between ourselves and Mrs. Younge. When I looked back, he laughed and said, "Have you grown into such a Darcy that you fear even the hint of scandal?"

"With you?" I said. "Of course not. Don't I call you brother?"

"Do you still?" he said. "I should hope not." Which would have made me sad had he not looked upon me with such delight.

Listening to this account, my brother had turned red in the face. I think he was too angry to speak. Finally, he said, "This never should have happened. I blame myself."

That's when he'd gone into the next room to have words with Mrs. Younge. I couldn't hear what he said, but his tone of voice alarmed me. When he returned, he told me that there had been a prior acquaintance between George Wickham and Mrs. Younge, in whose character we were cruelly deceived. It was by her connivance and aid that Wickham had come to Margate, where, at his request, she had orchestrated our time together and done everything possible to persuade me to elope with him. The "chance" encounter on the seawall had been nothing of the kind.

This was a blow. I went over all my interactions with George and Mrs. Younge, shocked that they'd colluded to trick me. I'd happily have given all my fortune to a good and honest man who promised me his love and was grateful to accept mine. But George Wickham was not who he presented himself to be. He was duplicitous and insincere. A liar. I learned that then and know it now.

So why—at seven and twenty years and well settled as a wife and mother—am I consumed with thoughts of this unworthy man?

If Lizzie were here, she would tell me to get outside and take a walk. The world is more beautiful on foot, she's declared more than once, and more manageable, too. I heed her advice and leave the house, thankful that the sky hasn't darkened as Miss Rookwood feared. I walk briskly, as if I can outpace the thoughts that haunt me. I'm halfway down the grassy slope to the rose garden when Thomas dashes up to me, tears streaking his pudgy cheeks.

"I was only pretending!" he says. "Why can't I play make believe?"

Anne, looking peeved, trots up behind him. She is trailed by the governess, who looks nearly as distraught as the children. Anne holds out a garland made of daisies.

"Look, Mama, I made this for his veil." She tries to place the garland on her brother's head, but Miss Rookwood steps up and takes it from her.

"I've no objections to the game, my lady," Miss Rookwood says, holding the garland behind her back.

"What game?" I wish they hadn't seen me.

"They were playing wedding," the governess says. "But Thomas insisted"—here she drops her voice to a whisper—"he insisted on playing the part of the bride."

"It's my turn to be the bride," Thomas says, trying unsuccessfully to grab the garland. "I want to marry Annie."

He is so sweet and silly; it's hard not to laugh. He's always pretending at something; last week it was a vicar, and before that a snake charmer. But I can't be bothered with this right now.

"Anne and Thomas, whatever the game was, it's over now. If you don't listen to Miss Rookwood, there will be no play at all."

I turn and walk away, thinking how benign my children's upsets are. If only mine could be vanished by an outburst of tears or a prolonged, sullen pout.

At the bottom of the hill, I follow the winding path that leads to Edmund's grandmother's private garden. She was considered a "great eccentric," Edmund had told me the first time he'd shown me Headsworth. He'd been so proud of his family and its traditions and so eager to share them with me. His grandmother, he'd said, had not only designed a garden to spark the five senses of sight, sound, touch, taste, and smell, but had kept the garden gate locked. There were only two keys—one that she kept on a chain around her neck and one that was entrusted to her head gardener. And she never welcomed visitors. Edmund had stepped into his grandmother's garden for the first time when he was nineteen, shortly after she died.

"I'd expected something more unusual," he'd told me. "It was just flowers."

We'd laughed about that then. I was eighteen and he twenty-four when we married, and after George Wickham's rakish ways, Edmund seemed the perfect gentleman. He was everything I thought a husband should be—handsome, respectful, kind, and mature. He was so sure of himself, both in the world and in the sphere of his own home. And he was honest. His opinions could be strong, but he always expressed them with a mild-mannered elegance that blunted their edge. Edmund's fortune overshadowed mine, which comforted me. My brother said we were a perfect match. From my engagement and wedding and through my early years of raising children, I was content.

As I push open the gate to the garden, which is no longer locked, I imagine Edmund's grandmother relishing her private oasis, where rich soil brought forth flowers for her pleasure alone. Maybe she wasn't eccentric at all but knew herself and what she needed. And yet, now that I think of it, there was the issue of the gate and the lock. Were they meant to keep everyone out, or were they holding something in?

As I move through the garden, a whiff of citrus tickles my nose. Lemon verbena, maybe? I brush my hand through a rosemary bush, which releases an herby odor. Its sticky scent clings to my fingers. The garden is lush and pretty, but since I was last here it's become so overgrown that I can barely breathe. The bushes and flowers fight for space and sunlight. And there is sound, as promised—a low buzz from the bumblebees that circle over a honeysuckle plant and the quick murmur of tiny hummingbirds hovering over a delphinium bush, their wings flapping so rapidly their movement is nearly imperceptible. It's too much. Deep orange daylilies emit a sweet, sickly smell that makes me dizzy. What is this place? Whatever it is, it's not "just flowers." I need to get out. I don't want to be in this unfettered explosion of color and beauty.

As I leave, the gate swings behind me. I head toward the hedge maze, drawn to its dark, narrow paths, so clipped and orderly. I have always been superstitious about the garden maze; I believe, or I want to believe, that if I find my way to the center without making any wrong turns, all will be well. Today, it matters more than ever. If I take the right route, my obsession of the past few weeks will dissipate and I will be calm, as I once was.

I enter the maze slowly, running a hand along the prickly hedge, which reaches far above my head. The first turns are easy, and I take them instinctively, confident that I know the way. But at the next branch, I hesitate. Do I go left or right? I take a few steps to the left before feeling that it's wrong. I turn back the other way. So far, I'm doing well. I know I am close to the center—I can feel it. At the heart of the maze, there is a stone pedestal upon which I can stand in triumph and enjoy the view over the hedges and beyond. One more turn—yes, this is right—and another. I am almost there. But a sound stops me. I'm not sure what it is. I step forward and peer around the hedge. I've found the center. But there's someone there, a man, standing close to the far hedge with his back to me. His shoulders are hunched. I can tell from the way his jacket flaps behind him that it is unbuttoned in the front. He reaches one arm down and brings up the folds of a skirt. There is a woman with him, mostly hidden, but now I can see her hair and her shoes. Who are they? Are they visitors? From the village? I should turn back, but I can't look away. The man shifts his stance, and I can see the woman's dark hair tumbling over her shoulder. And now her face. Her eyes are closed, and she is smiling as the man nuzzles her neck. Her hands, pale and delicate, grip his shoulders. He has one arm around her waist, I think. The other is moving down below. She opens her mouth, says "Oh," and sighs. And opens her eyes and looks at me.

I turn away, my heart racing. I start walking, but I'm not sure of the way out. I reach a dead end. I turn back, only to take another path that leads to nowhere. I go faster but lose my balance, and when I reach out to steady myself, my arm shoots through a gap in the hedge and a branch scratches my cheek. I want to get out of the maze and far away from what I saw. I press on until I see an opening and stumble out of the maze. The sunlight is harsh and the crunch of my boots on the gravel too loud.

I don't go back the way I came, by the gated garden, but head for the great lawn that will take me directly up to the house. I run, keeping my eyes cast downward to maintain my footing. I'm desperate to get inside without being seen, to be in my bed chamber, where I can calm myself. But when I look up, there is Edmund, handing off his horse to the stable hand.

"Has something happened?" he asks. "You don't look yourself."

"I'm fine." I force a smile and touch my cheek. "I slipped; that is all."

"You must be more careful, Georgiana." He notices something in my hair and gently pulls out a twig. "I don't want my dear wife running wild. Anything could happen."

Once I've changed my clothes, Edmund reminds me that his Aunt Alice is coming to tea. That I've forgotten attests to my strange state. Lady Atherton's visits, which are thankfully infrequent, are a trial. She is particular about her comfort—whether the assortment of tea cakes and sandwiches is balanced between savory and sweet, if the room is too drafty or warm. Worse, she notices everything about me. She tells me if I look tired, or if I'm smiling too little, which she thinks is selfish, or too much, which she deems infantile. Though I come from a family of considerable fortune and was raised in a grand home, she faults me for entering my marriage without a title. Edmund has more patience with his aunt, who rarely criticizes him and demands little of his time. He usually sits with her for no more than a quarter hour, during which he inquires after her health and that of her dogs. When she isn't looking, he shoots sheepishly apologetic looks my way, seeking permission to leave. After Edmund excuses himself today, Aunt Alice sneers at her tea and then turns her attention to me.

"You've been in the sun. It's not becoming."

"I had a walk this morning," I say. "I stayed out longer than expected."

"You mean you let yourself forget the time," she says. "You must maintain a regular routine, as I do, and walk the same path every day at the same time. In this way, you will find you always will be home when expected."

"I'll keep that in mind," I say.

She sets down her cup and saucer.

"I saw your sister last week when I was in Bath."

"You saw Elizabeth?" I ask.

"Not Elizabeth. Mrs. Wickham."

My cup slips, splashing tea onto the saucer. I reach for a serviette so I can look away and hide my face. My cheeks are burning.

"Mrs. Wickham is *not* my sister," I manage to say.

"Do you not call Elizabeth Darcy sister?"

"Of course. She is my brother's wife."

"And is Mrs. Wickham not Elizabeth Darcy's sister, as she told me?"

"She is."

"Then I am correct. Your sister's sister is *your* sister. Therefore, Mrs. Wickham is your sister."

This is ridiculous. Lydia Wickham is nothing to me. She is never spoken of to me. My brother has not uttered George Wickham's name in my presence since the day he came to London to inform me that George had married. I remember not knowing how to interpret the racing of my heart.

"To someone with a great fortune?" I'd asked.

"On the contrary, she has practically nothing."

"He married for love?" It came out more plaintively than I wished.

"Do not trouble yourself on that account," my brother said gently. "George Wickham is incapable of loving anyone but himself. I cannot reveal how the union came to be. But trust me when I tell you that Wickham's aims were base and that my involvement in the matter was solely to protect the reputation of the young woman as well as that of her family."

He seemed embarrassed. When I asked about the bride, he said it was Lydia Bennet, the younger sister of Elizabeth Bennet, to whom he'd recently introduced me. I understood that my brother had been involved in making this marriage happen and that he had done so on Elizabeth Bennet's behalf. It was my first inkling that my brother hadn't just taken a fancy to Elizabeth but had found love at last.

"Georgiana, are you listening?" Aunt Alice says. "You must be more attentive. I *said* that Mrs. Wickham addressed me in an unforgivably familiar manner. She called herself a distant relation of mine—because of *you*. Can you imagine? Me, Lady Atherton, a relation of Mrs. Wickham's? Elizabeth Darcy must tell her sister to have greater deference for her superiors. You must tell Elizabeth to do so."

Lydia Wickham's behavior is my responsibility? This is unbearable.

"Would you like to see the children?" I ask.

"Whatever for?"

"They've grown since you last saw them. Anne is becoming proficient on the piano."

"I expect nothing less."

"Thomas is nearly as tall as his sister."

"Hmm." She squints at the sun as if it's chosen to shine through the window at this particular angle specifically to vex her.

"They're both very imaginative," I say.

"You speak with unfortunate pride," Aunt Alice says. "You must disabuse yourself of the notion that imagination will serve them well."

"They're children." I know I shouldn't provoke Lady Atherton, but I am unable to defer to her today. "They like to pretend. Their latest game was playing at getting married."

"Such nonsense." Aunt Alice picks up a sugar biscuit.

I tell myself not to speak but disregard my own counsel.

"Thomas played the part of the bride."

Aunt Alice freezes, biscuit halfway to her mouth.

"I trust you put a stop to that immediately."

"He's five years old, Aunt. I don't see the harm in his playing make believe. He does it all the time."

"Georgiana, you disappoint me. Have you not fully comprehended the responsibilities of a child born into this family? Your son will be the seventh Earl of Covington. He cannot, *must* not, play such absurd games. You must make sure it never happens again. I remind you of your obligations. You are not Georgiana Darcy anymore. You are Lady Stoughton. You must do better."

I must, I must. I must control my children and not lose track of time. I must stay out of the sun. I must not be too soft or too loud or smile too much or too little. I must not think about past mistakes, or someone who once loved me, or said he did. I must not think wistfully of being young and how exciting it was to be wooed, to have a hand brush mine unexpectedly or feel soft lips pressed under my ear. I must not remember a finger running along my collarbone or how a tress of hair, when lifted, once made me tremble. I must not have memories or give in to meandering, nostalgic, or inappropriate thoughts. I must not have a body that craves something I don't fully understand and someone who is not my husband. I must not be at a loss as to how to numb it. I must not be riveted when I come upon strangers in blissful intimacy in the center of a hedge maze.

For the rest of the visit, it takes all my strength to remain calm, despite my rapid pulse. I say "Yes, Aunt" and "Of course, Aunt" and "More tea, Aunt?"

When, finally, she leaves, I walk directly to the library, where I find the children practicing their letters with the governess. I tell her she is free to go.

"Have I done something wrong?" she asks.

"Of course not," I say. "I want to play with the children."

"You do?" Anne and Thomas say in unison. Miss Rookwood slips out of the room.

"Yes," I say, sitting down and pulling Anne and Thomas close to me. "What shall we play?"

"Knights," Thomas says, leaping up and pretending to brandish a sword.

I stand and jump back.

"You'll never catch me!" I say.

For a moment, the children are too stunned to move, and I understand that they've noticed my dark mood of late and that it has changed. Then, laughing, they launch themselves into the game, chasing me around the room, imaginary weapons slicing the air.

"En garde!" Anne shouts, nearly catching me.

I fall onto the couch, pretending to be mortally wounded. The children are delighted.

"Again!" Thomas says. "I want you to die again."

"It's my turn to kill her," Anne says.

We fence until we're breathless and red in the face. Thomas is so excited that he's spinning in circles.

"Let's have a rest, my little puppies," I say, which starts a new game. Anne and Thomas are animals, whimpering and scampering, standing on their knees and begging for food. They are fully immersed in their play, more devoted than the best of stage actors, deep in their worlds of make believe. And why shouldn't they be? Their imaginings are as insubstantial as the air, invisible, existing only in their minds, giving them nothing but joy. They have taken themselves out of the library and into a battlefield, a kennel, a meadow. They are playing because it delights them. It is beautiful and pure.

At supper, I am still flushed and giddy from our games.

"You look well," Edmund says. "Am I to infer that you had a good visit with Aunt Alice?"

"I wouldn't call it good," I say, smiling back at my husband. "But it was inspiring."

"I don't believe it. Aunt Alice, the esteemed Lady Atherton, inspired you?"

I take a sip of my wine, which is succulent and warm.

"Let's just say her poor example was stimulating."

Edmund, looking amused, raises his glass.

"To stimulation, then," he says. "And to my lovely wife."

The supper is ordinary, soup and venison and roasted potatoes, but the tastes hit my tongue with unusual pungency. I finish my glass of wine and ask for another.

"Is there an occasion I've forgotten about?" Edmund asks, smiling at my thirst.

"Just a good end to the day," I say.

I carry the mood with me into my bed. I am buzzing with energy. I wait for Edmund to join me. He presses a palm to my shoulder, a gesture I have come to understand. I turn toward him, and he kisses me. It is familiar and not unpleasant. My mind goes to another kiss, barely a whisper, and others, more urgent, on the settee by the window in Margate. I roll toward my husband. He runs a hand down my side. I know where he will touch me and how. I am thinking about George's hand on my thigh beneath my skirt as I press into Edmund and find his lips. I am not afraid of the scenes that play out in my head. They are memories, and fantasies, as ephemeral as make believe and as harmless. They are mine to do with what I wish.

As Edmund's body finds a rhythm with mine, the thoughts that have frightened me are now at my service. They are not about George Wickham, really, and perhaps they never were. This is about me and what I want and will let myself have. The thrills I remember goad me on, give strength to what is happening here. I am not afraid and not burdened by questions of the past. I stretch my neck back, cresting like the notes on a scale, and I gasp. My mind is clear because it is free.

Sense, Sensibility, and Snapdragons

ELOISA JAMES

Margaret, the other sister, was a good-humoured well-disposed girl; but as she had already imbibed a good deal of Marianne's romance, without having much of her sense, she did not, at thirteen, bid fair to equal her sisters at a more advanced period of life.

Jane Austen, *Sense and Sensibility*

I grew up in a literary household; my father wrote poetry and my mother short stories. Literature was a serious matter—which meant that the romance genre, like TV and white sugar, was banned. Thankfully, my mother's polka-dotted Austen hardcovers were jammed in a bookshelf, left over from college.

I read and reread Austen's novels with a critical eye; unbeknownst to myself, I was preparing for a lifetime of writing historical romance. To my mind, *Sense and Sensibility*'s claim to romance was dubious. Marianne was young and beautiful, albeit brokenhearted. Why should she give up and marry a man twenty years older? I fiercely disliked seeing her "sensibility" flattened into "sense."

I was particularly indignant about Austen's disdain for Marianne's little sister. Margaret is described as having "imbibed" Marianne's sensibility "without having much of her sense." Who would want the pragmatism that sent Marianne into the colonel's arms? Austen concludes with biting condescension that Margaret "did not, at thirteen, bid fair to equal her sisters at a more advanced period of life."

I wrote this novella for my thirteen-year-old self, indignant at not being allowed to read "real" romances and critical of the literary romances I was allowed. My Margaret is a version of myself, a young woman with a lifetime of writing novels ahead of her. Her sensibility—not her sense—leads a gentleman to fall in love with her.

Back then, I had no idea how much my rereading of Austen would teach me about the art of writing novels about love. I am endlessly grateful.

Delaford, Dorsetshire, the estate of Colonel Brandon and his wife, Marianne, née Dashwood

I sit down to begin my memoir at four o'clock in the afternoon on September 1, 1816.

(Or is it *memoirs*? For some reason that sounds better.)

My name is Miss Margaret Dashwood, and this account is fodder for my first novel. I plan to write a romance akin to those of Miss Jane Austen, but—to be frank, as a novelist must—the material I have at hand inclines toward tragedy.

My eldest sister, Elinor, claims to have married for love, but one would never know, given the lack of affection she and her husband display in public. Mr. Ferrars is a cleric, but would it injure his dignity to touch her hand or do more than smile at her across the table? I am frightfully fond of him, but he's no romantic hero: His face is long, his jaw angular, and his eyes never flash or spit fire, even when Elinor is snubbed by a cantankerous parishioner.

My second sister, Marianne, decided at the age of fourteen that her married household must encompass two carriages, a full complement of staff, and a stable of hunters (which means a gamekeeper and grooms)—which considerably narrowed the field of prospective spouses, given her lack of dowry. She fell violently in love with a lout named Willoughby, who did keep hunters, but after he jilted her for an heiress, Marianne married a wealthy, albeit somewhat elderly, suitor.

I am certain that Delaford, Colonel Brandon's estate, trumped love—and what's more, his income is three times Willoughby's, which must have been very satisfying. He doesn't have just a gamekeeper, but five sitting rooms! Her marriage proved a good turn for the whole family, as Colonel Brandon gave Mr. Ferrars a parish and me a handsome dowry. (Thank goodness!)

Unlike my sisters, I intend to be the romantic heroine of my own life and marry for passion rather than settle for sensible affection. To love is to be *on fire*, the way Juliet was. Marianne described her love for Willoughby as striking her like lightning, a description I've never forgotten. There should be burning and raging. Eyes should blaze like meteors. No, *hearts* should blaze like meteors.

The only problem is that I haven't experienced it, and no one has blazed at the sight of me, either. My family laughs at my ambition, judging Elinor intelligent, whereas I'm supposedly silly and romantic. I think they also secretly consider me selfish because I rejected a future marquess during my only Season in London.

Apparently, my worth as a woman is shackled to my future spouse's title and wealth—but after I publish this novel to great acclaim, they'll eat their words.

I plan to use these memoirs to report every detail of Marianne's upcoming hunting party so that I can use it later for romantic detail. My sister has invited any number of eligible young gentlemen and ladies, so I'm certain to witness Cupid's flaming arrows, even if I don't fall in love myself. She has invited two barons and two knights (the peerage is judged above my touch), supposedly for hunting and shooting, but in reality, to size me up. Of course, she's invited another girl or two to make it less obvious, but everyone knows.

Hunt for pigeons in the morning; assess the heiress in the evening. I sometimes wonder if the reason I haven't fallen in love is because I've become frightfully cynical (I'm romantic in ambition but cynical in spirit). Or perhaps I'm not attracting the right men. I wish I were as smart as Marianne is sensitive, or as stunning as Elinor is sensible. Alas, rather than having a romantic heroine's rippling hair and a nymphlike figure, I share the woes of many of my countrywomen: I have red hair, a plumpish figure, and large feet.

When I was seven years old, my friend Squibby told me that I resembled a tomato with carrot legs and beetroot feet. The horror of his assessment has weighed on me ever since. My hair color I can do nothing about; I'd blame the beets on my favorite red boots, but my lower half's similarity to root vegetables has only grown since. I have slender legs and blocky feet.

I write this with composure, but my feet have caused me many tears. It's unfair that gentlemen happily stomp around in Hessian boots, flaunting their feet, whereas ladies are supposed to tiptoe on their dainty toes. I hide my feet as much as possible, by tucking them under a chair, for example.

On the plus side, I'm quite pretty (I take after Marianne), and Colonel Brandon's dowry makes me an heiress. I plan to model my novel on Mrs. Frances Burney's *Cecilia, or Memoirs of an Heiress*, given that Cecilia's dowry and mine are identical— but my novel will be more realistic. For example, Mortimer finds out that Cecilia loves him after she confides in a dog. Absurd! I could have told Mrs. Burney that readers would roll their eyes at that ploy.

My main suitor to this point has been he of the tomato metaphor, Baron Hugh Skelmers Vaughan, whose family owns the estate next to Norland Park, where I grew up. Being sadly fixated on the trappings of wealth, Marianne keeps pointing out that Squibby will be a marquess someday and has a personal fortune of thirty thousand pounds, as well as whatever else he inherits.

Unfortunately, I couldn't marry Squibby, dear friend though he is. For one thing, I don't think he really wants to; I suspect his mother forced him to propose. For another, there's nothing romantic about a man who thinks of you as a tomato and remembers you eating worms—which was entirely his fault, I might add. When I was three and he was six, he dared me to eat a worm and shrieked with delight when I obliged. Our nannies came running, and we were banished to the nursery for the rest of the day.

He hadn't learned to read, so I read him a book, which I made up, as I didn't know my letters, either. Since then, he has routinely overestimated my intelligence, which I appreciate, given my family's withering assessment.

My debut Season in London two years ago climaxed with Squibby offering me a diamond ring and eternal devotion, which I rejected for the above reasons, along with my determination to marry for love. He was clearly unmoved by my refusal—I had scarcely seen him all Season (he loathes balls), so his proposal was certainly not prompted by a passionate wish to be with me.

The wretched truth is that I thought he'd try again, or at the least court me. Send a bouquet of violets or ask me for a waltz. Instead, he left for France without saying goodbye, which made his feelings clear. He'd been there a few months when war was declared (again), after which he traveled around Europe for another year. I'm glad he wasn't imprisoned like Frances Burney's husband, but I was poisonously jealous, all the same. More than anything—perhaps even romance—I would love to travel.

I plan to send my fictional heroine to picturesque areas such as Corsica, which is somewhere in Italy and reportedly full of craggy cliffs and men wielding daggers. This gives me an idea: I shall copy some of Squibby's letters from his Grand Tour into this journal so that I can use them later. An author must ruthlessly steal the material she needs. I've noticed any number of authors steal from Miss Austen, for example. How many Darcys can be insolently strolling around ballrooms, scowling because the ladies aren't pretty enough for them? (As a fervent reader: The answer is *lots*.)

That reminds me that a novelist can't merely drop people into a room and set them sneering at one another. Miss Austen, for example, routinely uses rain to nearly kill off her heroines, but I can do better. My heroine would climb a (craggy) cliff with a dagger clenched in her teeth and not get a cold, even though the rocks were crusted with snow.

Anyway, this morning Squibby dragged me along to watch the shooting party, so here's a description of Delaford woods—or "hanger," as the Colonel has it. (An aside: You'd think Squibby would be transformed by two years of unrelenting culture on the Continent, but other than a truly exquisite coat, he seems unchanged.)

We came through the yew arbor, its tree trunks dark and wreathed with fog. A bird (rook? wood pigeon?) was singing, until the retrievers started barking as loudly as pie sellers at the county fair. At least fifty men beat the underbrush to make pheasants fly up and be shot. The hills around were gray and lonely. Perhaps gray and naked.

Novels are all about detail, so I must do better. Words I should use: bold, uncouth, rugged, hazy, promentary. Or is it "promontory"? Neither looks right.

Another try: Clouds cast lowering shadows over the pheasants that cowered in the shrubbery before flinging themselves at the sky in a frantic attempt to avoid being shot in cold blood.

I expect I'll do better when describing drawing rooms, because dead pigeons lying in a row are uninspiring. I was disturbed by the way they had been set down with their thin necks all crooked to the right, especially after Squibby remarked they reminded him of opera dancers in Paris (a stinging reminder of his foreign experiences). Apparently, those dancers stand in a line, balancing on one leg and kicking the other over their heads.

Another detail: the revolting smell of blood mingled with gun oil. The beaters threw their oily rags onto the wagon, right on top of the bleeding pheasants.

That is not a romantic detail; I must aim at more flowery descriptions.

In the interest of accurate detail, here are the gowns by which I intend to entrance my suitors:

My new tea gown is pale thrush-egg blue. (I wonder if thrushes were making all that noise in the woods?) It is caught up under my breasts and drapes over my slippers. The modiste wanted to hem it above my ankles but I refused, since my skirts must disguise my feet. I have practiced tucking them back so that only the tips peek out from my gown.

I'll describe more gowns later, as I must go down to tea. I've been hearing carriages arrive all morning, rumbling over the gravel with a sound like a hailstorm. (Cliché: must do better.)

June 5, 1814, sent by Baron Hugh Skelmers Vaughan to Miss Margaret Dashwood:

Snaps, I've reached Florence, Italy. I know you want me to write about museums (and I will), but I came across people dancing in a piazza last night. You know how much I hate dancing, but a strange woman grabbed my hands and whirled me around. She reminded me of you, scolding me for being so awkward while waltzing.

Later That Afternoon

I have now met all the eligible men summoned to look me over. Marianne is determined to trade my dowry for a title, so they're mostly future knights, along with one future marquess (Squibby). Due to my passion for culture, Marianne included a poet and a novelist (future barons). It occurred to me when we were sitting around chirping over cups of tea that everyone is a "future," because I am a future wife.

Sadly, the conversation hadn't a shred of culture and centered on the likelihood of pigeon pie for dinner, given the morning's successful shoot. If I were as sensitive as Marianne used to be, the thought would have made me long for death. I comforted myself by thinking that somewhere in the world people were discussing Chaucer and Raphael, but it didn't help much, especially when the conversation turned to pig farming.

I smiled so much that my cheek muscles hurt. At some point, Squibby brought me a fresh cup of tea—he's awfully good at noticing empty cups—and asked me why I was grimacing so much. Rude! I scowled and made him go away, and after that Miss Feodora Wintresse confessed that she was devastatingly in love with him.

With Squibby!

I didn't ask why, but I must have looked astonished, because she waxed poetic about his cheekbones and the way his dark hair curls over his brow. (*Brow* is a good word for a hero. Of course, we all have one, but I shall reserve the word for my hero.) When I noted that his thirty thousand pounds are also very attractive, she turned pink and said that I needn't be vulgar. I almost retorted that I was too high*brow* to be vulgar, but luckily I didn't, because now that sounds rather stupid.

At any rate: a description of Miss Feodora Wintresse. She has flaxen hair and small earlobes to go with her very small feet. Her nose is small, too. Her heart is probably small, and as Squibby's true friend, I should warn him. But I shan't. Likely he will be entranced by the way her feet steal in and out of her petticoats like little mice. (Is that a poem? I'm sure I read it somewhere.) Her gown was so light that the line of her French stays was perfectly visible.

I wore my thrush-egg blue tea gown with a corset as confining as my grandmother might have worn, thanks to my mother's dislike of everything French. As soon as I'm married, I shall throw out my corsets and wear only stays, with no boning.

At any rate, I inquired about Feodora's reading habits, and she confessed to reading novels, but only in secret, as her mother disapproves. I would have pulled out *Cecilia* and starting reading then and there, but my sister banished everyone to rest before dinner.

We all obediently filed out of the room, but I saw Squibby saunter off toward the back of the house, so I expect he was going to the stables. He's obsessed with horses, though, to his credit, he doesn't bore one to tears talking about it. I was tempted to follow, but, of course, one mustn't. I might be caught and my reputation dented.

I suspect he was going to the stables to see if my darling mare, Bobbin, was in good form. Squibby and I share a passion for hunting—though it has nothing to do with killing a fox. We love tearing over hedges and leaping stone walls on horseback. Bobbin is smaller than his mount, Belial, but she's wily and clever. We often manage to bump Belial from the path because he's too well bred to bump *us*. On occasion, Bobbin will even bite at his flank.

Back to the novel.

Novels are never confined to the exploits of lords and ladies, so I shall practice by describing my maid, Sally. I know girls who are horribly bullied by their French maids, but, thanks to my mother's provincialism, Sally is from Northamptonshire. She has blue eyes and bigger feet than me. She claims to be grateful for her feet, because otherwise they would ache after a long day—which is a salutary reminder that most people work, whereas I am feckless and haven't completed a single petit point chair. Another important point: Sally has a much larger bosom than mine, supposedly the reason why most of the footmen are in love with her.

I considered making my heroine an impoverished orphan with a fanciable bosom, but I am unnerved by the idea of fictionalizing (if that's a word) a life I don't know much about and which can be so arduous. Sally gets frightfully tired, though she assures me that Colonel Brandon's butler is fair, and no one is overworked.

I expect I'll end up with someone like Feodora as my heroine. But smarter. Like me, but with small feet.

I won't be able to write again until after supper and dancing, but I'll just say that tonight I shall wear a fir-green evening gown with the tiniest bodice you can imagine. Sally has managed to trade one of my lace-trimmed handkerchiefs for some lip color—my mother refused to buy me any—so my lips won't look grimly pale compared to other girls.

July 25, 1814, sent by Baron Hugh Skelmers Vaughan to Miss Margaret Dashwood:

Dear Snaps, I ran into Bobby Peel in Florence (he says to remind you that he partnered you in a waltz at Fulham Palace). His father requires he stay with people of "worth and substance" rather than in coaching inns, so we're in the Villa di Castello right now. The garden is fed by a series of fascinating aqueducts leading from two springs that I might copy someday to bring water to the north cornfields. Thinking of you, I looked around at the paintings. There's one of a lady without a stitch of clothing standing in a conch shell. Bobby claims to be impressed by her gilded locks, though they're not nearly as pretty as yours.

Very Late That Night

It's three in the morning, but authors cannot give in to exhaustion, so I am sitting down to write my impressions of the evening. The moment I came down the stairs, I saw Squibby, draped against the wall like the leaning Tower of Pisa. I greeted him with that simile, and he argued that he was more like a statue of Bacchus that he saw in Rome. I was distracted by his explanation of Bacchus (the god of wine and implicitly all sorts of depraved activities) and remarked that I'd never seen him in his cups, to which Squibby responded that no lady sees a gentleman in his cups, unless it's their wedding night and they're sharing a bottle of champagne to celebrate.

I was silenced by that idea and couldn't help turning red. I've never given the wedding night much thought, other than noting Juliet's undignified wish to keep Romeo in her bed. I suppose, when the time comes, I'll be forced to ask Elinor about it, since she's too sensible to allow me to be embarrassed by ignorance.

I couldn't help wondering what Squibby's unclothed chest looked like, no matter how inappropriate that was. Not that he would rival a Roman god like Bacchus, but I got the distinct impression that he would look quite good draped in a few grapevines.

Obviously, he realized his impropriety, because he changed the subject and asked if I'd read Cowper's poetry. I was quite surprised. "No, I haven't," I said. "Have you?"

"He wrote a good one called 'Epitaph for a Pheasant,' that I thought you might enjoy," he replied.

The truth is that I have intentionally avoided Cowper's poetry, because it sounds depressing. I struggled for a moment, deciding whether to reveal the truth about my propensity for cheerful literature, but I finally did. "I made up that title," Squibby said, after I confessed. My mouth fell open, and I let out an unladylike squeak. Or squeal. "You what?"

"Made it up," Squibby said, smiling at me. "The way you read me that book, years ago. Though Cowper did write 'Epitaph for a Hare,' so I wasn't far off."

I shan't elaborate on my reaction, but I experienced a burning feeling under my breast bone that did not come from eating too much cake.

Squibby was seated far away from me at the dinner table; I was sandwiched between two knights, of which Sir Roderick Muckrose was the less annoying. He said that a thrush sounds like a wooden flute and may well have been singing in the woods. He wouldn't mind reading a novel now and then, except the House of Lords keeps him busy. That seemed a reasonable excuse. Unfortunately, one couldn't describe his eyes as "flashing"—perhaps bovine?

I expect he will ask me to marry him tomorrow, as he informed me that I was the prettiest girl he'd seen for years and told me three times that he'd like to be the first to lead me into a dance. I wish he hadn't a maddening habit of beginning nearly every sentence with "I say!" Who else is saying it, if not him?

You'll be thinking I'm a snob, and I *am* a snob. I want to marry an intellectual or, if that's impossible, a man who reads novels. Colonel Brandon claims to enjoy music far more than literature, and has read only one novel, *Pamela; or Virtue Rewarded*, by

Samuel Richardson. If the subject comes up, he wreathes his arms around his chest ("wreathes" is a good word for a man with a narrow chest) and declares that *Pamela* was "so vulgar" that he's "never bothered to read another."

He considers novelists dubious, if not outright immoral, but hopefully he will change his mind when my novel is published.

While we were eating, the footmen set up the drawing room for dancing, so after the meal, we all traipsed across the hall. I couldn't help noticing that Squibby was frightfully well dressed in a coat of steel gray; in fact, he was the most elegant man in the room, and much admired by all the ladies. He professes to dislike dancing, but he was forever bowing before someone and then guiding them around the room. By the time he came around to ask me to dance, I was in a terrible mood, so I told him that Roderick danced like a cloud.

Squibby didn't look the slightest bit annoyed at my comment and pointed out that my married name would be "Lady Margaret Muckrose," as if I hadn't already considered that drawback. He gave me a thoughtful look and said it suited me, which we both recognized was a tremendous insult. He wandered off, chortling, and I didn't see him again until the last dance, which he suggested we sit out. I have to say that he always seems to guess when I'm tired. I blame myself when gentlemen trample on my large feet, but whatever the reason, by the end of the evening, my toes inevitably feel blue.

We could have had an intellectual conversation, because I happen to know that Squibby has read reams of literature (he'd reportedly embarrassed his father by taking a first at Oxford in Litterae Humaniores—rather than a more respectable subject, such as math). But instead he confided that his second cousin Albertina had run away with her father's coachman and was last seen heading for the Scottish border.

I just realized that from now on I should transcribe dialogue in novelistic form, since my novel may be a roman à clef, which means "taken from life."

"Are you certain the coachman was the groom?" I asked, fascinated by Albertina's boldness. My mother would die if I widened my search for true love to the household staff.

"He stole the family carriage."

"Well, if I were writing Albertina's story," I said, "that would be a ruse. You believe it was the coachman because he was driving, but who knows who was seated beside her? She may have eloped with someone even more ineligible."

Squibby was very struck by this idea and kept asking me questions. I could see that he had a smile tucked in the corners of his lips, but we were both having so much fun making up a truly scandalous story that I couldn't scold him for mockery.

We concluded that Albertina had run away with a divorced man, because I once saw her dancing with a divorced duke while ignoring the scandal that erupted in the ballroom. Apparently, she had always been startlingly unconventional. "My mother," Squibby said, "is unsurprised, based on her tempestuous watercolors. She labeled Albertina 'high-spirited' based on Highland crags and storm clouds." I know just what the countess was talking about: Most girls paint daisies, so when someone ventures into Scotland, her work does stand out.

"Perhaps the groom was not only divorced, but French," I suggested, thinking of my mother's distaste for the nation. Squibby wrinkled his nose and started telling me stories about the Parisian gentlemen who wore tight beige trousers and had terrible complexions due to drinking too much Pernod, a variation of the emerald-colored drink also called absinthe.

I would love to travel to France and see pale-faced men

clutching glasses of green liqueur. I said as much, and Squibby—that wretch—said that I'd better look elsewhere than Roderick Muckrose, because they had been at Eton and Oxford together, and Roddie didn't even like traveling to Bath.

"Of course, you could marry a Frenchman, move to that country, and stock your drinks cabinet with Pernod," Squibby suggested, nodding toward the only Frenchman in the room, Monsieur Antoine Barbier. Marianne had invited him to add "flair." And also because Antoine claimed to have narrowly escaped being guillotined, which everyone assumed meant he used to have a title.

I couldn't summon up any enthusiasm for Antoine, even given the allure of green liqueur. Every time he doffed his hat, the whole world could see that his valet combed such hair as remained over the top of his head. "Absolutely not," I said, without explanation.

"You're frightfully demanding," Squibby said, sighing. "I am glad we're not marrying. I'm sure you would exhaust me."

My heart squeezed, because that implied that I wouldn't make a good wife. It was one thing to turn down a proposal and quite another to learn that the man in question counted himself lucky.

"I shall send one of my grooms to London for some Pernod," he said.

That was absurd. I pointed out the poor man would be on horseback all day.

"I know the ride sounds unpleasantly strenuous," said Squibby, "but I assure you that my grooms are paid a fortune, and they don't mind the odd errand."

I did believe it, because anyone can tell that his servants like him. Sally tells me that Squibby's valet is pleased with his position, whereas Antoine's is miserable. The man speaks only French and refuses to eat meat, so he is likely starving to death. I suggested that he might not know English, but Sally says that he's been in this country ever since the near-guillotining years ago and should have learned how to say "egg" by now.

"Did you meet lots of Frenchwomen in Europe?" I asked Squibby, realizing a moment too late how improper that question was.

"I lived on the Continent for two years," he pointed out, rather evasively.

"I know that. We wrote to each other, remember?" I wrote to him every week, even though it is frightfully inappropriate to write to an unmarried man who isn't a family member. Colonel Brandon never said a word against it and stamped all my letters, so I felt that the head of the household had (so to speak) given me permission.

"I never wrote to you about ladies," Squibby said, his eyes glinting at me.

He'd grown a lot in the last two years; I couldn't help noticing that his shoulders were much wider. Plus, there was something indefinable about his face that suggested he gained all kinds of experience he hadn't had before.

"I have no wish to learn about them," I said, striving for dignity.

Then I retired *with alacrity*. That's a great phrase that I must use somehow. It perfectly conveys the speed that sends a person running from the room, their ears burning with embarrassment.

August 16, 1814, sent by Baron Hugh Skelmers Vaughan to Miss Margaret Dashwood:

Dear Snaps, Bobby Peel's father wants to start a police force in London, so he asked us to visit a Florentine prison called the Bargello. It turns out that paying a fine will commute a death sentence. I thought you'd want me to do it, so Bobby and I pooled our money and bought out a fellow for the crime of blasphemy. The three of us are in a pub, having drunk the better part of a cask of wine. Bobby is writing his father about police corruption but says Peel senior will ignore him. I hope this is legible. I miss you.

September 2
Morning

The men went out shooting again, so I breakfasted with Feodora and two other eligible damsels before making my excuses and dashing up to my room to write while my impressions are fresh.

Feodora is even more in love with Squibby than she was yesterday afternoon. Apparently, she danced three times with him—against the rules, but her mother had retired with a headache—so now she considers them to be virtually betrothed.

"His eyes are punishingly blue," she rhapsodized, clutching her hands together.

I found the revelation of her future spouse disagreeable, and the reference to "*punishingly* blue eyes" absurd. It seems I have fallen into the habit of considering Squibby my own, which is foolish, given that I rejected his hand. I almost pointed out that their children would be oversized with floppy curls, but dismissed it as sour grapes. Instead, I asked Feodora whether she liked to travel (no), or ride to the hounds (no), or read classic literature in English or the original language (no). Those are Squibby's favorite occupations.

"Why do you call him such a frightful nickname?" she asked. "According to Debrett's, Baron Vaughan's given name is Hugh."

"Hugh *Skelmers* Vaughan," I said. "I couldn't pronounce Skelmers when I was three years old."

She looked blank, which isn't unusual for her—I'm definitely getting sour in my old age. Why should marriage be based on conjunctive interests, after all? Colonel Brandon and Marianne have nothing in common. The other day I was a reluctant witness to a long conversation about drainage—to think that Marianne used to pride herself on being romantic! That subject was followed by a thoughtful exploration of the state of Cook's nerves, as reflected in overdone beef. I suppose this sort of exchange is a trade-off one has to make to marry a man with a large estate.

I will say this: The Colonel listens patiently to Marianne cooing about their children. I remember rolling my eyes at Squibby a couple of years ago, when she was raving about their first baby's intelligence.

He leaned over and whispered in my ear, "When I have children, I shall leave them alone to grow, the way you do a lemon tree."

"A lemon tree?" I asked.

"You can't expect fruit for a few years. I met an old farmer who said that only in Sicily do lemons bear fruit immediately."

Once we had sorted out where Sicily was—and agreed that we'd both like to see untended lemon groves—I knew precisely what he was talking about, because Marianne's maternal accolades are necessarily limited and repetitive. Even now, her first still can't read or say more than a few sentences.

"My sister drags her children to London and back for the Season, when the House of Lords is in session," Squibby elaborated. "It's absurd. She should leave them in the country breathing fresh air and growing at their own pace, rather than insisting that they be constantly under the parental eye."

I completely agree. I've noticed that people with children fall into two camps: either they treat the children as an extension of themselves ("Freddy is such an intelligent little chap") or as some sort of benign growth that took over the nursery ("Margery is growing like a weed, though I admit I haven't caught sight of her in months; I really must ask Nanny to bring her down before tea").

My sisters are resolutely in the first camp, and I am certain I shall be the second. I find children frightfully boring and shall leave mine in the country until—at the very least—they can read and speak in full sentences.

At any rate, Squibby and I aren't friends merely because of the massacred earthworm (yes, it was alive—but honestly, did it suffer more than if I'd stepped on it?). We shared any number of adventures as children. For example, once when he was home from Eton, we found a dead weasel and cut it open to see what it was made of (blobby bits that are hard to separate with a twig).

All this ancient history has made me feel maudlin, so I think I'll go down and interview a suitor. Sally reported that one of the knights didn't join the shoot. Apparently, his valet failed to polish his boots, which curtailed his participation.

October 1, 1814, sent by Baron Hugh Skelmers Vaughan to Miss Margaret Dashwood:

Dear Snaps, According to custom—but not reason— the Grand Tour completes an English education. Most fellows spend their time buying snuffboxes and statues of naked goddesses to ship home. Bobby and I are trying to broaden our minds by observing local customs. Here's our summary, carved out last night over copious wine: French courteous. Spanish lordly. Italian amorous. German clownish. I actually don't know about the last, but Bobby has already been in Germany and swears the natives are poisoned by something called apple beer.

Late Afternoon

I had a feeling that Roderick Muckrose had stayed back from the shoot, and I was right. Roderick told me that he remained home in hopes of talking to me, which was a much better excuse than the "scuffed top boots" reported by our butler. Though it turned out that his valet had suffered an attack and expired on the spot, which is rather grim.

"You should ask Lord Vaughan to share his valet," I suggested, rather liking the idea of Squibby having to appear in the drawing room without being polished from head to foot.

Roderick proceeded to tell me a story meant to prove that Squibby would never give up his valet. When they were both at Oxford, Squibby installed a Venetian chandelier draped in crystals in his university sitting room, where it hangs to this day. Roderick considers the chandelier outrageously affected ("I say! Practically French of him").

I know that Squibby can't read if a room isn't very bright, but I merely agreed that it was questionable taste to insist on such grandiosity in university chambers. Even more so, Roderick claimed, because Squibby had been given the exact set of chambers in Christ Church that his father and grandfather previously occupied.

"If his father didn't need a chandelier, why should he?" Roderick demanded. "We were on the same staircase, and I made do with oil lamps."

Since I was wearing a lovely walking gown—rose with lace trim—I dragged him into the gardens, ignoring his complaints about venturing out of doors without boots.

"I say," Roderick said rather bashfully, "I do like your curls, Miss Dashwood. They're so round."

Of course they're round; Sally creates them with a poking iron. Without her help, my hair curls with wild and unfashionable abandon. I didn't enlighten him, because I take comfort in being kind to balance out my (private) unkind thoughts.

"Thank you," I said. "I find your sideburns quite agreeable."

He stroked them as if he were trying to remember what the word meant. "I say! My valet spent many careful hours shaping these to perfection. Now what am I to do?"

We were strolling in the garden arm in arm, discussing the shortage of valets who could meet Sir Roderick's exacting standards, when the men returned from the shoot, entering the garden through a side gate. They were splashed all over with mud, cheeks ruddied ("ruddied?" Is that a word?) by the wind. Squibby was hatless, and his black hair stood up on top of his head.

"You should have come with us, Snaps," he said, striding over. "It was much more fun than yesterday."

"Snaps!" Roderick exclaimed. "Are you referring to Miss Dashwood?"

"We're childhood friends," Squibby said. "I named her Snapdragon when we were both young."

"What an extraordinary nickname," Roderick said disapprovingly.

At that point I intervened because while Roderick was not proving to be a fanciable suitor, I had no interest in informing him about the origins of "Snaps" (only slightly better than the tomato). I cleared my throat and gave Squibby a stern look. "I've just been telling Sir Roderick that you would be happy to share your valet, given that his has suffered an unfortunate incident and expired."

"Happy to, old chap," Squibby said, surprising me. "You can have him for the week. I didn't take Barton with me when I traveled abroad, so I'm used to doing without him."

I would have thought all that calculated elegance took hours of anxious preparation. Apparently not.

An accurate description of Roderick's face would include a *gape*. He gaped. He had a gape. He was shocked to the toenails. "Oh, I say! How could you go on without a valet?" he stammered. "That takes me back to the horrors of Eton. I had to recruit two footmen this morning, and I still feel disheveled."

Squibby stood before us with mud splashed to his knees and laughed. "He's yours." Then he took himself off with a careless farewell.

"I can't say that I like his negligence," Roderick said, "even though we all know you and Vaughan are old friends."

We do? I was dying to ask more, but that would be too revealing. Roderick might conclude that I had set my cap for Squibby—a humiliating thought. I could hardly announce that I'd already rejected his proposal.

"A lady of your charms ought to be treated like the finest . . ." Roderick seemed to run out of inspiration.

"Finest what?" I inquired, after the silence grew uncomfortable. "China or porcelain," he said. His eye lighted on the garden before us. "A lady of your beauty ought to be treated like the fairest rose that by any name would smell as sweet."

That didn't make sense, but Roderick was gazing at me triumphantly. "*Romeo and Juliet*," I said obediently.

"Oh, I say! I knew *you'd* get it," he said. "Vaughan told all of us how intelligent you are, back at Oxford. Said you'd have got a First if girls were allowed to attend university."

I gracefully demurred, but my heart thumped. I had never imagined that Squibby said a word about me when he was away at university. We did send letters back and forth, though he told me it was just because he didn't have a little sister.

For the sake of honesty: I would have died before I got a Second, since Squibby got a First.

I should add here that I examined the garden very carefully while perambulating with Roderick. I don't have much to say about the flowers, unfortunately. What really caught my attention was the way the swallows dove into their little mud houses under the eaves. They could have been bullets, unerringly striking home.

Once again, I have failed to sound romantic.

Like Cupid's arrows, unerringly striking the breast of a young woman named Feodora.

January 20, 1815, sent by Baron Hugh Skelmers Vaughan to Miss Margaret Dashwood:

Dear Snaps, I'm going on to Vienna without Bobby. Remember how we termed the Italians *amorous*? Suffice to say, he is more enamored than I am (in truth, his father may have to travel over to separate him from a lady of dubious morals). An old fellow in the Vatican yesterday predicted that the Holy Roman Empire will be dissolved in the next year—which he compared to the Fall of Troy. I can tell you more about the empire when I'm home, but essentially the Emperor of Austria will no longer rule the whole thing, but just his tiny country. I want to see Vienna while it's still the center of the empire.

That Night

It's two in the morning, and I've had an extraordinary evening: *two* proposals of marriage! I turned both of them down, but there's something very heartening about a proposal. It's like turning up late for breakfast and discovering that all the bacon hasn't been eaten.

Around midnight I found myself on the terrace with Squibby and shared that simile. He understood it instantly. "Did you accept either of them?" he inquired. He needn't have made it quite so clear that he didn't give a damn what I did, and I almost fibbed, but then I confessed the truth.

"Excellent," Squibby said. "If you were betrothed, we'd have to stop meeting on the terrace like this."

That comment was *most* unwelcome. "I intend to meet you on the terrace many times in my life," I declared. (Had I drunk more than was strictly advisable? Yes, I had.)

"Not after you're married, Snaps," Squibby said. He was leaning against the marble railing, glancing down at me with a sort of negligent, sardonic expression.

"Are you thinking that I will marry a jealous man?" I demanded. "I shan't. Jealousy is frightfully tiresome. A woman should be allowed to live her life as she pleases." I finished my glass of champagne with an air of bravado.

He stepped closer to me and put his hand on the marble, just beside mine. I couldn't help noticing that, valet or not, his hands were beautifully kept. "Jealousy is not something that any woman can prevent," he said.

"Her husband can and should stifle his feelings," I pointed out.

He shook his head. "Not if he's in love with his wife. He won't be happy to find her chatting with another man in the middle of the night."

I chewed on my bottom lip for a while, because I reckoned he was right. At the same time, *I* was right. A woman should be able to do whatever she wanted.

"Perhaps you won't want to meet me," Squibby suggested.

Inconceivable, though I wouldn't want to flatter him by blurting it out.

"Why not?" I asked.

"Because you'll be in love with your husband, and you'll want to be talking to him. You'll find him fascinating, and when you look at him with those green eyes of yours, he won't want to stop talking. He'll make a fool of himself trying to keep you interested, just like poor Freddie is doing, not to mention the rest of the fools in there."

That wasn't a very nice way to refer to his friends, since all the men seemed to know one another from school. More to the point, I felt a wave of emotion at his description, which I can only sum up as a passionate wish that he, Squibby, would make a fool of himself to keep me talking.

Alas, the poet, Lord Dulloch, showed up and offered to recite a poem he had written for me. Squibby turned to go, and I caught the hem of his coat just in time.

"Snaps!" he complained. "I promised this dance to Miss Feodora."

I gave his coat a tug. "What if Lord Dulloch and I are discovered alone on the terrace?" I hissed.

It was unlikely, because Marianne is a lax chaperone, to say the least. In fact, I think she had dashed off to the nursery an hour prior and never returned, but the last thing I wanted was to be forced to marry a man simply because we were discovered in improper proximity.

Thankfully, Squibby groaned and folded his arms over his chest. "Are you any better at poetry than you were at university?" he asked Lord Dulloch.

The poet scowled at him. "This poem is entitled 'For Margaret.'"

"Original," Squibby said grumpily.

I beamed, because even though I could not imagine falling in love with Lord Dulloch—his sparse beard, if nothing else, would preclude it—a poem written in my honor was grist for the mill. (The mill being *Memoirs of an Heiress*, obviously.)

"For Margaret," Lord Dulloch said again, with dignity. "Tell me not, Sweet, that I am unkind."

Squibby intervened. "Are you joking? You're calling Snaps here 'sweet'?"

"Be quiet!" I exclaimed. "I *am* sweet."

Sometimes.

Squibby's laugh rumbled over the garden. "No, you're not. You're snappy and bad-tempered and endlessly curious."

Was that a compliment? My foolish heart thought maybe it was. "Please, Lord Dulloch, continue," I said, with just as much dignity as the poet.

"Tell me not, Sweet, that I am unkind, for from the nunnery of thy chaste bosom—"

Squibby interrupted that line before I even absorbed it. His voice is normally low, but it dropped an octave. "How dare you refer to Miss Dashwood's person?"

"It's poetic license," I explained, though I wasn't actually in favor of the line. I couldn't help thinking that Sally's breast would never be called "chaste," which implied that mine was flat enough to warrant the adjective.

"From the nunnery of thy *chaste bosom* and quiet mind, I fly," Lord Dulloch said doggedly.

"'Quiet mind?' You're blurting out poetry you wrote for some other woman," Squibby said, interrupting again. "Did this used to be called 'For Molly'? Wasn't that the name of the barmaid you were so obsessed with at university? Though 'chaste bosom' might be a stretch."

See what I mean?

Obviously, no woman wants a chaste bosom.

Lord Dulloch's lips thinned until he looked as indignant as a bird whose worm got away. As grumpy as an owl. As sour as a beetle.

(The problem with nature similes is that I have no idea how to interpret a beetle's mood.)

"I was inspired on first glimpsing Miss Dashwood's face," he declared.

At least he didn't refer to his first glance at my bosom. I had the feeling Squibby might have knocked him down.

"We all have attacks of strong emotion now and then," Squibby said more kindly. "Snaps here is doubtless responsible for any number of men losing their heads. But writing poetry about her bosom is *not on*, old chap."

Lord Dulloch cleared his throat. His face had gone rather red. "I shall rewrite that line and recite it to you tomorrow, Miss Dashwood." He cast a nasty look at Squibby. "When such a flippant critic is not present."

"I shall look forward to it," I said, giving him my kindest smile.

"You've never had a 'quiet mind,'" Squibby said, chuckling to himself, as his lordship disappeared into the ballroom. "Dulloch always was a fool."

"I don't suppose you would ever court anyone with a poem," I said, because (again) I had drunk too much champagne, and it made me giddy.

"Not my own," Squibby agreed. "If I was to court you—which I won't, because we are only friends—I'd use Andrew Marvell. There's a brilliant one called 'To His Coy Mistress.'"

"I am never *coy*," I said indignantly.

"And I glory in that," he retorted obscurely. "Come on. I can't play chaperone all night." He caught up my hand and drew me through the tall doors leading to the ballroom.

To my profound annoyance, he paused for a moment on the threshold. He's tall and has a commanding way about him, so a great many people turned and saw us hand in hand.

I felt a spasm of embarrassment, but at the same time, I liked the feeling of his hand around mine. My hands match my feet, but Squibby's fingers make me feel delicate.

"There she is," he said, dropping my hand as if *it* were a beetle.

He headed straight over to Feodora, whose silly face was wreathed in smiles. Imagining herself as the Countess of Vaughan, no doubt.

I felt an unladylike stab of jealousy along with embarrassment. One moment he was holding my hand, and the next he was paying particular attention to another woman. Not that I wanted him to hold my hand. . . . It was frightfully annoying, and I was glad when the dancing concluded.

If he hadn't let go of my hand, I would have pulled away, of course. I thought it through on the way up the stairs to my bed-chamber. I would have pulled away *and* given him a stern glance that said, "I am not your little sister."

Tomorrow afternoon the entire party will visit Barton Place, the estate of Sir John Middleton, one of my relatives. I mean to steal into Sir John's library and see whether I can find any poetry other than Shakespeare's.

I am positively writhing with curiosity about Andrew Marvel and his "coy" mistress. Colonel Brandon's opinion of poetry is as low as that of novels, so I shan't find it here.

February 3, 1815, sent by Baron Hugh Skelmers Vaughan to Miss Margaret Dashwood:

Dear Snaps, No one in Vienna seems to care whether the city is termed the capital of the Austrian Empire or the Holy Roman Empire. They are mad about dancing, so my waltz has improved. When a lady enters a ball here, they give her a miniature of a new invention to pin onto her dress. I wanted to bring one home to show you, so I talked a young princess into giving me her tiny telescope. It turned out her present was the sign of great favor, so I am leaving Vienna at first light before I am coerced into marriage.

September 3
Very Early Morning

Even though it is practically dawn, I am sitting down to narrativize my experiences at Barton Place, because Feodora was once told that Miss Austen was a "husband-hunting butterfly," who took all her novels from her own life. That suggests there was a Darcy in Miss Austen's life. She must have been madly in love with him, and he rejected her. Then she wrote the novel in which *he* falls madly in love for the pure satisfaction of crushing his dreams, albeit in fiction.

I approve, and so does Feodora.

Directly after luncheon, I drifted over to Lord Boucheron, the only other novelist in the party besides myself (I've decided Lord Dulloch's claims to literary prowess are dubious at best). Lord Boucheron published one novel a year ago, and Marianne reports that he has a second one on the way.

I meant to engage him in literary conversation on the way to Barton Place, but somehow Squibby ended up in our carriage as well. It turned out that he knows Lord Boucheron just as well as Roderick and the rest.

"I didn't realize that you were 'Snaps,'" Lord Boucheron exclaimed, turning to me. "I know all about you. Why didn't you tell me, old chap?" he asked Squibby, reaching out and picking up my gloved hand to bring to his lips. "I would have been kneeling at your feet, Miss Dashwood, any number of times in the last year."

"Just what did you tell your friends about me?" I asked, turning to Squibby.

(Yes, I knew that he had claimed I would get a First, but "all about me"? I couldn't stop myself from inquiring.)

Squibby was leaning back in the corner of the carriage. "Nothing more than the truth."

I narrowed my eyes.

"He talked about you all the time," Lord Boucheron said, his mouth quirked in a smile that was not unlike Squibby's at his most infuriating.

My heart thumped because—*he did?* I didn't think Squibby cared at all. I had imagined him blithely sauntering through Oxford, rarely sparing a thought for the childhood friend he termed his little sister. I had to swallow back the impulse to demand an accounting of every word.

"We had nothing else to talk about back then," Squibby said, smiling. "Thank God for the Grand Tour. The Tour finishes a man's education, you know."

That gave me a sour feeling that could be described as a "throb of rage." The Tour allows gentlemen to jaunt around the world, whereas young ladies have to stay at home and attend the Queen's drawing rooms and musicales.

Back when my family moved away from Norland Park, I had to leave behind my favorite book—an atlas. When we were little, Squibby and I would sit in my treehouse and plan long voyages around the world. It broke my heart to leave it behind. Later I heard that all the walnut trees had been cut, which surely included my treehouse.

The memory reminded me how affected I had been by Squibby's letters, the ones I'm excerpting for my book. Every time I got a letter, I would read it over and over, and then traipse listlessly around the countryside trying to find anything interesting to write to him about.

"Darling boy," Lord Boucheron said (quite as if they weren't the same age), "you are such a liar." He turned to me. "I ran into him in Prague just after he'd had one of your letters. He could talk of nothing else."

"Prague? I never mailed a letter to Prague."

"I left a groom behind to collect letters whenever I traveled on," Squibby said. I was puzzled until he added, "My father's none too young. Luckily for me, he stayed hale and hearty, and I didn't have to dash back home."

He certainly wouldn't have wanted to miss a notice of his father's illness.

"Hearty?" Boucheron snorted. "Your father was riding to the hounds for ten hours last Friday. I was exhausted, but the man wouldn't give up without catching a fox."

"I'm guessing he didn't catch anything." Squibby raised an eyebrow.

Boucheron shook his head.

"He never does, because the marquess is too loud for his own good," I explained. "Every fox living within forty miles of

Vaughan Hall knows that bellow and stays snug until he returns home. It's the same at Delaford, so I hope you aren't longing to be in at the kill tomorrow, Lord Boucheron."

"Luckily, my father finds the delights of fresh air as pleasing as a dead fox, so he isn't bothered by failure," Squibby said.

True, the marquess is always cheerful. Rumor has it that his lordship maintains dozens of mistresses, all at the same time, but I have never dared ask about that.

"I have a literary question," Squibby said. He was sprawled across the carriage in such a way that his thigh was touching my leg. I would have edged away, but then it would be obvious that I felt the press of his leg.

Which I didn't. Or shouldn't have.

Except I did. His breeches were very tight, and his leg seemed disgracefully muscled, perhaps because of a familial propensity for outdoor exercise.

"Ask me anything," Boucheron said, waving his hand languidly in the air.

"Why are larks always *merry*? Nightingales *gentle* and, for that matter, why is their song *silvery*? I've never seen a bosom *heave*, but they do it all the time in print."

I couldn't help laughing. "A robin is always *perky*, and a serpent's tooth is always *sharp*."

Squibby's eyes lit up, but before he could throw in more adjectives, Boucheron tossed his forelock like an agitated horse and demanded, "Are you implying that my novel was clichéd?"

"I didn't read it," Squibby said. "Not for want of trying. My father bought four copies and gave them all away, and my understanding is that it sold out."

"True," Boucheron said, unable to suppress a triumphant smile. "Four hundred and fifty copies, gone within the month."

"I'm sorry not to have read it," I said. "What was the title? Perhaps Colonel Brandon has a copy in his library."

"He hasn't," Boucheron said, the smile falling from his face. "I asked him, but he said that novels are secular and unedifying."

"I know," I said with a sigh. "He read one novel and will never read another, but I thought he might have bought one out of politeness."

"He is not a man of culture," Boucheron said in a brooding sort of way.

"He is extremely fond of music and has a well-informed mind," I said, feeling a spasm of loyalty. "He can tell you all about the East Indies."

"Never mind about his being a man of culture," Squibby said to Boucheron. "Neither are you."

"I certainly am!"

I decided it was time to intervene. "We have arrived," I said. "Squibby, stop being so rude."

Boucheron scrambled out and then paused, waiting to assist me from the carriage.

"Do you suppose you might call me Hugh?" Squibby asked, blocking me from leaving.

I stared at him, perplexed. No more Snaps and Squibby?

"Perhaps just in public?" he qualified. "You addressed me as Hugh in your letters, and I quite liked it."

A horrible thought occurred to me. "Did I just embarrass you?" I tried to remember whether I'd addressed him as Squibby in front of Lord Boucheron. "Would you prefer Lord Vaughan?"

"For Christ's sake," he growled, turning and jumping out of the carriage.

Which was not helpful.

Boucheron poked his head in. "Miss Dashwood, may I assist you to alight?"

It was absurd to feel so hurt by Squibby's—no, by *Hugh's*—response. I should stop thinking of him as Squibby, obviously. He is Hugh, a future marquess.

Only best friends call each other by nicknames. That time is over. Squibby and Snaps are as dated as childhood toys. We are history.

Of course, he doesn't want anyone to think that we had been so intimate. The fact that my heart felt pierced was absurd. ("Pierced?" It is hard to describe the peculiar nature of the pain.)

Sir John lives in a large, gracious manor that he invariably refers to as his "ancestral home" and sometimes, more grandly, a "stately home." He is a cheerfully gossipy sort of man whom I've always liked, and the feeling is mutual.

"There's the prettiest girl in the county!" he boomed when I entered the drawing room.

Details: a huge room, also used for dancing, with oak paneling topped with blue brocade wallpaper. One end has an enormous fireplace, and the other has double doors that lead onto a terrace.

The Middletons used to have a peacock that would march up and down screaming until someone threw him bread, but he died after eating rat poison, and Lady Middleton couldn't bear to replace him.

"I expect you've been collecting marriage proposals the way other people collect butterflies," Sir John said after we'd curtsied and bowed at each other.

"Yes, killing each one, exactly as one does with a butterfly," Squibby—*Hugh*—said, suddenly looming behind me.

I startled. Surely he wasn't talking about my rejection of his proposal? It had been so casual that it hardly deserved the title. He *laughed* after I refused him, which hurt. In fact, I cried myself to sleep that night. How dare he imply that I was frivolously rejecting proposals, given his slapdash approach?

I turned slightly and curtsied. "Lord Vaughan."

He bowed in a very minatory manner. I suppose he didn't care for the formality, but we're both grown up now.

No more Squibby and Snaps.

Lord Boucheron promptly joined us, Feodora on his arm.

"Another lovely young lady," Sir John boomed. "Lucky fellows these, to have such blooming flowers to choose from. I love a bit of matchmaking. I'll have to decide which two of you should be mated, the way bees do with blossoms."

Blank silence greeted this sally. I'm not sure that Feodora understood, but I didn't care for the idea.

"I shall anticipate your meddling," Hugh said, only the faintest tone in his voice revealing that he was on the verge of bursting into laughter.

"I fully expect that you will leave Colonel Brandon's house party betrothed," Sir John told him with satisfaction. "I've done it any number of times. Why, matrimonial plans are like confetti to me!"

Whatever that meant.

"Tomorrow, my dear lady and I shall join you for the dinner and dance after the hunt, and I vow that the week will see any number of new pairings. I've often thought that a matchmaker holds the power—the future—of the nation in his hands, since the well-being of the country depends on those of high degree making appropriate unions."

"Indeed," Hugh said, greatly amused. Perhaps not everyone

recognized that look in his eyes, but I could see the enjoyment he was taking in the conversation.

Apparently, Lord Boucheron wasn't inclined to be forcibly paired off, as he marched over to the butler and demanded sherry. Feodora, on the other hand, was gazing at Sir John with the awe usually reserved for a conjuror at the county fair.

"Lord Boucheron has good bloodlines, but a novelist will never do for a lady as pretty as you," Sir John said to her. "I shall keep a special eye out, my dear. You need to be *cherished*. I can see it with a mere glance."

She peeked at Hugh under her lashes and turned pink.

"Surely Miss Dashwood also deserves to be cherished," Hugh said in a silky voice that suggested he felt like being troublesome.

The lout!

(Though my heart jumped at the sound of his voice.)

"My darling Miss Dashwood may be suited to a novelist," Sir John said thoughtfully. "She may look docile, but she is made of sterner stuff."

"Not gentle," Hugh agreed.

I didn't know what to make of that.

"But a gentlewoman," Sir John said, frowning at him from under bushy brows. "I shall look over all the young bucks at the hunt before I reach any conclusions. Matchmaking is a serious business. Just look at all the fuss that followed Colonel Brandon's older brother's divorce."

Feodora's eyes rounded as if she'd never heard the word. Divorce is supposedly a forbidden subject in the presence of innocent maidens—but frankly, ladies rarely discuss anything else, what with reviewing recent divorces and predicting new ones.

Hugh's mouth was quirking at the corners again, and he nudged my shoe with his boot. But since we weren't friends anymore, I moved my foot to the side.

"I am never bored," Sir John continued, with an air of self-congratulation. "Not when my skills and talent are so desperately needed amongst my young acquaintances. I can't tell you how many happy marriages I am responsible for."

His wife popped up at his elbow. "Come along, dear. It's time to retire to the dining room."

"I'm just telling these pretty young ladies that I mean to stir myself on their behalf and ensure they marry well," Sir John told her.

Lady Middleton patted his arm. "It really isn't up to you, dear." She looked at me and Feodora. "I always advise young women that the most important calculation a woman can make is weighing money against boredom."

With that extraordinary comment, she sailed away, leading her husband over to the door to head up the procession to the dining room, followed by Marianne and the Colonel.

At the butler's prompting, Roderick came over to fetch Feodora, who walked away with one lingering glance over her shoulder at Hugh (I really must give her lessons on disguising her feelings).

"May I escort you to dinner?" Hugh asked me.

"No, you may not," Lord Boucheron said indignantly. "I've already been told that Miss Dashwood will sit to my right."

"Ah, but I have more money, *and* I'm less boring than you," Hugh said.

Just in the nick of time, Sir John's butler loomed up before us. "We have unequal numbers this evening, so I would be grateful if both of you would escort Miss Dashwood to the table."

Right.

I suppose I should recount the dinner, but honestly, it was just like every other meal at Sir John's house. He prides himself on offering an orgy of food and drink, all of it served on silver platters. By unfortunate chance, a boar's head was plunked down on the table just in front me, festively attired with a circlet of rosemary and bay leaves.

"Would you like me to ask a footman to remove it?" Hugh asked, following my gaze.

"No, because I am trying to figure out how to describe it," I confessed, which led to my telling him about my novel. Even though I had been ferociously hurt by the demise of Squibby and Snaps, his eyes were so interested and intent that I couldn't stop myself.

"The boar looks like a statue of Bacchus," Hugh offered.

"That Roman god, the one who loves wine?"

"Precisely. A little tipsy, with a wreath of grape leaves over one eye."

"I thought *you* were playing the role of Bacchus," I retorted, starting to enjoy myself.

"That was yesterday. Today I'm more like Eros."

Even I knew that Eros was the Roman god of love, so I was preparing a riposte, when Lady Middleton turned her head to talk to the person on her left, which meant that all of us had to do the same, like the clockwork mechanism on a chiming clock.

I took the opportunity to ask Lord Boucheron—as a published novelist—how he would describe the boar's head.

He squinted. "Ugly, isn't it? I don't care for the boiled look of its eyeballs."

"That is so observant!" I cried, perhaps a little louder than necessary, because Hugh turned from his conversation with Feodora and threw me a sardonic look.

"I don't care about eyeballs," Boucheron said. "Or eat them, either. Why should an exquisite lady like yourself be interested in something as ugly as a boar's head?"

To my other side, Hugh let out a distinct groan, which implied he was ignoring *his* conversation in favor of ours.

"I am writing a novel," I told Boucheron. Hugh couldn't expect to be my only confidant, now that he'd thrown away Squibby and Snaps.

Boucheron eyed me. "I didn't know that."

"No one does," I assured him. "I've only just begun. Actually, I haven't quite begun."

"Don't," Boucheron said.

"Why not?" I asked.

"It's a fool's business. I did it to prove my wits, but it turns out that writing a book makes you stupider."

That was surprising. "How so?"

"Getting all those words down on the page changes your brain," he elaborated. "Pretty soon you'll find yourself looking at a mere acquaintance and imagining he's villainous, when in fact he's grimacing after drinking cheap sherry. It isn't gentlemanly. Or ladylike," he added, for my benefit.

"Miss Jane Austen doesn't write about villains," I pointed out.

"Haven't read her stuff," Boucheron said. "I like a novel with some meat, if you know what I mean."

I didn't.

"Good novels need a monster," he continued, recognizing that I was perplexed. "A villain of untold cruelty. Readers expect to read about someone ravishing women and poisoning people right and left. The problem is that once you've done it, you see monsters everywhere."

That didn't sound comfortable.

He lowered his voice. "Did you hear that Vaughan's cousin ran away with a coachman?"

I nodded.

"I can't help thinking that she's lying decapitated in a ditch."

I blinked.

He pointed his fork. "I look at that boar and think about decapitated women. The *eyeballs* of decapitated women whose heads have been boiled."

Hugh cleared his throat and said, "That is an utterly inappropriate subject for dinner conversation, you fool."

I admit to being rather glad of the interruption; I sat back and let the two of them fling insults at each other until Lady Middleton turned her head once again.

"May I apologize for my pigheaded friend?" Hugh asked, as Lord Boucheron turned away. "I use that adjective knowingly."

Hugh did have a lovely smile. "There is no need," I said. "Amongst themselves, ladies constantly talk about terrible things."

"You do?"

I sorted through the recent conversations I'd been party to and picked a subject that wasn't too embarrassing. "Eating brains for breakfast is excellent for regularity," I told him.

He made a face.

"I'm serious. Drains and digestion are discussed almost every day."

"No wonder you looked so blue when I first arrived," he said. "Nothing but drains and digestion since I left for France?"

"To the contrary," I retorted. "I've had heaps of suitors, who discuss all manner of fascinating subjects."

That was an exaggeration, but I couldn't help it.

He tactfully didn't ask me to elaborate. "Tell me more about your novel."

"Lord Boucheron was quite discouraging," I admitted.

"Don't listen to him," Hugh said. "You were always going to be a novelist. It was only a matter of when you decided to put a quill to paper."

I have to admit that his statement was so baldly said that it flew to my heart and nestled there. (*Not a bad sentence.*)

"What were you always going to be?" I asked.

"Don't you know?"

I shook my head.

"You will," he said, but the conversation was interrupted by Sir John rousing himself to offer a long series of toasts to the health of the King and Queen, the Duke of Wellington, the Prime Minister, and each of his unmarried guests and their future spouses, to be determined by him.

It occurred to me that Sir John was likely responsible for Marianne marrying Colonel Brandon, since the Colonel is one of his closest friends. While love didn't bring them together, I must admit that they are well matched.

Toward the end of the meal, Marianne bored everyone to tears by declaring that her second daughter, Delphinium, was showing clear signs of genius along with her first tooth. The Colonel didn't precisely agree with her, but he did pat her hand and make approving noises.

Hugh whispered that when he had children, he expected them to have all their teeth at birth because they would be that brilliant. In fact, they might rival the birth of Venus and come out fully formed.

"Babies are not meant to have teeth," I pointed out.

"Why not?"

"Because they are fed from the breast," I said, before I thought better of mentioning body parts. Once I realized, I felt myself turning pink.

His eyes did fall to my "chaste bosom," almost entirely on display thanks to my tiny bodice. But then he looked directly back into my eyes. Maybe his color heightened. Slightly.

"I didn't think about that," he said.

The whole conversation was improper, but we ended up discussing an article from the *Times* that argued that most wet nurses addle babies' brains by drinking too much beer.

"It may explain why arguments in the House of Lords are so turgid," Hugh said.

"Will you take up your seat in Lords?"

"After my father passes away," he said. "Until then, I mean to travel."

I couldn't help sighing.

Hugh looked sympathetic. "Remember how you loved that old atlas they had in Norland Park?"

"I was just thinking about it," I said. "I'll never forgive my aunt for insisting that every single book must remain in the Norland library. She was critical of 'foreign parts,' so she had no need for an atlas."

"Like body parts," Hugh said, nodding. "Ones she found improper."

Exactly.

But we were dangerously close to breasts and bodices again, so I turned to Lord Boucheron.

After the meal concluded, Sir John ushered us all into the ballroom, where he spent the evening pacing around the dance floor, squinting at the dancers. He was clearly playing the part of a bee and deciding which of us to pair off.

Hugh said that he was reminded not of a bee but of a trout, a fish that rises to the surface of the water to eat flies. The way Sir John lurked by the wall reminded him of a trout lurking at the side of a Scottish stream.

Apparently, Scottish lakes are called "lochs." I would love to throw out my line on a foggy morning to catch a fish. Colonel Brandon uses stew ponds to house fish over the winter, and I used to enjoy scooping out a fish with a net. Lochs sounded much more sporting. To tell the truth, I felt sick with envy. Before I could confess as much, the dance concluded, and I found Roderick at my elbow.

"I'll escort Miss Dashwood in this country dance," he said to Hugh (*not* to me).

Hugh said negligently, "Do just as you wish, old chap. I've no claim on Miss Dashwood."

Which he didn't, of course.

To make up for a lowering feeling in my belly, after dancing with Roderick I allowed Lord Dulloch to draw me to the side of the room and recite his poem instead—which still included a reference to my bosom, by the way. In an amusing turn of events, later in the evening I encountered Feodora in the lady's retiring room, waiting while a maid sewed up her hem. A simple inquiry led to the revelation that she, too, had been praised for her "chaste bosom"—her poem was a match to mine!

She didn't like her bosom being described as "chaste" any more than I did.

"Lord Lewes went on about pig-breeding until I was ready to collapse from tedium," she said sadly, "and Lord Boucheron was insulted because I didn't know he'd written a novel. Did you realize that his subject is a merchant who murders people because he can't get enough fat for his soaps? Any large person on the street was in danger of being dragged off to his basement and boiled down."

I shuddered.

"His future wife might find herself scented with jasmine and sold to the luxury market," Feodora said.

I grinned at her, because I'd been unfairly mean in my assessment. She had a sense of humor, which is the clearest indicator of intelligence.

"The only man worth balancing money and boredom is Lord Vaughan," Feodora said.

I cleared my throat.

"And he's yours," she said, before I could comment. "We can all see it."

"Poppycock," I said, thinking with a pang of Squibby and Snaps.

"Whenever you're dancing with someone else, he watches with great feeling."

Which meant what, exactly?

Modesty meant that I had to insist she was wrong, wrong, wrong, and likely Hugh was staring at someone with a less-chaste bosom than either of us.

"I don't think he cares about that," Feodora said.

"Of course, he cares," I said, somewhat crossly. "He once said that I have a tomato for a head, carrots for legs, and beets for feet."

"How old was he?" Feodora inquired.

"Young," I admitted.

"Then I would listen to Sir John, rather than to such a silly description," she said comfortably. "It's a matter of self-respect, isn't it? My head was as bald as a billiard ball when I first appeared in the nursery, and my brother told Nanny to exchange me for a better-looking baby, but I don't hold it against him."

It was good advice, and I took it. No more thoughts of tomatoes.

The rest of the evening, I watched from the corner of my eye, but I never saw Hugh stare at me broodingly, the way a romance hero might. He danced the night away with Feodora, who kept laughing, so I am certain that Sir John will decide to pair the two of them.

I had no chance to steal off to the library, because the business of courting took up every minute. When we returned home, I ducked into Colonel Brandon's library to search for poetry (one never knows), but found Roderick scribbling a poem. I asked if he was inspired by jealousy of Lord Dulloch, but he insisted that the muse had struck him, and "he must obey."

He won't be joining us on the hunt tomorrow, because he had resolved that one shouldn't kill foxes. I thoroughly sympathized with the emotion, but it's amazing how fast one's convictions go out the window when considering a delightful day spent tearing around the countryside on horseback. I told Roderick that the Colonel doesn't think it's sporting to search out foxholes beforehand, so I can't remember the last time that we caught an animal. They are far too clever for us.

"It's the ethics, not the death," Roderick said, somewhat obscurely.

He only remembered the first line of "To His Coy Mistress": *"Had we but world enough and time, this coyness, lady, were no crime."*

After that we discussed whether direct address—i.e., "lady"— was insulting or not. Roderick pointed out that the word was needed for the syllabic rhythm of the line.

I argued that perhaps "lady" was balancing out the "mistress" in the title, because if his beloved was well born, she would likely be peeved to find herself referred to with such a pejorative term.

"We should ask Vaughan," Roderick said, after we thrashed the question for a bit. "He knows everything. Used to correct the Oxford dons on occasion."

I flinched at the idea of Hugh learning about my inquiry regarding the poem that he said he would have used to woo me—except he isn't wooing me. "Absolutely not," I said fiercely, and excused myself.

The cultural content of our exchange was almost enough to make me reconsider marrying Roderick, but though he had quickly covered up his poem, I noticed that it was addressed "To Diana." Since no Diana was invited to the party, I suspect the lady is back in London.

I am wildly looking forward to the hunt tomorrow. My mare, Bobbin, is in fine form, and Sally employed one of her admiring footmen to discover that Hugh had indeed brought Belial with him. Bobbin and I have raced Belial numerous times, and lost only twice.

What's more, my riding habit is magnificent. Given Mother's poor health, Marianne had accompanied me to the modiste, which meant Mother didn't know that we frequented the establishment of a Frenchwoman.

My habit is daringly styled after men's riding coats. The sleeves go past my fingers, just as do gentlemen's jackets. The seams give it a glove-like fit on top, and the skirt has a long enough drape to cover my boots. Plus, I have a darling little cap like a jockey would wear, the brim turned up in back. All of it is dark emerald green, which flatters my hair. Tomato-colored it may be, but I have to make the best of it.

August 14, 1815, sent by Baron Hugh Skelmers Vaughan to Miss Margaret Dashwood:

Dear Snaps, I've arrived in Salzburg. The musician Mozart was born here, though he lived most of his life in Vienna. In his honor, they sell special cakes with violins etched in icing on top. They're the kind of cakes that look better than they taste, which is rather dry. That's how I feel about this Grand Tour. I'm coming home, Snaps.

Early Evening September 4, the Best Day of My Life

I'm home.

I'm not sure how to describe the day.

First of all, when we gathered in the courtyard, the sky began frizzling (*such* a better word than *drizzling*), so half the party turned around directly (Feodora in the lead) and returned to the house. Colonel Brandon and Sir William never allow rainwater to stop their pursuit of a fox, so thankfully there was no talk about canceling the hunt, even when it turned out I was the only lady willing to ride.

"You won't have a chaperone. Be *sensible*, darling," Marianne said, trying to persuade me to return to the house—which was the final straw. *Sensible* I shall never be, and the grin on Hugh's face when Bobbin and I pranced up beside him was worth her disapproval.

I suppose I ought to describe the hunt for my novel, but it's all a blur, a glorious, happy blur. We began by riding through the woods, the dogs braying like mad, but it turned out they had startled a flock of pheasants, not a fox. We came out onto a grouse meadow with a low stone wall at the far end.

Hugh looked at me, and I looked at him, and then we flew across it. Belial has longer legs, but Bobbin managed to win because she edged up to him and nipped at his ear. Belial turned his head away rather than bite back (a gentlemanly mount, indeed!), which meant we were able to take the stone wall, and of course Hugh had to pull up or run the risk of running into me.

I couldn't stop myself from laughing as I drew up on the other side. Hugh doffed his hat and counted it a win on my side. Have I noted that instead of a few strands combed across his head, his black hair is wildly unruly? It's also surprisingly soft, with ringlets like silk.

I'm not sure what sort of novel I'm writing, but I'll keep that detail for my memoirs. *Private* memoirs.

He and Belial backed up and neatly cleared the wall, which is when we realized that the hunt had taken a different route. Off in the distance, I heard the Colonel bellow "*Tally-ho!*"

"Do you suppose your brother-in-law actually sighted a fox?" Hugh asked, glancing in that direction, although the hunt was out of sight.

I shook my head. "The Colonel feels it's unsporting to admit that all the foxes migrated to the next county long ago, so he shouts it once or twice an hour to keep people's spirits up."

Sure enough, no other voices echoed Colonel Brandon's. The only sounds in the meadow were a lark singing and our horses snuffling each other in a friendly sort of way.

Hugh leaped off his horse and came over to me. I know I'm under the spell of romance novels, but I am telling the strict truth when I say that the expression in his eyes made me shiver, in a good way.

"May I help you to dismount?" he asked.

A moment of decision.

I suddenly realized that my future hung on my response. The *future me* hung in the balance. I either climbed down from the horse, or we kept riding, and he would never ask me to marry him again.

Hugh looked up at me without a trace of expression in his face: either I knew what was happening, or I didn't.

I did know, of course.

All sorts of things were suddenly clear to me: my feelings for him, his for me, and the nature of our love.

He had always been able to read my eyes, so he did this time, too. He reached up and put his hands around my waist, and without a word, I leaned toward him. His hands wrapped around my waist was a sensation that I won't forget.

He proved to be frightfully strong, because he didn't drop me to the ground like a lead weight.

"Do you remember how you were always climbing trees when you were small?" he asked, rather surprisingly.

"Of course," I said—or something like that. I find that my memory is blurred by what happened next. I had a treehouse at Norland Park, and then Sir John had one built for me when we moved to Barton Cottage, because he found out that I was constantly up in trees or under tables.

"You used to curl up in the treehouse and study French in your red boots."

"Beet-colored boots," I said.

He frowned at that. We discussed beets for a while, before discovering that he had no memory of calling me a tomato with carrot legs and beetroot feet.

"Do you truly still believe I think of you that way, or even that I thought of you that way back then? I said those things in jest. I was young and stupid and wanted your attention any way I could get it. I've always thought you were beautiful."

I forgot to mention that he had led me over to the old stone wall, and now boosted me on top so that our heads were at the same height. That involved wrapping his hands around my waist once again, which I liked even better the second time. Then we both pulled off our riding gloves, without saying a word about it.

I am beginning to realize that it's hard to move characters around a space, because you have to constantly be reminding the reader where they are. So: once our gloves were off, Hugh leaned his hip against the wall, standing quite close to me, and I thought my heart would pound out of my chest.

I unpinned my hat and put it to the side because I was so happy to hear that he thought my hair beautiful, and also because this conversation might lead to kissing.

I do like kissing, and I've done enough to know that hats get in the way. When Hugh tossed his hat down on the wall, I had to work hard to suppress my lips from shaping into a wholly improper smile.

I know I had already turned down his marriage proposal, but at that moment there was nothing in the world I wanted more than to kiss him.

"I only studied French because I thought we'd travel together," Hugh said. "Squibby and Snaps in Paris."

"You said—"

I stopped. He waited until I was forced to keep talking. "You said no more Squibby and Snaps," I said, my voice huskier than I would have liked. I was aiming for an airy tone, but I didn't get there.

He looked astonished. "What are you talking about?" he repeated.

"You don't want me to call you Squibby," I pointed out. If I had to describe it, I'd say that I swallowed "painfully," because I did feel sick.

"Snaps."

He reached out and tugged at a lock of hair that had fallen down onto my shoulder. Sally had wound it all up rather than shaping ringlets, so it had a disorderly curl that is particularly my own.

"What are you talking about?" he asked.

"You requested that I address you as Hugh," I reminded him. "I understand, and I'm not complaining. I do know that it is improper for me to address you so informally. Especially once you marry someone else," I added.

He moved a little closer, and that smile was lurking in the corners of his lips again.

"But what if I don't marry anyone else?"

My mind was boggling, to be frank. I could hear my heart beating in my ears, and my entire body was tingling. I could *feel* his gaze in my fingers. In my toes.

"Feodora is quite certain that the two of you are virtually betrothed," I blurted out.

He raised an eyebrow. "Are you referring to the girl with sandy-colored hair?"

I didn't believe for a moment that he wasn't sure who Feodora was.

"I only like hair the color of a sunset," Hugh said, wrapping the curl round his finger. "I have hardly paid attention to Feodora."

"You danced with her numerous times. You smiled at her." I couldn't stop myself from brushing a shock of hair off his brow. "She didn't have a chance."

"Actually, she had *no* chance. You see, a young woman named Snaps came along and caught my heart years ago. It is my dearest wish that Squibby and Snaps will be inscribed on my tombstone. Our *shared* tombstone."

"Is that a proposal?" I demanded. "Because it is *not romantic* to talk about tombstones, Hugh."

His leg was pressed against mine by now. To be precise, as a novelist must, I had both my hands braced on the stone wall. He still had one hip leaning on the wall, but he was as close to me as possible, and somehow when he swung round and put a hand on both sides of my hips, it felt utterly natural.

I took in a quick breath and hoped that my peppermint tooth powder was still effective. Sally has assured me that Pearl Dentifrice is de rigueur for a lady hoping for kisses.

"I've always loved your hair," Hugh said, more romantically. "It isn't the color of a tomato. It gleams like marmalade in the sunshine, with darker bits and lighter streaks."

I wasn't marrying a poet, which is my way of saying that I knew exactly what was happening here. I felt a wave of that crashing joy that one feels when a long orchestral piece is coming to an end.

It was the most delightful compliment that had ever been given to me. When I looked up to examine his hair more closely, planning to be equally admiring, my eyes were caught by his (as they say).

I drew in a breath and found myself without words. Which is *not normal* for me.

"If my hair was the color of butter, we would be perfect together," Hugh said thoughtfully.

I almost—*almost*—blurted out that we were already perfect together, but luckily I caught back the words.

"Even with my hair being the wrong color, I still think we are perfect," Hugh said conversationally, as if he were discussing breakfast. "Particularly you."

I gulped. Everything I always believed about love—the burning meteors and raging eyes—reeled through my head, along with the conviction that I'd been wrong.

It might be that love was two people who went together like butter and marmalade. Like the end of a symphony, when you turn to your favorite person in the world, free to go home with him.

"You turned me down last time," Hugh went on. "I don't mind telling you that I was pretty shattered afterward."

"You were?" I blurted out. "You put the ring back in your pocket, shrugged, and said, 'Oh well.'"

I realized that his large hand had wrapped around one of mine, because he brought it to his lips.

"I couldn't make myself vulnerable," he said.

"Vulnerable? You *whistled* as you walked out."

"Did I ever tell you why I read classics at Oxford?"

I shook my head.

"Because I knew you'd want a man who knew literature," he said, shocking me to the core. "If you had left me alone, if we had never met, I'd be like any other peer, Snaps. I'd be riding to the hounds every week, if not every day. I'd take up my seat in the House of Lords when I was forced and spend the rest of the time bothering about drains. Actually, I may still bother about drains, because sanitation is important. That's probably the biggest lesson I brought back from the Tour."

"I do realize that," I said, not wanting to sound like a complete lout.

"I read literature in order to win your hand, which included a great many love poems, but I couldn't share any of them with you because you were too young. Then when you debuted, I tried to give you freedom in case you found someone you liked better, but you didn't seem to, so I showed up and tried my luck."

"There's no one I like better," I said flatly.

I could hear the lark singing again. I suppose I really am a novelist, because I was in the midst of the most important conversation of my life, and I found myself cataloguing everything: not just the lark (shades of *Romeo and Juliet!*), but the way the rough stones felt underneath my rear and the warmth of his legs against mine. The clouds had blown away, and the sky was blue behind him, but I couldn't stop looking at his face.

Hugh's pupils are rimmed with a thin line of black, and his jaw is frightfully manly. His eyes didn't precisely flash at me, but the expression in them made me feel hot all over. And happy. Happy deep inside my body.

"At the time, I thought," I said rather shyly, "that you would ask me again. Or try to make me fall in love with you. After all, you had scarcely danced with me during the Season."

"I couldn't," he said.

My smile was faltering, when he clarified, "I loved you too much, and it made me bad-tempered to see other fellows flirting with you. The night of your debut ball, I was tempted to knock one of my oldest friends down for daring to waltz with you."

"Oh," I breathed, seeing that evening in a whole new light. I had thought that Hugh was bored and showed up only out of friendliness. "I thought you asked me because your mother forced you to."

He shook his head. "She knew, of course. I had to ask her for the ring that's always given to the next countess, but she had nothing to do with it. I got on a boat for France the day after you turned me down, which is where I meant to take you if we married."

My heart thumped. "Because I know French?"

"Because you long to travel, and I want to travel with you. We would have started there and gone wherever you wish. As it was, I walked around cataloguing things that you would love and waiting for you to write me. Then I would take off for a new place, leaving a groom behind me to make sure that I didn't miss a single one of your letters."

"I had no idea," I croaked. "Why didn't you tell me?"

"You refused me so briskly, as if the idea of our marriage was inconceivable. The morning before, I told my sister that I meant to propose, and she said, 'No woman could possibly fall in love with someone called Squibby. She's not in love with you.'"

"We bungled the whole thing," I breathed.

"The only thing that gave me hope was that your letters were addressed to 'Hugh.'"

"Your sister is probably right," I said, feeling as if I was over-flowing with emotion. "Except it was too late for me. You don't think that I'd eat a worm for just any old fellow, do you?"

Hugh breathed something that sounded like a grateful curse, and then he leaned even closer and kissed me.

I *have* been kissed, remember? Any number of times in the last year. I didn't let anyone kiss me in my debut Season because . . . well, because. I was waiting. After Squibby left for France, I went through a phase of reckless kissing, trying to find out if love was a lightning bolt spurred by desire.

"You're so beautiful," Hugh said, sometime later, his hands cupped around my face. "You're so damned beautiful."

What I was feeling was so big—and so precious—that I couldn't shape words.

"Your hair is like a flame," Hugh said, clearly not as dazed as I. "I adore your legs and your toes."

"My chaste bosom?"

We kissed for a while longer, and then he told me exactly how much he loved my bosom, and it turned out that he had paid very close attention to my every curve, and thought none of them chaste.

In fact, he recited most of that poem Andrew Marvell wrote. I mean to memorize it, but for the moment, this line stuck with me:

An hundred years should go to praise
Thine eyes, and on thy forehead gaze;
Two hundred to adore each breast,
But thirty thousand to the rest.

I shall never again worry about whether my "chaste bosom" isn't large enough.

After more kissing and some promiscuous closeness, Hugh drew back and pulled a small book from his breast pocket. It was bound in worn leather, with his initials stamped in gold on the front.

I was surprised as, frankly, I was expecting the diamond to make another appearance.

I turned the book over and looked up at him. "May I?"

"I wrote it for you."

It took me a moment to understand what I was reading. "It's the record of your Grand Tour!"

(Gentlemen keep a commonplace book of memories, and if they are very clever, watercolors. It hardly needs to be said that Hugh's was merely a list of scrawled notes with places and dates.)

He nodded.

I bent my head, feeling sun on the back of my neck because my hat was off, and read one page and then another, and then a page from the middle of the book. By then I felt as if I might burst with happiness.

"You really didn't forget me when you were traveling," I whispered.

His blunt finger came down on the page I was looking at. "Everywhere I went, I thought about what you would think of the place. This was when I visited that villa outside Florence, the one with *The Birth of Venus*."

Botticelli's Primavera *has three red-haired women who are thin as shooting sticks and not nearly as beautiful as Snaps. The one with her back to me has hair most like Snaps's but the one to the left has an odd expression. Snaps would say, a frightfully odd expression. The one to the right has a nose like a poker.*

"Oh," I said softly. Whenever I turned the pages, I discovered that Hugh was having a conversation with me, except I didn't happen to be next to him.

"I went to Fontainebleau, but I came away without going inside, as I didn't want to see it without you."

"Also because you don't like Napoleon," I said, poking him.

"Who could? Not a sporting sort of fellow at all. I wanted to travel on to Greece and Portugal, but not without you, so I came home to fetch you instead. I thought perhaps we might complete the Grand Tour together, Snaps. We could even start over, because it wasn't as much fun as it could have been. With you."

Happiness was burning like a comet in my chest.

"What if I had married another man while you were traveling?"

His jaw firmed. "Colonel Brandon would have dispatched the groom that I left in your household to fetch me, and I would have returned home immediately."

I gaped, just like a romantic heroine on seeing a ghost. "*That's* why the Colonel stamped all my letters and never mentioned the impropriety of our correspondence!"

"I asked him for your hand at the beginning of your Season, but I wanted to give you time to look about," Hugh said, running a hand through his hair. "Then I realized that your 'looking about' turned me feral, so I stopped going to balls. You might as well know that I'm jealous, Snaps. No talking to other men on the terrace at midnight."

"I was always looking for you," I admitted, which led to more kissing.

"It seemed to me that you didn't bother to dance with me during the Season," I said later, "and then when you hadn't anything else to do, you pulled out a ring and gave it to me."

"It wasn't just that I wanted to knock down your dance partners. I wanted to kiss you, which would have been monstrously improper. It seemed best to stay away. I was so afraid that you would reject me that I couldn't express myself at all."

A long time later, I came back to my senses to find that Hugh and I were pressed together.

"I adore you," he said in a raspy voice, pulling away just enough so that our eyes could meet. "With a passion that is the backbone of my life, Snaps. I decided to marry you as soon as I realized that people could pair off, like animals in the ark. You were there when I learned about Noah and his ark. Do you remember?"

I swallowed hard. "When I was three and supposedly read the story to you?"

"Exactly. I bought Norland Park's entire library so that I can give you your atlas back."

"You *what*?"

"That foolish woman Fanny Dashwood decided to have the library torn out so she could do up a salon in the Chinese style, so I sent our estate manager over and scooped up all the books."

"Oh, Hugh." My eyes grew hazy with tears.

"I bought Dashwood's hunters, too, as she's decided they're too expensive. Dashwood lives a dog's life, that poor sod."

"Poor fellow," I said, gurgling with laughter.

And happiness.

"I have never wanted anything in this life except to be with you, to laugh with you, to learn with you, to argue and share things with you."

"I didn't let myself admit it, but I feel the same way," I said. "You are magnificent, and I am hopelessly besotted. If you left now, for France or even for Bath, it would break my heart."

His arms tightened around me. "You asked me a couple of days ago what I was meant to be, Snaps. Do you remember?"

"Yes. You said I was meant to be a novelist," I said with a happy glow of memory. "And you didn't tell me about you."

"I was meant to be your husband, Miss Dashwood. Even when I was six years old and chasing you around the garden making blossoms snap at you, I knew it."

He stepped back and turned to Belial, peacefully cropping grass. From a saddlebag, he pulled a slightly crumpled bouquet of snapdragons. "For my fiery snapdragon."

As I took it from him, my lip trembled, and I almost started to cry. The only reason I didn't is that he uncorked a small bottle of green liqueur and put it into my hand. One gulp of Pernod had me coughing so hard that tears really did come to my eyes.

A while later Hugh said, "After you read me the story of No-ah's ark, I told my mother that I was going to take you on board or not go at all—which is why she had nothing to do with my proposal years later."

"You told the countess that?" I gasped. Then I realized that it might explain why she had always been so very kind to me, even when I was a little girl.

Everything he'd said had gone to my head, so much so that *I* reached up and drew down his head and kissed him, instead of the other way around. A very long time later, I realized that I was no longer sitting on the wall, but instead on Hugh's lap.

"It's my turn," I said huskily, arms around his neck. "Will you marry me, Hugh?"

His eyes widened, and that beautiful, wicked smile spread over his face. "Yes, but only if you call me Squibby, and I call you Snaps."

I nodded, because his expression made me unusually shy.

"Even on our tombstone," I promised.

This time, I let him put the ring on my finger.

EPILOGUE

Y ou once told me that children should sprout like lemon trees, far from their parents," I remarked to my husband.

Hugh grinned at me. He had a boy clinging to his back like a limpet, and two smaller girls—the twins—wreathed around each leg as he (a giant) "fee-fi-fo-fummed" across the lawn. Finally, he managed to shake them off and collapsed into a chair.

"Feodora and I shall be entirely civilized about child-rearing," Lord Boucheron said, his eyes resting proudly on Feodora's balloon-like waist. "We've made up our mind to raise the little chap the way the French do."

"Not that Bouchie is unenthusiastic about your lovely family," Feodora said, "but coming at this juncture later than our friends has allowed us to make careful plans."

Hugh reached out and wrapped his fingers through mine. His eyes were gleaming with laughter. "Oh? It's not too late for us, if you care to share a few choice recommendations."

"Do you know how a gardener trains a tree to grow flat against a wall? They call it espalier," Boucheron said.

I knew all about it because Colonel Brandon prided himself on his garden walls, covered with (he claimed) the best fruit trees in the country.

"The tree supposedly makes a better display," I replied. I couldn't help thinking that it was a grim but apropos metaphor for a young lady's debut.

"Bouchie thinks that's the perfect way to raise a child," Feodora said. I could interpret my best friend's eyes almost as well as my husband's, and the idea had her in fits of laughter. Though she was too kind to crush her husband's dreams.

"The gardener trains the tree to grow on the best wall, one that faces east," Boucheron reported. "It doesn't hurt the tree in the slightest, and in fact, they bear more fruit as all their branches are in the sun."

"Hmmm," my husband said. "What do you think, Snaps?"

"I think that your son and heir is eating a grasshopper," I said, nodding at Peter.

Hugh turned his head and bellowed, "Sally! He's murdering insects again." Peter was only a few hours old when my beloved maid decided that she'd prefer to be a nanny.

Sally dashed over, one of the twins dangling under her arm like a sack of flour. "Peter, don't eat that. Now how will it be able to sing to us at night?"

"It won't because Peter has eaten its brains," Elsbeth said, her head hanging as she tried to brush the grass with her fingertips. She was the most like me, without a spark of romance in her soul. I'd finally accepted that the novels I was inclined to write didn't talk about blazing hearts.

"I believe you can train a child so that its mind sparkles with delicacy and charm," Boucheron said, as Sally started back to Vaughan Hall.

"Did you hear that my darling husband's latest book is a best-seller?" Feodora asked, tactfully changing the subject.

"As is my wife's," Hugh said, kissing each one of my fingers. "You and I, Feodora, married above our touch."

Remember when I thought that love was like a meteor and a fiery sun?

I was right. Love burns the whole world until you create a new one, you and your beloved, and your children who grow lanky as lemon trees.

It persists through a couple of years jaunting around the world, and then coming home to conversations about drains and efforts to train children to use the water closet (or, at the least, a chamber pot).

I never imagined that someone could be so in love that a day out of their sight felt like a thousand years, but it's true. Hugh had to join the House of Lords when he inherited the title. I missed him so much that the whole family moves to London when the session opens.

"Nap time," Hugh said, hoisting his grasshopper-eating heir into his arms and holding out his hand for me.

"Do forgive us," I said to Feodora and her husband, who looked rather surprised. "We find napping one of the most delightful aspects of child-rearing."

Hugh and I left them on the lawn and retired to our bedchamber to dance in the marital sheets. And if I was like Juliet and didn't want my Romeo to get out of bed, even when it was time to dress for dinner, who would blame me?

We were in love, after all.

My husband likes to remind me that his favorite poem promised a hundred years to praise my eyes, two hundred for each breast. . . .

And thirty thousand for the rest.

The Elizas

AUDREY BELLEZZA
AND EMILY HARDING

"I cannot remember the time when I did not love Eliza; and my affection for her, as we grew up, was such, as perhaps, judging from my present forlorn and cheerless gravity, you might think me incapable of having ever felt. Hers, for me, was, I believe, fervent as the attachment of your sister to Mr. Willoughby, and it was, though from a different cause, no less unfortunate. At seventeen she was lost to me for ever. . . ."

Jane Austen, *Sense and Sensibility*

No character shaped *Sense and Sensibility* more than Eliza Brandon. What's more astounding: As readers, we never even meet her. Colonel Brandon's first love, Eliza met a tragic end before the novel begins, forced to marry the Colonel's brother, then abandoned when she falls pregnant with another man's child. Like so many women of the time, she is a victim of her circumstances, while having control over none of them. After she dies from consumption, the Colonel raises her baby as his own.

This all happens well over a decade before Mr. Dashwood dies at the start of *Sense and Sensibility*. In fact, it's revealed in only about two paragraphs' worth of exposition. But her life, and that of her daughter (also named Eliza), shape the lives of everyone else we encounter in the story. Colonel Brandon falls in love with Marianne because she reminds him of his childhood love. Willoughby loses his inheritance because he impregnates the younger Eliza (who we also never meet), then leaves Marianne to find his fortune with someone else.

The Elizas are integral to the story, but they're also so much more than just a plot device. Jane Austen made sure that we knew their names, their struggles, and we're certain, if given a chance, she would have told their story, too. This is our attempt to do just that.

ELIZA BRANDON

Circa 1797

Eliza Brandon came from a long line of Elizas, an unbroken thread of life that spanned all the way to the beginning of time itself. Of course, Eliza herself was unaware of such a thread or, in any case, was never allowed to consider it. There had always been far too many things to do and books to read to get bogged down by her lineage, especially since she had no particular connection to it. After all, her parents had died before she even learned to walk, before she could even remember their faces. Back then she had been Eliza Fowler, daughter of George and Mary Fowler of Derbyshire. Then, after, she was Eliza the orphan. Eliza the heiress. But as far as Eliza had been concerned, she was still just Eliza.

Even now, years later, it seemed strange to think of her name. It didn't reflect any of those women who had come before, just a road map of the men hell-bent on their legacy. Funny then, where hers had led. In a world where a woman's appellation was really nothing more than something to be traded and changed, it had never occurred to her that the name she dreamed of someday having would end up being hers, but with cruel undertones. A source of disappointment. Eliza Brandon. Either a joke or a punishment from divine circles, she still wasn't sure.

Goodness, how tragic. She almost wanted to laugh. There had been a time not too long ago when it would have all sounded so terribly romantic, like something from one of her favorite books. Strange how much can change in just a few years.

The sound of her daughter's laughter pulled Eliza from her thoughts and back to the small room where she had been bedridden for the past few weeks, to the open window just a few feet away. The smell of flowers and turned soil in the air wafted in as the little girl ran across the sunny garden, dark curls flying in every direction, just like Eliza's had done years before when she would spend the day climbing trees and turning over rocks in the creek before returning to Delaford House with a skirt full of thistles and a smile on her face.

How odd. Eliza hadn't thought about Delaford in ages. She had hated it for even longer. Yet, in that moment, with her head swimming with fever and her small daughter's laughter echoing in her ears, Eliza was struck with her early memories of that grand house and how she had loved it once. A childhood spent roaming its labyrinthine grounds, hiding from her governess in the library with a pile of books, exploring the garden with its tall stone walls that she convinced herself were like a castle's bailey protecting her from all manner of evils just beyond it.

She never thought to question why she didn't leave the premises, or why she barely saw her guardian, an elderly man named Louis Brandon, who was a distant cousin of her mother's. It was a relation in marriage only; from the stories Eliza gathered from eavesdropping on the servants, his wife, who had been much younger and much richer, had died giving birth to their second son. She left her fortune to her husband, and he promptly squandered it over the next five years. Perhaps that was why he stepped in to take Eliza upon her parents' death. It was not out of altruism but a bid to control the immense fortune Eliza brought with her.

Of course, the details were never explained to her then. What would have been the point? She didn't have a choice in the matter. She barely had any choice at all. Mr. Brandon was simply the master of the house, the one she needed to avoid, though that was rarely necessary since he was never really home.

Neither was his eldest son, William, which was a blessing. Eliza's few interactions with him seemed always to involve a cutting insult about her appearance or her orphanhood. Fortunately, he wasn't smart enough to devise anything particularly original, so when he was home from boarding school or the gambling dens in London, his taunts were predictable. And, thankfully, rare. In fact, months could go by at a time without seeing Mr. Brandon or William. But Eliza was never lonely. After all, her imagination kept her company, fantasies fueled by the books she found in the immense library, novels by Frances Burney and Henry Fielding, Charlotte Lennox and Daniel Defoe. And, more importantly, she had the younger Christopher, the younger Brandon son.

Back then he hadn't been Christopher, though. He was Kit. Her Kit. Eliza couldn't recall her first memory of him. He had simply always been there, a permanent fixture in her life. But surely there was a moment they met? She closed her eyes now, groping through her fevered mind to try to grasp hold of the moment. Was it that morning he found her hidden in the branches of the apple tree? It had been late August, cool enough that her small feet had crunched along the frost in the garden as she snuck out of the house at dawn. She knew her governess would be looking for her, but she also knew the branches would do a good job of hiding her skirts. By the time she reached the top limb and had filled her lap with a half dozen apples, she had convinced herself that she could happily live in that spot for the rest of her life, or at the very least until her ninth birthday. That's when she had heard his voice from below.

"What are you doing up there?"

Even then, his voice had been deep, vibrating at a timbre that should have been too low for a boy only two years older than her. She looked down to the base of the tree and found him staring up at her. He was already dressed in his breeches and a waistcoat, a miniature version of what Eliza had seen his father wear a handful of times, but his dark hair was always just a bit unkempt. And his brown eyes always contained a small bit of mirth.

"Nothing," she replied, then took another bite of her apple.

"So, not stealing one of my father's apples, then," he replied.

"It is impossible to steal an apple," she replied around her mouthful. "God said so."

"Did he?"

There was a hint of jest in his voice. It spurred her on as she raised her chin and recited the Bible verse she had heard at church the week before. "'The Lord is good to all: and his tender mercies are over all his works. . . . The eyes of all wait upon thee, and thou givest them their meat in due season. Thou openest thine hand, and satisfiest the desire of every living thing.'"

He didn't look convinced.

She frowned. "What?"

"Nothing," he replied, his head cocked ever so slightly to the side as he looked back up at her again. "It's just a pity Eve didn't have your working knowledge of Psalms."

Eliza had been shocked, not only by his cheek, but to be considered a worthy recipient of it. So shocked, in fact, she couldn't immediately think of a reply.

Then he had smiled. "Care for some company?"

From then on, he was her Kit, and she was his Eve. It was the name she would hear him call out across the garden, the one whispered when he found her in the library after she had fallen asleep with a pile of books.

"Hello, Eve."

live with me and be my love, / And we will all the pleasures prove, / That Valleys, groves, hills, and fields, / Woods, or steepy mountain yields.'"

Kit watched her, his expression unreadable, like he was seeing something in her that she hadn't meant to reveal.

"'If these delights thy mind may move,'" he murmured, almost to himself. "'Then live with me, and be my love.'"

She smiled. "That's not the next line of the poem, Kit."

"I know, Eve," he replied, his eyes still locked on her so intensely that it felt as if her heart would stop.

Perhaps that was why, with her breath labored and the end so near, this memory had come to her. Because that was the moment she knew. She was his Eve and he was her Kit, and they were in love. They always had been. Nothing in the world felt more natural than that.

Yet, she hadn't said anything. It felt too precious, too sacred to share, even with him. So she kept it a secret, thinking she could lock that love away in her heart so no one would find out.

How naive she had been.

"You're in love with her, aren't you?" William had asked his brother one evening, then scoffed. "How pathetic."

Eliza wasn't meant to hear it. She had merely been hoping to steal a book of poetry from the library's mezzanine unnoticed. It was only once she was in the room, her hand creeping up to the leather-bound copy of Spenser, that she paused at the voices below.

"I'm not sure why it should concern you either way," Kit's voice replied from somewhere below.

"You can't possibly be so stupid," William replied with his typically venomous tone. "Father intends for me to marry her, not you. It's the entire reason she's here."

Silence descended.

"Have either of you bothered to ask what she wants?" Kit finally asked.

"Why the hell does that matter?"

The statement was punctuated by his slithering laugh.

William retreated to Cambridge the following day, but his accusation remained, growing in her chest until it had consumed her. Kit loved her, too. But along with the epiphany came another, more pressing one. Her future was being decided without her.

It wasn't surprising, exactly. Somehow, she had always known that she was intended to become Eliza Brandon. It was one of the few things Mr. Brandon had ever communicated in her presence. Eliza Fowler—and her immense fortune—would remain under the Brandon roof. She would stay at Delaford, and she would eventually become lady of the house. But how that would be cemented hadn't been of serious concern. At least, not as a child. But at seventeen years old, it was a question that suddenly felt urgent.

That night she was stirred from sleep, opening her eyes to the thick darkness of her bedroom. She didn't move for a long moment, letting her eyes adjust as she tried to pinpoint what had roused her. Then she saw something move in the chair in the far corner of her room.

She sat up. "Who's there?"

"It's me," Kit's voice vibrated from the shadows.

Eliza was suddenly aware of her thin nightdress, her long hair falling around her exposed shoulder.

"What's wrong?" she asked.

He didn't say anything for a long moment, and with every second that ticked by, the sense of dread in her chest grew.

"What do you want, Eve?" he finally asked.

She could have feigned ignorance. Pretended she hadn't been

privy to the conversation earlier that day. But she also didn't know how to lie. Not to him.

"You know what I want, Kit. To be happy. To have the chance at happiness, at least. To experience life and all its pleasures, however small," she replied. "And I want you there with me for all of it."

She could make out the shape of him now, the silhouette of his long body leaning back in the chair, his hand at his temple as he stared at her, his gaze so intense her breath caught. "My father purchased a commission for me," he said. "I'm leaving tomorrow."

Her heart tumbled down deep in her chest. "Where?"

"Bombay," he replied.

There was nothing that could have prepared her for that answer. "But university—"

"I'm the second son, Eve," he replied, as if forcing a bit of levity in his voice. "William will inherit our father's name, his fortune. I must make my own way in the world."

"What of my fortune?"

A muscle in his jaw ticked. "Your fortune is my father's until you marry. And you were always intended for—"

"You," she said. "I love you, Kit. Above all things."

She knew she had said the words, but they still sounded like they had emerged from a dream, too ethereal to be real.

"You love me?" he asked, so low she barely heard it.

"Yes," she whispered, before she could stop herself. "So much I feel like I could forget to breathe if you're not near."

A moment passed, then Kit rose and stalked slowly to the bed. He came to a stop at the end of it, looking down at where she still sat.

"Then marry me, Eve," he said softly, almost pleading. "Not

because my father wants your fortune, or because of my brother's plans. Marry me because you love me."

She didn't have the chance to say yes before his lips were on hers. Then words seemed so superfluous. All she could think about were his arms around her body, their sighs and kisses and moans until morning.

They were so naive to think their plan would work. They hadn't anticipated the maid overhearing their plans, alerting Mr. Brandon, and sending Kit away before they even had a chance to say goodbye.

She waited. She did. The weeks turned into months, but still, she waited. For what, she wasn't entirely sure. She knew he was thousands of miles away, but she had hoped for word of his arrival, a letter, something. But nothing arrived. And then, six months after he was gone, half a year of hiding in her room and avoiding every corner of Delaford that reminded her of him, Mr. Brandon knocked on her door for the first time in seventeen years.

He didn't wait for her to give him permission to enter. He didn't ask her how she was. He merely stared past her to the wall and said, "You are to marry William tomorrow."

"But Kit—"

"Christopher is gone."

She hadn't backed down, merely raised her chin. "Then I will wait."

"You don't have a choice," he said offhandedly, as if it were a sidenote and not the most devastating statement in the entire world.

Then he closed her door and left.

Eliza didn't remember the wedding. In fact, those following weeks still felt like a blur. Perhaps that was on purpose, a way to make the pain more manageable.

Eliza had grown up with William and his vicious tongue, but

with marriage came the introduction of clumsy fists. Maybe it was because Kit was gone. Maybe it was because he hated how much she hated him. Or maybe there was no reason at all. Maybe William was just a sad, pathetic man who was grasping at straws to feel strong and important, and one of those straws just happened to be her throat.

"Uppity bitch," he used to mumble, usually after he had come into her room unannounced and forced himself into her bed without another word.

Thankfully, he grew bored of her quickly. The relief was short-lived, though, as stories of her husband's dalliances began to find her ear. Eliza had never expected him to be loyal, but she had expected discretion. Perhaps that was her mistake. Discretion required respect, and William never offered that. So she flirted. Any man who so much as looked at her got a smile, a laugh, anything to poke alive that part of her that had once felt vital and loved and worthy. It was always just that, a flirtation, a passing glance.

Then she met Geoffrey Williams, an officer from a regiment stationed nearby, and he had indulged her more than any man ever had. There was conversation and compliments over the course of the Season, until it all came to a head at a concert at Delaford. After the music was finished, he had asked for a tour of the gallery, and Eliza obliged, showing him the collection of family portraits and landscapes. At the end of the long room, he had taken her hand, pulling her close to the window so they were hidden by the curtain, and he kissed her.

It had been so long since she had been the recipient of affection that she hadn't even thought of pushing him away until they heard a door close nearby.

"We should go," she whispered.

"And where should we go, Mrs. Brandon?" he had whispered

in her ear. "Back to the party, or out to the garden? It's your choice."

Your choice. It was such an intoxicating proposition. When was the last time she had been given a choice? How much different would her life be if she had? And if this was it, the one opportunity she had to be master of her own life, then she would take it. So she chose the garden.

She let him take her, right there against the ivy-covered wall where she used to explore as a child. And as her legs went around his waist, as he forced her back up against the cold stone, she gripped his red coat and let herself imagine that he was Kit. That he had come back from his war and saved her from this loneliness, this desolate excuse for a life.

Afterward, she learned quickly that no one comes to save you. That when you end up pregnant with another man's child, and your husband finds out and beats you to the point of almost killing you, then throws you out onto the streets, while keeping your fortune and your home, you must navigate that yourself.

For the briefest of moments, she had felt free. Yes, she had no money, no prospects, but she hadn't worried. For the first time in her life, she had free will. She had a choice. And when she gave birth to a little girl a few months later, she was confident enough to name her Eliza, after herself, because men shouldn't be the only ones allowed to honor themselves in their progeny. Because women's survival was just as important.

But Eliza quickly learned that the world wasn't designed that way. Where she thought she would have a choice, she soon found only condemnation. The responsibility of all those choices that had been made for her now landed squarely at her feet, and all she could do was take what menial jobs she could find to keep her and her daughter out of the poorhouse. But then the cough arrived in her chest, and even that became impossible.

She wasn't Eliza Brandon, lady of Delaford House. She was just Eliza. And she was dying.

The physician said it was consumption, and by the time he came to see her at the small room she had rented in the East End of London, he said it was too far advanced to offer anything but prayers. Two weeks later she could barely get out of bed to take care of her baby, let alone find work. The bills accrued quickly, but there was nothing to be done. No one wanted to hire an unmarried woman with a small child, let alone one who was deathly ill. So she and her baby were hauled off to a debtor's prison.

When Eliza was a child, she had thought dying young would be romantic somehow, like a character in one of her novels, but that was only because she thought it would always be inspired by romance, the ultimate genuflection to love. But no, this was just pain and loneliness and fatigue. A slow atrophy of life in a tiny room with a single bed and one stale meal a day. Not the ending she intended.

That's where Kit found her, after she had been there for three months. The sickness had taken hold of her lungs, and she had begun to find blood in her handkerchief after a coughing fit. She had convinced herself that she would never leave that place when she heard that familiar voice again. "Hello, Eve."

She used the last bit of her energy to turn her head, and there he was. Standing in the doorway of her dilapidated room.

"Hello, Kit," she had said, tears already forming in her eyes.

Except he wasn't her Kit anymore. He was Colonel Christopher Brandon, a moniker that brought with it new creases to his forehead, a sad turn to his lips. The voice that had always carried a hint of amusement was now grave, and his eyes serious. Had his military service done that? It had been only a few years, but then, she knew how much a person could go through in that period of time. Who knows what war and bloodshed he had been forced to witness.

But he had come back to her. She hadn't asked how, and she didn't inquire about the swiftness with which he had her out of that place, how much he had paid to clear her debts. She knew only that he smiled when he held her daughter and made her laugh. And for the first time in almost two years, Eliza felt hopeful.

A few days later, she woke up here, a cottage north of London. Being saved was nothing like it was written in her old novels. What had once seemed so romantic and sweeping was, in reality, quite perfunctory and logical. Her things were new, but she had no idea from where. There was a governess watching her daughter, but Eliza didn't know the woman's name. It was all so much better than it had been, but she also understood the motive even if Kit didn't have the courage to tell her: It was in anticipation for the moment she was gone.

"I want to marry you," he said one day as he sat beside her bed and held her hand.

She tried to smile, even though she barely had the energy. "I'm still technically married to your brother, you know."

"Then I will force him to give you a divorce. I don't care if it takes a hundred years."

"I fear I don't have anything close to that left." She had hoped the words sounded light, like a joke and not a harbinger of doom. But she still felt his breath quiver from where her head rested against his chest.

After a long moment, she looked up and met his tear-lined eyes.

"I want you to take care of little Eliza," she said. "I know she's not your daughter, but she should have been and—"

"I already love her as my own," he said. "She will never know want or pain. . . ."

His voice cracked, and she knew she couldn't survive it if he did start to cry. Everything else hadn't broken her, but that just might. So she tried to smile again. This time she managed it.

"All right," she said softly. "So long as she has agency, too. Let her have choice in her life, Kit."

It could have been so different. What if he hadn't gone away? They would have been married, surely. The army would never have stolen that spark from his eye, and she wouldn't be dying right now. Her little girl would be his.

What if.

"I'm so sorry, Eve," he had whispered, hugging her tightly, like she might slip away right then. "I should have protected you."

If Eliza had had the strength, she would have protested. She didn't want protection. Not from her guardian, or her husband, or the world, which seemed so intent on grounding her down to nothing at all. She only wanted a choice. Was that too much to ask?

Even Eve herself had a choice. And while the world still railed against her for the one she made in the Garden of Eden, in the end, God had still granted her free will to make it.

Was it so wrong to want agency over her life, too?

She was so tired. Even now, she could barely keep her eyes open to spy her daughter as she ran by the window again, her squeals of glee mingling with Christopher's laughter.

That's when Eliza considered that thread again. The long one that spanned to the beginning of time, the line she was now throwing forward for her daughter to catch.

Maybe, in that way, it wasn't an ending. Her Eliza would grow up without her, yes, but perhaps she would have a chance at happiness. At love. At independence and choice and everything she had once dreamed of.

That was the last thought that floated through her mind before she passed, her last breath exiting her lips, and her eyes locked on the window of her room. Hope that the next Eliza would have a chance at discovering her own happily ever after.

ELIZA WILLIAMS

Circa 1812

Eliza Williams came from a long line of Elizas, an unbroken thread of life that spanned all the way to the beginning of time. Of course, Eliza herself was unaware of such a thread or, in any case, was never allowed to consider it. At eighteen years old, it already felt like she had lived a lifetime, yet there never seemed to be a moment to ponder such questions. At school, there were far too many other things to learn, facts to recite, and books to read to get distracted by her lineage. And later . . . well, it hadn't been the most pressing concern.

Still, she would sometimes look in the mirror and wonder about the origins of her brown curls, her dark eyes. Only that there was no one available to ask. Not her mother, who had died before Eliza turned three, or her father, whose identity was a mystery. There was her guardian, Colonel Brandon, of course, but he was not a blood relation. From what Eliza had gathered, he was a friend of the family who had stepped in to take her upon her mother's death and whom she now called her uncle. Besides, he spent most of the year on the Continent fighting Napoleon, which was why, at first, he had sent her to live at Ms. Goddard's School for Girls when she was just a young child.

There were no answers at the school, either. At least, not the ones she was looking for. But even with her limited familial knowledge, she recognized the rumors whispered among the other girls.

Eliza the orphan. Eliza the bastard. But as far as Eliza had been concerned, she was still just Eliza.

Even now, as she stood on the creaking deck of a merchant ship bound for New York, the scent from the sea and brine filling the air, it seemed strange to think of her name. It had been scrawled there on her ticket, but that had only made it feel more alien. Eliza, the name of a mother she never knew, and Williams, the surname of a man who didn't even know she existed. Either a joke or a punishment from divine circles, she still wasn't sure.

Of course, it hadn't felt like that when she was young. Not until she had stumbled upon her mother's books. She had found them one Christmas while visiting the Colonel. She had wandered into his library, desperate for something to read, and had recognized the title of an Ann Radcliffe novel stashed on the top shelf. At the time she had almost laughed at the idea of her stoic guardian reading such a sweeping romance, but then she had opened it and found a name carefully scrawled on the first page: Eliza Fowler.

She found the same name in a half dozen others and promptly scooped them up, stowing them in her trunk to bring back to school. For the next few years, the books lived under Eliza's bed. Each night she would pore over them—*The Romance of the Forest* and *Evelina*, *The Mysteries of Udolpho* and *The Decameron*. At first, she had hoped to imbibe something of her mother, as if the stories hid some of the truth Eliza had been starving for, but then the stories themselves became too good. Romance and violence, death and mourning, but always wrapped up in a happy ending. Despite the trials and tribulations, love always won.

How odd. Just a few years ago, she couldn't imagine anything more romantic than those happy endings. Then, after last year, she had almost resented them, as if they had sold her a false bill of goods. But in that moment, as she held her newborn daughter to her chest and stared out across the Atlantic, the ship swaying beneath her feet, she was struck with the memory of those books and how she had loved them once. After all, they were the reason she made her first friend.

When she was fourteen, the Colonel had pulled her from boarding school. He had inherited the estate after the death of his brother, William—a man Eliza never met but who, by all accounts, would not be missed, particularly since he left behind no wife or children—and with their new status came new expectations. Therefore, the Colonel was sending her to live at the prestigious home of Mr. and Mrs. Carrington, a family whose estate took up a good amount of Dorsetshire. There, in their residence and under the tutelage of Mrs. Carrington, Eliza would receive a more thorough education on what was expected from a young lady of landed gentry.

The rationale had been sound, even if Eliza hadn't entirely agreed. Her books had told her about the tumultuous world beyond the small patch of countryside she knew, had promised adventure and love beyond anything she had yet experienced. But she also knew that in order to live a life that was in any way acceptable, she had to conform to societal norms. Her sex dictated a prodigious amount of her future, if not all of it, and whatever she wanted was less important than what was expected. So she arrived at Mrs. Carrington's with her trunk as directed—her mother's precious books safe from prying eyes—and she hid away in her room as she always had done at school before.

Perhaps that was why, a few days later, when Eliza returned to her room after a morning spent on the piano and found a girl about her own age lounging on her bed, she was so startled.

"Is this yours?" the girl asked. It was only then that Eliza saw that she was leafing through her mother's copy of *The Mysteries of Udolpho*.

"Yes," Eliza replied nervously.

"I've been dying to read it," the girl replied. "I only have *The Romance of the Forest*, and I've read it so much I think I've broken the spine."

Eliza straightened. "You have *The Romance of the Forest*?"

"Yes." The girl sat up. "Do you have that, too?"

"No, I haven't been able to secure a copy."

"Then I will lend it to you, and you will let me read this, and then we will have something to talk about."

Eliza smiled brightly. "All right."

That was the first time she met Mrs. Carrington's daughter, Charlotte. For the next two years, they shared books about lost loves and stories of haunted castles, dissected the fictional affairs, and swooned over the heroes. She was Eliza's first true friend.

But that was two years ago. Two years that felt like a lifetime. Where was Charlotte now? Eliza had been staring at the ocean for so long, she was almost grateful for the new thought. A break in the anxiety and tension. But with memories of Charlotte's friendship came another wave of sadness. It was yet another thing she had lost along the way.

And it all began with that invitation to Bath. Eliza remembered the day well—she had been reading *The Castles of Athlin and Dunbayne* for the third time, trying to keep her mind occupied, when Charlotte poked her head into her room.

"Any news?" she had asked.

Eliza had been staying at the Carrington home for two years by that point. It had been lovely, truly, but now, at sixteen, she was beginning to wonder at the world beyond the walled garden, at what life looked like in places where new people existed every day. That's when the often-absent Mr. Carrington appeared from his sickbed and announced he was going away to treat his episodic dyspnea.

It wasn't that Eliza was glad for Mr. Carrington's breathing difficulties. Only that the ailment presented a unique opportunity. The gentleman was going to Bath in the hopes that taking the waters would relieve his suffering, and his eldest daughter had been invited to accompany him, along with a friend.

"Nothing yet," Eliza replied and fell back dramatically on the bed. "Sneak me in your trunk. I beg you. I'm small."

"I'm sure your uncle will send word soon," Charlotte said, even as she sent a nervous look to the window.

"But what could be taking him so long to reply? He's not on the Continent anymore. He's in Surrey!"

"Maybe there were . . . bandits," Charlotte said, turning to give her friend a conspiratorial look.

Eliza recognized the reference to the latest novel they had read, *The Orphan of the Rhine*, and bit back a smile as she feigned concern. "Or a nefarious monk."

"And the messenger was kidnapped . . ." Charlotte whispered.

"Hidden away in a mysterious castle . . ."

"With a surprisingly attractive Italian nobleman."

That was as much as they could take before they both dissolved into laughter. It was short-lived, though, as the sound of hooves rose up from the lane. Eliza scrambled to the window, with Charlotte close behind, just as a rider emerged over the hill, galloping toward the house.

Charlotte was clutching onto Eliza's shoulders with such strength, her friend's nails digging into her yellow school dress, Eliza thought she'd soon draw blood.

"That has to be it," Charlotte said, as if trying to convince the both of them. "Don't you think?"

Eliza didn't know. But she watched closely as the rider came to a stop at the door below. Then the girls waited, barely breathing. A few minutes later, a knock on the door.

"Miss Williams?" the housemaid asked. "The lady wishes for you to get your things together for the journey."

Eliza turned back to her friend, smiling even more broadly. "We're going to Bath!"

Despite the excitement of packing and planning for a summer away, the following two weeks had also been filled with letters from her uncle, outlining expectations and rules, as if Eliza could forget that her freedom had limitations. She was born a girl, after all, and if that wasn't bad enough, she was also an orphan, two unfortunate strikes against her. Luckily, she was also the beneficiary of her wealthy caring uncle. Without him, she would be out on the streets, like a character from one of her novels.

But that danger immediately vanished from her mind the moment their carriage arrived in Bath.

"'No place in England, in a full season, affords so brilliant a circle of polite company as Bath,'" Charlotte read aloud from her new copy of *The New Bath Guide* by Christopher Anstey, which she had ordered from London especially for the occasion. "'The young, the old, the grave, the gay, the infirm, and the healthy, all resort to this place of amusement. Ceremony beyond the essential rules of politeness is totally exploded; everyone mixes in the Rooms upon an equality; and the entertainments are so widely regulated, that although there is never a cessation of them, neither is there a lassitude from bad hours, or from an excess of dissipation.'" Then she squealed. "It's perfect!"

It is, Eliza had thought, staring out the small window, awe-struck. People paraded down the narrow sidewalk, in and out of shops occupying the tall limestone buildings lining the street. It was unlike anywhere she had ever been before.

The Carrington family had let 13 Queen Square, a substantial townhouse not far from the Royal Crescent. Not only did it come with a housekeeper and a little black kitten that ran about the staircase, but each girl had her own room away from Mr. Carrington's dwellings in the parlor on the second floor. Eliza's bed was larger than the one at Ivy House, and she had a nice chest of drawers and a closet full of shelves—so full that there was nothing else and it should really be called a cupboard. Regardless, she loved the room, not just for the shelves or the bed, or the view from her window of three Lombardy poplars in the park across the street. But because this room, this summer, meant freedom.

Every night at dinner, they ate rich meat stews and drank fine wines, and talked about a myriad of subjects from the academic to the absurd. Mr. Carrington made it a point of making plans for them afterward each evening, assuming it was only a matter of time before he would be feeling better and could enjoy a ball or the theater. Unfortunately, such a miraculous recovery never occurred, so Charlotte and Eliza found themselves very often on their own.

Suddenly, there were people—men and women her own age!—laughing and talking and discussing the world and opinions entirely their own. It was like a world had opened up to Eliza, bright and alive, and just waiting to show her all it had to offer. Theater and art, music and debate.

And then there was him.

Even now, she hated how her heart raced at the thought of their first meeting. How his dark eyes locked with hers at the theater and stayed there so she missed the end of *Twelfth Night*. How he found her the next day at the Pump Room, and offered to escort her around the room with a smile, as if they were old friends. How they talked about books and poetry until they were called to dinner, only to meet again the following day. Then the day after.

His name was John Willoughby. He looked like the men she pictured in the novels she read: dashing, tall, with thick brown hair that he always had perfectly coiffed, and only a few years older than herself. She'd never met a person who took such care of his appearance, and he appreciated her dark curls and bright eyes because he told her so, and she believed him.

His letters began to arrive at 13 Queen Square the following week.

Your laugh, your wit, your beauty, it lives in my very soul. . . .

Your beauty is unparalleled and haunts me day and night. . . .

I only wish I could see you again because I fear you have won over my heart; my affection for you is unwavering. . . .

Eliza was careful in her responses. She knew enough not to give her heart away too easily. She guarded those details about her life that were so sacred—her mother's history, her uncle's name— but as the weeks wore on, she found her defenses falling.

It all seemed to culminate on the eve of their final night in Bath.

"You're looking flushed," he had murmured to her as they played cards around a crowded table in the Assembly Rooms. The sounds of loud chatter and a lively jig tune echoed throughout the space while Charlotte sat across from her, laughing with another young man they had met a few weeks before and oblivious to just how close Willoughby's lips were to Eliza's neck.

"Am I?" Eliza breathed, and she swore he brushed his hand over her knee under the table. Her entire body heated.

"You are," he said with a slight smirk, his dark eyes unflinching. "I distinctly remember your beautifully pale cheeks being a lighter shade of pink, and now they are most definitely a deeper tone. Almost scarlet red, I'd say. You either have a very good hand, or you're in dire need of some fresh air."

"The culprit is definitely not these cards," she replied, folding them in front of her.

He smiled. "Well, then, may I be so presumptuous as to escort you about the garden, my dear Eliza?"

Her heart soared when he said her name, his voice so gravelly and low. Then his hand landed on her knee, and all the oxygen went out of the room.

"I could use some air," she whispered, barely recognizing her own voice.

The next second, she was excusing herself and following him into the hallway that led outside to the small grove attached to the building. Tall trees lined the lawn, offering seclusion against the towering walls that enclosed it. After just a few steps, Willoughby turned and leaned her against the cool stone. Her heart hammered in her chest as he slowly bent forward and brought his lips to hers. Letting out a sharp gasp, her eyes fluttered closed as she gripped onto his coat. She lifted up onto her toes when his arm wrapped around her waist, pulling her against him. Her lips parted, and he deepened the kiss. The night air seemed to still, the world stopped, and all Eliza thought was: *Oh, so this is what I've been missing.*

"I love you, Eliza," he murmured against her skin. "God, how I love you. Say you'll be mine, or I might perish on this very spot."

She had been so stupid. She had believed him when he said they would one day be married and she would become Mrs. Eliza Willoughby, a name she could proudly claim as part of her own legacy. She hadn't stopped to ask why the plans had been made so quickly, why they had to go to London first before setting off to Scotland to be married. She hadn't even been given the opportunity to write to the Colonel to let him know about their impending nuptials. She had only said yes, and trusted that he knew what to do. At the time, it had all felt so terribly romantic, like a scene from one of her books, where the dashing gentleman stole the heroine away in the dead of night and they lived happily ever after.

Except, in the harsh light of morning, ever after turned out to be a small apartment near Cheapside in London.

"I should write Charlotte," she had said after their bags and trunks had been delivered and they were finally alone. The rowdy sounds from the pub across the street filled her ears even as she did her best to ignore them. "Let her know our plans."

"Of course," he said, walking forward and wrapping his arms around her waist.

"And that I'm safe," she continued, trying to maintain her continence as his mouth traveled down her neck. "I've never been to London before, and I can only imagine my uncle will be concerned when he finds out where we are. . . ."

"Don't worry," Willoughby said, leaning back enough so she could see that familiar smile on his lips. "I'll protect you."

And she had trusted him.

As the days rolled into weeks, she trusted he was doing what was best for both of them. Even as she looked back now, she couldn't fault herself for that. How could she be blamed when she had spent her entire life being told to trust that the men around her knew what was best? So she hadn't questioned why they never left the apartment. She simply used the time to write a letter to Charlotte, recounting events and including clear instructions: Her friend should deliver the enclosed letter to her uncle, which ex-

plained everything to him, all the happy news. And Eliza hadn't
paused when she gave that letter to Willoughby to mail.

The weeks turned into months. She found it troubling that
Charlotte hadn't written back, and that her uncle hadn't arrived,
but her concern was soon overshadowed by a much larger problem. She was pregnant.

There had been joy, at first. Yes, they weren't married yet,
but they would be soon and then Willoughby would not only be
her husband but a father. Surely he would see the happiness that
awaited them in that. And to his credit, when he arrived home one
night after spending hours at a gentlemen's club nearby and she
told him the news, he had smiled. And as he stoked the small fire
in their room, drinking whiskey straight from a bottle, he claimed
to be celebrating.

Yet somewhere in her heart, she knew better.

He was gone by the time she woke the following morning. It
wasn't the earliest instance when he had left before dawn, so she
hadn't thought too much of it. But then his absence continued
the day after, and the day after. Two weeks later, she sat in front
of the dying fire in their small apartment, trying her best to think
of where he could be, when she noticed something buried beneath a month's worth of ash and embers. She was almost thankful she didn't have enough money to pay the maid to clean out the
fireplace or she would have missed it. A small white corner, like
a piece of paper half hidden under the soot. She used the long
poker to pull it out from beneath the grate. After a few moments,
she had it close enough to the mantel that she could reach for it
with her bare hand, but she didn't need to. She could already tell
what it was. She recognized her handwriting, the swiftness with
which it was written.

Her letter to Charlotte.

Willoughby had never sent it.

"Coward," she whispered at the glowing embers, tears in her eyes.

The reality of her predicament hit her quickly then. Her friend had never received her instructions, had never delivered her note to the Colonel. No one knew where she was, what had happened over the past few months. Now she was a pregnant, penniless girl in an inn that had yet to be paid.

But she didn't have time to wallow.

She ran through her limited options, then eventually went to the desk, wrote out a note, and hurried outside to find a postrider to deliver it to Delaford House in Dorset as quickly as possible. She used her most charming smile to reassure the impatient landlord that her husband had simply been delayed and would be there by the next day with payment, that there was truly no need to call upon the authorities. Wouldn't he like a song or two on the piano? She knew a wonderful jig.

The next day, after a restless night alone, there was a frantic knock on her door at the inn. Eliza rushed to it, tears already falling down her cheeks as she flung it open and found a disheveled Colonial Brandon staring back at her.

The look in his eyes was not anger, as she had expected; there was only sadness. Such utter sorrow that, for the first time, her guilt overshadowed her pain.

"I'm so sorry—"

"Stop." He held up his hand and pulled her in for a tight hug. "Eliza, it will be all right."

No, it won't, she thought. But she didn't say it. She just let him usher her outside and into his waiting carriage.

She had been at Delaford House only a few days before she heard the staff gossiping. And a few days later, their whispers were confirmed by a letter from Charlotte, with news from their friends in Bath.

John Willoughby was in love with someone else.

Eliza tried to get information about the young woman—her name, her family, anything she could. She thought that perhaps facts would help it make sense, and sever her connection to him. Alas, they didn't. She learned the woman was named Marianne Dashwood. She lived in a cottage on the outskirts of Barton Park, just a few miles from Delaford. And she was beautiful and curious, clever and bright.

Eliza couldn't hate her. In truth, she sounded like someone she would have quite liked. Perhaps someone she would have been friends with.

If only that were the way the world had been architected. One where women's voices were adhered to, where their opinions were respected and their choices were trusted to dictate the future ahead. Perhaps then Willoughby would have listened to his aunt and proposed marriage to Eliza. Perhaps Eliza could have been the one to spurn him. Perhaps she could even have met Marianne and told her of her history with the man, and the two of them could have laughed at his expense. They could have truly become friends, one at Delaford and one at Barton Park, and they could have visited and together warned her daughter of such men in the world.

But it wasn't.

So here she was. Repeating mistakes that felt inevitable, simply because she had no other option.

For all the talk of women's irrationality and extreme emotions, it was the Colonel who was in London now, challenging her former lover to a duel. It was Willoughby who had followed his whims to another woman as soon as real sense was required. Men reacting only to emotion, while the women stayed home, carefully planning for the aftermath.

As she walked the halls of the Colonel's home, forced to avoid the outside world and their judgmental words, her hand absently cradled her swollen belly. That long thread of women who had come before was about to get a bit longer, a line thrown to the future in the hopes that the next woman might know what to do with it. That it might be better for her, then.

Maybe, in that way, it wasn't an ending, really. Eliza had made mistakes, but her baby could have a chance at happiness. At love. At independence and choice and everything her books had once promised her. The need for it came from somewhere bone-deep. Maybe she could carry her mother's name, but also something deeper, an instinct that had been passed down to her, too, which Eliza now began to listen to.

She could do it on her own.

Thankfully, it was winter, which meant Eliza could keep the pregnancy a relative secret under blankets and thick dresses while she made arrangements. She could hide it from the staff at her uncle's estate quite easily under large wool blankets while writing letters, setting things in place. By the time the leaves started to peek out on the branches of the apple trees in the garden, and Colonel Brandon was down to just his very trusted help for the start of summer, Eliza knew it was time to share her plans.

"America?" Colonel Brandon asked one day, looking up from his book. The weather had warmed and the sun was out for the first time in days, so they were both sitting outside in the gardens.

"Yes," Eliza replied.

They couldn't keep this secret forever. She knew it was only a matter of time before a rumor spread—*Did you hear? Like mother, like daughter*—and she would be cast out of proper society, taking Colonel Brandon along with her. She could never allow that to happen.

"But I've already made arrangements," he replied patiently. "You will go to the country, far away from prying eyes and news of Willoughby's—"

"You once told me of a family connection, an old friend with some prominence in the Americas, in New York," Eliza interrupted, desperate to shift the conversation forward. "The Van Rensselaers."

"Yes," Uncle Brandon said, sitting up straighter. "It's been many years, but yes."

"I took the liberty of writing to them to see if they might hire a newly widowed mother as a governess and sent my credentials along with your recommendation."

"Eliza," he replied firmly. "I would have seen to it myself, offered to—"

"They wrote back."

She handed him the letter that had arrived that morning. He read it slowly, then took a long moment before looking up at her again. "You are suggesting a transatlantic move with a newborn and . . . working for an esteemed family I haven't had contact with in over a decade?"

"Yes."

"But—"

"This is my choice," she said, willing her voice to sound confident.

His expression changed slightly—a mix of shock, sadness, and something that looked like admiration. "My God," he murmured. "You sound so much like your mother."

Then he agreed.

Eliza had been so thrilled that the realities of what lay ahead weren't realized then. Now, aboard a ship somewhere in the Atlantic, she allowed herself a moment's panic. But just a moment. Then the baby cooed, staring up at her, baby Eliza's little hand wrapped around her mother's pale finger. It was the first day it hadn't rained on their journey, and mother and daughter were finally able to leave their cabin belowdecks. Standing above the ship's hull of their transatlantic ocean liner, Eliza was able to view the horizon, and the vast sea before her, as she held her newborn. The ship's passengers were milling about, nodding to her as they passed. She wore all black, and no one gave her pause, as she was clearly a widow with a young baby hoping to make it across the sea to America to meet her respectable relatives at the port in New York.

"It's an adventure," she reminded herself.

Yes, but it was nothing like the grand adventures she had read about in any book. This was terrifying and so painfully lonely that she hugged her daughter to her chest a little tighter. When the baby cooed in response, Eliza looked down and smiled.

"But not you," she whispered. "You will do scary things, too, but you will be brave. So much braver than I. And maybe that means you won't have to do them alone. And if you find yourself alone, in a place where even I can't protect you, make sure you have a choice in how your story unfolds. Because you always have a choice."

There were so many forces keeping her in place that it was almost overwhelming. But maybe this choice, this one decision would be enough to throw that line forward. And maybe her daughter would catch it and bring it forward. Maybe she could find something close to a happily ever after.

ELIZA CARTER

Circa 2025

Eliza Carter came from a long line of Elizas, an unbroken thread of life that spanned all the way to the beginning of time. Of course, Eliza herself was unaware of such a thread or, in any case, had no way to investigate it.

Not that she hadn't tried. Her parents had never hidden the fact that she was adopted, but it wasn't a topic that was openly discussed, either. When she was a child, the details were simply glossed over with smiles and assurances of their love. Then, later, everything between her parents began to fall apart before she could find the courage to ask. Fights echoing down the hall late at night. Days of silence that were almost just as painful.

Eliza had tried to save it. Salvage the moments of love and tenderness as if they were broken pieces of a plate scattered on the floor. If she made sure to collect every single one, she was sure she could put them back together herself and her parents wouldn't notice the cracks. It hadn't worked, though. By the time she was sixteen, she was Eliza Carter, child of divorce, subject of endless custody hearings. But as far as Eliza had been concerned, she was still just Eliza.

Even now, years later, it seemed strange to think about her name. How it connected her to two people whose lineage didn't match her own. Her adoptive parents loved her, of course. She had never questioned that. But after the divorce, she could never shake one nagging question—was she the daughter they hoped for when they made the choice to adopt? Yes, their marriage had failed, but she could still be the silver lining. Perhaps that was why she worked so hard to make them proud, to live up to the potential they so often told her she had. She had learned to measure her life by their lens, so by the time she graduated from college, she couldn't quite tell where their dreams ended and her own began.

That's when she began to wonder about her birth mother. She had before then, obviously, but when she was young, it was usually a curiosity about her reflection. Sometimes she would spend too long looking in the mirror, studying her long, straight nose. Her brown curls and her large dark eyes. Where did those eyes come from? she would wonder. Had they been her mother's? Passed down from the women who came before her? She had no way to be sure. And, really, who was there to ask?

Sometimes, on a particularly sad day, if she was consumed with self-pity, Eliza obsessed over her birth mother's choice to give her away. Did she even have a choice? She often wondered, if faced with the same situation, would she make the same decision?

After Eliza graduated from college and moved to New York, she tried to get answers. She had reached out to the adoption agency to see if there were any breadcrumbs they could share about her birth parents. She tried not to hope but couldn't help the crushing disappointment when she received the form letter back stating what she already knew: The adoption was closed, and they were unable to share any details. Eliza had no choice in the matter at all.

She tried to remind herself that it didn't really matter. Most people didn't know much about their family history, either, despite knowing exactly who their parents were. This was America—a jumble of people made up of other people who came from every corner of the world. But that hadn't stopped her from getting one of those ancestry kits online a few years later, one that asked you to swab the inside of your cheek, then send it back to receive your results. She had done so, waiting patiently for three weeks until the email arrived. She had expected more fanfare, but in the end she had opened it in her pajamas while in bed, staring at the results while waiting to feel something. But instead of elation or joy, there was just mild confusion as she worked out how to read the information: 38 percent Iberian Peninsula; 29 percent Great Britain; 25 percent Eastern Europe; 8 percent South Asia. Numbers listed and explained thoroughly, yes, but there were no names. No pictures. Nothing personal to connect her to any of those statistics that somehow made up her whole being.

In the end, she stopped caring. At least, that's what she told herself.

Then she met Ben Capshaw.

Eliza had noticed him around the office at work. How could she not? As soon as he stepped off the elevator, every woman on the floor locked eyes with his six-foot-tall frame, lopsided smile, and curly black hair. The casual way he strode to the conference room and the deep laugh when he left.

He joined the company in October, and by February, his visits to the fifth floor for the executive meetings became the highlight of Eliza's week. But she never talked to him. Even the thought of it sent panic through her chest. What would she even say? For the past three years, she had been working so hard she had barely made any friends there, let alone dated. Which was fine. She was content to watch from afar and let her imagination do the rest.

Except, Ben Capshaw had other plans.

Eliza had stayed late at work, per usual, and hadn't expected to find anyone in the elevator when she pressed the call button.

That's why she walked in without looking up, and straight into Ben's broad chest.

"Sorry!" she said, eyes darting to his, then away, then to the buttons, then to the floor. "Sorry."

"It's all right," he said, that lopsided smile on his face. "Serves me right for standing smack in the middle like that. I just didn't expect anyone else to be here this late."

Eliza let out a breathy laugh. "Me, either."

He leaned down a bit, making sure to catch her gaze with his before he asked, "You work on the fifth floor, right?"

"I do," she replied, so dumbfounded that she forgot to be nervous anymore. "How do you know that?"

His smile broadened, so warm and kind that her heart stumbled in her chest.

"Because walking by your desk is the highlight of my week," he said.

He asked her to grab a drink, which led to dinner, which led to his walking her home and kissing her so thoroughly that she forgot to take things slow. To safeguard her heart and set boundaries. All she knew was that her hand fit perfectly in his, and for the first time in her entire life, she felt like she truly belonged to someone.

She moved in with him just a few months later. Met his family at Christmas. Got a birthday card from his parents in March. Without even realizing it, her hopes, her dreams, her future became inextricably enmeshed with his. His dreams became her dreams; her life was measured by his lens, just as it had been by her parents.

The worst part was that she hadn't even noticed she was doing it. Not until the following August, when Ben suggested they head out to the Hamptons for a long weekend to celebrate their one-year anniversary. Even though they had both lived in the city for years, neither had ever made the journey out to the eastern tip of Long Island, and they spent the weekend enjoying the beaches and small seafood shacks along the narrow roads, even while laughing about how out of place they were amid the sprawling mansions and luxury cars. Their final night, they found a dive bar along Montauk Highway, just down the road from their hotel, and wandered in just as a band took the stage. They were dressed like ABBA but had face makeup like KISS, and when they started singing "Dancing Queen" over thundering drums, Eliza had laughed so hard she almost snorted her drink out her nose.

"Is this okay?" Ben had asked.

"This is perfect," she finally said through her smile.

He had smiled, too, then leaned down to steal a kiss. Then he laughed.

"What?" she asked.

"I just realized that when we get married and have kids, their first exposure to KISS is through stories about tonight," he said close to her ear.

It was an innocent comment. Sweet, really. But it fell against her chest like a lead weight, stealing the air in her lungs.

"How many kids do you think you want to have?" he continued, his lips so close he could get away with almost whispering. "I'm thinking two. And a dog. We definitely need a dog."

She could feel her smile flatten, and the sound of the music suddenly felt very far away.

Ben noticed a moment later. He leaned back, his forehead creasing. "You okay?"

Was she? It was the first time they had ever broached the idea of marriage, let alone children. She had barely thought about it. But that didn't mean that he hadn't. So why did that fact make her want to recoil? Why had those simple words triggered such a panic deep in her bones? "Fine. I just . . . I need a minute."

Then she disappeared into the bathroom, keeping the tears at bay until she reached the sink. And now, here she was, standing in front of the bathroom mirror in a dive bar somewhere in East Hampton, tears in her eyes and mascara running down her face. She studied her long, straight nose again. Her brown hair and her large dark eyes. For the first time, she wished it were her mother's face. That if she stared long enough, she could ask it for advice. Had she had a similar moment herself? An instant when she woke up and realized she was locked in a social contract that she had never actually signed? Was this same blind panic the reason why she gave Eliza up? Did she ever end up regretting it?

God, what was wrong with her? She loved Ben. She loved him so much that the thought of losing him was almost unbearable. But at the same time, she couldn't ignore how her body reacted, like a generational muscle had awakened and was forcing her to pull away.

Another sob wretched itself from her chest, and she let her head fall into her hands.

Behind her, Eliza heard the bathroom door open, but she didn't bother to look to see who had come in. Not until a moment later, when she heard a clear, light voice behind her.

"Do you want a Clé de Peau Beauté towelette?"

Eliza blinked away her tears to look up into the mirror. There was a brunette woman standing behind her, statuesque and gorgeous in heels and a short sundress that looked distinctly out of place against the mustard yellow walls and bathroom graffiti.

"I'm sorry?" Eliza asked.

"They're makeup wipes," the woman repeated. She balanced a martini glass in one hand as she used the other to pull a small tissue from her mini Chanel handbag. "These are phenomenal. Just a quick touch up here and there, and no one will even know."

It was such a small gesture. Insignificant really. Eliza felt silly that it struck her with such profundity.

"Are you sure?" she asked.

The woman rolled her eyes as if it was a silly question. "Of course. What's the point in spending a small fortune on Japanese skin-care products if you can't share?"

Eliza tried to smile and took it. "Thank you."

The band had just begun playing a guitar-laden chorus of "Dancing Queen" when the woman gave Eliza a third makeup wipe. Then the door to the bathroom flew open.

Two women entered, one with red hair piled on top of her head and a Guns N' Roses T-shirt half-hidden under a pair of denim overalls, and the other with a perfectly fitted navy sweater and blond hair pulled back in a neat ponytail.

"Who thought it was a good idea to create a hair metal version of ABBA?" the redhead groaned.

The blonde laughed. "Oh, come on. It's ABBA and KISS. And their name is AbbaKiss. Like the ancient calculator. Get it?"

The redhead snorted and looked like she was about to reply with a sarcastic remark, but stopped short when she saw Eliza's reflection in the mirror, with the brunette leaning against the counter next to her.

"Everything okay in here, Emma?" she asked.

The brunette waved her martini glass in the air, sending small droplets of vodka over Eliza's arm. "I haven't gotten that far yet. We're only on the mascara."

"It's fine. I'm fine," Eliza said, her voice wavering. "I'm sorry."

The blonde frowned. "Why are you apologizing?"

"It's just . . . so stupid." Eliza shook her head, as if it might ward off another sob. "My boyfriend and I are out here for the weekend, and we've been having such a good time. It's been perfect. But then we were out listening to the band, and he said he loved me and . . ."

The redhead's eyebrows knitted together. "And?"

Eliza could feel her face crumbling again. "He started talking about when we get married. When we have kids and . . ."

Silence fell, with only the sound of the band's lead singer belting out the opening lyrics to "Super Trouper" echoing off the walls. Then the blonde came up to Eliza's side and gave her an encouraging smile in the mirror. "That sounds sweet."

The woman with the Chanel bag rolled her eyes again. "Yes, Anne, because you're getting married. Personally, I'd rather have my nails plucked out with—"

"Okay, Emma, we get your point," the redhead cut her off.

Emma shrugged as she slid to sit on the counter, balancing her drink in front of her.

"It was nothing," Eliza said, more to herself than to the women now surrounding her. "I'm probably a little drunk, and it just caught me by surprise. To be fair, we've never really talked about what he wanted before."

The blonde—Eliza thought she remembered that her name was Anne—seemed to consider the point. Then she asked, "And what do you want?"

That was the crux of it. The neglected heart of it that she was only just recognizing now.

"I don't know," Eliza said. "I'm twenty-seven years old, and I have absolutely no idea. I've been so focused for so long on what everyone else wanted for me that I've based every choice on that. I never stopped to think if I want it. Do I want to get married?

Have kids? Get a *dog*? Or have I just been told I want those things for so long that I never took the time to think about it until now?"

"Does it matter?" Emma said with a shrug.

The redhead frowned. "That's a little harsh."

"No, I'm serious, Lizzy." Emma slid off the counter, then turned her attention to Eliza. "Even if you had wanted those things, it doesn't matter. You can change your mind. You have a choice."

"But it doesn't just affect me—it affects Ben, too," Eliza said, her head swimming with vodka and panic. "What will he do?"

"Marvel at your ability to evolve and change," Emma replied, raising her drink above her head so small splashes of vodka scattered on the floor.

"Hear, hear," Anne said with a smile.

"I still can't believe you ordered a martini at a dive bar," Lizzy murmured, glaring at Emma's glass now perched above their heads.

Eliza smiled, but it faded just as quickly as it had come. "And if he doesn't?"

Lizzy opened her mouth to speak just as the bathroom door flew open again and two more women entered, laughing to each other drunkenly as they started for the mirror, but they stopped abruptly when they saw the four women already there.

"Her boyfriend wants to get married, and she doesn't know if she wants to," Emma said, answering their unspoken questions.

"Ohhhh," they said in unison, as if that was all the background information they needed.

"It's fine," Eliza said, wiping the last of her tears away and giving the women an apologetic smile. "I just don't know how to tell him. I don't want to hurt—"

"Oh, please." The taller of the two women who had just entered rolled her eyes as she pulled a lipstick from her bag and reapplied the cherry red. "Never set yourself on fire so someone else can stay warm."

"That's a good one," Anne said, eyes wide.

The woman winked. "Thanks."

"But what if that's not what he wants?" Eliza asked. "What if that's enough to make him walk away?"

"Then you'll know," Lizzy said with a shrug.

"It's like my mom always said," the tall woman's companion said, her words slightly slurred as she tried to straighten her very crooked skirt. "'It takes a mighty good man to be better than no man at all.'"

The door opened again, and more women came in. Within a few minutes there was a crowd of women surrounding the bathroom counter, all sharing their insights and advice while Anne used the towelettes to fix Eliza's makeup.

"Whether you get married or not, always make sure you keep your own checking account, just in case!" a woman said over the din of the hand dryer.

"Never second-guess your gut, sweetie!" a man in a mesh shirt called out from the hallway, where he held open the door.

"Don't work so hard to get chosen when you're the one who chooses, m'kay?" another woman said as she stood in front of the sink, dabbing a mojito off her shirt.

"You don't owe anyone anything!" someone yelled from a stall.

It should have felt overwhelming. The idea of not knowing what she wanted, of telling Ben, of choosing her own future for what felt like the first time in her life? It was terrifying. Except it didn't feel terrifying. In that moment, it felt electric. The gates open, her soul free, with the weight of expectation and life and history dissolved.

Or maybe this was history. These women all carrying their own different threads, passed down from the women before them, bound together for a moment in that mustard-colored bathroom in a dive bar somewhere between East Hampton and Montauk, to make something so much stronger than they were on their own.

Maybe this was what her birth mother had wanted for her all along, she thought as Emma fixed her mascara, and Lizzy offered her some gloss. Sisterhood. Support. But most of all, the opportunity to have a choice. One she never had.

Eliza didn't know how much time passed, but by the time she left the bathroom, she had twenty new best friends and, inexplicably, a half-finished Long Island iced tea in her hand.

She found Ben at the edge of the dance floor. He was bobbing his head to the music, and when he saw her, his expression lit up.

"Hey, you," he yelled over the band's thumping rendition of "Fernando," hooking his arm around her waist. "I was about to call a search party."

She took another sip of her drink for liquid courage. *Here we go.*

"I need to tell you something," she yelled back.

He waited, his attention wholly on her.

"I don't think I want to get married," she said.

He blinked. A small grin turned up the corners of his mouth again. "Okay."

"And I don't know if I want kids."

"Okay."

"Or a dog. I might not even want my job—I don't know," she continued. She was on a roll now. "I'm not sure what I want at all, but I want to figure it out."

His grin turned into a broad smile. "Okay."

She frowned. "Okay?"

"Yeah, okay. I don't need to marry you to love you, Eliza," he said, squeezing her waist. "I just want to be there with you through all of it. That's it."

She smiled, too, so broad and unfiltered that she would probably be embarrassed if she had less to drink, but in the moment, it didn't matter. She threw her arms around his shoulders and kissed him.

"I love you," she said against his lips.

"I love you, too," he replied.

Then the cover band began playing a mash-up of "Waterloo" and "Detroit Rock City," and Eliza pulled Ben to the center of the dance floor. They danced to the music, and Eliza waved at the familiar faces of the women from the bathroom, some also on the dance floor, others at the bar. Suddenly, those percentage points of her history, geographic metrics printed out on a piece of paper, didn't feel two-dimensional anymore, but like a long thread attached to her sternum, a thousand hands pulling on it, forcing her forward. Each unique and different and none of them wrong. Just threads to hold on to, to bind together to make something so much stronger than each on its own. A happily ever after on their own terms. Because, really, what other kind was there?

Lydia's Story

DIANA QUINCY

"Unhappy as the event must be for Lydia, we may draw from it this useful lesson: that loss of virtue in a female is irretrievable—that one false step involves her in endless ruin—that her reputation is no less brittle than it is beautiful—and that she cannot be too much guarded in her behaviour towards the undeserving of the other sex."

"I am going to Gretna Green, and if you cannot guess with who, I shall think you a simpleton, for there is but one man in the world I love, and he is an angel. I should never be happy without him, so think it no harm to be off. You need not send them word at Longbourn of my going, if you do not like it, for it will make the surprise the greater, when I write to them and sign my name Lydia Wickham. What a good joke it will be! I can hardly write for laughing. . . ."

Jane Austen, *Pride and Prejudice*

It's a treat to be celebrating Jane Austen's 250th birthday by envisioning what happened to her most memorable secondary characters. I immediately knew that I wanted to tell Lydia's story. Like many readers, I had always found Lizzy Bennet's silly, spoiled younger sister to be entertainingly annoying. However, as I delved deeper into her story, I empathized with the immature teenage girl whose impulsive decision condemned her to an unhappy marriage. I conjured up "Lydia's Story" by imagining what resentments a grown-up Lydia might harbor and how she might finally find her happily ever after. I hope you enjoy revisiting one of Austen's indelible side characters as much as I did!

It is a widely accepted reality that society does not truly respect a woman until she is someone's wife. In my case, however, the exact opposite was true. Marriage made me a laughingstock.

"Look! It's the Widow Wickham," the boy and his friend taunted as I walked across the village green after dropping off a basketful of my prized vegetables at the nearby church. "Whaddya say? Are you up for a jig at the tavern?"

"A merry widow should want to dance the night away!" his companion laughingly called out as he trotted beside me.

Ignoring them, I kept a brisk pace. Spine straight. Chin down so that the brim of my bonnet shielded my face. Petty harassment wouldn't break me. I was a mature woman of thirty-six with four almost-grown children. I'd dealt with far worse than the jeers of schoolboys who were barely off the apron strings.

Even my own sister Elizabeth was loath to have me at her home for extended periods of time for fear my presence would stain the precious Darcy name. All of respectable society was more than eager to judge me harshly *now*. Yet in the beginning, when I was a young teen, few could fault me for immediately falling for George Wickham's considerable charms. Many others had been struck by his impressive person as well. Including my sister Lizzy.

A dashing officer who wore his red coat and military prestige with effortless charm, Wickham's good looks and excellent manners instantly enchanted me. As a child of just fifteen, I knew nothing of men and was over the moon at the thought of becoming Mrs. George Wickham. Having grown up in a respectable family, which included a matchmaking-obsessed mama, I had no clue just how far and brutal the fall from grace could be.

But I quickly learned.

"Get away from her!" a deep voice commanded. The pestering boys immediately stilled. And no wonder, the man's forceful voice was made for being listened to, for obeying without question, for reverberating from the rafters. And, apparently, for rumbling through a person's insides. "How dare you insult a lady quietly going about her business?"

"She's no lady, Vicar," one of the boys protested. "You're new to the village of Castleberry; otherwise, you would understand."

Vicar? My face heated. If only the ground would swallow me whole. I'd gone to great lengths to steer clear of the new vicar, to avoid tainting him with the presence of the village's most scandalous widow.

"There is never cause to treat a fellow human being with anything short of kindness and respect. We are all God's children." The vicar spoke calmly and deliberately, striking each word in a way that made even the most mundane term sound like the keynote in a symphony. "Be on your way now."

"But, Vicar," one boy dared to protest.

"That will be enough." The vicar's manner was firm. "Good day to you."

The sounds of scuffling feet sounded against the dirt path as the boys scampered away. I finally lifted my chin, relinquishing the shield of my bonnet brim to have a look at my unlikely champion.

Kind eyes blinked back at me. He was olive-skinned, with luminous midnight eyes framed by thick, long lashes. And filled with such compassion that my chest swelled. It was rare that anyone in Castleberry looked upon me with warmth.

"Are you all right?" he asked. My cheeks were hot as I nodded. Normally, I would immediately lower my gaze. But it had been a very long time since I'd glimpsed such an arresting figure of a man.

It was hard to look away from the gentle strength of his gaze. His eyes were set amidst the sharp planes of his face, including a strong nose that, on someone else, might appear a tad too prominent but, on this man, enhanced a perfectly imperfect handsomeness. It took me a moment to realize what he held in his hands.

"I thought I would return your basket, Mrs. Wickham." His tone was both kind and respectful as he held the straw receptacle out to me. "I'm glad to have the opportunity to thank you for your generosity."

"All of these weeks, you've known the offerings came from me?" I took back my basket, which was now empty of the fruits and vegetables I'd just left on the church doorstep. "And you still accepted my donation?"

"Of course. Your very fine produce is put to good use every week to feed the poor families of our parish."

I'd expected a pious man to reject any offering from a disreputable woman. "If you knew it was me, why have you not said anything?"

He smiled, and a dimple appeared in his right cheek. "You made it clear that you preferred not to be interfered with."

He had the right of it. For the past several weeks, when I thought no one would be at the church, I surreptitiously left a basket of fresh produce from my garden. As an avid gardener, I harvested far more berries, cucumbers, and tomatoes than I could ever hope to eat, since my children were spending the summer with Lizzy and Darcy. Each week, I returned early the following morning to retrieve my empty basket, thoughtfully placed exactly where I'd left it, not far from the church door.

"Your donations have helped to feed hungry people in need. You could have sold that produce to improve your own situation," he noted.

My cheeks burned. "Few people will want to purchase food tainted by scandal."

"Food is food." He quirked a smile, drawing my attention to his beautifully molded mouth. "And none of us is without sin."

I could not imagine this angelic-seeming man doing anything sinful. "Not even you?" I could not resist asking.

He laughed outright. "*Especially* not me."

The vibrant sound stirred something sinful in my belly. I was aghast at my carnal response. The way my body responded to a man of God surely confirmed my proclivity for improper behavior. After all, a handsome man had been the source of my downfall before.

In the early years of my marriage, I followed my husband's unfortunate example, enjoying drink and cards and dancing with abandon, living beyond my means, cementing my disgraceful reputation, even though I abandoned all carousing by my twenty-fifth year, more than a decade ago.

"Some of us," I said tartly, "particularly of the female persuasion, are held more accountable than others."

"That is unfortunate."

"Very."

"Allow me to introduce myself. I'm Michael. Michael Haddad."

Michael Haddad. Why did the name sound vaguely familiar? "I'm Lydia Wickham."

"I know who you are."

My face burned. Naturally, he'd heard of my wretched past, which unfortunately followed me into the present.

"I can only imagine what you've been told." Since Wickham died, more than one man assumed I'd eagerly entertain male companions when my children were away. "Believe what you will"—I despised the defensive edge that crept into my tone—"but most of what you've heard is untrue."

I usually didn't bother to defend my soiled reputation. I'd grown accustomed to keeping to myself, spending hours in welcome solitude tending to my garden, especially as my children grew older and passed more time at Pemberley with Lizzy and Darcy. As the years went by, I became indifferent to the townspeople's low opinion of the outrageous Mrs. Wickham. But not this time. Strangely, I couldn't abide allowing the handsome young vicar to hold me in low regard.

He studied me. "I suppose that I shouldn't be surprised that you don't remember me."

I blinked. "Remember you?"

"We have met."

My gaze narrowed. "Truly?" He was not a forgettable man. "I think I would remember."

"It was a long time ago. When we were children."

My eyes rounded. "We were acquainted in Meryton?" The market village was near Longbourn, my father's estate, where I grew up with my four sisters.

"We didn't exactly know each other. It would be far more accurate to say I admired you from afar."

"Me?" This splendid specimen once thought highly of me?

"Everyone knew of the five Bennet sisters of Longbourn. But you were the one who caught my attention. You were so lively and energetic."

"That feels very long ago."

"You are still much the same."

I laughed at the absurdity of that observation. "You are too kind."

"Would a vicar lie to you?"

"I don't know," I answered honestly. At the age of thirty-six, I no longer had the patience to temper my words. "Anyhow, thank you for coming to my rescue."

"It was the least I could do." And then he added, "I was happy to return the favor."

"I beg your pardon?"

"You came to my rescue once."

"I did?"

"It was after church. I was new to the neighborhood. I had no friends and was feeling very left out. You were among the children playing cricket on the green. The other children would not let me play. But you insisted that I be included. You said you would quit the game if I could not play."

"Did I?"

"I believe you said something to the effect of, 'The more, the merrier.'"

"That does sound like me." Well, it was what the original Lydia would have uttered. The one full of joy and laughter, who was always up for a bit of fun. A child who had no idea what the world did to silly girls who made rash decisions.

"I was instantly smitten," he told me.

All of a sudden, a memory floated back to me. Of a short, scrawny, dark-haired child who'd followed me around for a bit. *Michael.* "Goodness," I said. "I believe that I do remember. But you were such a small boy."

He laughed. "As you can see, I have grown a little since then."

He certainly had. I could never have imagined that slight, narrow-faced boy I'd barely noticed could transform into the fine model of a man before me.

"May I see you home safely?" he asked.

He wanted to walk me to my cottage? "I appreciate your gallantry, but I am not in need of protection."

"Are you often accosted by Peter and Matthew?" he asked, referring to the young tormentors he'd just run off.

Pride kept me from detailing how most of my neighbors shunned me and instructed their children to do the same.

"I can take care of myself." Tucking my basket firmly in the crook of my arm, I resumed walking across the green, heading in the direction of my cottage. "Thank you for returning my basket. Good day to you."

"Good day, Mrs. Wickham," he called after me.

I was surprised to find my second-oldest sister waiting for me when I arrived home.

"There you are." Lizzy greeted me with a kiss on each cheek. "I was wondering where you were."

"Don't worry," I responded. "I wasn't out doing something scandalous."

"I never thought you were," she protested.

Lizzy was the sister who'd married most advantageously. Our eldest sister, Jane, was happily wed to Charles Bingley, but his wealth did not compare to Darcy's. I liked Charles, who was friendly and good-natured. Darcy was the opposite—aloof, judgmental, and arrogant. His union with my sister was supposedly a love match, which I would never understand. But it was obvious that Lizzy was smitten.

I put the tea on. "What brings you to Castleberry?"

She settled at my small kitchen worktable. "Can I not visit my sister?"

"You didn't bring the children?" I had four in all. Three sons and a daughter. The boys, George, Edward, and James, would be fine under Darcy's tutelage. He paid the tuition at Oxford for George and Edward, as well as the fees at Harrow, the exclusive boarding school James attended along with Darcy and Lizzy's own son.

It was my daughter, Georgina (my husband insisted on naming both our eldest son and our only daughter after himself), who I fretted would be the most negatively affected by her parents' dubious reputation. Girls always bore the brunt of society's judgment. But Darcy intended to settle a generous dowry on her, and I trusted he and Lizzy would see that she married well.

Fortunately for Georgie, she'd inherited her father's good looks and charm, which would be advantageous on the marriage mart. Young men overlooked many detractions if a woman possessed beauty and magnetism. Thankfully, Georgie did not have her father's poor character and lack of integrity.

"They're at a garden party with their friends," Lizzy informed me. "I know you miss them terribly."

"But it is for the best," I said firmly, ignoring the painful twinge in my heart as I set a plate of biscuits on the table. "The less associated they are with me and their father, the better for their futures."

"Actually," she said after a pause, "that is why I am here."

"Oh?" The kettle whistled. Lizzy continued talking as I prepared our tea.

"There is a widower, a neighbor in Lambton, who is seeking a wife."

I set out two teacups. "And?"

"He is very well respected and willing to overlook certain shortcomings."

I set a steaming cup of tea in front of my sister and settled across from her with my own. I immediately understood her purpose. "You do comprehend that I will never marry again?"

"Not even for the sake of your children?"

"Isn't it enough that I absent myself from my children's lives?" As much as I resented Darcy's supercilious nature, I appreciated all he and Lizzy had done for George, Edward, James, and Georgie. "I allow you to be more of a mother to them than I am."

"They know you are their mama."

"I deprive myself of the people I value most in this world to assure their futures. Do not ask me to also throw my life away on another man. I will spend the rest of my years recovering from Wickham."

George had turned out to be a drinker, liar, and cheat. He ran out on his bills and caroused away from home while I looked after the children.

I learned that, before our marriage, George tried to compromise the daughter of his benefactor, Darcy's sister, in hopes of getting his hands on her considerable dowry. He was a spendthrift (well, so was I, but I had the excuse of being a hapless girl who knew nothing of finances), an unfortunate habit that left us destitute. The only reason we had a roof over our heads was because Darcy stepped in to pay the rent and continued to do so since Wickham's demise.

To say that I was relieved when George finally drank himself to death after twenty years of marriage was an understatement. I'd barely been widowed for a year and wasn't about to give up the newfound freedom that I relished.

"I've just gotten out from under one terrible marriage," I told my sister. "I have no intention of condemning myself to another."

"But Mr. Wilson is exceedingly agreeable."

"So was Wickham," I reminded her.

"You could spend more time at Pemberley if you marry Mr. Wilson," Lizzy pointed out. "You would see the children far more often."

"Not necessarily," I countered. "They are almost grown. It won't be long before they are wed." And who knew how their spouses' families would react to a mother-in-law with a name as disreputable as mine.

My children were born barely a year apart until I learned how to avoid conception. George was twenty; Edward, almost nineteen; James had just celebrated his seventeenth birthday; and, in the fall, Georgie would be fifteen, the same age as I was when I foolishly married her father.

"You would like Mr. Wilson," Lizzy assured me. "Darcy is very fond of him."

Which was reason enough for me to avoid the man. Any friend of Darcy's risked being as insufferable as the man himself.

"He is a bit older," Lizzy continued, "but he has retained his handsome looks."

My sister presumed an appealing face was still enough to entice a race to the altar? I wasn't fifteen anymore. "How old is he?"

"Fifty-five," she answered, quickly adding, "but he's still a fine figure of a man."

There again was the assumption that a physically appealing specimen would be enough for me to willingly become someone's wife again. "Almost twenty years older than me."

"And reasonably wealthy," she added. "He and his first wife had no children. And his property is not entailed."

Meaning his second wife stood to inherit upon his death. But as pleasant as the thought of never worrying about money again was, I just couldn't bring myself to consider being shackled to another man. "I cannot endure another loveless marriage." A shiver of revulsion went through me. "The thought of a strange old man rutting over me is not to be borne."

Lizzy's eyes widened. "You did not enjoy Wickham's attentions?"

"Why in the world should that surprise you?"

"I suppose I assumed, despite Wickham's many lesser qualities, that his prowess and charms extended to the bedchamber."

I stared at her. "Are you saying you actually enjoy having Darcy do *that* to you?" I asked incredulously. Surely Darcy was as much of a prig in bed as he was in public.

Lizzy flushed and reached for her tea. "Let's just say that I do not find the marriage bed to be disagreeable in the least."

"You enjoy it!" I sputtered in disbelief.

She sipped her tea. "With the right man, you can as well."

"Ha!" I bit into a biscuit with a satisfying crunch, enjoying the sweet buttery flavor on my tongue, a treat that gave me far more pleasure than any man ever could. "I doubt that."

"At least allow Mr. Wilson to call upon you here."

"What have you told him about me?"

"The truth. That you married at fifteen to a man who set an unfortunate example for his impressionable young wife."

"A bachelor visiting the home of a disreputable widow will outrage the entire village."

"I shall make certain to be here to chaperone. What harm is there in meeting him?" she pressed.

I knew Lizzy well enough to comprehend that she would not let go of any issue she felt strongly about. Besides, for years my sister sent me all of her pin money so that I could keep the children clothed and fed as Wickham's debts piled up. Meeting Mr. Wilson was a way to show my appreciation. Even though I resented owing her or anyone anything.

"Very well," I relented. "Mr. Wilson can come for tea. Just don't expect to hear wedding bells anytime soon."

"There you go," I said to the cucumber plant as I secured it to the trellis. "Now you should grow tall and strong." I checked to make certain the soil around the plant was moist. Cucumbers required a great deal of water, especially during the flowering stage.

"Do you always speak with your plants?" asked a voice from behind me.

I immediately recognized Mr. Haddad, even though I'd spoken to him only once. I straightened, embarrassed to be caught in my shabby gardening dress and the floppy ancient bonnet I used for outdoor work.

"Good day, Vicar." I removed my gloves and swiped the perspiration on my upper lip with the back of my hand. "I do find plants are often more reliably good company than people."

His eyes twinkled. "I myself never understood the allure of gardening, except, of course, for the food that results."

"I enjoy being in nature and feel a keen sense of accomplishment when the plants grow and prosper," I told him. "I began gardening out of need, in order to put food on the table for my children. But now I find respite, and much-needed solitude, among my fruits and vegetables."

He surveyed my flourishing garden. "You seem to have a bountiful harvest."

"Yes, indeed." I did not bother to hide the pride I felt in the abundant garden I'd created. And my neighbors noticed as well.

Although they did not speak to me, except for a stiff nod, I did observe how they lingered whenever they passed my garden. I grew flowers, too. Ribbons of color that streamed across my modest property. "I pretend not to notice when some of the young men in the neighborhood pluck a few flowers for the girls they hope to court."

"That is generous of you. Considering how they treat you."

I shrugged. "They learn from their parents, as all children do." I added some cucumbers to my straw basket. "I will have far more berries, cucumbers, and tomatoes than I could ever hope to eat since my children are spending the summer with my sister."

"Ah, the estimable Mrs. Darcy. I trust she is well?"

"Well enough to meddle in my life," I retorted before catching myself too late. "You must forgive my impertinence. I have never been good at holding my tongue."

"If your sister is meddling, surely she means well."

"Lizzy always means well." Not only was Lizzy wealthy and generous, she was also pretty—second in looks only to our eldest sister, Jane—and easily won people over with her intelligence and gentle, teasing manner. By contrast, I was not only considered compromised but also brainless and impulsive. A reputation I could not shake no matter how many years had passed since I'd behaved recklessly. "I usually allow Lizzy to interfere, but this time I must draw the line."

He regarded me with interest. "Why is that, if I may ask?"

"She thinks I should remarry in order to salvage my reputation as well as my future."

"And you do not wish to take another husband?"

"One was quite enough for me." I aggressively pinched off the flowers of the cucumber plant. "But Lizzy can be most persuasive.

I have agreed to allow her to bring Mr. Wilson for tea the day after tomorrow."

"Mr. Wilson is the name of your suitor? Perhaps you will find him appealing."

"He is twenty years my senior, but Lizzy insists he is very respectable." I tore off a couple more flowers. "Respectable enough for me to be able to visit Pemberley more often."

Little frown lines appeared between his brows. "You are not welcome at your sister's home?"

"I am welcome in small increments, but my character is too compromised for me to live there."

"That is . . . unfortunate." I registered the banked anger in his voice.

I smiled at him. "We cannot all be as forgiving as a vicar." Mr. Haddad was surprisingly easy to speak to. I couldn't remember the last time I had an actual conversation consisting of more than a few sentences with any of my Castleberry neighbors.

He followed the motions of my hands as I cleared out the flowers. "Are you taking your frustration out on the cucumber plant?"

"Only the male ones," I said as I added a flourish to pinching the flowers.

"Ouch," he replied, and I heard the smile in his voice.

"One picks off the male flowers to encourage the production of female flowers, resulting in more fruit. Which means," I added, "that I will have more vegetables to donate to the parish."

"As it happens, that is why I have come."

"To make sure I am tending to my garden?"

"To save you the trip to the vicarage to drop off the vegetables."

"I see." A chill passed through me. "You've come here so that I won't go to the church."

He smiled. "Precisely. Given that you are kind enough to donate so generously, the least I can do is come and pick them up rather than expecting you to deliver these heavy loads in your basket."

"I understand." And I did. He didn't want me anywhere near the church or his respectable parishioners. "Your timing is fortuitous." I cooled my tone. "As you can see, the basket is almost full. I'll just add some tomatoes and berries, and then you can be on your way."

"May I help? I'm not much of a farmer, but I can pick fruit."

"That's not necessary." I quickly gathered the remainder of my donation. "Here you go." I handed him the laden basket.

"That's a very generous portion. The parish will be grateful."

I doubted that. "Good day, Vicar." Without giving him another glance, I turned on my heel and walked back to my cottage, where I firmly closed the door behind me.

Lizzy gazed out my cottage window. "Mr. Wilson should be here at any moment."

I set the porcelain teacups out on the tray. "Hopefully, he will not stay too long."

She shot me an accusing look. "You agreed to give Mr. Wilson a chance."

"And I will."

"You could endeavor to at least pretend to be a little excited."

I reached for the tin containing biscuits I'd baked that morning. "You forget that I'm no longer a boy-crazy fifteen-year-old."

"That is not true. I see who you are now." Her words were gentle. "You have made an effort to be more responsible, and you live a quiet life. And I truly admire all of the work you've put into your garden."

I bristled. I didn't require anyone's approval. Yes, Lizzy married well, even if the man was insufferable, but that did not mean that she was better than me. Of course, society thought that Lizzy was miles above me and admired her for looking after her wayward sister. But the truth was that Lizzy wasn't superior to anyone. She'd just chosen more judiciously.

My feelings for my sister were complicated. I loved her—everyone did—but I resented being in the position of needing her assistance. We'd grown closer over the years because Lizzy came by more often than my other sisters. I did see Jane, but she was busy with Bingley and their children. I visited with Kitty and Mary the least. Kitty, the wife of a clergyman, was occupied with church activities. And dour Mary, who married last of all of the sisters, had finally found a husband among one of our Uncle Phillips's clerks.

I was received at Longbourn, my late father's estate, which was now in the possession of Mr. William Collins, our distant cousin. Although I was fond of his wife, Charlotte, Mr. Collins was an absurd character, and I avoided Longbourn due to his insufferable sense of self-importance.

"You look very pretty," Lizzy remarked.

"I promised to make an effort, did I not?" I wore one of my better gowns, which was plain compared to the selections in Lizzy's extensive wardrobe. But I adored my long-sleeved gown of the palest gold with pretty bows adorning each wrist.

"I am certain Mr. Wilson will appreciate how fine you look," she said.

I changed the subject. "Do you remember someone named Michael Haddad from Meryton?"

Lizzy looked thoughtful. "I remember the Haddad family. It was a large family, six children, if I remember correctly. Why do you ask?"

"Because one of those children is the new vicar in Castleberry."

Lizzy's eyes rounded. "You've met the vicar? Does that mean you're attending church again after all of these years? That is encouraging."

"No. I had occasion to meet Mr. Haddad when I dropped off produce from my garden for the parish."

"Oh, well. What is he like?"

"He is young." I thought of dark liquid eyes and perfectly molded lips framing a slightly arrogant nose. My insides went warm and fluttery. "And quite agreeable."

Our conversation was interrupted by a knock at the door. Delight lit Lizzy's face. "Your future husband awaits!"

"Stop teasing me. This meeting is uncomfortable enough as it is." The last time I'd interacted with a man as a potential mate was with Wickham when I was barely more than a child. I might be twenty years older now, but I absolutely was not any more experienced when it came to the opposite sex. I still had no sense when it came to men. My body's lamentable reaction to the young vicar was proof of that.

"Mr. Wilson." Lizzy greeted the new visitor warmly as she opened the cottage door. "Welcome. Do come in."

"Mrs. Darcy." The man's voice was deep and not unpleasant. I got my first look at him when he stepped inside and his gaze immediately found me. "Good day. Thank you for allowing me to visit."

I was tongue-tied and profoundly embarrassed. I really had no idea how to behave around men, especially those with noble intentions.

Lizzy broke the silence. "Lydia, this is Mr. Wilson, a delightful acquaintance of ours from Lambton. This is my sister, Lydia Wickham."

"Mr. Wilson"—I finally found my voice—"welcome to Castleberry."

He gave me a nervous smile. "Thank you, Mrs. Wickham. It is a lovely village."

We settled in the parlor. I could see what Lizzy meant about the man's lingering appeal. Mr. Wilson had obviously cut a fine figure of a man back in his prime. Even now, in his fifties and well past middle age, despite his jaw no longer retaining the sharpness of youth, Mr. Wilson's good looks were still in evidence. He retained a full head of hair, now liberally streaked with gray.

"I could not help but notice your garden," Mr. Wilson said. "It is impressive."

"Thank you. Do you garden?"

"I do. I am very fond of spending time with my plants."

Lizzy beamed. "You both enjoy gardening. How fortuitous!"

Having found a subject in common, Mr. Wilson and I managed to carry on a slightly less stilted conversation about properly preparing the ground before planting cucumbers and strawberries. I'd just served the tea and biscuits when a knock sounded at the door.

Lizzy looked at me. "Are you expecting someone?"

"No." I rarely had visitors, except for Lizzy or another of my sisters. Both of my parents had passed in recent years. And obviously my neighbors never called on me.

I was shocked to find Mr. Haddad on my doorstep. "Vicar. This is a surprise."

"A pleasant one, I hope." He held my basket in his hand. "I thought I'd return this."

"How considerate," I said without enthusiasm. I'd gotten the message. He did not need to keep reiterating his desire for me to steer clear of his precious church.

"Who is it?" Lizzy appeared in the small foyer.

I had no choice but to introduce Lizzy to the vicar when all I truly wanted was for the man to make a hasty retreat. I'd misjudged his kindness. Deep down, the vicar was like everyone else in Castleberry who wanted to avoid being seen with me.

"Mr. Haddad," I said with a sigh, "you might remember my sister, Mrs. Darcy."

"Of course." He stepped inside even though I hadn't invited him to do so. "How lovely to see you again."

Lizzy's eyes widened almost imperceptibly as she took him in. I couldn't blame her. Michael Haddad was a striking man. "I think you were a very small boy when we last met," she said.

"Probably no older than thirteen. I have told Mrs. Wickham that all of us admired the famous Bennet sisters of Longbourn."

"How charming." Lizzy gestured toward the parlor. "You must join us."

If she'd been near enough to me, I would have kicked her.

He hesitated. "I don't mean to interrupt."

"Don't be silly," she insisted. "Please do join us in the parlor."

"If you insist," he said, with a slight smile on his lips, which suggested he was more than happy to be asked to stay. As he went in ahead of us, I held my sister back with hard pinch on her arm.

"Ouch!" Lizzy exclaimed. "What was that for?"

"Why did you invite him to linger?" I whispered furiously.

"Lydia! Do you not see how fortuitous this is? Now Mr. Wilson will see that you are respectable enough for the vicar to condescend to be seen visiting you."

I shook my head, frustrated. After entertaining no male visitors at all, I was suddenly forced to play hostess to two men. "When did you become our mother? First I had to endure her matchmaking, and now I must deal with you."

"You will thank me one day," Lizzy said, all confidence. "Just wait and see."

I sighed and fetched another teacup for the vicar, introductions were made all around, and I retook my seat, hoping Mr. Haddad would drink quickly so this interminable visit could come to a hasty end.

"Haddad? I do not believe I have heard that name before," Mr. Wilson said. "Where is your family from?"

"My parents were born in Ramallah, a small town in Palestine not far from Jerusalem. They came to England before I was born."

"Palestine? Your parents are Turks? From the Levant?"

"Arabs, yes," Mr. Haddad said.

Mr. Wilson frowned. "And you are the vicar here in Castleberry?"

"Yes," Mr. Haddad said. "I am, indeed."

"Hmm." Mr. Wilson's frown deepened. "Did your family convert to Christianity once they came to England?"

"No, my family has been Christian for centuries." Mr. Haddad was all patience as he explained. "We are descendants of the original Christians, and we have retained and practiced our faith for centuries."

"How interesting." Mr. Wilson sipped his tea. "I thought all Turks . . . erm . . . Arabs . . . were Mohammedans."

"That is understandable," Mr. Haddad replied. "While the majority of Arabs in the Levant are indeed Muslims, there are, naturally, many Christians in the birthplace of Jesus."

I listened with great interest. I vaguely recalled that the Haddad parents came from foreign lands, but I hadn't known where they were from until now. That explained the vicar's lovely dark curls and liquid midnight eyes.

"It is so considerate of the vicar to visit," Lizzy piped in. "Do you often visit all of your parishioners?"

"I do try," he answered. "But I had occasion to call on Mrs. Wickham today in order to return her basket."

Lizzy blinked her eyes, all innocence. "And why, pray tell, were you in possession of my sister's basket?"

"Mrs. Wickham is kind enough to donate the harvest from her garden to the local parish."

Mr. Wilson shot me an admiring glance. "How commendable."

"Isn't it?" Lizzy said with a pert smile. My sister knew perfectly well why the vicar had my basket. I sighed when I realized she was attempting to coax the man into singing my praises in front of my potential suitor. Another echo of our mother.

Mr. Haddad obliged. "Mrs. Wickham delivers fruits and vegetables every week. She has helped to feed many of our poorer families. But," he added, "I would not have come had I known I would be interrupting."

I narrowed my eyes. The vicar should be aware that I was entertaining a potential suitor this afternoon because I'd told him as much. But I suppose my schedule was of so little interest to him that he'd forgotten.

Mr. Wilson studied the vicar. "I wonder if you know my great friend Squire Worsley."

Michael sipped his tea. "I do, indeed. He is the district's leading landowner and our magistrate. As it happens, he is also responsible for giving me the living at Castleberry."

"Yes, he is a very influential man," Mr. Wilson said. "Worsley and I are longtime acquaintances. We attended Eton together."

It made sense that Michael had sought a living. His father was not a landowner, which meant that each of his sons would have to make their own way. A church living was a permanent job that included a home to live in, income, and some farmland. All in all, the position offered a modest but comfortable life.

Mr. Wilson turned the conversation back to the subject of gardening. "How far apart do you plant your strawberries?" he asked me.

"At least two foot lengths apart," I answered gamely, in order to contribute to the conversation, "to give them the space they need to grow. Naturally I remove some of the runners throughout the growing season so that they don't overtake the other plants."

The conversation continued for almost another hour—to my horror—well past the time for a polite visit. I breathed a quiet sigh of relief when both men finally rose to depart.

I happily closed the door behind them and fell back against it with a long exhale. "I thought they'd never leave."

Lizzy's eyes twinkled. "They did stay quite a while."

"I realize that I have not been in polite society for ages, but when did afternoon calls become so interminably long?"

"They didn't." Lizzy shot me a contemplative look. "Mr. Wilson is well known for his courtesy and decorum, and yet he lingered much longer than a polite visit requires. He must be very drawn to you."

"I have done as you asked." I went to gather up the tea tray. "I met your Mr. Wilson."

"Did you like him?"

"Not enough to marry him."

"Come now, Lydia. You agreed to give him a chance."

"I did give him a chance."

"Your vicar also stayed for a very long time."

I'd noticed that as well. "At any rate, I am relieved that that is over."

"How long did you say you've been reacquainted with the vicar?"

I picked up the tray. "We met twice in the last week. And then again today."

She followed me into the kitchen. "Did you notice how he looks at you?"

"Notice how who looks at me?"

"The vicar, silly. Who else?"

"How does he look at me?" I began rinsing out the teacups.

"With great interest."

My heart skipped a beat. "Don't be absurd. The man barely knows I exist."

"Oh, he definitely takes notice of you."

"Lizzy, you are being ridiculous. The vicar didn't even remember that Mr. Wilson was calling today."

"You told him that a potential suitor was coming to see you this afternoon?"

"Yes, and he forgot. That's why he ended up accidentally interrupting the visit."

"Is that so," she said with a thoughtful expression on her face. "Anyhow, let us return to the subject of Mr. Wilson. He is most amiable, is he not?"

"Not amiable enough to marry, no matter how much Darcy longs for this match to make me respectable."

"What does Darcy have to do with this?" she asked, her tone a little sharp.

"He already ensured my first terrible marriage. And while I am grateful for all he has done for me and the children, I do not require his input on a second husband."

Lizzy's mouth dropped open. "What are you talking about?"

"I haven't forgotten that Darcy was at my wedding, that he indeed paid for it."

"You had run off with Wickham. We, all of your sisters, would have been ruined if Wickham hadn't wed you."

I thought of my own daughter. My sweet Georgie. "I used to think I was obliged to be grateful for Darcy's interference. All of you certainly told me that I should be." Fire flared in my belly. "But I look at Georgie, and I see that she is still just a little girl. A child of fifteen should be reprimanded and sent back to her parents. Not forced to marry a man that Darcy knew better than anyone would be the ruin of any girl."

Lizzy flushed. "Darcy saved you from ruin!"

"No, he saved you, his future wife, from disgrace so that you wouldn't be tainted when he wed you. He sacrificed my happiness and well-being to ensure that his future wife's reputation would remain spotless."

"That's absurd!" she burst out. "Darcy is all that is good and kind. He acted as he did to salvage the Bennet name after you ran off with Wickham. Do you think any of your sisters would be respectably wed if Darcy hadn't paid Wickham a fortune to make you his wife?"

"I beg your pardon." I blinked. "What did you say?"

Lizzy stilled. "Nothing. The story of your marriage is long in the past, where it should stay."

"Darcy *paid* Wickham to marry me?" I asked, incredulous. "He didn't just cover the wedding expenses?"

Lizzy shook her head. "I don't know what I was saying. I misspoke—"

"Stop lying to me!" I slammed down the cup I was rinsing, and it shattered to the floor. "I want the truth. I demand it. You owe me that at least."

"I don't know why I said that." Pale, Lizzy sank into a wooden ladder-back chair at the table. "I'm an idiot. Forgive me."

I felt sick. "What did you mean when you said Darcy paid

Wickham a fortune to marry me? We eloped. Darcy caught up to us after we ran off but before we could wed."

"Oh, Lydia." Sorrow filled Lizzy's voice. "Wickham never intended to marry you. He was going to desert you once he tired of you."

Horror rippled through me. George intended to use me and then cast me aside? I plopped down into the chair opposite her as the implications of her revelation sank in. "George didn't wish to marry me."

The unhappy alliance. The fights. The drinking. The tears. George constantly being gone from home. His unending womanizing. His indifference. All of it made sense now. My husband hadn't wanted me. He'd been forced to wed me. I blinked back tears of humiliation. "Does everyone know?" I whispered.

"No, dearest, Darcy didn't even tell me. I found out quite by accident."

"Were Mama and Papa aware?"

"Papa was."

"Who told him?"

"I did. When Darcy asked for my hand, I explained to Papa what Darcy had done for our family."

"What did Papa say?"

"That we owed Darcy a great debt, but I insisted to Papa that he must never mention it to anyone, least of all Darcy, who didn't want anyone to know of his kind act."

"I see." I was mortified. Especially about Papa, who'd never really had much use for me. To the end, he saw me as a silly girl who'd tarnished the family name. Lizzy was always his favorite and remained so until the day he died.

Throughout my marriage, the one thing that sustained me at least a little was the fact that Wickham fancied me enough to wed me, that he chose me over my more sophisticated older sister. I'd held on to his desire for me no matter how badly our marriage turned out.

Now I didn't even have that.

I did not leave my cottage for the next several days. I barely managed to get out of bed most mornings, and I napped a great deal in the afternoons. I couldn't bear to see anyone. I did not know how I would face Lizzy or Darcy again. Years ago, I had thought my humiliation was complete, and now that Lizzy revealed the truth, shame and embarrassment overtook me.

On the fifth day of my self-imposed exile, a firm knock sounded at the door. I ignored it, but the tapping persisted for several minutes.

"Mrs. Wickham, are you in there?"

I recognized the voice. It was the vicar. I couldn't bear to face him or anyone else. "I am fine," I said through the door.

"Are you certain?" he said. "I have been worried."

Michael Haddad was concerned about my absence? First, he tried to keep me from coming near his precious church, and then he worried when I obliged him. I had had it with all men. Wickham. The vicar. Even Darcy. I resented him for helping me. For knowing of my humiliation and keeping it from me. I could not abide being pitied by Lizzy and Darcy. I abhorred how it made me feel.

"There is no need to worry about my well-being. My thanks to you for coming by. Good day," I said firmly.

I peeked through the window and watched as he walked down the walk, pausing at the gate to look back at the house. Then he continued on his way, and I breathed a sigh of relief.

But he came back the next day and the day after that. Apparently, there was no discouraging him. On the third day, I finally relented and faced him.

Surprise lit his face. "You opened the door."

"It not as if you gave me any choice."

"I've been concerned about you."

"Why? I am perfectly well," I lied.

He cocked his head. "Forgive me, but I do not believe you."

I huffed. "You, sir, are impudent. A gentleman would take a lady at her word."

"Your garden tells a different story."

"What do you mean?"

"It is overgrown and looks like it hasn't been tended to in at least a week."

I peered out at my garden and was aghast by what I saw. The plants showed signs of stress, growing tall and thin, sure indications of overcrowding. I chastised myself for wallowing about a transaction that was long in the past—even if I had just become aware of it. Meanwhile, my prized garden, the one place where I excelled and was the envy of my neighbors, had suffered.

Another gardener might not be alarmed by a little overgrowth, but I kept my garden in pristine condition. That's why it was the model of the neighborhood. Eight days of neglect had taken a toll on my plants. I hadn't given the garden much thought while I came to terms with Lizzy's revelation that my husband was forced to wed me. But now I could think of nothing else.

I grabbed my work bonnet off the nearby hook. "Well, I must remedy that posthaste before everything is ruined."

He followed me into the garden. "Surely a few days of neglect won't destroy everything."

"Stressed plants will never produce as well as ones that are cosseted. I have hours of work ahead of me."

"Hours?" he said dubiously. "It doesn't look that overgrown."

"It is late summer, which means the weeds are out in force. I must tend to them immediately."

"Tell me how I can help." He shrugged out of his somber black tailcoat, leaving just his white linen shirt and waistcoat. I tried not to notice how finely formed he was, with wide shoulders, a trim waist, and the athletic thighs of an expert horseman.

"Don't be ridiculous." I started with pulling the weeds around my cucumbers. "You don't know the first thing about gardening."

"Surely you can direct me." He rolled up his sleeves, just slightly, baring strong forearms generously dusted with dark hair. "It is the least I can do, given how generous you've been to the community."

I averted my eyes. How had I never before noticed how attractive a man's arms could be? "Can you identify a weed?"

"Naturally." He watched my progress. "I can assume that task."

"Very well." I stepped aside, moving over to the tomatoes. "You may weed so that I may focus on pruning."

He immediately took my place, pulling the weeds with the necessary care, the cords in his forearms flexing. The weather wasn't overly warm, but I certainly felt heated. Forcing myself to concentrate on the tomatoes, I trimmed and tied back the plants to train them to grow in the proper manner. Mostly, we worked in amiable silence, with the vicar asking the occasional question about his task. I was a little sad when it came time for Mr. Haddad to take his leave after a couple of hours.

"My thanks for your help," I said.

"It was my pleasure," he said, rolling down his sleeves, covering those lightly muscled forearms. "Will you work in the garden again tomorrow?"

"Most definitely. There is much work to do."

He surveyed the rows of plants. "Is there?"

"I am very particular. More so than most gardeners."

Amusement lit his eyes. "I am beginning to see that."

To my surprise and delight, he came again the next morning, insisting on being put to work. He returned again the following day, and I began to look forward to our time in the garden. We worked side by side, sometimes in silence, other times chatting about Meryton and his five brothers and sisters. He told me about each of his siblings and spoke fondly of his nieces and nephews. He asked me about my children and appeared genuinely interested in my answers.

"Why did you become a vicar?" I asked on our second afternoon weeding and cropping together.

He paused, looking out over the garden. "I felt a calling, and I cherish developing meaningful relationships with my parishioners. It is an honor to be of service to people during the most significant periods in their lives—such as marriage, illness, and death."

I admired his commitment to good works. Michael Haddad was a truly decent man. "If only my late husband had had a calling beyond gambling and carousing."

His understanding gaze met mine. "Was your marriage very difficult?"

"It was." Again, I noted how easy it was to talk with Mr. Haddad. Perhaps it was on account of his being a vicar accustomed to hearing people's problems. He listened without judgment, which, in my experience, was exceedingly rare. "Darcy, my sister's husband, saw to it that we were married after I was foolish enough to run away with Wickham."

"You were very young and, I imagine, quite sheltered from the machinations of scoundrels like George Wickham."

His defense of my reckless youthful actions warmed my insides. "It is ironic that Darcy made certain that Wickham married me to save my family's reputation," I remarked. "But Wickham turned out to be such a disreputable character that being his wife was perhaps even more damaging to my good name."

"I am truly sorry you've had such a difficult time."

"My union with Wickham gave me my children, so I cannot regret it."

Later, when I set him to work on the squash, he said, "My mother would covet your squash."

"Then you must take her some once they are ripe."

"Oh no, these small ones are perfect for kousa mahshee."

"What is that?"

"It's my favorite Arabic dish. Squash stuffed with seasoned rice and meat cooked in a tomato broth."

"That sounds delicious," I said. "You must pick enough to take to your mother."

"One day," he said, "I will ask Mama to prepare some for you to taste."

I couldn't imagine the vicar telling his mother he wanted to bring her food to me. But I was touched all the same. We were developing a friendship, and I appreciated every moment of the conversation and companionship we enjoyed as we worked among my plants. It was nice to have a friend.

By the third day, we'd managed to clean up the garden to my exacting standards.

"It gives me great satisfaction to see you regularly in the company of your plants again," Mr. Haddad said as we finished up. "I was extremely worried when you did not deliver your basket of produce."

"Men!" I said, exasperated. "There is no pleasing you."

He blinked. "It is not a matter of pleasing me. I know how fond you are of your garden. I became alarmed when I saw it was not being cared for. I thought you might be sick or hurt."

"I didn't deliver the produce because you told me not to."

He looked affronted. "I most certainly did not."

"There's no need to try to spare my feelings. I am well aware that I am not the most respectable woman in Castleberry. It is understandable that you do not want me anywhere near the church."

"Everyone is welcome at church. I wish you would come. Not just to drop off the produce, but to attend my sermon on Sunday."

He seemed so earnest in his manner that I was taken aback. "But you came to pick up the produce so that I would not be seen at the church."

He shook his head. "That was not the reason at all."

"What other motive could there be?"

"I came because I wanted an excuse to call on you."

"You did?" I frowned. "Why?"

He flushed. "Is it not obvious?"

"If it were, I would not be asking."

"I find you very appealing."

"I beg your pardon?" My surprise quickly gave way to outrage. Reality slammed through me, and the vicar's daily visits took on an unsavory twist. So that was what he was after. I should have known. "Just because I am a widow with a scandalous past, that does not mean I want to entertain men."

"What?" He gaped at me. "That is not my intent at all."

I stomped out of the garden and into the house, eager to slam the door in his face. But his scuffed black boot appeared in the door to prevent it from closing. Instead, it bounced open. I flounced away from him into the kitchen. "Go away."

He followed me. "I cannot allow you to believe that I have the worst of intentions. My aims are completely honorable."

"What do you want from me?"

"I am thirty-four. A parish expects its vicar to be married."

"What does that have to do with me?"

"You are a widow. I find you to be most amiable."

"You want to *marry* me?" I asked incredulously.

"Of course," he said, as if it was the most obvious thing in the world. "What else? Do you think I would spend hours gardening for just anyone? It might not be the most conventional way to court a woman, but I hoped it would help me capture your heart."

"Capture my heart? Are you mad?" As if it wasn't bad enough that Darcy and Lizzy pitied me. "I am not your charity case."

His eyes sparked, and his smile was slow. "Taking you to wife would most definitely have nothing to do with charity."

Heat flushed through my body. I backed up against the kitchen table. "I do not understand."

"I have admired you since I was eleven. At thirteen, I was heartbroken when Wickham stole you away before we came of age, depriving me of the chance to win your heart."

"Don't be ridiculous. Thirteen-year-olds know nothing of matters of the heart. I thought I loved Wickham, and it ruined my life."

"You may have noticed that I am no longer thirteen." His voice was a low rumble that vibrated through me. "I am a grown man who knows what he wants with complete certainty. When we became reacquainted after all these years, I realized I still find you as appealing as ever. Perhaps even more so. And our time together in the garden has only served to deepen my feelings."

"But," I spluttered, "a vicar cannot marry a woman like me!"

He stepped closer. "Whyever not?"

"Isn't it obvious? I am not respectable. You need to wed a young lady with an unblemished reputation."

"I have had such opportunities. Squire Worsley once hoped I'd wed his daughter."

Jealousy, hot and potent, slashed through me. "Miss Worsley is an only child. She stands to inherit everything."

"The only woman who interests me is standing right here."

His ardent manner flustered, and flattered, me. "But we are barely acquainted."

"I know you well enough."

"Perhaps working in the sun these last few days has affected your judgment."

He smiled. "You have been in my thoughts since the day we met again. Why do you think I returned your basket the other day?"

"Because you wanted me to refill it?"

"No. I knew you were entertaining a potential suitor. I lost my chance once before when Wickham came between us. I refuse to lose my opportunity again by allowing another man to steal you away before I declare myself."

It took me a moment to digest his words. "Have you been drinking, Vicar?"

He laughed. "My name is Michael, and no, I have not imbibed spirits of any kind."

The intensity of his gaze threatened to blaze a path straight to my heart. I looked away. "I don't know what to say."

"Say you will at least consider my offer."

"I vowed never to remarry."

"Why?"

"Because Wickham was a terrible husband. He was a gambler and a philanderer. He was never home."

"I am neither a gamer nor a cheater. When not busy with church business, I will be home."

He stepped close enough that the lemony scent of his shaving soap filled my nostrils. My knees lost their strength. What was happening to me? I settled my hips against the kitchen table.

"I would treat you with the kindness, care, and respect you deserve," he said. "I have long admired you. I believe that I might already love you. Most fervently."

"Stop saying such impossible things!"

"Why does it surprise you that a man could admire you?"

"Because I am not a lovable person. My husband never loved me. My own father had no use for me."

"You are very deserving of love." He pressed his lips against my temple. "And you have mine." My skin burned with sensation at the feel of his mouth against my flesh. "Promise me that you will at least consider my offer. Think of the advantages of choosing me over Mr. Wilson. I am considerably younger . . . and more vigorous."

The following morning I awoke full of hope. I'd pledged never to remarry, but Michael made me reconsider. I could not help wondering what it would be like to be the wife of such a man, who was decent and generous. A man who made my blood swirl.

I even hummed as I made myself a cup of tea and wondered what Lizzy would say. I would take satisfaction in telling her that a man of quality, a young, handsome man of virtue, wanted to make me his wife. I could imagine her surprise that a man like Mr. Wilson, who was old enough to be my father, was not my only option. But was I really considering remarrying?

I was.

And the thought of it made excitement course through my veins. I prepared a quick breakfast of tea and toast before going to check on the garden. I reached down to pull an errant weed when a supercilious male voice sounded behind me.

"Mrs. Wickham, I presume?"

"I am she." Facing the well-dressed man, I wondered who he could be. He was in his forties, with a flushed round face. How had I gone from receiving no visitors, outside of family, to this constant stream of people appearing on my doorstep?

"I am Squire Worsley."

I immediately recognized the name. This man was Michael's benefactor. Worsley was the village magistrate and largest local landowner. He'd given Michael the church living in Castleberry. "How do you do?"

"Not very well, I am afraid. Do you have a moment to speak?"

I could not imagine what business a man of the squire's influence could have with me. "Of course. Would you care to come in?"

He made a moue of distaste. He possessed full, wet lips. "I suppose it is necessary because I do require a word with you."

I took an immediate dislike to the man and his high-handed manner, but he was Michael's employer, so I forced myself to behave in a courteous manner. I led him to my tiny parlor. "May I offer you some tea?"

He pursed his lips. "No, thank you. This is not a social call."

"What kind of call is it?"

"One in which I attempt to talk sense into you."

"Into me?" I asked, confused.

"You are aware that Michael Haddad serves as the vicar of Castleberry at my pleasure."

"I don't see what that has to do with me."

"It has come to my attention that he hopes to make you his wife."

"It has?" Despite my surprise, I forced myself to maintain a neutral expression. "Where did you hear that?"

"Do you deny that he has made you an offer?"

"I will neither confirm nor deny it."

His eyes flashed. "You are impertinent."

"I cannot imagine where you would have heard such a thing." I could not fathom Michael telling anyone, especially considering that I had yet to accept his offer.

"The vicar informed me that he hopes to marry soon. Although he did not name the . . . erm . . . female he has in mind, it has been noted by many that the vicar has recently made several visits to your home."

I shouldn't be surprised that the townspeople had noticed Michael working in the garden with me. I barely contained my temper. "If you are suggesting that anything untoward has occurred—"

"I am not. I know the vicar to be a virtuous man, and it is my expectation that he will remain so."

"And you believe that the scandalous widow of Castleberry has turned her wiles on a defenseless man?"

"Mrs. Wickham. You do realize that the vicar has a modest income."

"I hadn't given it a thought."

"Mr. Haddad supplements his rather meager salary by tutoring some of the village youth. Were he to align himself with you, respectable village families would naturally reconsider that arrangement, causing the loss of a vital source of revenue."

My heart sank. The last thing I wanted was to hurt Michael. I should have known that happiness was not for me. One mistake at fifteen, a lifetime of ruin.

"It is well known that you are not welcome at your sister's home of Pemberley for long periods of time. Her husband, Mr. Darcy, is the largest landowner in several counties and very respectable. Of course I, as well as all decent people, would follow his lead."

I felt the sting of his words. They reminded me of my separation from my children. And of a family that took care of me financially but never publicly stood behind me.

The squire continued. "A promising man with as much appeal as Mr. Haddad should marry a respectable young woman of unblemished reputation. In other words, someone who is worthy of him. Surely you understand."

"Perfectly."

"Furthermore, I cannot be expected to employ a vicar whose standing in the community is lower than it should be. A vicar should set the moral standard rather than flouting it in the service of his baser desires."

Disappointment panged through me. Michael thought wedding me would envelop me in a cloak of respectability. The squire made clear that the opposite was true; my questionable reputation would limit Michael's future prospects. I swallowed against the soreness in my throat.

I could never ruin Michael's life.

"I take your meaning very clearly." I stood, no longer able to bear another second in this man's company. "Thank you for coming. I am certain you can see yourself out."

And then I fled to my bedchamber before the tears fell.

* * *

Michael returned the following day bearing a basket.

"That is not my basket," I said, putting off the inevitable conversation that would end these delightful visits forever.

"No indeed," he said cheerfully. "This is from my mother. I hope you are hungry. Arab mothers insist on feeding their loved ones well past the point of satiety."

The unmistakable smell of fresh summer squash and seasoned lamb wafted over me. He came in and set the basket on the table. He wore a dark fitted suit, his typical somber vicar clothing, which I had come to find exceedingly attractive. His brown curls were ruffled as usual. He'd never looked more handsome. Disappointment welled up in my chest. How lovely it would have been to spend a lifetime with this man. After the squire's visit, I realized how much I wanted a life with Michael.

What would it be like to have a husband who wanted to come home to his wife and actually did so? To have a life mate who shared his thoughts with me? I'd come to look forward to our conversations while we gardened. Wickham had never wanted to talk about anything beyond what I was serving for dinner.

"This is kousa mahshee," Michael said with pride in his voice. "Do you have plates?"

I nodded and set out the plates and utensils. He carefully placed two stuffed yellow squashes on each plate and spooned the tomato sauce broth over them.

"It smells heavenly," I said, hoping he did not note the catch in my voice.

"Come and sit," he urged, pulling a chair out for me. I couldn't remember the last time a man did that for me. Wickham, for all the fine manners he displayed on first acquaintance, dropped all pretense of chivalry once we married.

"Eat up," he instructed. "I would not want to have to report back to Mama that my future wife doesn't care for mahshee.

Alarm trilled through me. "You told your mother about me?"

"I couldn't resist. I did not name you." His dark eyes twinkled. "I told her you have not accepted my offer as of yet, but, because she thinks I am the catch of the county, she's certain your answer will be yes."

"Michael," I began, "about that—"

"I insist that you eat first, and then we can discuss what I hope will be our life together."

I marveled at his confidence in our future. Blinking back tears, I focused on my plate and tried a bite of the stuffed squash.

"Well?" he prompted, watching me carefully.

The food was delicious, and he was so wonderful—I could not help myself. I burst into tears.

Alarm stamped his face. "It cannot possibly taste as bad as that."

"No, it's very flavorful," I said through my tears. The squash was tender and the rice and meat filling perfectly seasoned. "I love it."

"Am I to understand that these are tears of joy?" he asked dubiously, offering me his kerchief. "Will you tell me what is vexing you?"

I took it and blew my nose. "I've had a visitor."

"Did Mr. Wilson return?" His lips thinned. "Have you accepted his offer in favor of mine?"

"Squire Worsley was here." I proceeded to repeat everything that odious man said. "And so," I said in conclusion, "there is no way we can marry."

His face reddened. "He had no right to come and speak with you," he said angrily. "I will have a word with him."

"To what end?"

"If necessary, I shall find a church living elsewhere."

"Who will employ you with me as your wife? You must think about your future."

"*You* are my future. If you will have me, I'll stand for nothing less."

"You must be reasonable."

"Worsley is being difficult because he wants me to wed his daughter."

Although the squire had been a stranger to me, I'd seen his daughter before. An only child, she was in her late twenties, shy and a bit plain. She had not had success on the marriage market. "Maybe you should. If you wed her, your future would be assured."

"As would my misery. I have nothing against Miss Worsley, but my heart is already taken."

"The squire must think highly of you to want you for a son-in-law."

"It is not as great an honor as you might think. He realizes his daughter will likely be a spinster and thinks, due to my less-than-porcelain-like skin and my parents' foreign connections, that I should be grateful to make such a match."

I was outraged. "Your wife will be the most fortunate woman in all of England."

He rose and came over to me. "If you truly believe that, then say you will marry me, Lydia, please."

I shook my head. "I followed my heart once, and it led to great unhappiness. I am a grown woman now. I cannot follow my whims and desires."

His eyes sparked. "So you do desire me."

I looked away. "It means nothing."

"It means everything. I am offering myself to you, body and soul."

"I cannot." I stood and moved away because I couldn't think rationally when Michael was physically close to me, when all I wanted to do was throw myself into his arms. But for once, I needed to lead with my head and not my heart. "My impulsive actions ruined my future. I am not willing to destroy yours as well."

He came to stand in front of me. "When will you start believing that you deserve good things?" He brushed a kiss across my temple, his masculine scent enveloping me. "When will you believe that you are most worthy?" His lips feathered across my cheek. "That an honorable man can love you and is willing to fight for the privilege of taking you to wife?"

Emotion roiled in my chest as his lips found mine. Moving in soft yet assured motions, his soulful mouth was a gentle pressure against mine, sliding from the top of my lip to the bottom, exploring, stealing the air from my lungs. Strong, warm hands caressed my face with delicate care, as if I were a great treasure. The floor beneath my feet fell away, and I was floating on a tide of pleasure and sensation.

He broke the kiss, his breath coming fast and hard, and set his forehead against mine. "That," he said, "is a mere taste of what we have to look forward to. If you are willing to fight for us. For our future."

Sensation still streaking through my body, I marveled at this man's effect on me. Wickham, in the beginning, had kissed me more forcefully with tongue and hands roaming everywhere. Yet Michael's almost-chaste kiss affected me much more profoundly.

How could I ever let him go?

* * *

Lizzy made a surprise appearance later that afternoon. "Oh, dear Lydia, do not cry!" she exclaimed as soon as she took note of my swollen red eyes.

"I cannot help it." I slumped into a stuffed parlor chair.

"I am overcome with guilt," she said. "I never intended to upset you by disclosing Darcy's agreement with Wickham. It was my natural instinct to protect my husband. People always misjudge Darcy. Please say you'll forgive me."

I waved a miserable hand. "I haven't a care about that. Oh, Lizzy, I am wretchedly unhappy."

She frowned. "If this is not about Darcy and Wickham, then what is upsetting you so?"

"The vicar."

"Mr. Haddad? What has he done?"

"He has made me a proposal of marriage."

"The vicar wants to marry *you*?"

"You needn't look so surprised," I said scornfully. "I understand you think I cannot do better than to marry a pensioner."

She clapped her hands together. "This is the most marvelous news! Mr. Haddad is very appealing. When will you wed?"

"We won't. The squire here in Castleberry forbids it."

"Can he do that?"

"He is Michael's employer, the biggest landowner and the wealthiest gentleman in the county. And yes, the richest among us have tremendous power over other people's lives. As you, of all people, should be aware, Mrs. *Darcy*."

Lizzie wore a contemplative look on her face. "That power can also be a force for good."

"If you are referring to Darcy paying off Wickham to wed me, I am no longer angry about that. I recognize that Darcy was trying to do the right thing. Just as you both try to do the right thing by helping me financially."

"Thank you for saying that." She paused. "I thought you said you'd never remarry."

"I believed no gentleman of good character, who wasn't decrepit, would ever offer for me. Michael's integrity made me reconsider."

Lizzy raised a pointy brow. "His integrity or his handsome looks?"

"Both, I suppose. But it is of no matter now. I turned down his offer."

Lizzy looked at me sharply. "And does it end there? People do change their minds."

"He said he wasn't giving up."

Lizzy grinned. "Commendable."

"Or foolish. The squire pointed out that if I am not respectable enough to be received in my own sister's house, why would the village of Castleberry accept me as the wife of their vicar?"

Lizzy's face dropped. "Oh, Lydia."

"Women like me are not meant to live happily ever after."

"That is not true." She reached for her wrap. "I must go."

"So quickly? You just arrived."

"I have a matter that needs to be urgently attended to."

"What is it?" It was unlike Lizzy to leave so abruptly when she knew I was feeling low.

"I'll be back Sunday morning," she said briskly.

"You will? It is not as though you live nearby. Pemberley is two hours away. You certainly are visiting more frequently than usual."

"I am a woman on a mission. Be ready."

"For what?"

"To go out."

"Where?"

"You'll see," she said breezily as she strolled out the door.

"Come along," Lizzy said. "We mustn't be late."

She appeared at my door bright and early, dressed in her Sunday finest, a navy pelisse over a sky-blue gown with a fitted bodice. I yawned. I hadn't slept well. Thoughts of Michael—and that kiss—kept me tossing and turning. "Where are we going at this hour?"

"You will see soon enough," she said. "Don't dally."

I grabbed my pelisse and accompanied my sister to the coach, a stately affair with red velvet seats.

To my surprise, Darcy emerged from within. He was impeccably dressed, as usual, with his prominent sideburns flawlessly trimmed. My brother-in-law's midnight tailcoat topped a dark-patterned waistcoat, and his snowy cravat was tied in an artful knot. "My dearest sister," he said with a frosty kiss on my cheek. "I trust you are well."

"Well enough, thank you," I lied as we all climbed back into the conveyance. "Where are we going?"

"You shall soon see," Lizzy said.

We were silent for most of the ride. Darcy and I rarely had much to say to each other, mostly because I sensed his disdain. Lizzy said it was just Darcy being shy and a bit awkward, but I remained skeptical. Although the coach was quiet, a sense of anticipation buzzed off of Lizzy.

I nervously adjusted my bonnet. I'd dressed with care, donning an emerald-green gown with a round neck and a dark green band just above my waist. My bonnet was adorned with a matching ribbon.

Darcy finally spoke. "Your sister tells me that the local vicar has made you a proposal of marriage," he remarked in his usual solemn manner.

"He has," I replied, not at all surprised by Lizzy's loose tongue. I had the impression she kept few secrets from her husband. "But I turned him down."

"It that because you don't care for the man, or due to Squire Worsley's interference? If I may ask."

"I find the vicar to be most amiable, but, as you know, my reputation precedes me. The squire has made it very clear that he will not abide the marriage."

"If it were not for the squire, am I to understand that you should like to marry Mr. Haddad?"

Why did he insist on twisting the knife? "Yes," I said, remembering the feel of Michael's lips pressing against mine. "I believe I would."

"I see." Darcy remained expressionless.

The carriage came to a stop. I glanced out the window. We were at the church. *Michael's* church.

Alarm rippled through me. "What are we doing here?"

Lizzy's eyes twinkled. "We are attending Sunday services."

"We?"

"Yes." She grinned. "*We.*"

"I am not," I said furiously. "I no longer attend church."

"That won't do for the future wife of a vicar," she said.

"I told you that I am not marrying Michael."

"Why won't you go to church?" she asked.

"You know perfectly well why," I said. "I am not welcome."

"Instead of hiding yourself in shame, when will you hold your head up high and claim your rightful place in Castleberry?" she asked. "You blame everyone for not accepting you, but the truth is you hide yourself away so much that your absence fosters even more gossip."

Darcy remained silent while he watched our exchange.

Panic gripped me. "I cannot go in there."

"You can," Lizzy urged. "The squire said we don't support you. Let us show him and all of Castleberry that we do."

I shook my head. I couldn't face the disapproving looks I was bound to receive from a church full of people. "I cannot."

"If you will not do it for yourself, then do it for Mr. Haddad."

"My attending church will hurt Michael, not help him. Why are you asking me to provoke a scandal?"

Lizzy tried a different approach. "If your alliance has damaged the vicar's reputation in any way, having Darcy and myself attend his service will help bolster his standing in this community."

I wanted to assist and protect Michael in any way I could. "Then go on in," I said. "I shall wait here."

Lizzy remained right where she was. "I'm not attending the service without you, and neither is Darcy."

For once, I looked to Darcy for help. "Please talk some sense into your wife."

"Would that I could," he said in a mild tone. "But once Lizzy gets something into her mind, she is difficult to dissuade."

"Very well," I snapped. "Do not blame me if the entire congregation walks out in protest."

We alighted from the coach. Darcy offered his arm. "We are beside you."

Dread filled me as I allowed Darcy to escort me into the church. Most people had already been seated. A hush came over the pews as I proceeded down the aisle. And then the whispering began.

"The audacity," someone said.

"How can she show her face in church?" another remarked in a loud whisper that was clearly meant to be overheard.

But instead of making me cower, the comments fueled me. I lifted my chin and pulled back my shoulders. I wasn't doing this just for Michael any longer. It was now for me as well. I wouldn't allow these people to make me feel shame. I'd done that for years. But no longer. I was tired of lowering my head to satisfy these people. Whether they approved or not, I was part of this community. I had shared my flowers with many a young suitor and fed even more of the villagers.

Darcy led us to the front row, as if it were the most natural thing in the world for him to take the best seat. We arrived late enough that the service began almost as soon as we were seated. Squire Worsley's eyes widened when he realized who'd joined him in the front pew, which had low walls around it, and he dipped his head in respectful acknowledgment to Darcy just as Michael began the service.

He approached the pulpit wearing a black cassock and a shorter white surplice over his black suit. I had never seen him in his robes. They made him seem larger than life and more out of my humble reach than ever.

He began with a call for confession and repentance, a rite I remembered from the days before I met Wickham. As a girl, I viewed church as mostly an opportunity to socialize, which, of course, I adored. It had been many years since I'd attended Sunday services.

"We ought, at all times, to humbly acknowledge our sins," Michael began. I'd kept my head lowered, but his vibrant voice compelled me to look up to fully experience Michael in all of his glory. My anticipation grew, my breath coming in shorter spurts, as I waited for him to realize that I was in attendance. When our eyes finally met, his smile widened, and I felt the full force of his welcome. I envied the parishioners who were fortunate to hear his sermon every Sunday.

The congregation knelt, reading a prayer aloud that confessed our sins and asked for forgiveness. "We have erred and strayed from our ways," Michael said.

As I recited the prayer, a powerful feeling came over me. I felt the full effects of the words. The realization dawned that I was deserving of forgiveness.

Michael was compelling as he led us through the service. He came even more alive, his voice, loud and clear, carrying throughout the church. He made eye contact with his audience, and his expression was not severe and dour. He smiled and was welcoming. We could all feel his joy, and it was infectious. In that moment, I vowed never to do anything that would rob Michael of his ability to do what he was clearly born to do.

The service went by quickly, a huge change from girlhood when the hours-long services seemed like they would never end. But with Michael, I could easily listen forever. Once the final prayers were recited and the service ended, Squire Worsley was the first to hurry over and introduce himself.

"Mr. Darcy, welcome to our humble church. You honor us with your presence."

"Worsley," Darcy acknowledged the man in a tone that suggested he was doing him a great favor. For once, I appreciated Darcy's distant dignity. "Allow me to make known my wife, Mrs. Darcy, and my sister in marriage, Mrs. Wickham."

"We have had the pleasure of meeting," Worsley said, darting a fleeting look in my general direction. Michael joined us, and I proudly introduced him to Lizzy and Darcy.

"How do you do?" Darcy said. "It gives me great joy to meet the man who is betrothed to my wife's beloved sister."

The air left my lungs. For Darcy to publicly express his approval of the union carried great power in a society that revered men of wealth and standing. Michael's eyes lit with surprise, and then happiness.

"I am the most fortunate of men," Michael said. He looked at me askance. Darcy's approval was not sufficient; he needed to hear my acceptance of his proposal directly from me.

Our gazes locked. "And I am the most fortunate of women."

Michael smiled widely at this acknowledgment, and I grinned back, exhilarated that we could be together after all.

Darcy, and Lizzy, had made it so.

Darcy turned to Worsley. "I trust you have heard the excellent news?"

Worsley flushed. "I offer my deepest congratulations to you both." He dared not defy someone of Darcy's stature. His circumstances in life were dwarfed by Darcy's. By escorting me to church, Darcy had publicly acknowledged my role as a treasured member of his family. In doing so, he shielded me with the full force of his influence. And made my marriage to Michael possible.

Lizzy beamed. "They truly make a lovely couple. Wouldn't you agree, Squire?"

"Yes," Worsley said tightly. "I certainly do."

Michael offered his arm, and I excitedly took it. The parishioners, who'd closely followed the conversation, shocked me with murmurs of congratulations as Michael led me up the aisle toward the exit.

"I look forward with great anticipation," Michael said as he tucked my hand deeper into his elbow, "to your walking the opposite way down the aisle, to the altar."

Anticipation rippled through me. "I cannot wait to meet you there."

"Three weeks," he said, "just long enough to read the banns, and then I will make you mine."

"And you," I said, "will be mine. Forever and always."

I glanced back over my shoulder and caught Darcy's eye. He dipped his chin, and, despite his dour expression, I registered the smile in his eyes.

At long last, after many years of wondering why Lizzy tolerated the man, I finally glimpsed what my sister saw in Mr. Darcy.

Lace and Larceny

NIKKI PAYNE

"I cannot boast of knowing more than half-a-dozen, in the whole range of my acquaintance, that are really accomplished."

"Nor I, I am sure," said Miss Bingley.

"Then," observed Elizabeth, "you must comprehend a great deal in your idea of an accomplished woman."

"Yes, I do comprehend a great deal of it."

"Oh! certainly," cried his faithful assistant, "no one can be really esteemed accomplished who does not greatly surpass what is usually met with. A woman must have a thorough knowledge of music, singing, drawing, dancing, and the modern languages, to deserve the word; and besides all this, she must possess a certain something in her air and manner of walking, the tone of her voice, her address and expressions, or the word will be but half deserved."

"All this she must possess," added Darcy, "and to all this she must yet add something more substantial, in the improvement of her mind by extensive reading."

"I am no longer surprised at your knowing only six accomplished women. I rather wonder now at your knowing any."

Jane Austen, *Pride and Prejudice*

Caroline Bingley, Elizabeth Bennet's famously snobbish foil in *Pride and Prejudice*, deserves a second look. If I may play anthropologist for a moment, Caroline constructed her entire sense of meaning by mastering the narrow avenues of power available to women within the rigid class structures of Regency England. As a member of the gentry without title or fortune, her currency was performance—of gentility, of refinement, of perfect social positioning. So how jarring it must have been to watch Elizabeth Bennet—who neither genuflected nor performed ideal womanhood—win the very proximity to male wealth Caroline had been trained to secure.

That's why I had such fun placing my Caroline in a Western road-trip narrative. The wide-open frontier dislocates her from the polite rituals and quiet hierarchies of drawing room society. In the dust and uncertainty of the American West, she's forced to trade performance for survival, wit for warmth, and control for connection. Can she do it?

In my version, Caroline is also a white-passing woman of color from high-status New Orleans society—someone who thrived under a strict and specific social code, only to find those codes warped, inverted, or erased entirely out west. It is in this liminal space that her rigidity is tested, her ambitions recontextualized in the form of a bounty hunter she would have never set her sights on in New Orleans. Through him and other new connections, Caroline finds her best, and most scandalous, chance to transform.

And let's be honest: What's a reinvention story without scandalizing a whole town on the way?

HOODOO

"Y ou ought to be ashamed of yourself, coming here looking like you do, Caroline Bliguet," Sister Slidell hissed at me while pretending to look for her seat in St. Mary's Church.

New Orleans was sweating through its corset by nine o'clock—the magnolias wilting, the streetcars moaning, and every woman at this shock wedding patting her pressed hair, praying it wouldn't rise up and embarrass her.

I didn't so much as blink, just kept fanning myself. There was nothing to do about it now but die of heatstroke. Through the gauzy gloom of my black mourning veil, I glanced down at my bodice, which was stiff enough to chafe the soul. The only thing more oppressive than the Louisiana heat was the rough starch on this dress.

St. Mary's was packed to the rafters with people pretending to love the bride. No one looked toward the altar. No one cared about the exchange of vows. Every eye in the building was trained on me.

Sister Slidell leaned in over my pew; her voice was low but sharp enough to cut ribbon. "Why don't you get up and dance for coins, if you're so determined to steal the show?"

"I'm mourning"—I paused, dabbing my forehead with a handkerchief—"the death of good sense around here."

She clicked her tongue. "Mean as a snake. It's the poor girl's wedding day, and you've come dressed like your maman done passed for the second time."

I turned my fan toward her with slow ceremony. "Poor girl?" I echoed.

Sure, she didn't have two red beans to rub together, but the bride Eliza Benoît was no *poor girl*. She had swept into their parish like yellow fever: unwelcome and inevitable. Too brown for polite circles and too unbothered to care. Not a beauty by traditional measure, no. But when she walked into a room, people adjusted their postures.

New Orleans society was a narrow little kingdom, where sometimes the right shade of skin mattered more than the right heart. It was the kind of world you could live in your whole life and still not belong to—unless you married well, and never, ever forgot your place.

I had hoped to marry into it. To take my rightful place as the pinnacle of a scholarly woman—genteel, educated, admired in all the proper rooms. But now, sitting in this heat-drenched church, watching Eliza Benoît—who had *no* private tutors, no finishing school, and called herself *autodidactic*—I wondered:

Did she have any idea what she'd signed up for?

"She'll embarrass him. Embarrass all of us," I whispered. "You know she cussed out Lady D—"

"Didn't Lady D say *you* weren't pretty enough for Toussaint?" Sister Slidell cocked her head.

I stiffened. "Well. Maybe Lady D deserved a good cussing out. Still," I amended, smoothing my skirt, "those wild sisters . . . married or not, I know the youngest ran off with that card counter before Toussaint tracked him down. That's the stock she comes from. They're not *our* kind of people."

Up front, her family was wailing like they'd buried the bride instead of married her off. Some of them were brown as chicory coffee and dressed like they were headed to revival. One sister was taking notes on the sermon, raising her hand like the priest might call on her mid-blessing. I half expected someone to fry catfish on the front pew and call it a reception.

And still—they were. Loud. Joyful. Unapologetic. I simply couldn't imagine Toussaint *ever* being happy among them.

Sister Slidell looked at me then, tight-lipped. As if reading my mind. "That family is yours now, too, Caroline. Don't forget your brother Lil' Charlie married her sister Janey not three months ago. *That* table's set."

The blade of my fan snapped shut with high theatricality. "Well, *I* won't sit at it."

Eliza was unnatural. I suspected hoodoo. Or, at the very least, she'd tampered with Toussaint's food—stirred something unspeakable into his sauce piquante.

We had grown up together, Toussaint and I, two shining stars in the carefully calibrated constellation of New Orleans's gens de couleur. It was a world with rules, unspoken but ironclad. Our pairing was practically preordained, like the tides or Lent. I'd known him as a boy, tousled and mischievous, and as a man, polished and aloof.

We had an *understanding*. Not formally spoken, of course, but understood nonetheless.

The first crack in my certainty came when Eliza arrived, catching crawfish in the bayou in her bare feet at a low-country boil we attended only out of politeness. Eliza was a mess. The muddy Mississippi on the bottom of her skirt, her wild sisters making merry. You wouldn't know it from the way he acted, but Toussaint had been lost to me even then.

Defied logic. And I was nothing if not a logical woman.

"That's a mighty high horse you're on," Sister Slidell said. "I just hope your Ealy Washington is worth the climb."

In these instances, it's best not to respond. Silence does more damage than wit. I simply let her comment settle into the heat-heavy air of St. Mary's.

The woman huffed and walked away, and my sister Louisa elbowed me sharply. "Caroline Elizabeth Bliguet. Really. You've been some kind of terrible since you said yes to that man. Sight *unseen*, I might add."

This again.

"Lordy," Louisa went on, eyes darting toward the altar. "What if he's ugly as sin?"

I sighed, adjusting the angle of my veil to block both her and the altar.

"It's not about his face. I'm restoring our name. I'd marry a haint to keep from smiling in their faces for the next fifty years. You will never see a scandal attached to my name."

My engagement to Ealy Washington was a declaration. Let the world see how a Bliguet recovers. With poise. With purpose. With monogrammed gloves and a railway ticket out of this collapsing soufflé.

I unfolded the telegram for the hundredth time, its corners softening from wear. I didn't need to read it. I knew every word.

MISS CAROLINE BLIGUET STOP
ARRIVAL EXPECTED AND ACCOMMODATIONS
PREPARED STOP
A NEW LIFE AWAITS IN CARSONDALE STOP
— E. WASHINGTON

Five short lines, but it read like scripture. It promised structure. Placement. A version of myself with title and dignity intact. It said *someone* was waiting. That the table had been set. That I still belonged somewhere.

"I don't want to see that old paper again, Caroline. It's breaking my heart," Louisa said, sniffing into her sleeve. "What kind of name is Ealy anyway?"

I hadn't met him yet, but Ealy's telegrams were spelled correctly, and his mother was "Dearly Departed." If that isn't the foundation of a strong marriage, I don't know what is.

"I just don't understand what went wrong," Louisa continued, looking ahead to Eliza stumbling shakily over her vows.

"Nothing," I say, and I mean it. I had followed *every* rule. No scandals. No musicians. I cut out articles from *Woman's Home Companion*. I earned a nursing certificate from Spelman Seminary, and my hair obeyed a comb with the proper amount of docility. I *excelled* at order.

Toussaint was the one who had done wrong. Men like him didn't marry women like her. Not in public. Not with a brass band.

Now Eliza, with her too-loud laugh and dirty hems, gets to occupy Pemberly House. She would bring them low with scandal. I knew it.

If the world insisted on descending into chaos, I didn't have to follow it.

Let Toussaint D'Arcy and his brown bride keep New Orleans. I was choosing the world. The wide one. The untamed one.

But scandal—well, scandal has a way of chasing you clear across the country, doesn't it?

What follows is the entirely true (and only slightly embellished) account of how I, Caroline Bliguet, a cautious girl from a *very* proper family, became embroiled in the most whispered-about scandal west of the Mississippi.

And honestly?

I regret very little.

TAME THE WILDERNESS

For all my grand declarations about being done with New Orleans, when the day came to leave, I was misty-eyed. In one gloved hand, I held a ticket to Colorado, folded three times and wilting in the heat. At my feet: three valises, each the size of a small person. My family stood in a semicircle, awkward and expectant. I felt more like I was departing for war rather than the West.

First, Louisa, my sister—moonfaced and round with pregnancy. She clutched her belly then pressed my hand to it.

"I'll write you as soon as the baby comes," she said. I looked up to blink away wetness. Her husband stood beside her, simple and good-natured. I wished them both well.

Next came my brother—smiling, softhearted, and entirely unprepared for the weight of marriage to that Damned Benoît Family. His arm was looped through that of his wife: Janey Benoît. Too sweet to be openly cruel to, though God knows I had tried. But if there was one principle I believed in: If you cannot do something wholeheartedly, don't do it at all.

I had failed to hate her properly. So I stopped.

Though I did not cry, my vision took on a slight shimmer when I saw Toussaint. He hugged me the way a gentleman might brush crumbs off a tablecloth—swift, impersonal. His cheek never touched mine. No breath, no scent. Just the quiet, final words between us: "Bon temps."

Good times.

As if we were passing acquaintances who once shared a table at a picnic. As if our entire lives hadn't unfolded together, layer by layer.

I was trying to stifle an untoward sob. When Eliza walked up with that strange, ungodly magnetism, like a natural lodestone, I swallowed nervously. You could feel people shifting in her direction—shoulders angling, eyes following, necks craning. I might as well have been part of the luggage. Even the train hushed its groaning. The whole world wanted to hear what she would say.

When her cheek pressed against mine—velvet and warm—my spine stiffened.

And my mind, the traitor, flashed to a memory I did not want: Toussaint's hand, his knuckles grazing Eliza's cheek with casual reverence. Had she closed her eyes when he did?

No. Stop.

There was no room for that. The past was dead. I was not. I was heading toward the future, toward the territories. Toward Ealy Washington and land and respect and a wardrobe worthy of reinvention.

Eliza pulled back. When she spoke, her voice had that maddening, bell-clear resonance.

"You'll do wonderfully in the wilds of Colorado, I'm sure."

And before I could even process the meaning, Louisa, always the echo, patted my shoulder and added, "Yes, it takes a special kind of person to tame the wilderness."

Eliza extended one hand, gesturing graciously to the little circle of family behind me.

"It's a shame she couldn't start right here."

The crowd erupted.

My idiot brother guffawed like someone had lit a firecracker in his boot, and even Louisa snorted into her lace gloves. It was a charming little moment, for them. A laugh line in someone else's play.

But *I* felt it. A tight pinch, like a mosquito bite.

You were unsuccessful here.

Eliza is the wilderness you cannot tame.

She hadn't said those words, but I'd heard them all the same.

I swallowed the sting and summoned the smile I'd practiced at Dillard Finishing School under Miss Dorothea Hamilton's merciless tutelage.

"A shame," I managed quietly. But no one heard me.

I had just placed one patent-leather boot on the train's cast-iron step when I collided—quite literally—with a wall of wool and cologne.

The man was tall. Broad-shouldered. Skin the color of burnished mahogany, with a jaw that looked carved. His porter's uniform was crisp and suspiciously well fitted, as though tailored not just for functionality but for . . . effect.

I opened my mouth to protest, but before a single word could escape, he plucked the folded ticket from my glove with one smooth motion.

"You won't need all of that where you're going, Miss Bliguet."

He pronounced my name *Blee-GET*, and I corrected. "Blee-GAY rhymes with beignet." I followed his form through the train. "And what do you mean I won't need all of that?" I asked.

I wasn't sure if he meant my family or my ticket or the uncharitable thought I was having about Eliza, but either way, it felt a little *on time.*

I was losing him in the crowd. "Excuse me—!" I managed. I'm sure my face was burning. "Sir—"

But the man was already striding down the platform, disappearing into the crowd like fog. The train let out another hiss, the door clanged shut behind me, and I found myself in the narrow corridor of the colored Pullman car—fuming, flustered, and entirely unsure where my luggage had gone.

Only then did it strike me: He knew my name.

I clutched the brim of my hat like it might keep my entire life from blowing away.

When I looked down at the ticket in my gloved hand—creased now, handled too many times—I realized something was terribly wrong. My ticket. This wasn't mine. My comfortable seat, paid for in full, had been switched.

To the colored car.

Colored!

I wasn't under any illusions. I knew exactly who I was. But I had *paid* for second class. A seat with real upholstery, a porter, a window that closed properly. In New Orleans, people made allowances, looked the other way.

But I was being herded toward the back of the train, behind the day laborers and traveling musicians. Past the respectable noise of second class and straight into a boxcar with rusted hinges and the ghost of livestock. Wooden benches. No service.

Lordy, there was a hen in a crate under one of the benches!

I had left New Orleans to escape unpredictability.

So naturally, it followed me onto the train.

REAL MUSTARD

I adjusted the crisp folds of my traveling dress, already regretting how fine it was. Every dart and button screamed of better company than the one I was currently keeping. The cabin smelled like chicken fat and something pickled. I sat bolt upright, back like a ruler, like my posture alone might protect me from the indignity of it all.

The seats were stiff and narrow, upholstered in a coarse fabric that scratched even through my gloves. Every face looked hard up, but it was surprisingly worldly in this cabin. I counted at least four languages. Across the aisle, a woman cradled a baby wrapped in a quilt that—God help me—smelled like onions. Actual onions. The baby wept as if it knew where we were.

I don't hate traveling. I love the idea of it—trains especially. The glamour of departure, the suggestion of progress, the elegant inevitability of arrival. But this was *not* that kind of train. This was penance on wheels.

I was supposed to be riding first class. Well, not *first* first class but Negro first class: second class. My monogrammed trunk should have been tucked away in a proper compartment, my hat carefully stored, and a porter—preferably well spoken and deferential— should have been offering me tea or a blanket by now. Instead, I was wedged between a farmer who kept spitting into a tin and a woman whose hat looked like it had been sat on by a mule.

I hated this train.

I hated the grimy windows, the ticket I no longer even had, and the man—the porter, or whoever he was—who'd snatched it from me like he owned my whole journey. I kept scanning the aisle, waiting to catch another glimpse of him. How had he known my name? Why had he pushed me aboard like he'd been expecting me?

No answers. Just soot-streaked glass and a view of the bayou slowly dissolving into fields. I curled my fingers around the hem of my dress, right where the emergency cash was sewn into the lining. My little fortress of forethought.

The train shuddered. My past billowed behind me like the smoke curling from the engine, gray and impossible to hold.

The baby across the aisle wailed again, and the mother hushed it with a sweet little rhythm.

The train lurched to a stop, throwing her forward. The farmer disembarked—*thank God*—with his spit tin and his molasses breath, muttering something about "feed" and "cousins." I resisted the urge to wipe the seat with my handkerchief. The mother and her screaming baby stayed, though.

No sooner had he cleared the threshold than a woman heaved herself onto the train. She was either pregnant or stealing an entire ham.

She wore a shapeless muslin dress and carried a small square suitcase. The box thudded onto the floor as she lowered herself beside me with a grunt.

Without a word, she reached across me—*across me*—and held something over the squalling baby. A small glass dropper.

"Sugar water," she muttered.

The mother nodded, desperate, and opened the child's mouth. The pregnant woman squeezed the dropper and miraculously, the baby went quiet. Not a fuss, not a hiccup. And for hours everyone in our row could breathe again.

"Lessie Mae," the woman beside me finally said, nodding once before popping open the suitcase—which turned out to be a tin lunch box.

Inside: warm buttered biscuits. Ham sandwiches. A holy scent lifted into the air like a hymn. Half the compartment swooned on instinct.

A man reached out to grab one, and Lessie Mae snapped the tin shut like a bear trap.

"Ten cents, please."

He reared back. "Ten cents? I could get a whole box of biscuits for thirty cents!"

"You're welcome to the box then," she said.

He blinked. Then shuffled off. But others surged forward—coins clinking in open palms, some throwing nickels, others dimes, one dramatic woman dropping a silver dollar like she expected applause. Lessie worked the aisle like a practiced showgirl, taking orders, making change, never once standing up.

I turned just in time to catch the mother across from us—baby now passed out in sugar-soaked bliss—staring at the last biscuits in the tin like they might sprout wings and fly into her mouth. Then she looked away, ashamed of the wanting.

Without thinking, I reached into my reticule and flicked a quarter into Lessie's open hand.

"Last two," I said. "Plus, a tip for your trouble."

Lessie winked. "Whew. Sorry folks, I'm sold out." But she looked proud. As well she should. The train staff hadn't so much as offered our section a glass of water, let alone ham on warm bread. I studied her sidelong. She was sharp. Resourceful.

Wordlessly, I passed one of the sandwiches to the baby's mother. She hesitated—because that's what pride does—but the baby stirred, and hunger does not argue long.

She took it. Tore into it with the quiet ferocity of a woman who knew this was the best meal she'd get for days.

I looked out through the cracked partition, pretending not to watch her.

I had a nice view of second class, though. Too fine to be poor, too poor to be fine. I caught sight of the man. The man who had robbed me, shoved me, named me. The so-called porter. I moved toward him like a bullet.

He was sitting in a sunbeam, positively lounging and eating a sandwich like someone without a single regret in the world. Roast beef, from the looks of it. Thick bread. *Real* mustard.

I slapped it out of his hands.

He didn't even look surprised.

"I was wondering when you'd find me," he said.

"This is my seat, you louse," I hissed, arms folded, voice low enough to remain respectable. "Shouldn't you be serving the passengers?"

He raised an eyebrow, chewing slowly. "Oh, you mean that porter's suit?" He glanced down at the blue coat, now rumpled and unbuttoned. "Bit too tight, wasn't it?"

I froze.

He *wasn't even* a porter.

He wasn't employed by this train. He was just some stranger in a borrowed uniform, a walking scandal, a thief with good posture.

"*You*—you stole a uniform!"

"Technically," he said, licking mustard off his thumb, "I borrowed it. I'll be returning it at the next major station. In better condition than I found it, I might add."

"I—I could have you arrested!"

"Yes," he said, nodding agreeably. "Or you could sit down here and talk to me, Caroline."

I glared at him. "How do you know my name?" I demanded.

He looked up at me then, eyes dark and gleaming, like he found me terribly amusing—which, frankly, I couldn't allow.

He stood and dusted off his coat. I thought he was leaving.

Instead, he reached into the inside pocket and pulled out . . . my ticket.

Neatly folded. Unsullied.

He pressed it into my glove like a love letter.

"I just wanted to look out the window for a spell," he said.

He slipped past me and out the back of the car. I noticed something else tucked in with the ticket: a calling card. No name. Just a hand-drawn sketch of a crow in flight, and on the back, in that same neat hand:

Major Washington
Bounty Hunter

THE DEATH OF NUANCE

I sat in my paid-for seat in second class, legs crossed just so, gloved fingers resting on my reticule like it might fly away if left unsupervised.

And I felt like a thief.

I smoothed my skirt again, for the hundredth time, then uncrossed my legs just to recross them the other way, as if that might realign something in the universe. It did not.

Those women in the back. Lessie Mae and the mother. The others with their bundles and shawls and biscuit crumbs. They'd laughed, shared food, even smiled at one another.

The least I could do was bring them something.

So I stood and made my way to the small refreshment station near the end of the cabin. It wasn't much: a crooked counter, a half-bored attendant, and a row of sweating bottles.

"Soda water," I said. "Two, please."

I carried them carefully, cradled like fragile gifts. My gloves smudged slightly with condensation, which annoyed me more than it should have.

When I reached the rear compartment, the women were where I'd left them—Lessie Mae with her feet up now, fanning herself with yesterday's newspaper; the mother half dozing while the baby teethed on its own sleeve.

I cleared my throat.

Two heads turned. One smile bloomed—Lessie, of course— and the other looked startled to be addressed at all.

"Thought you went off and joined the white folks," Lessie teased.

I didn't reply, setting one bottle beside her and the other in front of the mother, who blinked down at it like it might explode. "It's not much," I said. "But . . . it's cold."

"Cold's a blessing," Lessie said, already cracking hers open with the corner of a button. The mother nodded, quietly murmuring her thanks. I gave a little smile and turned to go—not wanting to linger too long.

As I stepped back across the threshold into the second-class car, I caught him watching me.

The not-porter. Sandwich thief. He sat in the corner of the rear car, legs crossed, arms folded, chewing on a toothpick. I felt caught in the act of decency.

"Well," I sniffed, adjusting my gloves again, "I'd better go."

He raised an eyebrow. "Why don't you stay a spell? You'll be sitting pretty soon enough in Carsondale."

So he knew my name *and* my final stop. Was this bounty hunter hunting *me*?

So I sat in the rear car, between a now-calmed baby, a pregnant entrepreneur, and a bounty hunter watching my every move. It had been hours, and the porters had come to the rear car only with clinking jars of cloudy water. My loyalty to the rear car, already hanging by a crinoline thread, was beginning to wane.

"Well, ladies," I said, beginning to rise, intending to find a cleaner death elsewhere when he spoke.

"You know they throw out the old sandwiches and trade 'em in for new ones when we stop in St. Louis."

I blinked and nodded politely, the way one does when a child tells you how many teeth they've lost.

"If we could get Lessie some of those sandwiches," he continued, eyes on me like he'd been reading ahead in the script, "it might help a lot of folks back here make it a little farther down the line."

"Those sandwiches are twenty cents up there," I said, adjusting the angle of my hat. "This car could barely scrape together the ten cents Lessie charged for biscuits."

"Not everyone's paying twenty cents," he said, and then gestured with his chin like we were conspiring. "The VIP car's got heaps of them. Just rotting. On platters."

I scoffed. "Do any of us look like VIPs?"

I meant it as a joke. But the entire car fell silent and stared at me like I'd confessed to stealing from the tithing basket.

"I can see blue veins in your wrist," the bounty hunter said flatly.

"You're crazy, Mr. . . ." I scream-whispered, forgetting what was on the card.

"Major. Call me Major. And we're not in New Orleans anymore, darlin'," the bounty hunter muttered. "I'd have to step aside if I saw you on the street."

Even Lessie nodded.

I closed my mouth, stunned. *This* was the death of nuance. My whole identity as a gens de couleur—a complex, cultivated thing built on careful speech, finishing schools, and knowing which fork was for olives—reduced to the sudden fact that a few miles outside New Orleans, no one gave a fig about pedigree or politics.

Now they want me to pretend to be some . . . brunette from Lake Charles?

In the back of this train, I was either helpful or I wasn't. Hungry or I wasn't.

"Ms. Caroline," Lessie said gently, "if you get the materials, I can make the sandwiches and a fine sun tea to boot. I'll charge five cents for my trouble. That could go a long way toward paying my room and board where I'm headed."

So I was, against all odds and class expectations, an accomplice in the Great Sandwich Heist of 1893.

The first part of the ruse was almost offensively easy, like the good Lord had planned it himself. I stepped outside to stretch my legs and take in a bit of the bustling St. Louis I'd heard about when I saw a ticket—first class to Denver—fluttering out of a white woman's embroidered purse as she collapsed into the waiting arms of a man. The debutante, who clearly had no intention of meeting whoever her family had selected for her in Colorado, flitted off without so much as a backward glance at the small square of paper that now lay trembling on the platform, a tiny bird with nowhere to land.

I waited. Timing was everything. Not when the train was boarding, not when the platform swarmed with people, and not when the woman's perfume still hung in the air.

No, I waited until the chatter thinned, until the whistles began to blow and the train groaned to life, and I slipped inside the whites-only first-class rail cart like a needle in fabric.

I had to admit to a tiny libidinal thrill at sitting here unnoticed. I'd once walked into a candy shop on Canal Street, with its gleaming jars and suspicious white eyes that tracked my every movement. The trick, I'd learned, was not stealth but entitlement. Chin up, eyes forward, move like you've got a moral right to take up space, even when you know you don't. Especially when you know you don't. What was a white woman, anyway, but the right nose in the right context?

Still, my pulse betrayed my confidence. It raced wildly as I passed through the narrow corridor of the railcar, my hand gripping the ticket like it might dissolve at any moment. When I finally reached my seat, a plush thing upholstered in green velvet, I lowered myself with the grace of a queen and the pounding heart of a thief.

The train pulled out and, *Mon Dieu*, the cabin was whisper quiet and perfumed with the faint scent of lavender sachets. It was as peaceful as a Sunday morning, yet every time a shadow passed by the frosted window of my private car, my stomach tightened. I flinched reflexively, holding on to my borrowed dignity like a pastor's rag.

I was a VIP.

HEIST

I t started, as many of my worst ideas do, with perfect posture and a total lack of a backup plan.

The three of us—Lessie, the future tycoon; Major, the bounty hunter; and myself—pulled off what can only be described as a minor miracle of logistics.

Step one: I marched into the VIP cabin like I belonged there. Which, to be fair, I did. In spirit. I muttered something about my "uncle's urgent dietary needs" and fluttered a handkerchief.

Step two: Major, playing the role of bored staff and also, bafflingly, my "porter escort," lingered near the refreshment tables. Ushering foods out while I covered with over-the-top banter with patrons. So far, no one blinked an eye.

Step three: Lessie Mae waited at the rear of the train with a knife and spoon. *Mon Dieu*, that woman could do more with old bread than Jesus had done with loaves and fishes.

Together, we liberated no fewer than seventeen sandwiches, two wheels of cheese, and a decorative bowl of pickled things no one had touched since Arkansas.

We wrapped them in linens stolen from under a pyramid of teacups and slipped out just before a steward asked me for my card. I handed him the name of an entirely invented person. "Mrs. Adelaide F. Van Dorsen," I said, spelling it slowly. "You'll be hearing from my mother."

That seemed to scare the fire out of the poor boy.

We were getting away with it! Later that evening, as the sun fell over the Mississippi in a buttery collapse, the colored car feasted.

Lessie, radiant, laid out her bounty with a small flourish. She had added mustard and cured salami. I don't know how. I didn't ask.

And that *really* should have been the end of it.

But then the conductor caught Lessie swiping sugar—and all hell broke loose.

Apparently, sugar theft is the number one criminal threat to the American railroad industry. Which felt like a bit of drama on the conductor's part. Regardless, he came upon her red-handed—or rather, sticky-fingered—palming lumps of cane sugar from the refreshment table. She froze, of course. Guilty. Mid-pocket. The cubes glinted in the light like criminal diamonds.

This was a test of my umbrage. I was up for it. I straightened my shoulders, squared my hat, and marched up to the conductor with the full, brittle force of righteous indignation.

"Unhand m-my—" I stammered. "My maid. Just who do you think you are?"

It came out weaker than intended. More breathless than commanding. I was going for "imperious dowager," but I landed somewhere closer to "unwell niece."

The conductor turned to look me over.

Not at me. *Over* me. A slow sweep from hat to hem to my full lips and the soft roundness of my nose. I suddenly wished I had a lace veil.

He's going to know, I thought.

His eyes narrowed.

"Ma'am," he said, "we've had reports of missing cold cuts, and I now see this . . . woman, pawing at the sugar service."

I looked at Lessie. Then at her pockets. Lord, there were no fewer than fifty sugar cubes stuffed into her skirt. She looked like she was smuggling marbles.

"I require quite a bit of sugar," I said, voice trembling slightly. "For my tea."

"Quite a bit?" he asked, eyebrows raised.

"Quite," I said, planting my feet like that might stop me from sinking into the floor.

He didn't blink.

I know what you're thinking. This is it. This is the moment—the scandal that made me the subject of every parlor whisper from Denver to Durango. Stealing sandwiches? How provincial.

Reader, no.

This was not the scandal. This was merely . . . the appetizer.

"May I see your ticket?"

"Ah."

I reached delicately into my handbag and pulled out the other woman's ticket—the one I had borrowed . . . repurposed . . . stolen, depending on how you interpret minor crimes. My heart was now pounding SOS in Morse code.

He studied it.

"Yes. You," he said slowly. "This makes sense now. Your father did say you might try to flee."

"I— What?"

"Nice try," he said, plucking the sugar cubes from Lessie's person. "You're not going anywhere.

"I want you and your two Negro escorts back in your cabin. You're not leaving this train until Denver."

So there it was.

Not arrested. Just . . . sent back to my parlor cabin? Like we were misbehaving children. All three of us. Me, Lessie, and Major. The bed was large enough for Lessie and me, but surely we wouldn't be expected to sleep with Major in the room. And as the door clicked shut behind us, Lessie sank onto the chaise, pulled a sugar cube from her shoe, and popped it into her mouth.

"Worth it," she said through a grin.

Major just looked at me, amused as ever, then picked up a deck of cards.

And that is how we ended up under lock and lace in the finest cabin on the train—with nothing to do, nowhere to go, and far too much man in the room for me to sleep.

THE OLD CAROLINE

The VIP cabin was—naturally—nicer than my actual apartments in New Orleans. Mahogany trim. Sconces. Cushions filled with what I can only assume was crushed angel feathers. I tried to stay annoyed. Why did that fool girl want to take so much sugar?

But Lessie fell asleep almost immediately on a velvet chaise, hands resting on her rounded belly. She snored delicately, like a woman who had earned her peace. I would have allowed her the rest, except that left me alone. With him.

Major leaned against the opposite wall, his arms crossed, one boot resting lightly against the trim like a villain from a novel.

"So," I said, attempting nonchalance, "is this the part where you arrest me?"

"Would you like to be arrested?" he asked, too casually.

"I— No."

"Sounded like a maybe."

"It wasn't."

He twitched his shoulder.

I folded and refolded my gloves in my lap. "How did you know my name?" I ask.

"Everybody in Carsondale knows your name," he said quietly.

"How?" I asked.

"You"—his eyes caught mine—"are marrying my fool brother."

I had gotten engaged accidentally. A perfectly innocent act of showing off.

Eliza's sister Janey had taken ill at my family's borrowed country house—No. 7 Netherfield, a name far too grand for a place with peeling shutters and chickens in the front yard—and the whole neighborhood had taken it as an opportunity to hover. There were broths and herbs and overlong visits. Lil' Charlie, of course, was there every afternoon, sitting by the fire like some tragic suitor.

Toussaint D'Arcy came, and at first, I thought we would commiserate over the Benoîts—their loud voices, their borrowed house, their endless parade of mismatched tea sets. I thought he'd sit beside me, sigh meaningfully, and remember who he was supposed to choose.

He arrived with stationery. Cream stock, monogrammed. A stack of correspondence he needed to send on behalf of the family. I offered to help. I'd always had the neatest script, the sharpest French, the most gracious turns of phrase. That day, I wrote to Toussaint's little sister. To distant cousins. A minister. A retired teacher. And at the very bottom of the pile, to a bachelor cousin out west—a man in Carsondale looking for a wife.

Ealy Washington.

I addressed the letter with the soft authority of a woman doing someone a favor. I signed it on behalf of the family, of course—but I suppose a little too much of my charm slipped between the lines. I mentioned myself as a *lovely intellect*. I had imagined Toussaint reading it aloud, like he had done the others. Maybe pausing at a turn of phrase and smiling.

But then Eliza came through the door, all bluster and wind, and his attention evaporated like steam from a teacup.

Still, I must have made an impression. Because three weeks later, a reply arrived.

Not for Toussaint.

For me.

A letter from Ealy Washington, addressed to Miss Caroline Bliguet, full of admiration for my clarity, my elegance, my "refined thought." He said I sounded like a woman who would make a fine wife.

Two weeks after that, the proposal came. Tidy. Respectful. Practical.

And I said yes.

Because I wanted to wake Toussaint from whatever spell he was under.

Because I thought it might make Eliza blink.

Because I'd spent years being excellent with nothing to show for it.

And now I'm supposed to believe Ealy—the man who chose *correctly*—was the fool?

I would not.

On the train, I narrowed my eyes at Major. "What's so foolish about your brother? He's got good-enough taste." And I finally stopped folding my gloves and placed them on the table.

"He was desperate, you see," he said at last. "Sent out letters to five exceptionally classy women. Thought he'd get one. Maybe two, if fortune was kind. He had no idea so many would say yes."

My heart slowed to a crawl. Not shattered. Just . . . stunned. Why was it always me being forced to prove myself in a crowded field?

I sank into the overstuffed mattress of the sleeper cabin, letting my head tilt back against the velvet cushion. The train's rhythm, that quiet mechanical lull, worked its way into my chest like a spell. *Calm me, please.*

How did women manage these infernal clothes on long train rides? I imagined myself in the back with the chickens, easing the stays on my bodice to rest. The corset pressed like an iron band against my ribs, my petticoat bunched uncomfortably under my legs. There was no grace in this, no ease. This was the price of pretending to belong in first class: The performance never stopped. Not even when you were alone.

I unpinned my hat and sighed. Let the hair fall, dark and straightened, loose around my shoulders. My scalp sang at the release.

Correction. I wasn't alone. Lessie was passed out asleep on the chair, and Major was . . . well, looking.

His gaze flicked to my hair. It stayed there. Then back to my eyes.

"So you're here to turn me right around?" I asked, massaging my scalp. "Tell me your brother doesn't want me anymore?"

My voice was strong, like the old me.

Lordy, why am I already calling myself the *old* Caroline. I had been on this train for four days, and New Orleans already felt like a lifetime away.

He shrugged, and it was a heavy slow roll of his shoulders. "Not turning you around. Worse. I'm here to tell him you are the best of them." Major's Adam's apple bobbed. "You're the one he told everyone about. You are the prize. The others were insurance. He's a wealthy man, and he wanted to be cautious."

His words landed like a slap. Cautious was what *I* was. Before I started running around with fake porters/bounty hunters and teenage entrepreneurs.

"How many women are on their way to Carsondale?"

"Three now."

"Now?" My eyes bugged out, and my mind raced.

"It was seven, but four were unsuitable. I just met you and couldn't intercept the other two. Bertha Wallace and Elle Mae."

"So Bertha and Elle are both on their way to Colorado? From God knows where, thinking they're marrying Ealy next week?"

My voice pitched high, wild around the edges. "Is that what you're telling me?"

I stared at him, at the unbothered calm in his face, while my future unraveled like cheap thread. Everything I had planned—every step, every calculated yes—slipping through my fingers like cloudy bathwater.

"I can't believe this," I whispered.

Major stepped forward. Just one step. But in the lush, compact VIP parlor room it was a scandalous proximity. "It won't happen like that. I'm going to tell Ealy of all the women, it's you. I will make sure *you're* the woman he chooses."

"Why?" I asked. My voice was thinner than I meant it to be. "Because you met me?"

His gaze held mine for just a breath too long. And it made me feel like a train was going right through my belly.

"No. Because I've seen you."

I straightened my spine. I wasn't some trembling damsel, even if my hands were shaking. I meant to scoff. Truly. I meant to lift my chin and make some clever remark about his needing spectacles.

Instead, I swallowed, and the sound seemed loud in my ears.

The train groaned beneath us, iron wheels grinding toward a future I no longer recognized.

"Well," I said, smoothing the front of my skirt, though there wasn't a wrinkle to be found. "Let's hope Ealy's eyesight is just as sharp."

And I turned to fold down the bed before I could see if Major was still watching me.

But I felt it. The heat of it. The pull.

Something had shifted. And I couldn't say then whether I was stepping toward safety or straight into the fire of a scandal.

EVERYTHING BUT A CHILD OF GOD

The West stretched out before me like a messy unframed canvas. Unruly. Brown. Like God had spilled His drink and decided to call it a territory.

Major and I had urged Lessie into the bed last night, and he took the chaise. I had rocked in the bed barely able to breathe with the knowledge that there was a man in this tiny room, boots falling over the velvet chaise, tight belly rising and falling, and eyes always finding mine in the night. This morning, I turned to watch Lessie and Major eating cold shrimp. I didn't trust seafood this far from the gulf, so I let them have it. Lessie made notes in her little book after she tasted something she liked.

"I'll tell him it's you." Major had the audacity to say this like I'd won some bayou beauty contest. Good sir, I didn't board this train to be crowned Miss Prairie Dust 1893 by a bounty hunter.

Was I supposed to be flattered? Swept away? I was far from fainting.

I'm not romantic. Not *desperately*.

But I did think—just briefly—about the way Toussaint had looked at Eliza. That man trembled at the altar. Like love was the Holy Ghost and he'd just caught it in both hands. No one's ever trembled for me.

I *did* want it, though. I had twisted myself into knots—so many, so tightly—that I was unrecognizable to myself. The way I'd started tousling my hair and taking those long, useless walks around my French Quarter apartment, waiting to bump into a miracle. I had lost *myself* trying to be *her*.

And I could never live that way again.

We'd been confined to the VIP cabin for the last twenty-four hours of the journey—me, Major, and Lessie, like debutantes in detention. Our meals were delivered to the door with the suspicious energy of a jailhouse slop line. Some father *really* didn't trust his daughter. The conductor watched Major and Lessie like they were planning an armed rebellion.

But did they care? Absolutely not. They ate like royalty. I watched the world change outside. I thought about Ealy. And then Toussaint. And then, annoyingly, Major. His eyes on my hair. His hand on mine as we swapped sandwiches.

At least the view wasn't confusing.

It was vast and wild, unruly in a way that both thrilled and unsettled me. The train ride from New Orleans had its moments of stunning clarity: the endless expanse of prairie grass shimmering in the light, the red rock mesas standing defiantly against the horizon, and the jagged peaks of distant mountains. I *wanted* to see the grandeur. I *tried* to see the grandeur.

But all I saw was chaos. No order, no sense, no society. Just land and sky and nerve.

And honestly, it made my stomach twist.

I tried to find the hidden order in the randomness. The way the grasses bent uniformly with the wind, like wispy dancers. Even the train itself, though grimy and rattling, kept a steady tempo as it cut through the West. I clung to these patterns, like tiny anchors.

By the time the train pulled into the last stop, where a fancy Wells Fargo stagecoach waited to take the remaining passengers farther west, I was already mentally cataloging the next steps. I avoided Major's gaze, keeping to myself as I busied my hands, readying my supplies for the transition to the coach. The stagecoach gleamed, its rich red panels trimmed in polished gold.

In Denver, an expectant husband stood swaying at the platform, scanning faces for a bride I knew was never coming.

I was just about to step forward, tell him she'd gotten off in St. Louis with her skirts hitched and her lover in tow, when the man staggered toward a stack of packing crates and smashed them with a single blow. Wood splintered. A child nearby started crying.

Then came the shouting. He called her everything but the child of God, each word meaner than the last.

So I stopped. Because maybe that rich girl hadn't run *toward* romance after all.

Maybe she was running *away from* this.

I kept my mouth shut and boarded the stagecoach. Like any other woman minding her own business.

NEVER GETTING TO CARSONDALE

The interior of the stagecoach was surprisingly plush, with leather seats that bore the faint scent of saddle oil and windows shielded by delicate lace curtains. I'd prepared for discomfort, but this was decadence on wheels, or at least the frontier version of it. There were six passengers, far fewer than the coach's maximum capacity, and this made all the difference. Profit had triumphed over propriety; the company, eager to fill seats, had ignored the rigid segregation rules. For Wells Fargo, practicality outweighed prejudice, and white and Negro passengers rode side by side.

Major's broad back swayed outside the carriage, his spine straight, as if the least desirable seat on the entire stagecoach were some royal throne. When the carriage jolted, he didn't jolt inelegantly like they did inside. Instead, he merely shifted, letting the sun catch the sharp line of his jaw, looking every bit like the self-appointed King of the West instead of a lowly Negro forced to cling to the stoop for dear life.

Out here, in the yawning vastness of the frontier, everything was so aggressively large and unorganized. But Major was a pin in the map, a familiar grounding thing in an unfamiliar world. The land stretched out in every direction, unbothered by human concerns. There was simply too much of everything. The sky, a bottomless shade of blue. There was nowhere to contain it, no neat edges, no sense of proportion.

It was, frankly, sloppy.

Lessie groaned next to me, cutting through my internal complaints about God's maximalist architecture. Lessie had been pleasant enough, a hearty, cheerful sort in the back of the train, even while carrying what looked to be an entire family inside her swollen belly. But now, something was off. I noticed it immediately: the telltale darkness spreading around her neck, the unnatural sheen of sweat across her forehead. It was not the graceful, light perspiration of a genteel woman enduring discomfort but the soaked-through sort, the kind that spoke of something systemic failing in real time.

I frowned. "You all right?" I asked, though, judging by Lessie's complexion, she very much was not all right.

Lessie swayed slightly, her breath going shallow, and then, as the coach hit an obnoxiously large rut, one I was sure could have been avoided, she promptly collapsed onto my shoulder.

"Oh, come on, Lessie," I muttered. We were thirty hours away. Couldn't she hold on for two days?

I was never getting to Carsondale.

The coach gave another brutal lurch. Now actively holding up a full-grown woman, I whipped my head toward the front of the coach, motioning wildly at the nearest person who seemed to have some pull with the driver.

"Whoa!" I barked, waving my arms. "We have to stop!"

The driver did not immediately comply. Instead, he sucked his teeth, glanced over his shoulder, and then drawled, "We can't get off schedule."

I resisted the very real urge to throttle him. "Oh, well, let me just inform the baby that it's a bad time!" I snapped. "Maybe it'll climb back in for a few more miles."

The driver did not look impressed. He looked at me. Really looked at me, and I was once again all too aware of the wave of my hair in the stifling heat. He was likely weighing if this cargo was worth the trouble. The other passengers, previously content to ignore Lessie, now muttered nervously, concern bubbling up in unhelpful whispers.

I took a sharp breath, turning to look at Lessie, now fully unconscious and slipping farther down the seat. One of the many practical skills Spelman had equipped me with, including how to properly humiliate a man in polite conversation, kicked in.

I scanned the horizon, running calculations in my mind. Ten miles back, there had been an inn and a general store, meaning water and—if we were lucky—a set of clean cloths and someone with at least *one* useful medical opinion. This was a well-traveled route, which meant someone here had probably seen a baby being born before. Or at the very least, had the common decency to panic alongside me.

"If you don't stop," I said, "this woman may expire in your expensive little carriage. And passengers who have gone to meet their maker don't pay."

The driver blinked. That got his attention.

"There is a fort a few miles up, just outside Boulder. That fort can't supply an *empty* wagon, much less a wagon of nine souls. If we stop there, I'll have to continue on without you. The horses need feed and rest."

I sighed. "I'll take my chances."

"And it'll be hell finding a wagon to stop there for . . ."

He didn't have to finish: *for Negro women and a baby.*

When we reached what truly was an abandoned fort, the driver yanked the reins, pulling the coach to a shuddering halt. The dust kicked up in angry little swirls, but I barely noticed. Lessie had lost her water in a wet rush down her simple dress. Everyone in the carriage wanted this problem gone. I took her and was already moving, barking out orders, enlisting the help of whoever had the good sense to listen.

Major, solid thing on this whole journey, swung down from his perch and, without a word, moved to assist, his hands steady, his expression unreadable. I ignored him. Absolutely refused to acknowledge the embarrassing fact that I was damned grateful for his stabilizing presence.

UNBEARABLE COMPETENCE

The fort was a sorry thing, more suggestion than structure. They called it a fort, but I had been to church picnics more defensible. Supplies were low, and the first officer overcharged us for cold coffee. His buttons were mismatched; his face looked unfinished, like God had decided to scrap the project mid-creation.

The baby was coming, the mother was sick, and the whole ordeal was swiftly becoming the kind of situation I had spent my entire life avoiding. That is, one that required both improvisation and excessive sweating.

Major, bless him, had rolled up his sleeves and was now, utterly unbothered, boiling cloths like he'd been doing it since boyhood. It was both infuriating and helpful. I chose not to tell him which. When my hair was puffy from the sweat and fell in my face, Major pulled it away and tied it with his handkerchief. The soft brush of his fingertips on my neck made the hair rise there.

Lessie drifted between groaning and prayer.

"Why'd you get off with me?" she asked suddenly, voice tight with pain.

I shrugged, dabbing her brow with a clean cloth and pretending not to hear the honest note in her voice. I didn't have an answer I liked—at least not one that wouldn't lead to uncomfortable warmth or, worse, mutual respect. What would we do when we parted ways on this trip? Cry? I couldn't open myself up to that. And truth be told, she shouldn't be looking at me like I'm worth a hill of beans anyway. I don't know if a week ago I would have gotten off that wagon. Lessie was dark as a rubber tire and poor as a mouse, and a big part of me is ashamed to know that would've once been reason enough for me not to get involved.

"I suppose I like a challenge," I muttered, reaching for more rags and studiously not making eye contact. She snorted, then promptly grimaced into the next contraction.

She was tough in the way women are when life never gives them permission to be anything else. Just a body that knew how to survive.

"You hear this, Major? She"—Lessie groaned—"likes a challenge."

Major ran a hand over her forehead.

"Mean as a wet cat." Major said it with a warm smile. The combination of words versus his tone made her stomach wobble. He had been good during the labor, working wordlessly, boiling cloth, fetching water, and squeezing Lessie Mae's hand with patience.

It was an unbearable competence.

I did what Spelman Seminary had trained me to do: I stayed clean, calm, capable. I counted contractions, watched breath patterns, adjusted angles. It was one part science and two parts guts and heart.

And then, blessedly, it happened.

The baby, a slippery, wailing little miracle, emerged without ceremony or apology. Thank goodness, it lacked Lessie's talent for unnecessary dramatics. It screamed like it had already formed opinions about the world, and, if I'm honest, I respected that.

I wrapped it with one of the cloths from Major's pile and placed the bundle into Lessie's arms.

She blinked, eyes glassy with exhaustion, and then, with more pride than I'd seen from a queen in full regalia, she declared:

"Ferdinand Karol Montgomery."

I froze.

"Karol?" I asked, like I'd misheard or perhaps hallucinated it under pressure.

She looked at me. Smirked. "Karol. With a *K*."

My chest felt suddenly, ridiculously tight.

Major, standing beside me with a bowl of now-cold water, glanced over and said nothing. Just smiled in that solid way of his.

And I . . . I just patted the baby's head, cleared my throat, and said, "Well. At least he has impeccable taste in aunties."

I had delivered a *baby* in a fort held together by termite spit, and now there was a child with a name suspiciously close to my own to prove it. My eyes misted over slightly.

My name would mean something again, I had declared to myself. And so it did.

Major caught my eye, caught my wobbling chin, and his gaze wasn't full of amusement or challenge for once. Just quiet understanding.

There were too many small moments. The way he caught things before they fell. The way he knew when to pass me something before I asked. The way he had wordlessly handed me his own coffee ration after I spent the morning delivering a baby.

I looked away.

"You hold babies like you hold books," Major said, lighting a gas lantern. "Like they got chapters in 'em."

I turned, finally meeting Major's gaze in the flickering glow of the gas lantern.

"And you hold them like a pro. You probably have a wife in every territory."

"No wives, no young'uns, either. Just the son of a midwife."

"So that's why you're so insufferably good at everything," I murmured.

Major tilted his head, considering me. "You say that like it's a flaw."

"It *is* a flaw," I shot back, smoothing the creases in my skirts with precise, practiced fingers. "Competence is an invitation. It means people will ask things of you. Expect things of you. You can't just be good at something *one* time." I glanced down at the baby, now sleeping soundly against Lessie Mae's chest. "Look at me. I delivered *one* child, and if it gets out, I'm going to be sawing off legs in a second civil war."

Major chuckled, a rich, warm sound that ran straight through me. Tickled something buried. My pulse tripped over itself trying to catch up.

"You'll do it if you're asked, though, won't you? I told you before that I seen you," he said, and I wondered where he had gotten the straw between his teeth or why I was all of a sudden focused on his mouth.

I only sniffed. "Well, I see you, too."

He turned, brow lifted in amusement. "Do you now? 'Cause from where I was sitting, you've spent this whole wagon ride trying not to. What do you suddenly see?" he pressed, teasing but not unkind.

I gestured vaguely at his dusty shirt. "That you're smart enough to be a Negro doctor. Or know enough law to sit behind a desk, not chase fugitives through the brush. Why?"

Major considered me, the corner of his mouth twitching. That damn straw moved with it, lazily wicked.

"Same reason you're not some rich man's wife, living soft in Nawlins," he said.

I hadn't thought of Toussaint D'Arcy in so long. The face passed through me like water through a sieve. No residue.

"Poor decision-making?" I guessed.

"Insufferably good at everything," he countered, and damn it all, the man smiled.

I rolled my eyes, but the corner of my mouth betrayed me, twitching upward.

"Well," I said, standing and dusting off my skirts, "if you plan to keep up this infuriating habit of being good at things, you may as well make yourself useful. I'll need someone to steal some proper medical supplies next time we stop."

Major raised a brow. "Steal, is it?"

I arched a delicate brow in return. "They won't sell them to Negros." I looked at his amused face, then said, more softly, "Oh, please. Don't act scandalized. We were sandwich thieves once."

His grin, crooked at the corner, was lazy and private. I had this feeling of great anticipation like when the preacher is climbing to the high point in the sermon, and the organs start going. He stepped forward, just slightly, barely a shift of boots on dirt but suddenly I could feel it in the space just above my skin.

"And there's honor 'tween thieves?" he said, soft.

I let the question hang, but I suddenly needed a whole pitcher of tea.

Our eyes locked. Every nerve of mine was alive and listening.

He stepped a hair closer. "What else, I wonder," he said slowly, "might be between thieves?"

The world tipped.

He leaned in slow. His fingers brushed my waist, the edge of my glove, nothing that could be called scandal but everything that would've kept me up at night. The straw in his mouth was gone, and his nose grazed against the racing pulse at my neck.

My eyes closed.

And then—

Some first officer (where had he been when we needed supplies?) popped right out of hell to holler, "Wagon coming up fast
from the south!"

The moment cracked like porcelain.

Major stepped back with military precision, hands retreating
to his pockets. Behind us, Lessie swore under her breath as Freddie stirred. She may have been watching us because she turned
her eyes when I looked toward her.

I said nothing. Just briskly began to pack our things.

I was taking something that didn't belong to me. Something I
had no rightful claim to.

I had once believed my dreams were stolen from me, that Eliza
had swept in and taken the future I'd built piece by careful piece.

And now here I was, standing in her shoes.

It surprised me, how easy it was. No twirling mustaches, no
evil laughter. Just hot looks in a moving train with a man who
could guide a baby's shoulders through labor like he was shelling
peas.

Could I do that to someone else?

Apparently, yes.

If there's one thing I've learned about running up a tab with
God—it's that the bill always comes due.

A SINNER IN CHURCH

Carsondale. We were finally on our way. The journey required the hiring of another wagon, which meant I—occasional Negro, and now, apparently, plantation heiress—was forced to negotiate with the driver about the cost of transportation. He was trying to take advantage of me, and I was done being surprised at the naked opportunism of this place.

"Food's gotten dearer," the driver announced. "Can't be takin' passengers without accountin' for their meals. Three extra bellies to feed."

I sighed like a woman who had been forced to deal with the most indelicate of things, which, at present, was him. "Sir, surely you know that Negroes don't eat in the main chambers at the rest stops. It simply *isn't* done. They take their own meals elsewhere, usually in far humbler circumstances than whatever you're envisioning." I adjusted my gloves, making a show of their expensive cut, and, because I was nothing if not thorough, even wrinkled my nose just slightly, like the very idea of sharing a meal with my own traveling companions was laughable.

It worked. The man deflated instantly, his argument collapsing under the weight of his own prejudices. "Well," he grumbled, rubbing his jaw as if he had been the one tricked. "S'pose that's true."

Major, standing just behind me, shifted slightly.

"Good," I said, brisk now. "Then there's no need to increase the fare, is there?"

He grunted. "S'pose not."

I did not smile. Smiling was for women who were not entitled to this treatment. Instead, I stepped lightly into the wagon, not bothering to look back as Major and Lessie Mae climbed in behind me.

We set off, the wagon rocking over the uneven road, and I allowed myself a moment to bask in the ridiculousness of it all.

Because I knew one thing for sure and two things for certain: I could never have gotten away with that in Louisiana.

The moment I opened my mouth, the moment my lips formed an *r* too round or an *s* too sharp, they would have taken me apart like a sinner in church. It wouldn't have mattered that my dress was fine, that my manners were perfect. The rules were different there, and the ways of knowing were nuanced and perfectly calibrated.

But here? Everyone was too busy trying not to starve to bother enforcing nuanced race rules with any real conviction. Here, I was a woman in a delicate dress, traveling west with my servants. If I said so, it *was* so.

The absurdity of it was intoxicating.

Tucked primly into my seat, I did my best to focus on the road ahead, the long, sunlit stretch of dirt unraveling toward the horizon. A new town. A new name. A new life, supposedly.

But no matter where I looked, there he was.

Major was inside the wagon, for now hidden from the dust that rose around outside us in lazy spirals. Even in silence, he occupied space with a kind of heaviness.

Major leaned against the wooden side of the wagon, his arms crossed, his long legs stretched out before him. His hat was pushed low, shielding his face from passengers' stares.

I kept stealing glances, meaning only to confirm his calmness, to reassure myself that we had really pulled something off. But at that exact moment, his eyes popped open, dark, smoldering beneath heavy lashes, catching me in the act.

My breath got stuck somewhere in my chest, and my eyes made a circle around the wagon. But his gaze didn't waver; suddenly, the entire thing felt smaller.

Heat crawled up my neck. Caroline Bliguet did not fluster. It was ninety degrees. *Of course*, I was warm. I pressed a damp kerchief to my neck and smoothed the pleats of my skirts, tilting my chin just so, willing myself to be unbothered.

And yet, for the rest of the ride, I did not look at him again.

The road stretched ahead of me, and the wagon rattled on, and I had to contend with a new reality. Maybe Toussaint D'Arcy *hadn't* been a fool. His trembling hands, his vows spoken like prayer, made perfect, aching sense now.

Maybe he'd just been brave enough to fall.

THE LIE

Carsondale!" the driver hollered, his voice cutting through the thick, hot air.

We were here, or arriving. The wagon still rumbled beneath me, but the platform was already in view, blurred at first, then sharpening into a scene of bustling movement, men unloading crates, women clutching parcels, children darting underfoot.

Would he be here?

I imagined a tall, broad man in a fine coat, his boots polished to a mirror shine, standing at the edge of the platform with a bouquet of wildflowers in his hands. It's not strange that I'm imagining Major. It is his brother, after all. Wouldn't they favor? But Ealy would have a ridiculous bouquet. A grand gesture. A declaration. I hated flowers, useless, sneeze-inducing colorful grass, but I wanted the performance of them.

I wanted Major to see it, too. That I was not some reckless fool who'd let her heart get tangled up in the arms of a man who boiled cloths and looked at her like she was a gift he wanted to unwrap. The wagon lurched, sending my stomach dropping lower and lower.

Lessie Mae, ever practical, was already securing the two-day-old baby Freddie to her back, tying the fabric with a knot that looked like it could hold through a fall hurricane. She lifted her bundle of belongings, same small satchel, same remarkable resolve, and I realized I had never asked her where she was going. Or why.

"So," I said, brushing the soot from my skirts, "is your husband waiting for you here?"

"Hopefully my husband never finds me," she muttered, without looking up.

I nodded. Fair enough.

"Family?"

Lessie glanced over, and her face was remarkably suspicious. "I got Freddie here, and a suitcase full of my granny's recipes. Thought I'd get a cooking job somewhere."

I honestly couldn't believe it. The girl had no plan. No solid anything?

"That's"—I gestured vaguely at the sack—"hopeful of you. What if your granny's recipes are dreadful?"

Lessie laughed. "They ain't. She had a shop."

I said nothing. I had been to many a shop that should've reconsidered its ambition, but now didn't seem the time to offer my critique of under-seasoned grits. Had she always planned to come to Carsondale? Or was this just her following her gut? Following me?

I saw past the ingenuity and the baby. Lessie's soft face. The girl couldn't be a day over sixteen.

"Well, then," I said, adjusting the buttons on my cuff, "make me your granny's best meal, and my husband and I will be your first patrons."

"You still getting married?" She looked incredulous.

I nodded. "Of course . . . Of course," I said too quickly. I heard it, that touch of disaster in my voice, like a piano chord struck an inch off-key.

"I thought—"

"You thought what?" My words had grown teeth. My guilt, sharper than intended.

Lessie narrowed her eyes, looking past me to Major's broad back swaying on the perch. "You ain't gotta make up your mind now, do you? About your husband?" She looked toward the approaching crowd. "Ealy Washington ain't bought you, has he?"

Before I could answer, before I could even wonder how Lessie could have picked up my betrothed's name, the wagon rolled to a stop, and Major hopped down from his perch outside. Landed soft. Graceful. Catlike.

Of course he moved like that. The sneak.

That Lessie and I were disembarking into what appeared to be a completely Negro town was not lost on the driver. His lips curled in distaste as he hauled my valises onto the platform, making a spectacle of their weight before tossing them down with so much force the wood cracked open, leaving my petticoats exposed to the city dust.

I lifted a gloved hand, all politeness.

I reached into my reticule, pulled out a gleaming silver coin, and held it up just long enough for him to see it catch the light. Then, with a feigned fumble, I let it clatter onto the wooden platform at his feet.

"You don't mind picking that up," I said, voice thicker than sweet tea. "Since you seem so fond of throwing things down."

The hush that followed was exquisite. The driver's fists curled at his sides, but he did not move. The weight of the crowd, the town, the moment itself pressed down on him like a boot to the neck. He scrapped the coin up like a dog but not before he took a parting shot.

"Bitch," he spat out.

Lessie let out a low whistle, adjusting the baby on her back. I smoothed my gloves, the big smile on my face was real.

"I do try," I said.

Major had found his way behind me. Chest against my back as the wind picked up, tugging loose a puffy curl from my hasty chignon. He reached up, so casually, so terribly intimate—Lord have mercy—and tucked it behind my ear like he had seen me do. And it dawned on me that no one gives you flowers for what you *didn't* do. Restraint is never applauded.

There's no sash for *almost* kissing a man you shouldn't even like. No medal for *not* swooning in public.

But if there were, I would be Miss Prairie Dust 1893, proudly standing there on that podium.

He turned, brushing the dust from his sleeves, and looked at me, not long, just enough.

"I'm going to find my brother," he said, low and even.

My stomach dropped. Like I had passed a note in school, and now the teacher was reading it out loud.

I reached for his arm without thinking. Just the brush of my glove against the wool of his sleeve. "What," I began, but the words curled into silence on my tongue, "—will you tell him? That we shared something? And it surprised us both?"

I was here to marry his brother.

Come hell. Come high water. Come whatever this was between us.

His eyes flicked to where I held him.

Then, softly, he said, "I'll tell him a little bit of the truth and a little bit of a lie, Caroline. . . . That you're the best woman *he* could have hoped for."

His words echoed somewhere beneath my corset. God help me, I knew the lie.

WOMAN-SHAPED THING

I sat at the station for longer than I'd hoped, and it was long enough to start to comprehend the full breadth of my dishevelment. Dust had settled into the fine weave of my traveling dress, darkened the hem. My hair, once a sleek and careful arrangement of curls, had declared independence somewhere between day six and day sixteen of the journey, and now hung in stubborn, frizzy rebellion around my face.

I knew it was him before I even turned.

Ealy Washington did not arrive. He descended, in a swirl of voices. He was the color and sheen of boiled peanuts, and his hair was oiled to perfection. He was the most important person in any room.

And then, he blew right past me like I was a park bench. He scanned the platform, gaze slipping over me entirely.

Passed over. That phrase is going to be on my tombstone.

After a few slow steps, he stopped.

Seeing no other woman-shaped thing waiting for him, he turned back to us carefully, brows drawing together. It was a very strange thing, watching the man you were meant to marry walk right past you like you were a barrel crate. Not even a nice barrel crate. Just one of those cracked ones used to store rotting turnips.

Ealy scanned the platform, his gaze sliding clean over me and right onto some poor old widow behind me with a crooked bonnet. The townsfolk on the platform were hiding laughter behind their fans. He approached me finally, but it wasn't to embrace me.

"Have you two ladies seen—" he started. "Well, my brother told me a real fine lady was s'posed to be waitin' on me here," he said, laughing in a way that was mostly teeth and not a lot of joy. "I'm afraid if I don't come back with her, he'll draw up my last will and testament."

I couldn't even be offended. He looked so worried I almost pitied him. But it wasn't *me* he was worried about; it was his brother Major's wrath.

"This here's Miss Caroline." Lessie placed both hands against my back and shoved me forward.

A hush fell over the gathered townspeople, a collection of well-dressed businessmen and their corseted wives, shopkeepers peering from doorways, the odd dust-coated cowboy leaning against a post, all watching to see how the tall, important man would handle his less-than-impressive fiancée.

Ealy's gaze landed on me, and for a second—just a second—his lips pressed into a thin, disapproving line before he caught himself. He fixed it instantly, smoothing his features.

"Caroline, the . . . uh, beauty of New Orleans Caroline?" he said.

A line he must've practiced on the way over. "I waited for three days," he said. I knew he meant to sound devoted, but it landed a little closer to wounded pride. "I was worried sick."

"I'm so sorry. We were delayed," I said. Trying to match his pitch.

"Oh, dear. On Saturday, there were speeches. Toasts. Plans. Oh, it was grand."

Ealy took two measured steps forward and, instead of embracing me, brushed dust from my shoulders. "Caroline. I—" Then he said, "Let's get you changed and into a proper bath. Major says you're whip-smart. But I have to tell you—out here, it's cooking, cleaning, and refinement that matter. Not books."

He laughed.

It wasn't surprising. Men like that existed back in New Orleans, too, only with better waistcoats. But something about his words landed differently now. Not like a revelation, but like a final, definitive bad note on a trumpet someone should've retired years ago.

He pulled out a white handkerchief and held it to his nose, like my presence might carry the plague.

Heated embarrassment bloomed across my skin, crawling up my neck in sharp, mortifying waves. I wasn't what he'd imagined, and the look on his face was letting me know *live*, in front of a full audience, instead of through a letter weeks after the wedding.

This was the kind of story one of my friends would write me about in hushed tones, begging me to guess *what happened next*. But this wasn't a letter. This was me. And I already knew the ending.

When I wrote home, I'd tell them Ealy was charming. That the house was made of marble. That I was lucky. I'd write it the way I'd practiced it.

But standing there on that platform, I knew better.

He was still rattled by the delay. I could see it in his eyes. *My lateness disrupted the schedule.* The engagement had unfolded out of order. It should have been, a *beautiful woman* arriving precisely on time. A *grand engagement* unfolding precisely as planned. We were alike in that way. It was why I had agreed to be his bride from hundreds of miles away. Ealy did not forgive that sort of thing. Not easily.

The townspeople had started whispering. Pointing. Watching. I could feel their scrutiny gather and press into me. And Ealy, panic-stricken Ealy, only started walking faster, beads of sweat breaking across his upper lip.

Something else was going on here.

And it looked like *I* would be the last person to find out what it was.

OMELETTE

The bath, I would begrudgingly admit, *was* divine. The water was warm and thick with lavender oil, the kind that clung to your skin long after the steam cleared. The tub was deep enough to lose myself in, and for a few decadent minutes, I allowed the fantasy to bloom: I had arrived. This was it—the kind of life where things were soft and perfumed, where someone else boiled the water and love came in the form of silence and soap.

But even paradise feels odd when you're the only one living in it.

The towels were too white. The silence too curated. Not even the bathwater seemed to ripple unless I moved. It was like being wrapped in satin-lined museum glass.

Once I was scrubbed to gleam, powdered, and poured into a silk gown that cinched my waist into submission, Ealy returned to take me on a tour.

He beamed like a boy at a school presentation as we crossed the threshold of his home—the only marble house in Carsondale, he told me proudly, as if it had grown there naturally. In truth, it looked like a baby's first tooth: pale, sharp, and strangely out of place in the dry, red dirt of the West.

Inside, the house was just as grand. Silk curtains I suspected had never been drawn. Rugs imported from somewhere expensive. China so delicate it looked see-through. The whole house smelled faintly of lavender, lemon polish, and nothing at all.

I noticed the dining room first. The table was set for twelve, but not a single plate showed the faint trace of use—no scratches from a knife, no heat mark from a soup tureen. Pristine.

Looking around the kitchen, I thought of Lessie Mae at the boardinghouse. Her sleeves rolled. Her arms full. Baby Freddie Karol swaddled tight against her back while she kneaded bread with the same hands she'd used to catch him.

Ealy, meanwhile, had shifted into a monologue about efficiency, about how help should be quiet and skilled and preferably invisible.

"You know," I said, tapping a finger thoughtfully against the marble countertop, "I met a young woman on my way here—Lessie Mae. She's looking for work as a cook."

Ealy, mid-preening, turned to me, adjusting his lapel. "Well—this is what I wanted to talk to you about," he said, already fidgeting. "You were late and, well . . . someone came. A lovely woman, a chef. Bertha. She was trained in France. Studied under . . . um . . . Jefferson's people."

"Ealy. I know you wrote several letters to women."

He opened his mouth, no doubt ready with some fiction about mistaken identities or bulk postage. But he surprised me with the truth.

"No harm was meant," he said quickly. "Women get cold feet, you see? Four of the seven declined me at the last minute. You can't predict these things."

I said nothing, mostly because I wasn't sure which part to respond to.

"My brother didn't understand my process," he went on. "But you don't become the richest man in Carsondale by putting all your eggs in one basket. Only three women were bold enough to come. Could've been less."

"Bertha is one of the wives you sent for." I ticked one finger.

"Yes. And—"

"And the other?"

"She hasn't arrived. As of yet."

He was twisting his hat now, visibly sweating.

"And when she does?"

He paused. Thought about it. Not for drama, but because the wheels were truly grinding upstairs.

"Well, I thought we might . . . I don't know. Have some sort of contest. A chef. A book woman. A business lady."

"A business lady . . ." I repeated, flatly filing that bit of knowledge away. "You could've said that at the train station and saved me the time."

"That's the same thing I told Major," he blurted, his voice high with panic. "He made it seem like I had to—you know, like you'd come all this way. . . . And my brother is a terrible fright in a bad mood."

So Major hadn't just *convinced* Ealy to meet me at the station. He'd browbeat him like a wayward child. Like someone who couldn't be trusted to do the right thing on his own.

"I have no interest in a contest," I said. "Not for you. Not for anyone."

And I hadn't known how much I meant that until I heard it out loud.

For so long I had been wrapped up in status. Trying to make myself look better than Eliza in comparison—lighter, neater, more educated. I had been playing the game, believing there was a prize.

Ealy's shoulders dropped, and he let out an even breath.

"Well, that relieves me," he said, too quickly. "See, the townsfolk are keen to avoid scandal. This being one of the few colored towns so far west . . . And I only told them about a *Caroline*, so Bertha's been forced to be, well . . . under my hat, as it were, and it's a shame because . . ."

He looked me squarely in the face.

"Bertha's the one you want," I finished. Did I have to script my *own* rejection? Would the humiliations never cease? "Miss Trained in France?" I said, tone light as air.

He nodded.

"Mon Dieu," I murmured, my voice all velvet and venom. If he flinched—and I think he did—it was well earned.

"Then I must meet her."

Ealy lit up like he'd passed a test. He was so pleased with himself.

He gestured toward the far end of the kitchen. "Bertha, my love."

A stout, flour-dusted woman turned around, rolling pin in hand. She looked like she'd lost a fight with a sack of dough. Her sleeves were damp with kitchen heat, her apron streaked in batter. Her face, round and honest, was obscured in a cloud of flour. But even through the haze, I could see it: panic.

The fire was low, the knives dull, and the only food I could see was a slab of salted pork and a basket of potatoes, neither of which seemed to be doing anything particularly French.

"Ah! Mademoiselle Bertha!" I greeted her in my best, most-fluid Parisian French. "Que prévoyez-vous de cuisiner pour le dîner?"

The plump woman went stiff. Absolutely rigid. Her mouth opened, then closed. Her fingers twitched around the rolling pin. Her eyes darted to Ealy, then back to me.

"Uh . . . omelette." Bertha said it like she'd finally remembered a single word from a dream.

I blinked.

She blinked.

And we stood like that—two women who understood exactly what was happening, trapped on opposite ends of a lie.

Ealy beamed. "Bertha doesn't want to confuse you. She's more advanced than, say, your Louisiana Creole."

I saw the fear in her eyes. The *please don't* written all over her face. Bertha was now gripping the rolling pin like it might double as a weapon. Like if I told Ealy this woman didn't know any French, I would get my head cracked open for my trouble.

And I could've. God help me, I wanted to twist the knife. Play the clever girl. Blow the whole scheme open right there in the too-quiet kitchen, just so Ealy would know what he'd lost—and the whole town could hear it echo.

Ah, we are so close. But even this—almost bigamy, French chef fraud, all of it—is not the scandal that made me the most talked-about woman west of the Mississippi.

Besides, if I made a scene, ran straight into the square to announce what Ealy had done, what would I have won?

Ealy?

A man who had to be threatened with bodily harm even to greet me at the train station? Who couldn't tell a *bonjour* from a *bonsoir*? I'm not sure I'm motivated by that prize anymore.

And so I smiled. Sweetly. Magnanimously. And let the moment pass.

Bertha blinked once, slowly. She understood.

Ealy, of course, beamed. "See? The real thang," he said, smiling that piano-key smile. And I—Caroline Bliguet, Spelman graduate, daughter of a seamstress turned shopkeeper, orchestrator of the Great Sandwich Heist of 1893—stood there in that gown, in that polished house, and knew I had come all this way for nothing.

ELLE

I went to visit Lessie and Freddie the very next day at the boardinghouse.

"Why didn't you tell me?" I asked, skipping pleasantries entirely.

Lessie looked left, then right, as though checking for exits.

"Tell you what?" she asked, stalling so poorly I almost respected it.

"You are the *third* wife," I said. "The business lady. I found it curious that you seemed to have no plan and no destination. I have never met an entrepreneur without a plan."

"Oh, come on, Caroline," she sighed.

"I'm serious."

"Well, I wasn't exactly running an honest scheme," she said, folding a napkin too many times. "You saw the condition I was in. I couldn't let Major know before I got here, and everywhere you were, there was Major, so we never got around to talking honest. If he knew I was L. Mae and *this* pregnant, he'd have turned me around in Baton Rouge."

She pulled her shoulders back like a woman bracing for wind.

"And I can't go back to what I left, Caroline. I won't."

I knew that look. I'd worn that look.

"Did you *ever* plan on marrying him?" I asked softly.

She looked down at the floor like it might have answers.

"I don't plan on marrying ever again," she said, sliding three mismatched plates in my direction. "Taste these. I could really do something here. It wasn't for nothing." She gestured to me. "The trip. Got a trial here as a cook. Not many kids in the place, so the owner don't mind Freddie."

Of course he didn't. The baby was turning into quite the charming little butterball, full of grabby hands, wet giggles, and the kind of noisy joy that demanded to be shared.

The boardinghouse was loud and drafty, the table wobbled, and one of the chairs was standing only out of habit, but it was *warm*. It was honest. Sitting in that cramped kitchen, elbow to elbow over chipped plates, eating food that came from some-body's grandmother instead of a French pamphlet, I felt some-thing I hadn't let myself feel in weeks.

Something dangerously close to home.

I thought of my sister. Of the yawning distance between us.

Since the boardinghouse doubled as the town's postal hub (and also the candy counter, and also a place to buy secondhand hats), I sat down and wrote my sister a letter—the first one in weeks.

I wrote about the train ride. About roast beef sandwiches and delivering a baby in a run-down fort. About a grand marble house with a soul like a mausoleum, and a fake French chef named Ber-tha and the real chef Lessie, who had left me to my writing to take more orders. I was surprised at the wetness on my cheek as I folded the papers. So much had happened to me.

I kept making my way through samples of Lessie's grand-mother's dishes, and each was better than the last, including an étouffée so good it had made me stand up and praise the Lord. I called Lessie back over to the bar.

"The owner's going to be begging you to stay," I told her.

"Make him set aside space for individual goods. Handheld things, like this chicken pie." I pointed with my fork. "People will pay good money for food they can eat without a knife and fork."

I was mid-meal, my spoon deep in a bowl of oatmeal, when the door creaked open and Major walked in.

GLORIOUS

Polished, and entirely *too* handsome, Major locked his eyes on me. And my knees felt like crepes. Without the dust of the road on him, without the wind-whipped roughness, he was dangerous. He tipped his hat, and my throat worked to get the oatmeal down.

"Everywhere you are, there is Major," Lessie said pointedly.

I'd still not found my voice, but Major's eyes hadn't left the spoon in my mouth. He hadn't even looked up at Lessie. When I pulled the spoon out and placed it on the counter, his eyes did not follow it.

"Care to take a walk, Miss Caroline?"

"On the main street?" I asked.

He nodded.

"Lessie, I'll take Freddie Karol and let you work in peace for a spell," I said.

She had agreed too fast. And Lessie's eyes moved over me.

It was indecorous, entirely unbecoming of a woman of poise, and I knew it. Knew it the moment I had bundled little Freddie Karol too haphazardly, my hands unsteady, my movements rushed, until Lessie had to gently pull her baby near, securing the wrap herself, and said, "Daylight still gonna be there when you get outside."

I nodded and let her secure the baby on my back.

The walk was warm. Stifling.

I kept my chin high, my posture perfect, but my pulse was another thing entirely, wild and out of rhythm.

Beside me, Major walked with that maddening, unhurried grace of his, his presence stretching into the space between us, filling it with something too big to ignore.

"I thought I'd tell you something," he said, voice smooth. "Something that might help make your decision."

All around the little plaza, the good citizens of Carsondale were trying their very best not to stare while absolutely, unequivocally staring. The shopkeepers. The men tipping their hats like they had somewhere better to be. The wives pretending to be fascinated by cookie tins. All of them side-eyeing Major and me like we were a two-horse parade. No malice in it, not really. Just the lean of curiosity, of knowing something was happening, even if they didn't know what shape it would take yet.

Major didn't seem to notice. Or rather, he did, and simply didn't care.

"I'm settin' roots," he said, in that low, sturdy way of his that always seemed to start from the boots up. "I been reading law," he added. "Under the county judge. Figure I'll take the Colorado bar in a year's time, practice right here."

I blinked. "So . . . bounty hunter to barrister?" I laughed, and the sound came out lighter than intended, girlish, like something from someone with a ribbon in her hair. Even Freddie gurgled behind me.

Major smiled at the boy. "Gotta keep things interesting. Besides—"

And here he paused. The whole air around us shifted. He took a step closer, and the heat rushed up my neck.

"I need you to see I'm serious," he said. "That I'm stayin'. That I'm not just followin' you around like some stray dog who got too attached."

My gloves were damp. My brain knew I should say something

refined. But instead, my stomach dropped into the soles of my shoes.

"Major, your brother—"

He cut me off, already gearing up for rejection. "I know you came here to marry him," he said quickly. "But if there's even the smallest part of you—any part—that might give me a chance . . ."

I opened my mouth. "Your brother chose Bertha."

That stopped him.

"What?"

"Your brother," I said, "chose the French chef."

He blinked like I'd spoken another language myself.

"She's about as French as fried chicken," he said.

"And yet." I raised both brows.

He let that sit for a second, then shook his head. "So you're tellin' me," he said, softly now, "you came all the way to Carsondale, Colorado . . . and you don't even have a fiancé?"

"It's a tragedy," I said, trying to sound dry. It came out a little breathless.

And then . . .

He did it.

"Oh, marry me, Caroline," he said, blurting it like it had been bouncing around inside him for days. The raw, earnest truth of the question pulled at my navel. It wasn't a performance. He didn't angle his voice for the listening crowd. The question was for me alone.

"I can't make you the wife of the richest man in town. But I can make you the wife of the happiest."

I did not speak.

Mostly because I couldn't remember how.

He looked at me like he meant it.

"I figure we could use a trained nurse here," he added quickly, like that might tip the scale. "Or, if you didn't want to work, you wouldn't have to."

I saw the life he was offering, whole and tender and unplanned.

Slow Sundays and loud kitchens. Freddie growing tall and bossy. Lawbooks open on the table, buttered biscuits cooling beside them. Lessie visiting with new recipes and laughter that spilled into the hall. The hound we hadn't named yet. The little porch. The windows that steamed in winter.

It was—absurdly, achingly—perfect.

In New Orleans, marriage had been a gilded cage: you married the lightest man you could manage, roamed your three tidy blocks of the French Quarter, curtsied to your neighbors, repeated your schedule until death or scandal pried it open. Safety was the *whole* point. The sameness was the prize.

And I had told myself I wanted that.

But what Major was offering felt like something else entirely.

It felt like freedom.

"Caroline?" he said again, softer now. The crack in it undid me.

"Oh my goodness," I said, blinking at him, stunned at myself. "I thought I said yes already."

He laughed then, and Freddie caught and pulled a frizzy curl of my hair, tilting my face up toward Major.

And because I couldn't help myself, because I loved knowing things before other people did, I said, "By the way . . . Lessie is L. Mae."

He froze.

"You don't have to go looking for her," I added, grinning now. "She's been with us the whole time."

It took a second. Then—

"That—" he started, but I was already laughing. It was too good.

I reached for the folded ticket half hanging from his vest pocket.

I took it.

He blinked. "What are you—"

I folded it carefully, tucked it into the pocket of my dress like a keepsake.

"You won't need this where you're going," I said.

And then, right there in the center of Carsondale, under God, gossip, and the watchful eye of three shopkeepers and a cow, I found myself at the heart of the biggest scandal the town had seen since the traveling dentist ran off with the mayor's wife.

Because Major, the brother of the richest man in town, had just kissed his brother's fiancée full on the mouth. In broad daylight. With witnesses. *Children*.

And not just kissed me—*kissed* me. Like a man starving. Like he'd known me longer than my own mother, and was just now allowed to come home. There was no ring on my finger, no announcement in the paper. Just two people, holding nothing back, in the center of the square, like a pair of fools who'd finally figured it out.

The whispers started before we even pulled apart. I didn't have the good sense to care.

The town buzzed for weeks. I had neighbors dropping by with rhubarb pie and pretense, pretending to borrow sugar but really just angling to hear the story straight from the horse's mouth.

And I told it. Every time.

Because for once, it was my story to tell.

And next time you hear it back east—turned inside out, sharpened into scandal, passed around parlors like teacups— maybe I'll be a cunning mail-order bride who fell into a torrid affair with her intended's wicked brother, or a con artist, or a runaway heiress.

But just so you know:

It was me.

And it was glorious.

The Triumph of Hetty Jane Bates

SARAH MacLEAN

"I have none of the usual inducements of women to marry. Were I to fall in love, indeed, it would be a different thing! but I never have been in love; it is not my way, or my nature; and I do not think I ever shall. And, without love, I am sure I should be a fool to change such a situation as mine. Fortune I do not want; employment I do not want; consequence I do not want: I believe few married women are half as much mistress of their husband's house, as I am of Hartfield; and never, never could I expect to be so truly beloved and important; so always first and always right in any man's eyes as I am in my father's."

"But then, to be an old maid at last, like Miss Bates!"

"That is as formidable an image as you could present, Harriet; and if I thought I should ever be like Miss Bates! so silly—so satisfied—so smiling—so prosing—so undistinguishing and unfastidious—and so apt to tell every thing relative to every body about me, I would marry to-morrow. But between us, I am convinced there never can be any likeness, except in being unmarried."

"But still, you will be an old maid! and that's so dreadful!"

Jane Austen, *Emma*

A million years ago, when I was a brand-new author with one Regency under my belt, I was invited to speak to the Connecticut chapter of the Jane Austen Society of North America. After my presentation, I opened the floor to questions, and a single hand rose, belonging to a woman who had spent obvious years, lifetimes, with Austen. Did I have a favorite Austen novel? she asked.

Of course I did. Doesn't everyone? I replied with complete certainty. "*Emma*."

The room erupted into what I can only describe as disdainful murmurs, as the questioner cast a sidelong, knowing look at her companions. After their silent discussion of my shortcomings, she looked me dead in the eye and said, "You'll grow out of it."

Reader, I never grew out of it.

Emma is a banger. It's full of all the things I love in a romance—a deeply unlikable heroine who gets a real deal setdown, a mysterious relationship that is about to set the whole world aflame, a hero who is a particular flavor of Exasperated Man™, and a side character who deserves to be the heroine of the next book. Over the years, I've loved all of these aspects of *Emma*, but the romance reader in me keeps coming back to that last one.

If ever there is a character who deserves to be loved out loud, to be swept off her feet, to be the heroine of her own story, it's Miss Bates. Poor Miss Bates. Silly Miss Bates. Miss Bates, who deserves nothing but our condescension and pity, being, as Austen tells us (as Austen herself was), *neither young, handsome, rich, nor married*. Miss Bates, who is limited to three dull things in the picnic scene that has haunted me since I was fourteen years old and read it for the first time.

But what if we don't listen to Emma, that unreliable narrator who is so busy learning her lesson? What if, instead, we listen to Austen, who describes Miss Bates as *a happy woman, and a woman whom no one named without good-will*? Or what if we pay close attention to Mr. Woodhouse when he echoes his creator, describing *excellent Miss Bates* as a *thorough, worthy person*? What if we imagine Hetty Bates as the best of us?

She is worthy of such a lens: A devoted daughter. A good sister. An auntie for the ages. An excellent friend. And a capital citizen, worthy of a monument in the town square, if you ask me, for putting up with Emma and her outsized ego. In a different book, through a different lens, Miss Bates would have made an excellent heroine. She certainly deserves the treatment.

So, here we go. Justice for Miss Bates.

ONE

It was exhausting being so silly.

Harriet Jane Bates, aging spinster and oft-described flibber-tigibbet, entered the modest rental home on the edge of the town of Highbury, where she and her aging mother had lived since the death of her father, eager for quiet.

No one in the tiny village of Highbury would think Hetty interested in anything even close to quiet, what for all the ways she chirped and chattered when out in the High Street, always finding something to say—about the crispness of the air, the green of the trees, the clatter of carriage wheels, the handsomeness of a frock, the gleam of a shop window.

Hetty often found herself carrying conversations—as the eldest daughter of the village's third most recent vicar, she'd been raised to do just that, to be a listening ear, full of compassion and lacking in judgment. A kind ear. A sweet smile.

The conversations she'd been raised to have weren't supposed to be silly, though, and there'd been a time when they hadn't been. When they'd been just as she'd been raised. Soft, and sweet, and social. The kind of conversation that came with the tea and lemon-drizzle cakes vicars' wives and daughters were to excel at.

She'd been raised for the conversation of the good citizen. The welcome friend. The wife.

But somewhere between learning her mother's recipe for lemon cake and now, Hetty had made a mistake or two. Or a dozen. And with each one, what life was *supposed to have been* had given way to what life *was*.

And so, Hetty Bates lived here, quietly, on the edge of the village, a now only child of an aging mother, pretending she'd chosen this life rather than fallen into it.

Hetty did a lot of pretending. Pretending to have a lovely time at events she was invited to, thanks to the condescending kindness of others. Pretending not to notice when others rolled their eyes as she approached. Pretending not to want to scream when she was asked for the forty-third time that morning how she was, and wasn't she enjoying the lovely weather.

No one knew how to carry on a conversation with an aging spinster. Hetty imagined it was because they feared her affliction might be catching. An ague of the worst order, enough to send one to their bed. Alone. Forever.

Sometimes, she wondered if she could send a gaggle of young women scattering with a sneeze. Not that she would ever actually do it.

Instead, Hetty let them speak to her as though she was a child, with bright, false smiles and quick goodbyes and eye rolls kept at bay until backs were turned (mostly). After years of such treatment, Hetty stopped attempting to disabuse them of the idea. Instead, she let them think her a silly, featherbrained chatterbox.

Of course she was a chatterbox; noise was the only way Hetty knew to avoid silence.

Hetty had learned over the years that it was silence that carried the opinions of others. Opinions that came with a brutal sting. Things like disinterest. Or disdain. Or condescension. Or pity.

Or gratitude . . . for whatever ails anyone else in Highbury faced, at least they weren't poor Miss Bates.

Indeed, if one were to describe Miss Bates, in the plain bonnet and tiny spectacles that often convinced the uninformed that she was closer to sixty than her actual age of forty, they could have used something much worse than silly.

Silly was the best descriptor Hetty could hope for, and so she did her best to keep everyone believing that she was a kindly, aging chatterbox. Better silly than the other things she'd been called over the years. Naïve. Emptyheaded. Slow-witted.

Dull.

Yes, Hetty would take silly over the rest, because at least silly came with something that, if one squinted and tilted one's head, could look something like fondness.

That is, she could pretend it was fondness.

Just like, most days, she could pretend it didn't exhaust her to play the part of silly, poor Miss Bates, eldest, unmarried daughter of a forgotten vicar, a woman who required pity and compassion because, don't you see, girls, but for the grace of the Lord, you might be her.

There'd been a time, though. . . .

Hetty put the thought out of her mind and closed the door behind her with a quiet thump, setting her shopping basket down with the same—a bit of cheese, a loaf of yesterday's bread, two yellow apples. She reached for the fraying ribbons at her chin and called out to her mother, the sound loud in her ears as it echoed around the house, floors too hard and furniture too threadbare to mute the sharp edges of the vowels and the rising lilt at the end of her "Mummy?"

She did not expect the aging Mrs. Bates to respond—Hetty's mother had difficulty hearing without her horn and rarely had it nearby unless they had visitors. And yet—

"Hetty!" her mother called out from the front room.

Surprise flared, followed quickly by dread. Did they have visitors? She sucked in a breath and pasted a smile on her face, preparing to be silly once more, before stepping through the doorway to the front room.

Mrs. Bates was perched in the high-backed chair by the window that overlooked the High Street. The old woman squinted through the pince-nez at the bridge of her nose, staring down at a letter in her weathered hand. She was alone.

Relieved, Hetty raised her voice to a near bellow, "Is it from Jane?"

She crossed to her mother, eager for news of the newly married Jane Churchill, once Jane Fairfax, the only person who regularly wrote to the Bates women. There had been a time when Hetty had loved nothing more than doting upon young Jane, who'd been raised far from Highbury by Hetty's younger sister and her husband before she was orphaned and returned, like a gift, to Hetty and her mother for five wonderful years.

Unfortunately, when Jane turned eight, it was agreed she would be best served by living with a family of means—people with more to give her than a spinster aunt and a widowed grandmother in a tiny home on the outskirts of nowhere. Jane had moved to London and grown with knowledge and natural talents, and Hetty proudly told all who would listen (and many who preferred not to listen) about her brilliant niece.

Hetty's letters to Jane had been near religious in their regularity, filled with news of home and Highbury, and nearly a year ago, Jane had visited the little village and stunned its populace (though not Hetty) with her beauty, poise, and talent before it was revealed the young woman was also a party to a secret engagement. The engagement had quickly become marriage to a very handsome, vaguely roguish man, Mr. Frank Churchill, whose actions, though questionable, had been revealed to have noble motives, and now Jane and Frank were happily in love, preparing for a family of their own. Though Jane's letters were less frequent than they'd once been, they remained full of delightful news.

When Mrs. Bates did not respond to Hetty's question, she repeated it, closer and louder. The old woman looked up. "Oh! Hetty! It's you!"

Resisting the urge to snatch the letter from her mother's hands she tried one final time, "IS IT FROM JANE, MOTHER?"

"There's no need to shout, Hetty, really."

Hetty straightened. "Of course not."

"It's a letter from Jane."

With a prayer for sanity and patience, Hetty replied, "What does she say? Is she coming to Highbury?"

"She's coming to Highbury!"

Joy burst in Hetty's chest. "Lovely!"

"Isn't it lovely?"

A deep breath. "It is."

"She says," the old woman shouted, turning the letter to the light for better reading. "She and Mr. Churchill will stay with Mr. and Mrs. Weston for a fortnight, and she looks forward to seeing us."

"When?"

"Isn't it lovely?"

"It is," Hetty agreed. "And when will they arrive?"

"Of course we'll have to have them to tea. You shall have to make lemon-drizzle cakes!"

She raised her voice again. "Yes, of course! When?"

The old lady blinked. "We can't very well have them to tea before they arrive, can we, Hetty?"

"WHEN WILL THEY ARRIVE, MOTHER?"

As it was the first time the old woman heard the question, she calmly turned to check her source. "Thursday, three days' time."

Mrs. Bates looked up. "They've been invited to the Knightleys' Michaelmas Ball."

Hetty straightened. "Michaelmas."

Jane was returning on Michaelmas.

"Oh." Something stuttered in Hetty's chest, something she didn't dare linger on, or allow purchase. It had been too many Michaelmases since—

Her mother was still shouting the news. "Of course they have, what with how Mrs. Weston and Mrs. Knightley are so very close. She was her governess, as you know. No matter the history of Jane and Mrs. Knightley, Mrs. Knightley is too polite to allow past feelings to get in the way of present invitations to Hartfield."

Hetty had never thought Emma Knightley *too* polite, but she didn't say so. Not that she had to keep quiet—her mother couldn't hear her, anyway. "Jane also writes that Frank has news that a *baron* has let Lorimer House!" Mrs. Bates looked to Hetty. "Have you heard about such a thing? A *real* baron? In Highbury?"

"Are there such a thing as false barons?" Hetty asked, the question rhetorical as she crossed the room to fetch her mother's ear horn. If this was going to be a long conversation and Hetty was going to retain her sanity, the apparatus would be required. Hetty waited for her mother to lift the apparatus to her ear. "No, I have not heard anything of it." It was the truth. There was nothing silly about barons coming to Highbury, so no one would have thought to mention it to Miss Bates.

"No need to shout, Hetty. Please."

"Of course not."

"Jane says that Frank's father reports the baron has let the house for half a year, while he decides where he will set his seat! How exciting! Can you imagine! A baron!"

Hetty could not imagine.

"Isn't it exciting! Jane and a baron! I wonder if he is unmarried! Jane reports nothing of that!"

"If he is unmarried, Emma Knightley will surely make quick work of the poor man," Hetty said.

The wry tone was lost in the translation through her mother's ear horn. "Oh, you're right, of course. Mrs. Knightley will find him a proper match immediately. Likely at the Michaelmas Ball! How exciting that we shall be there to witness it! And with Jane, too!"

Hetty gave a little sigh at the reference to the newlyweds' first country dance. She'd been expecting to attend, obviously. It was impossible to avoid such a public event when one's aging mother required a chaperone for her favorite pastime—sitting on the sidelines of a ballroom sipping too warm ratafia in an even warmer room packed with the whole town.

But Hetty had been planning to make their appearance as quick as possible, as the hostess of this particular party had made it more than clear what she truly felt about Hetty Bates—that she was dull. So dull, indeed, that she couldn't keep herself from running her mouth with more dull things than any could manage. A champion dullardess.

With Jane in attendance, and whatever excitement was to come of the newly arrived baron, Hetty feared the ball would no longer be a quick diversion, but instead, hours of making too loud, too silly conversation. Quite dull, indeed.

Too consumed by her own dread, Hetty was barely listening to her mother when the old lady said, "Oh! And I nearly forgot. A package arrived while you were out."

Despite its casual delivery, the announcement was something of a shock. Packages did not arrive for Hetty. Ever. Packages required either expense the Bates ladies were unable to afford, or friendship to which the Bates ladies no longer laid claim.

Nevertheless, when the older woman waved a hand in the direction of the brown-paper-wrapped package in question, Hetty could not deny the truth. Someone had, indeed, sent her a package.

The large, flat box dwarfed the low table by the sitting room door, large enough that Hetty would not have missed it had she not been distracted earlier, eager for news of Jane. She did not miss it now, however, heart in her throat, pulse pounding for no clear reason as she removed the outside paper to reveal a box the color of fresh cream, a beautiful, golden *H*, stylized and swirling, and beneath it, a single word in gilded print: *Mayfair*.

There was no reason whatsoever for Hetty to have received a package from Mayfair. She'd never even been to London. Indeed, the only time she'd ever left Highbury had been twenty years earlier.

And still, here she was, staring down at the most extravagant box she'd ever seen. A box worth more than the Bates ladies lived on for an entire year. What could possibly be inside?

A card was inside, tucked into perfectly folded muslin. Hetty slid it from its seat, reading the single line of black text against stark ecru.

For the Michaelmas Ball.

Her brows knit in confusion, and she peered into the box.

"What is it?" Her mother, from a distance. From miles away.

"I don't . . ." Hetty shook her head and reached for the crisp muslin, tucked with precision, the folds hiding what was underneath. Pulling the ends loose, she opened the fabric, revealing more fabric, altogether different.

Her breath caught. It was a dress. She reached for it, hesitant, as though it might disappear.

It did not disappear, however. Not as she touched it, letting her fingertips trail over the silk of the dress, a pale, beautiful blue, the color of a robin's egg. Her confusion only compounded as she lifted it from the box, waves of silk and gossamer spilling to the floor, soft as butterfly wings.

And then the confusion disappeared, replaced with awe.

"Oh!" Mrs. Bates gave voice to Hetty's shock and surprise. "How pretty!"

It wasn't pretty, though. It was wildly more, with its cap sleeves embroidered with silver thread, and the tiny filigree of lace at the neck—a neck that was lower than anything Hetty had worn since her own coming-out twenty-one years earlier—and the embroidered panel marking its empire waist, and its layers of skirts that shimmered like moonstone.

No, it wasn't pretty. It was the most beautiful thing Hetty had ever seen, and the most magical—as it seemed to have arrived from nowhere, like a gift from a fairy godmother, bestowed with a promise of magic.

Except it was not from a fairy godmother, as old Mrs. Bates was quick to exclaim. "How very kind! A gift from Mrs. Knightley! How very kind. How very thoughtful. That she might condescend to us in such a way. A new dress! We haven't had one of those in the house in a decade! How very kind!"

Hetty winced at the words, loud and discordant and unwelcome and so obviously true. For who else in Highbury had the means to deliver such a frock to the doorstep of poor Miss Bates but Emma Woodhouse, who had surely felt the frock a proper penance.

And suddenly the dress wasn't so beautiful. Instead, it was a reminder of the truth of Emma's feelings about Hetty—of the whole village's feelings, really: Silly. Dull.

Hetty dropped the dress into the box, her fingertips singed with disappointment and frustration.

You see, there had been a time when Hetty Jane Bates had not been at all dull.

TWO

Twenty-One Years Earlier

There had never been such a lovely night, Hetty thought as she exited the Hartfield ballroom through the large open doors, breathless and laughing after a country reel, her seventh dance of the evening.

There were twelve on the dance card that hung from the end of Hetty's fan—the Woodhouses knew how to host a country ball—and every dance was claimed by a young man from the village. Hetty, nineteen and in her second year out, was by all accounts a success.

She'd be married by summer, her mother had pronounced in triumph earlier that morning. And what a triumph it was, with Jane, the youngest Bates sister, out and only weeks from becoming Mrs. Captain John Fairfax. This was Hetty's fifth proper dance of the season, and the fifth at which her card was entirely full—a gift horse Hetty knew she should not look in the mouth, but one that was quite tiring if she were being honest, for a full dance card made for very little fresh air.

And so, Hetty had finished her reel and weaved quickly through the throngs of revelers inside, begging Jane to play innocent about her sister's whereabouts as Hetty made her way to the fresh air beyond the ballroom. Somehow, miraculously, the balcony was empty, and Hetty stepped to its edge, taking a deep breath and releasing it in a long sigh to the night.

"That sounded glorious."

Hetty's spine shot straight at the words, coming bold and deep from the darkness. She turned toward them, peering into the shadows, where she could barely make out the figure of a man.

She should turn away. Head back inside.

Run back inside.

But no one cared less about *should* than a young woman heady with the power of a full dance card, which was the only explanation for her reply, decidedly un-vicar's-daughter-like. She lifted her chin and, practicing her most flirtatious tone, said, "I beg your pardon. We have not been properly introduced."

He stepped from the shadows at that, and Hetty immediately regretted the words. This man was not for practice. This man was for a proper hunt. He was tall and lean, clad in tight fawn breeches and a navy coat, his shirt bright white and his cravat perfectly, artfully tied. Hetty had never been to the coast, but she imagined his hair was the precise color of sand, falling in waves as though marked by the tide. And his face—there was a Roman statue in the fountain along the drive of the Knightley estate, and this man could have been cut from the same marble for the angle of his jaw and the line of his nose.

And perhaps Hetty could have resisted the sum of all these handsome parts, but to make it all worse—or better? She would need some time to consider which—he was smiling, youthful and perfect and disarming and winning and unexpected, and something flipped deep in her chest as he moved toward her, steps long and even and more confident than she'd ever been in her life.

"Edward Harris." He dipped his chin, a tiny, proper bow, and Hetty bit back a laugh. "Godson to Mrs. Weston. Now we've been introduced."

"On the contrary," she said. "Now you've been impertinent

enough to introduce yourself to me. We have not been introduced. We haven't met."

He grinned. "Yes, but you don't require introduction, Miss Bates."

"I beg your pardon—I absolutely require—" She blinked, surprise flooding her. "How is it that you know my name?"

"Not know the name of the prettiest girl in the room? What kind of gentleman do you think I am?"

She gave a little shocked laugh. "Not any kind of gentleman, if I'm being honest."

He laughed as well, placing a hand on his chest and smiling broadly. "I aim to convince you otherwise, Miss Harriet Bates," he said. "I know a great many things about you. You are eldest daughter of Silas Bates, Vicar of Highbury. Your sister, Jane, is one year younger and, in one month's time, will be married to Captain John Fairfax. And your dance card is tragically full, which is why I had to steal time on the balcony instead of during a quadrille." That chin dipped again. "Perhaps it's not a great deal of things."

Warmth flooded Hetty at the words, and she realized she much preferred meeting on the balcony than the to-and-fro and stolen seconds of conversation they would have had during the quadrille. "It is more than I know of you, Mr. Harris." She tilted her head to study him. "How long are you with the Westons?"

He tilted a chin toward the ballroom. "Three weeks. They have been kind enough to host me until I leave."

"Leave for where?"

He smiled. "I've a fortune to make, Miss Bates, if I'm to have a hope of winning a girl like you."

She couldn't help her laugh even as his bold words sent a blush over her cheeks. "With a tongue as silver as yours, I don't think you'll have any trouble winning a girl . . . like me or otherwise."

"Is that a promise?"

Oh, he was dangerous, this man—too young to take seriously, and anyway, too handsome for a vicar's daughter. This was the kind of man who would hie off to faraway lands and make himself a name before winning himself a wife worthy of it. The thought made Hetty strangely wistful, as though they'd already lived a life, and now it was gone, lost to a different future. A different woman.

It was an odd flight of fancy after a few stolen minutes on a balcony.

She smiled, and let the fancy continue. "It depends on how long you intend to take to make this fortune of yours and return."

He nodded, sagely. "You cannot be expected to wait. There are any number of men who would happily take my place." He reached for the dance card dangling from the end of her fan, glancing down at it. "Twelve, at least."

Her breath went shallow at his nearness; he was warm and smelled lovely, like cedar and spice. When she replied, it was quiet, like a secret between them. "You should have introduced yourself earlier in the evening."

His response was nearly a whisper. "And missed our moment on the balcony?"

"Where are you going?" she asked. "In three weeks?"

"I've a place on a merchant vessel; we're headed to America."

Her eyes went wide. "America!" A world away. "I would not have thought we'd be very welcome there."

"They're not so bad, now that the war is over and there is a need for trade on the wind," he said.

"It's a long journey." Long enough that he'd forget her.

"It's a good one for men like me, looking to buy my own vessel and make my own fortune."

"Well," she said, the wistfulness returned. "Sounds like you're headed for an adventure. I hope someday it brings you back to Highbury."

He watched her carefully. "Do you?"

"Though, if I may," she forced a teasing tone she did not feel, "I recommend doing away with this habit of lurking on balconies and startling unsuspecting ladies."

"It's been a successful habit tonight, Miss Bates."

She laughed. "Don't fret, Mr. Harris. I imagine you'll have no difficulty whatsoever getting American ladies to speak to you." She cast a glance back at the ballroom, the windows bright with golden light, revealing Mrs. Bates searching the crowd—for Hetty, no doubt. "In fact, I'm afraid if I speak any more to you tonight, your adventure will be cut very short, as my parents will think us more than passing strangers."

"Nonsense," he retorted. "We haven't even been introduced."

"My point exactly," she quipped, knowing she had to leave, because she was enjoying this too much. Enjoying *him* too much. Turning for the ballroom, she whispered, "It was very nice not to meet you, Mr. Harris."

Hetty made it only a few steps before he called after her. "Miss Bates."

She knew she shouldn't stop. Shouldn't look. But he was so tall and handsome and alive, and she couldn't resist.

When she did, it was to find his gaze on hers, steady and dark. "As I did not have a chance to secure a dance tonight . . ."

Her heart stuttered in her chest. "Yes?"

". . . perhaps you would let me call on you?"

"You're leaving," she said, without thinking. Too eager for thinking. "You said three weeks."

Bright white teeth flashed in the light, dangerous and tempt-
ing. "Much can happen in three weeks, Miss Bates."

Too much, Hetty thought. She should say no. She should forget about this beautiful young man and his beautiful smile and all
the promises she already wished he'd make to her.

She was to marry by summer, and he'd be on a boat then,
headed across the ocean, to the other side of the world.

But much could happen in three weeks.

And the promise of that was suddenly enough.

"You may call on me," she said, delighting in the way his lips
curved, pure satisfaction. And then she added, "If you can secure
a proper introduction."

Edward did secure a proper introduction, arriving at the vicarage
the next morning with Mr. Weston in tow, having no doubt been
coerced into fabricating a necessary conversation about the needs
of the Highbury church, and adding, "Oh, and may I introduce
my wife's godson, Mr. Harris?"

Reverend Bates was more than happy for the introduction, as
were his wife and daughters, the youngest immediately sensing
a game afoot and doing what sisters have done for eternity—
providing welcome parental distraction while their sibling
found reason to head into the gardens with a newly introduced
gentleman.

After that afternoon, Edward found his way to the vicarage
daily, always with a fresh reason for it. He offered help in the
churchyard, to oil the gears of the bell tower, and at one point
even arrived with a parcel of lamb (he'd somehow convinced
the butcher that the vicarage was on his way). But it did not take
long for everyone in the Bates family to see that Edward's motives

were not altogether pure. Indeed, as Jane pointed out one evening while drying a piece of crockery, his motives were Hetty.

Not that the Bateses seemed to mind such a thing. It was Hetty who had to remind them again and again that Edward wasn't forever. He was leaving in three weeks, and then two weeks, and then one week, and his motives were irrelevant. He would soon be on a ship, across an ocean, around the world. And Hetty was not invited.

It did not matter that her family had decided to like him.

It did not matter, either, that Hetty had fallen in love with him.

One really could not blame her, what with the way he charmed her mother, and befriended her future brother-in-law, and threw his back into whatever work her father found for him. Hetty was slightly ashamed to admit that she liked that last bit the most, the way his strong, sinewy frame moved as he easily shifted pews and lifted boxes and pushed wheelbarrows.

Apparently, working on a merchant ship made one very strong.

Strong enough that when they found themselves caught in a particularly soggy bit of pasture while walking the vicarage grounds, Edward didn't hesitate to lift Hetty up into his arms and carry her through, setting her down on solid earth before offering, "Your dress is too pretty to muddy the hem, I think, Miss Bates."

"Thank you."

"That blush is all the thanks I need," he said, reaching out to pass a thumb over her rosy cheek.

She leaned into the touch, giving them both what they wished, his palm warm against her face, cradling it carefully as their gazes met, and two weeks of daily walks and conversation and longing surfaced, and Hetty felt like she might go mad if she did not tell him what was in her heart.

Edward spoke first, however. "That's not true, though, is it? The blush isn't nearly enough. None of this is."

She recognized the emotion in his words. Longing. Desire. Frustration. "Edward," she whispered, lifting her hand to the back of his, wishing she could ask him to stay. Forever. "Don't . . ."

"I'm going to miss you terribly, you know," he said, his thumb still moving, stroking over her skin, setting fire to her.

"I am afraid," she replied.

His brows shot together, his jaw going hard as marble, readying for battle. "Of what?"

Pleasure thrummed through her at the warning in the question, like he'd defend her from whatever enemy appeared. "It's silly."

"Nothing about you is silly, Hetty Bates," he replied. "Tell me what ails you, love. I shall fight it off."

Love. He'd taken to calling her that over the weeks, and every time, it set Hetty's heart to racing. She knew it didn't mean anything. It was an endearment that some used so easily. He didn't mean it the way she did. The way she would if she said it to him. She pushed the thought away. "I know you're leaving," she said. "I know you're headed to the wide world. To adventure."

He didn't speak, but his warm brown eyes watched her with utter focus.

"But a part of me," she pressed on, "a part of me hopes you'll remember me. This. Even after you've seen the world. Even when the adventure is over."

"Hetty," he whispered, his other hand rising to cup her cheek, so he was cradling her face, tilting it up to the sun. To his gaze.

"I'm afraid you'll forget me," she whispered.

He was silent for a long moment, long enough that she wondered if she'd said the wrong thing. When embarrassment threatened to consume her, he shook his head. "No. Never."

And he kissed her.

If she were being honest, Hetty had been waiting for Edward to kiss her since the moment she'd met him on the balcony at the Woodhouse ball. She'd lain awake long after the candles had been snuffed, staring into the darkness, wondering what it would be like if he did, how it would feel if he touched her, whether the scent of him, cedar and spice, would wrap itself around her. Whether she'd like it.

She hadn't really had to worry about that last bit. Of course she would like it. She couldn't imagine Edward Harris doing anything at all, ever, that she didn't like. Except leave.

But he wasn't leaving. Not in that moment. In that moment, he was kissing her.

And it was magnificent.

Oh, she liked it. Very, very much. He was tall and warm and everything she'd imagined, and the kiss he gave her, it was everything kisses should be—at least, everything Hetty thought they should be. A taste of temptation. A taste of something else, something a vicar's daughter absolutely should not be able to identify. *Sin*.

Not that she was going to stop.

Instead, Hetty reveled in him, loving the way his hands slid into her hair, mussing her tightly pinned curls as she matched his caress, threading her own fingers through his soft, sandy waves.

And then he wrapped her in his arms and pulled her closer, tighter, sliding his tongue over her lower lip, a question she quickly answered, eager for more of him. Eager to be a part of him.

This kiss was dangerous. The kind that ruined a girl for all others. But Hetty didn't mind, for she was already ruined. Already gone for Edward Harris.

The kiss lingered, long and mind-altering, soft and sweet and so full of pleasure she forgot where they were. Why. For how long.

And when he released her, pressing soft kisses across her

cheek to her ear, and whispered, "You are perfect," she believed him. And when he added, "I'll never forget you, Hetty, because I'm never going to let you go," she believed that, too.

After the stolen time in the pasture, Hetty and Edward's walks became longer, farther afield. They strayed farther away from the vicarage, to the folly on the far ridge bordering the lands of Salterton Abbey, where no one would see them. Where no one would interrupt them if their kisses became more frequent, more ardent, more exciting, more consuming, *more*.

Where no one would find them if the kisses became something else, entirely.

Their last week together was remarkable, full of secrets and longing and the words Hetty had been too afraid to speak, now tumbling out of both of them. Honest and forthright in the way only first love could be—an adventure all of its own.

But love could not keep life at bay, and on Edward's final afternoon in Highbury, as they lay wrapped in each other's arms at the top of the folly, the springtime sun teasing them with warmth every time it emerged from the clouds, Hetty prayed for time to stop as she pressed her ear to Edward's chest, and he held her more tightly than he'd ever done before, and she listened to his heartbeat, strong and true and *hers*. Always hers.

"I'm coming back," he whispered, the sound seeming to come from deep in his chest. "For you."

"What if you didn't go? I don't need a fortune, Edward. I need you."

He pressed his brow to hers. "I need you, as well, my love. But I'm nothing close to the husband you deserve."

"We'll manage—" He stopped her words with a kiss, releasing her only when she melted into him.

"We won't have to manage. I'll be back by Michaelmas. We'll feed each other the last of the blackberries."

"Six months," she said, hating the words. The torture in them. "Half a year."

"Will you wait for me?"

It was a mad question. "Of course I'll wait for you." She'd wait a year. Ten. Longer, if she had to. Forever.

"Six months, and I'll have my own ship, and I'll ask your father proper, and we'll post banns, and we'll marry—and you'll wear blue."

She lifted her head. "I will?"

He nodded, the decision made. "You look beautiful in blue."

"I do?"

He kissed her nose. "You do. But I'm telling you your future."

"I didn't know you had such a gift." She grinned and let him.

"After we marry—it'll be a house for us. Here in Highbury, if you like, and a passel of babies if you like the sound of it."

She liked it very much, indeed. Six months. She could do that. "And everyone will call me Mrs. Harris."

He grinned. "Say it again."

"Mrs. Harris," she whispered. "Mrs. Edward Harris."

"Yes. They'll call you that," he said. "And when we're together, I shall call you my Hetty."

It was her turn to kiss. His to melt.

"I want it now," she said. "I don't want you to go."

"I'll make it up to you," he said. "Promise you'll let me. Promise you'll wait for me."

"Yes," she whispered, happier than she'd ever been, even as her heart was broken open with longing. Half a year wasn't so long. And then, they'd have forever. "Of course."

Another kiss, and another, and a dozen more throughout the afternoon, as the sun sank toward the horizon. Every one a promise. *Six months, and I'll be back. You'll have everything you ever dreamed.*

And she believed him.

THREE

He didn't come back.
　　　Not at Michaelmas.
Not for the October harvest.
Not in November, when the days turned short and the wind turned cold.
And by Christmas, Hetty realized he was not coming back.
Which meant she had to leave.

FOUR

Have you heard? There's a *baron* in Highbury!"

The Knightleys' Michaelmas Ball was every inch the crush Highbury had expected, everyone in the town eager to attend, eager to see their host and hostess in proper marital bliss. The Knightleys had married only half a year prior, and had immediately taken up residence at Hartfield to be closer to Mrs. Knightley's aging father, who enjoyed being caretaked more than most.

There might have been a time, years ago, when Hetty's own experience caretaking Mrs. Bates would have brought her closer to the newly wedded Mrs. Knightley, but it was difficult to see past what had transpired between them in the months and years leading up to Emma's marriage, and beyond. Hetty was perfectly aware of her lack of fortune, monetary or otherwise, but she couldn't help resenting Emma for drawing a line beneath it at every possible chance.

The dress, for example. What should have felt like a kindness instead felt like mockery when Hetty put it on earlier that evening.

It was exactly as beautiful as it had been in the box. The kind of dress a girl dreamed of having, because it made one feel just as beautiful as the frock. But Hetty Bates was no girl, and so when she peered into the looking glass in the front room of her threadbare home, she did not feel that she'd been made beautiful by the silk and gossamer and silver threads.

She felt silly.

Like a child, playing pretend in her mother's Sunday dress.

Before she could take it off, however, her mother had entered and gasped her delight at the thing with a too-loud "Oh, Hetty!" and "You look so youthful!" and "Why, I don't think I've ever seen you without a cap!"

"Of course you've seen me without a cap, Mother," she snapped. "I wasn't born a spinster." Luckily, the old lady didn't have her ear horn, so she did not catch the full blast of Hetty's irritation. She didn't deserve it. Not really.

"Is there something wrong with the frock?" her mother asked, replying to whatever she'd imagined Hetty had said.

"No," Hetty said. It was not the dress; it was the day.

It was the lifetime.

"I don't much care for Michaelmas," she admitted softly.

A long pause before her mother said, "That's nice."

"We should bring your ear horn, Mother," Hetty had replied as a knock sounded on the door, heralding a too-charming Frank Churchill, arrived with the Westons' second-best carriage to take them to Hartfield.

And now Hetty was posted at the far side of the ballroom, near a collection of potted ferns and the seats reserved for the event's most seasoned attendees, searching the crowd for Jane and listening to Charlotte Tilbury chirp about the mysterious baron in their midst.

"I had heard of the baron!" Hetty chirped in reply, falling easily into her role. "How very exciting! Darling Jane wrote to us and said he's let Lorimer House! It really is quite exciting."

"It is, isn't it?" Mrs. Tilbury said. "Have you heard anything of him? I do wonder if he is unmarried?"

Charlotte had three daughters, two of marriageable age, and was always on the lookout for eligible gentlemen upon whom to foist them, so Hetty knew the script. "One can hope, my dear!"

"Indeed!" Charlotte replied, breathless with dreams of a fresh, titled son-in-law.

"I heard he's not just a baron," Mrs. Pearson said, lifting her chin to peer through her spectacles at the assembly. Hetty held back a little smile at the words—as though a title in Highbury were *just* anything. "I heard he's *also* a military hero."

Of course he was. Mysterious new gentlemen in Highbury were always kings of men—titled, heroic, and the gossip would soon report he had fifty thousand pounds a year, no doubt. The truth would surely be less exciting. He would be revealed to be a man of middling age, interest, and fortune, and everyone would return to reason.

Hetty played her part, nonetheless. "A baron *and* a military hero," she said breathlessly. "How exciting! And I imagine he's quite wealthy, as well."

"Oh, I'm quite sure of that!"

The truth was, Hetty wasn't interested in the baron. Or the military hero. She was interested in Jane, as she hadn't yet seen the young woman and eagerly awaited their reunion.

"Aunt Hetty!" As though summoned by her thoughts, Jane appeared at her shoulder, tall and beautiful and bright-eyed, and joy burst in Hetty's chest at the look of her.

"Darling Jane!" she said, pulling her into a tight embrace before releasing the younger woman to study her carefully. "You look very well indeed."

"I am," Jane said. "And so happy. Wildly, wonderfully happy now that Frank and I are finally settled."

There was nothing Hetty liked so well as that news, and she turned to shout to Mrs. Bates, "LOOK, MOTHER! IT IS JANE!"

"Hello, Grandmama," Jane said, crouching to greet the older woman, pink silk skirts blooming around her. "You all look very deep in conversation!"

"Oh, Jane!" Mrs. Bates and Mrs. Pearson immediately drew Jane into their gossip. "We are discussing the new resident of Highbury!"

Jane looked to Hetty, who quickly explained. "The baron you wrote of. Everyone is wondering when he'll make an appearance."

"Well," Jane said, rising with a grace that never failed to send pride bursting in Hetty's chest, "I can answer that! He's here tonight!"

"Is he!" Charlotte Tilbury sounded as though she might require a smelling salt. "I must tell the girls!" She was gone before anyone could reply, and Hetty met Jane's gaze, sharing a silent laugh with her niece.

"She ought to be careful," Hetty said quietly. "A turned ankle will do her no favors in introducing her daughters to the man."

Jane leaned in quietly. "I don't think he is the type to be interested in meeting the Tilbury daughters, honestly, Auntie."

"Why not?" asked Mrs. Pearson.

"It's just that Captain Harris is rather . . . too distinguished for an ingenue, I think."

It took a moment for the name to find Hetty, but when it did, her breath caught in her throat. *Captain Harris.*

It was nonsense, of course. Harris was a perfectly normal name. She wouldn't have even noticed if it wasn't Michaelmas. He was always on her mind at Michaelmas. Besides, Jane said *Captain* Harris. Edward wasn't a captain of anything. He hadn't gone to war. He'd been on a merchant ship.

A ship, though.

No. Impossible.

"Distinguished," Mrs. Pearson repeated. "That means old."

"Not at all!" Jane replied. "He's no older than my father would have been. And a lovely man. Godson to the first Mrs. Weston. And he's been to Highbury before, apparently."

The temperature in the room was unbearable. Hetty was

finding it difficult to breathe. And then Jane said, "As a matter of fact, he asked after you, Auntie. Perhaps you—"

Hetty spun away from the conversation, desperate for air. Across the room, the large doors were open, the night sky beyond. She stepped toward them, barely containing the urge to make a mad dash for them. . . .

And there he was.

Older. Broader. Rougher somehow, despite the perfect cut of his clothing, each item tucked and hemmed and sewn to his exact dimensions. And they were magnificent dimensions. Twenty-one years had done Edward Harris very well, adding muscle to his lean frame and wisdom to his open face and silver to the hair at his temples, now darker brown than it had been. He was not *a lovely man*, as Jane had described him.

He was overwhelmingly handsome, damn him.

And he was staring directly at Hetty.

Hating herself for the weakness, she drank him in, this man she'd dreamed of for years, late at night, when she was alone and no one could judge her for it. But in those late hours, she dreamed of him young and safe and impossible.

There was nothing safe about this man.

Nothing young, either. He was well and truly grown.

He remained impossible, at least, swarmed with the citizenry of Highbury—fathers eager for a chat about whatever money and power he'd accrued in the last two decades, mothers eager to thrust their unmarried daughters in his path. Hetty watched them surround him with delight and curiosity, ignoring the twist of emotion that coiled through her. Refusing to confront that familiar wistfulness that had always marked their time together—a curling plume of what might have been, disappearing like smoke.

A young debutante was shoved into his path, the poor girl barely able to keep her balance, and he looked away from Hetty, setting her free as he delivered a patient smile to the sacrifice, inquiring about the young woman's well-being. At Hetty's elbow, someone heaved a feminine sigh.

She didn't look to see who. Hetty didn't begrudge the woman, as she would have done the same, truthfully, if she'd been able to breathe at all.

Because he was looking at Hetty again. No. Worse. He was crossing the room, headed for her. There was no escaping him, she realized. Nowhere to go in this room full of people—why did everyone have to like Emma Woodhouse so very much? Her gaze fell on the collection of palms in the corner. Perhaps she could—

"Hello, Hetty."

Even his voice had changed. It had gone deeper, richer. More seasoned. And her name on his tongue sent a shiver through her, just as it always had. She turned back to him. "You shouldn't—"

"No?" he asked. "Time may have passed, but we have been properly introduced, have we not? Is there a statute of limitations on introductions?"

How dare he joke? How dare he simply turn up after all this time? And looking like this? As though the world had done nothing but make him stronger, smarter, handsomer, more wonderful? And Hetty—she'd been left behind. She swallowed back the words, settling on "There is a statute of limitations on our friendship."

Something flashed in his gaze, familiar and fleeting. "Then we must begin again." His gazed flickered over her shoulder. "Mrs. Churchill, if you would be so kind as to introduce us?"

Jane stepped into view, looking absolutely delighted by whatever was to take place. *Oh, dear. Jane.* Before Hetty could stop her,

the young woman said, "Captain Edward Harris, Baron Courtenay, may I present my dear aunt, Miss Hetty Bates."

The irony of Jane reintroducing them was not lost on Hetty,
and she loosed a hysterical bit of laughter before he reached out
his hand and she was unable to make any sound at all, because
manners and habit and her own desire to please everyone around
her, at all times, had her placing her hand into his. Which was a
mistake, because when they touched, it made her think of all the
other times they'd touched. Of all the other *ways* they'd touched.
And she hated him for leaving her all over again.

She attempted to snatch her hand back.

He did not allow it, instead executing a perfect bow over it
and saying, "Miss Bates, it is a pleasure to meet you." He looked
up, his brown eyes sparkling as they'd done decades earlier. "And
may I say, you look beautiful in blue."

You look beautiful in blue.

He'd said it to her then, the night before he'd left. When he'd
told her future and predicted she'd wear blue on their wedding
day. Except there hadn't been a wedding day, or any other.

Realization dawned. "You sent it."

Edward didn't have to admit it. She could see it in his eyes,
along with a dozen other things she dared not name.

"Why?" Was it some kind of jest? With the world watching?
She looked around, a dozen people nearby, trying desperately to
look while appearing not to look. The Eltons. The Westons. The
Martins. The Knightleys. All of Highbury, here to inspect their
silly, dull neighbor and whatever nonsense this was. *Awful.*

She tried another snatch of the hand, but he once again
wouldn't allow it, instead inspecting her wrist. "Where is your
dance card?"

The snatch became a successful yank. "I don't have one."

"Why not?"

Because forty-year-old spinsters don't dance. They're lucky enough to be invited at all. She lifted a chin. "I don't dance."

"That's not true," he said, the words coming on an edge of something like frustration. "You love to dance. I've watched you dance."

"Well, I don't dance anymore."

"I want my dance, Hetty. I've been waiting for it."

But he hadn't been waiting for her, had he? Edward had lived a whole life without her. It had been *Hetty* who had waited. While her whole life had passed her by.

And whatever this game was, it was not entertaining. She shook her head. "You don't get one."

"Why?"

She could feel the heat of the assembly watching, growing more and more curious. And her mother. And Jane, who said with soft grace, "Go on, Auntie. You deserve a dance."

Jane.

Hetty shook her head. Not with Edward. No. Captain Harris. No. *Lord* Courtenay. *Lord!* How on earth had that happened? He'd had barely tuppence to rub together when they'd known each other. And now . . . he was so far above the aging spinster the whole town condescended to be kind to that it was a wonder she could see him.

But she could see him. And that lit a fire in her, a fire that arrived with a little, chaotic laugh. "Because you left, *my lord*, or *Captain*, or whoever you are. And I never danced again."

"Oh." A soft exhale of surprise from Jane, who'd certainly never seen Hetty say anything so forcefully ever before.

Edward, on the other hand, had seen it many times. He'd been the only person ever to see the truth in her. And he'd left. "Hetty," her name came on a soft, deep rumble, like he'd been saying it for twenty-one years in her mind. "Hetty. I'm back."

"No." She shook her head again, feeling sad and angry and a little bit wild. "You're too late."

She pushed past him then, crossing the room, pushing past the revelers, desperate for air. She found it beyond the large doors, out on the balcony, beneath the night sky, her hands gripping the cold marble balustrade tightly as she looked to the darkness and willed the tears that threatened not to come.

And it was only then, as she attempted to pull herself together, that Hetty realized her mistake. She hadn't left him.

She'd returned to the place where it had all begun.

"I'm sorry."

He'd followed her, of course. It seemed that one thing that had not changed about Lord/Baron/Captain/Harris/Courtenay/Whatever He Called Himself Now was that he did not take no for an answer.

At least he'd apologized.

She did not look to him as he drew close, coming to stand alongside her. Did not speak as he gripped the balustrade, his strong hand mere inches from her own. Instead, she stared down at that hand, wondering at the white scars that crossed the back of it. Wounds she might have cared for if he'd returned. If they'd had the life he'd teased her with.

"Let me explain," he said, deep and quiet, like a secret. "I came back."

She nodded. "So you said."

"No," he said, the word clipped, as though he wanted to say a dozen things but instead settled on, "Not today. Not now. I mean, I came back then."

Disbelief sent her gaze flying to his face in the shadows. "That's a lie. I was here. I was waiting for you. I stood by the window for hours. I waited. And waited. Through the autumn. Into the winter." *As long as I could.*

He nodded. "There were terrible seas on the voyage back—waves so high I'd never seen the like. We were tossed far off course and landed in Gibraltar, where we were commandeered and conscripted to fight."

She sucked in a breath. "You saw war."

He nodded. "Like my father and his father before him. A family business of sorts." He huffed a wry laugh. "But *I* didn't die."

Thank heavens.

"After we held the day at St. Vincent, I returned. I came straight to you. Here. In Highbury."

"When?" The question was more breath than sound.

"April the twelfth. In ninety-seven."

Her heart began to pound. "I wasn't here."

"Your mother wouldn't see me. Your father barely looked at me. I was told you were north with your sister. That you had met a man. That you were to be married." He looked away, to the darkness. "To a man of means, someone worthy of you, your father said." He looked away, lost to the memory. "I left that day. Returned to the navy. Became a captain of a different sort. Traveled the world for something I wanted as much as—"

You.

Her heart was in her throat, the words spilling out of her. "That April, I was not here. I was north, with . . . Jane. But the rest—it's not true. There was no man. There was no marriage. My father, he lied, and he shouldn't have. They never told me. I should have known. I deserved to know."

She had deserved to know, if not when he arrived, then after, when she returned to Highbury, devastated with sorrow and loss and longing for what could never be, before she packed it away and guarded it fiercely with chirping and chattering and nonsense.

"He was protecting you," Edward said, too kindly. Too decent. "I was not a safe wager for something so precious as his daughter. A sailor with nothing to show for it."

"What nonsense," Hetty said, letting the anger come. "There was no one else. Not then, or since. There was only—"

You.

His hand moved closer, the smallest of his fingers pressed against the smallest of hers, and he whispered fervently, "I thought it best. Had I known, Hetty . . . I would have moved heaven and earth to get back to you. To be with you. To keep my promise."

They stood like that, barely touching, staring into the darkness, for what felt like forever, stealing the quiet of company against the roar of the party inside and all the things they wished to say.

"You are a baron now," she said finally. "A far cry from the boy who left to find his fortune."

He scoffed. "I'm still that boy. No one is more surprised than I am about the title—a distant cousin of a distant cousin of a distant cousin died, and I was the last of a very long line."

"Lord Courtenay."

"Don't call me that," he said harshly. "Let me be Edward to you, still." A beat, as he looked to the sky and said, "Cor! The way my heart pounded when I heard young Frank was to marry, and to whom. *The Bateses*, Captain Weston wrote to me. *Perhaps you remember the old vicar.*"

He turned toward her, his face half shadow, half light. A tiny smile. "I've never in my life replied to a letter so quickly. A full page of nonsensical felicitations before allowing myself to inquire after the old vicar's daughter. Do you realize the strength it took not to ask all I wanted to know? Had you ever returned to Highbury? Had you married? Were you well? Happy? As happy as I might have made you?"

"I returned," she answered, her heart pounding in her chest. "I did not marry. I was well, but not very happy. How could I be?" His hand settled on hers, the warm weight shock and comfort, and such temptation. The only way he could touch her, in full view of God and Emma Knightley's assembly. Hetty lowered her voice to a whisper and lifted her gaze to his. "I was not with you."

"Hetty," her name came on a ragged whisper. "I should have found you. I wanted to. For years, I lay under the stars on ships around the world and imagined what would have been if I'd come for you and stolen you away from the man you married. I hated that man you married. I still do."

She smiled. "He does not exist."

"It doesn't matter. I hate him anyway. The number of times I marched into your estate house and laid him flat out, tossed you over my shoulder, and absconded with you."

"To the high seas? Like a pirate?"

"Finally putting all those years on the water to good use."

A little giggle bubbled up from deep within her, a sound she hadn't made in ages, since she was young and full of something like hope.

He lifted his hand in the wake of it, like he might be able to catch the sound. Keep it. He met her eyes. "You look just the same. Just as I dreamed."

It wasn't true, but she didn't correct him.

"And I was right. You do look beautiful in blue."

A blush bloomed high on her cheeks. "I am too old to look beautiful."

"No," he said, leaning toward her, the words infinitely soft, so close to her ear she shivered with the warmth of them. "You were beautiful then, you are beautiful now, and you shall be beautiful forever. And if you'll let me, I'd very much like to tell you that every day from now on—to make up for all the days I've missed."

She couldn't have stopped herself from turning toward him in that moment if everyone inside the ballroom had tumbled onto the balcony. When she did, he was there, so close, so warm, wrapping her in the scent of cedar and spice, casting her back to their youth, to when Hetty Jane Bates did wild, wonderful things.

Like kissing the man she loved.

Their lips touched and she sighed, and a deep rumble sounded in his chest, familiar and perfect, and Hetty set her hand to the new, wide expanse of him as though she could settle the beast within.

She woke it, instead. His hand came to her hair, holding her still as he took over the caress, deep and delicious until it felt like plunder, like the pirate he'd promised to be.

And it was magnificent.

After long moments, they broke the kiss, both of them gasping for air there, in the darkness, smiles on their faces, full of delight and discovery.

"I should warn you," he said finally, his thumb running along the edge of her jaw. "This time, I am not leaving. Not unless you are with me."

She came up on her toes at that, propelled by joy and hope and the undeniable promise of happy ever after he'd just made, and kissed him again, not caring that all of Highbury was mere feet away, no doubt aware of the scandal taking place on the Hartfield balcony.

Edward didn't care, either, another low rumble sounding in his chest as his arms came around her again, pulling her tight to him for another few minutes.

When they broke apart again, she said softly, "I've been wait-ing for this Michaelmas for twenty-one years, Mr. Harris. I should warn *you* that I've no intention of letting you leave."

"Thank God," he replied, his hands cradling her face just as they had years ago. "Do you think you can love me again, Hetty Bates?"

"Not again," she said. "Still."

He set his brow to hers and closed his eyes, whispering a thanks to the heavens. It was impossible to believe that the night had taken such a turn—that her life had taken such a turn. All that time, and finally, finally, this. This man she'd longed for. This future she'd packed away like spun glass, fragile and un-steady.

When they parted, she cast a glance toward the ballroom, where Jane and Frank danced past, bathed in golden light, well and happy and in love.

Jane.

"Edward," she said softly, loving the way he watched her, hanging on her words. As though everything she said had weight and power and import. "You must meet Jane."

"Mrs. Churchill?" he replied, a tease in his voice. "I have—she introduced us not an hour ago."

"Yes," she said. "But you must be properly introduced."

And though he did not understand—though no one could, in that moment—he nodded without hesitation, and something burst in Hetty's chest. Something like hope. Like happiness.

The future.

They returned to the ballroom, all of Highbury watching, each person assembled eager to begin long days of discussion as to the scandal that had transpired between Miss Bates and Baron Courtenay in the darkness—it must have been a scandal, mustn't it, for the couple to arrive so breathless and bright-eyed and joyful.

But to Hetty, it did not feel like a scandal. It felt like a triumph.

For that evening, not one person in Highbury thought Hetty Bates dull. In truth, no one ever thought her dull, ever again.

ABOUT THE AUTHORS

ELINOR LIPMAN's fifteenth novel, *Every Tom, Dick & Harry*, was published in 2025 by Harper. Her essays have appeared in *The New York Times*, *The Washington Post*, *The Boston Globe*, *The Wall Street Journal*, and many other publications. She was the 2011–2012 Elizabeth Drew professor of creative writing at Smith College, and a finalist for the 2023 Thurber Award for American Humor.

———

ADRIANA TRIGIANI is the *New York Times* bestselling author of twenty-one books of fiction and nonfiction. She is an award-winning filmmaker and television writer/producer who has loved Jane Austen from the start.

———

KAREN DUKESS is the author of *The Last Book Party* and *Welcome to Murder Week*. She lives outside New York City and on Cape Cod, where she hosts the Castle Hill Author Talks for the Truro Center for the Arts.

———

ELOISA JAMES is a *New York Times* and *USA Today* bestselling author of historical romance novels. Her books have been translated into twenty-six languages with sales worldwide of seven million. As Mary Bly, she is a Shakespeare professor at Fordham University. She lives in New York City and Florence, Italy. Find out more at EloisaJames.com.

————

AUDREY BELLEZZA is a two-time Emmy Award–nominated TV producer who has spent over twenty years writing, developing, and executive producing nonfiction television shows for a number of networks and streaming platforms. Audrey lives in New Jersey with her husband and two children.

EMILY HARDING is one-half of the writing duo behind the For the Love of Austen series, including *Emma of 83rd Street*, *Elizabeth of East Hampton*, and *Anne of Avenue A*. She is a graduate of Emerson College with degrees in both creative writing and film. After working over fifteen years in television development and production, she found her way back to writing. Emily lives in Dallas with her husband, two children, and an incredibly spoiled Texas heeler.

————

Bestselling author **DIANA QUINCY** is an award-winning former television journalist who decided to make up stories where a happy ending is always guaranteed. Her books have been included on "Best of" lists in *Library Journal*, *Entertainment Weekly*, and *The Washington Post*. As a US Foreign Service brat, Diana grew up all over the world, but she is now happily settled in Virginia. When she's not bent over her laptop, Diana reads, watches thrillers, and plots her next travel adventure.

————

NIKKI PAYNE is the author of *Pride and Protest* and *Sex, Lies, and Sensibility*. By day, Nikki is a curious tech anthropologist asking the right questions to deliver better digital services. By night, she dreams of ways to subvert canon literature. She's a member of Smut U, a premium feminist writing collective, and is a cat lady with no cats.

———

New York Times, *Washington Post*, and *USA Today* bestselling author **SARAH MACLEAN** wrote her first novel on a dare and never looked back. Translated into more than twenty-five languages, the books that make up "The MacLeaniverse" are beloved by readers worldwide. A former columnist for *The New York Times*, *The Washington Post*, and *Bustle*, she is a founding board member of Authors Against Book Bans and the cohost of the weekly romance podcast *Fated Mates*. Sarah lives in New York City.

HAVE YOU EVER PUT DOWN
AN AUSTEN NOVEL AND WONDERED:

*What about everyone
else's happy ending?*

Was Lydia Bennet happy with Wickham?
How did little Margaret Dashwood fare
when finding a husband? Did Miss Bates
ever meet someone who celebrates her?

In *Ladies in Waiting*, nine beloved and bestselling
authors across genres look beyond the pages of Austen's
classic novels to make her minor characters the stars of
their own stories. Written with plenty of love and wit, these
wildly imaginative reboots of the lives of Austen's "ladies
in waiting" take us from Regency England to 1860s New
Orleans to modern-day New York City.

This heartfelt collection is a celebration of Jane Austen
and her timeless masterpieces.

FICTION   1125

ISBN 978-1-6682-0417-7   **$19.00 U.S.**/$26.00 Can.

Simonandschuster.com
@GalleryBooks

GALLERY
BOOKS

COVER DESIGN BY EMMA A. VAN DEUN
COVER ILLUSTRATIONS BY REKHA GARTON/ARCANGEL